UNSEEN LOVE

Nancy Kimball

For Benjamin

Ex tenebris ad lumen
Out of darkness to light

Chapter 1

Rome

August, AD 79

Uncertainty is a vicious companion. Laelia Ricarri sat alone in her bedchamber clutching the jewel inlaid handle of her mother's dagger. The last coin she possessed was pressed tight to the roof of her mouth, the bitter metallic taste flooding the back of her throat. One well-placed slice to the forearm and she could join her mother in the underworld. Charon would collect his fee and ferry her across the river Styx into Hades. She would face her judgement secure in the knowledge she'd never offended the gods so grievously that eternal punishment would await her on the other side.

She positioned the blade against her inner arm and drew a shuddering breath. A good life in the Plains of Asphodel would be her reward. Her mother's embrace. Freedom from her father and his cruelty. Freedom from their defamed name and the scandal of her first betrothal. She squeezed her useless eyes tight and exhaled. *Do it. Do it now.*

"Laelia?" Father's voice boomed through their small house.

Her gasp sucked the coin in her mouth to the back of her throat and violent coughs shook her like a rag doll. She almost toppled from the stool and tears pricked her eyes as she gagged. Then as quickly as it had begun the coin relinquished its stranglehold and she spit it from her mouth. The single *sesterce* landed on the dressing table with a click barely audible between her coughs.

1

"Coming," she rasped, rising slowly and secreting the dagger between the swell of her breast and the linen bindings beneath the folds of her garment. With her free hand she found her walking stick, and then the plaster wall that guided her through the doorway.

"What kept you?" Father was closer than she'd expected.

"Forgive me." Her voice was mangled, and her throat felt like it was full of cinders and broken glass. "I was—"

"Come to the *atrium*. We have things to discuss."

The familiar scuff of sandals was already carrying him away. But there were too many feet. Oh gods. "Who's with you?"

"Mistress," a masculine voice answered.

Laelia clutched the dried cane of her walking stick with both hands. The man had addressed her as a mistress. Who was he? Why was he here?

"The atrium, Laelia. Now. I won't stand while I explain this to you. Bring her, slave."

Slave? Impossible. Naomi was the only one left.

"May I approach, Mistress?" the new voice asked.

"No." She clutched her stick tighter and drew up as tall as her short frame would allow. "Father, I can barely feed Naomi and myself. Another slave—"

The blow to her face knocked her sideways. Pain burned from her chin to her cheek as she regained her footing, refusing to rub the ache in her mouth.

"We *do not* speak of our situation in the hearing of others. Even slaves." Father grabbed her arm and yanked her forward. She struggled to keep her footing and in the process dropped her stick. He tugged her toward the front room with its empty fountain where he jerked her to a halt, spun her and pushed her down on the wide rim of the fountain pool.

Laelia folded her hands in her lap and waited, and let the familiar desire to poison him rehearse itself as she stayed silent.

"This is a slave for blind people. It's his job to try to help you find a husband."

She'd heard him very clearly, yet his words were impossible. He'd given up on that hope even before she had. She'd been beautiful once, but there was no amount of beauty that could overcome blindness.

"Say something." Father's tone was as hard as his slap had been.

"I'm grateful. But I fear no matter the man's talents I will be unable to secure a betrothal." Especially with just a single coin to her name.

"*Another* betrothal."

By the gods, he was never going to let that go. She slid her palms along the tops of her knees, smoothing the linen of her tunic. In the street beyond their door, a child was crying. Two women argued over the price of a chicken. How was a slave that served blind masters different from the hundreds of thousands of slaves that filled Rome? More perplexing was how did Father acquire him, and with what? Father never did anything that did not further his own ambitions. It was the reason he'd threatened to sell her to a brothel if she couldn't find a way to support herself—without begging.

"Master, may I speak?" The new voice again.

"Yes. Explain it to her. I've been away from Lady Fabiola's too long already. I will return in a few days to assess your progress."

Father departed and the thump of the entry door sounded. She and the man were alone. Surely Father has warned this man already against compromising her purity. But was the man worthy of such trust?

"Mistress, are you all right?"

"Yes." But the fear had rippled in her voice. She cleared her throat and projected a commanding tone. "I'm fine."

"Forgive me, but your lip is bleeding."

She touched the corner of her mouth, and then rubbed the wetness away on the thin wool of her tunic. "It's nothing."

The squeak of a cork sounded.

"A small wound is still a wound, Mistress. I've soaked the edge of a cloth in wine. May I clean it?"

He must have brought the wineskin with him. If he wished to tend the cut, did that mean he wouldn't hurt her?

"Mistress?"

Best to find out now. She nodded, and held still. Fingers touched her chin. Damp cloth dabbed the corner of her mouth while his thumb traced a tiny path back and forth along her jaw. The soothing stroke warred with her discomfort at his nearness.

3

"There." He released her, and she stepped back.

There'd been tenderness in his hands. His fingers hadn't felt small and boyish, and his voice held a mature, and comforting, quality. "How old are you?"

"Forgive me, Mistress, but I don't know. I was sold to my second master very young."

This was why she rarely left the house. If she could see, she wouldn't need to press. "If you had to guess."

"Then I would say a few summers more than you. Though you wear yours very well, if I may be allowed to say so this once."

He was a slave flattering his new mistress. Even so, the compliment was a bite of bread on a long-empty stomach. He'd shown her nothing but kindness so far. She would attempt to do the same. "What are you called?"

"Drusus, Mistress. If you'll permit me, I'll find the kitchen and leave my belongings there so we may begin."

"Begin what?"

"Our first lesson. I'll return shortly, and we'll begin learning from each other."

What did he possibly think to learn from her? How to take a slap in silence?

"May I put my things away for now?"

"The kitchen is down that hall." She pointed toward the right side of the atrium.

Footsteps carried him and his unique scent away. She rose from the fountain pool, crossed her arms and waited for him to return. She'd repressed hope for so long she feared opening the lid of that jar even a crack. She had no idea how she was going to feed him, or herself and Naomi past tomorrow. Tonight, if she did cut her vein, it wouldn't really matter.

Tonight. Tonight she could think. For now, she could at least see what this slave did, and if there was anything he could do for her. When he returned, she dropped her arms to her sides and faced him. "What did my father tell you about me?"

"I'm to accompany you throughout the day on errands and outings."

"I never leave the house. My servant Naomi does so for us."

"That's why I'm here." Laelia sensed him draw closer. "You prefer to remain within your house because you've learned its walls. But I will become your wall, so you may go anywhere you wish."

I will become your wall. Many nights since losing her sight, she wished to see again, but never more than this moment. What breed of man was Drusus, to possess such compassion?

"If I may take your hand, I will place it on my arm to begin."

She raised them both, and Drusus grasped her left hand and placed it above the bend of his arm. His fingers covered hers and she felt his hip against hers. The nearness was awkward, but not frightening. From the angle of his arm, he stood at least a head taller.

"We will always begin from this position. Squeeze my arm when you wish to go forward and again when you wish to stop. We'll learn this here in the hall, so you don't have to be concerned with turns and direction for now. Whenever you're ready."

She wasn't ready for any of this. But she didn't have to decide anything in this moment, other than to allow this man to teach her how to walk with him. "When Naomi or my father lead me, they hold my hand and pull me along. Is that not easier?"

"For them. Not for you."

Very true. With a confidence she didn't feel, she squeezed his arm. His hand over hers prevented her from letting go when he moved forward. Her foot shot out to keep from stumbling and became a step. Then another, and another.

"We're nearly to the far wall, Mistress."

She stopped abruptly and the angle of his arm changed as he fumbled to a stop beside her. She'd almost tripped him. "Apologies," she said.

"None required."

He moved around her, turning her with him so they faced the front of the house again.

A long moment passed. Why did he tarry? Ah, yes. She squeezed his arm and he moved forward, tugging her with him. For the first time in months, her gait turned steady. She was walking.

"We approach the far wall, Mistress."

This time she squeezed his arm before stopping, and he halted smoothly beside her.

"Well done."

"Yes. I've managed to walk the hall in my own house without breaking anything."

"We celebrate all triumphs, Mistress. Not only those of Caesar and his legions."

His high praise made her want to look away as her cheeks warmed. How long had it been since someone had been proud of her?

"A few more turns and you'll have mastered this. Then we practice the reverse. At times, I will need to ask you to stop and start again to allow a cart to pass or move away from some hazard. The pressure of my hand against yours asks you to move forward or stop with me, the same as your signal directs me. Are you ready?"

She nodded. Drusus turned her again, this time pressing his fingers firmly into the valleys of hers to start them forward. She knew so little about this man. Yet she felt safe with him. He didn't make her feel worthless. For the first time in eight years, her father had done her a true kindness.

As they walked, his mistress' stride lengthened and her grip on his arm eased. That she learned quickly revealed intelligence. He'd speculated at her abilities because of her appearance. Her black hair hung limp from a messy knot and the tunic had as many stains as the floor of the taverns he once frequented. She looked more like a slave than he did.

Then her father had struck her. Drusus had reached for the knife hidden in his belt on instinct. Thankfully he'd stopped before drawing the weapon. Master or not, a man should never strike a woman. If he could strike his daughter, how much easier a slave? The dust and dirt tracked across the stone floors as they walked told him the small house needed as much attention as its mistress. The mildew odor wafting from the walls had to be the culprit for the growing ache in his head.

"How did you learn to lead a blind person?"

"My last master. He died not long ago."

Every day for the last ten years, Master Pappus had occupied the arm she now held. The ache of his loss might sooner ease if Drusus understood why he'd been given away instead of being granted his freedom. Not even the coin he'd been given as an inheritance undid his disappointment. Since the laws of Rome forbade a slave from owning anything, he kept the coin well hidden, for it would become his master's if discovered. A few more steps and he stopped her. Together they turned back toward the opposite wall.

"I don't know what to say." She frowned as they walked. "Apologies are what everyone says to those left behind when another dies. But what if he was cruel and you're happy he's dead? That wouldn't make you a bad person."

"Master Pappus was a very good master who treated me as a son, Mistress."

She frowned again, and her steps slowed. "Then I mourn him with you."

"Thank you, Mistress."

"Please call me Laelia. Mistress makes me sound like a patrician noble, which you know I am not."

"Nobility isn't bestowed in name or wealth, but in courage. I already know you possess courage, Mistress."

Her cheek turned pink, a sign of life in her pale skin. "Thank you, but call me Laelia."

He wanted to please her but not at risk to them both. "I fear your father would disapprove."

"My father approves of his coin, un-watered wine, and his lover. Little else concerns him. Though the surest way to arouse his temper is to make mention of what does."

"Turn." Drusus lengthened his stride as Laelia shortened hers to pivot. "Well done." She'd skimmed the topic, so it should be safe for him to explore. "It grieved me to see him strike you. I wanted very much to intervene."

Her shoulders hunched, like she feared being struck again. "I'm glad for your sake you did not. My father hates anything resembling defiance. The only thing he hates worse is Christians."

Drusus stumbled and caused Laelia to misstep.

She stopped and gripped his arm tighter. "Was that my fault?"

"No, Mistress. Pardon my slip." They began again. After two strides, he resettled into a smooth gait with her. This time he urged her left to continue into the atrium. He had more reason now to fear the master—and to pray.

Her steps slowed. "It feels we've walked too far."

"We're in the atrium. The fountain is not working, or you would have known that."

"It hasn't worked in years. Since before my mother died."

"Apologies." The irony wasn't lost on him. She'd been right. That is what everyone says.

"Let us talk of happy things, Drusus. What news can you share?"

"Work continues day and night on the great amphitheater. I remember the first ring of stone being laid almost ten years ago. Now turn." A few more steps and they cleared the corner of the empty fountain pool. "A new shop has opened near the temple of Jupiter and the silversmith there—"

The heavy wooden entry door swung in. Before he could raise a hand or foot to stop it, it struck Laelia. She fell with a cry as an older woman tumbled in with a basket, too alarmed herself to be a threat. Drusus shoved the door shut as he knelt beside Laelia. "Are you injured, Mistress?"

"I don't know." Her voice trembled as she rubbed at her face.

"What's going on? Who are you?"

Drusus turned to the older woman, working to restrain his temper.

Her eyes widened as she turned and ran. "Master!"

Laelia shifted to pull her feet in and right herself on the floor. "Naomi, stop. Father is not here."

Drusus crouched near her. An unexpected touch would always startle a blind person. "May I help you rise?"

She shook her head and stood on her own, then held out her hand.

He took hold of her extended hand at once, placing it around his arm again.

The older women crept closer. "Who is this?"

"This is Drusus. Father bought him to guide me."

Her father had not bought him. Lady Pappus had gifted him to the man, but Drusus wouldn't correct her. He started to greet Naomi, but her glare stopped him.

"The master didn't say anything about another slave being added to the house." Naomi shifted the basket in her hand to her hip.

"Even so, I'm here now. It would be helpful if you would knock three times and wait a count of three before opening any closed door in the house. The mistress may be on the other side, as you witnessed a moment ago."

Her gaze narrowed, and she thrust a pointed finger at his chest. "You listen. I'm the head servant in this house—"

"Drusus means no insult," Laelia said. "I know it was an accident."

He observed the redness in Laelia's cheek and forehead. Those would be bruises by sunset. "Yes, but one easily avoided."

Naomi frowned as she too surveyed Laelia's face. "I'll try to remember to knock."

"Thank you. The mistress and I will appreciate that."

Naomi's frown deepened, and she mumbled something he couldn't discern as she departed. From the irritated tone, he wasn't sure he wanted to know.

After a moment to reposition, Laelia squeezed his arm and they resumed their walk. "Don't make an enemy of Naomi."

"Your safety matters more than her opinion of me. She'll have much to learn as well."

"You should be concerned if she doesn't like you. You'll be sharing the servant's chamber with her."

"I sleep armed."

She grinned as if that were a jest. If only it were. The concealed blades he carried could protect them from her father—and certainly from a bitter slave with a poor attitude. But the knives could never protect him from his past. A past they helped create.

Only God could do that.

Chapter 2

The *triclinium* reflected the neglected state of his new mistress. Inside the chamber, threadbare cushions covered the three-sided dining couch. Pottery shards littered the corners of a stone floor that hadn't felt the sweep of a broom in some time. Four lamps surrounded the dining couch and center table, but only one was lit. The single flame cast weak light and strong shadows across the face of his mistress. She wasn't unattractive, though to even consider her in that way was sticking a deep bowl beneath a fountain of trouble. He'd justified the one compliment of her earlier to sway her opinion of him. It had to be about the work now.

"I know it's not protocol, but will you allow me to dine with you while we're learning?"

"I'd enjoy that."

He reclined beside her just as Naomi carried in a platter of eggs and blackened fish. Their eyes met and her gaze became so tight her eyeballs disappeared. "You are the most insolent slave I have ever known."

Laelia stiffened beside him. "I permitted it."

A tense silence held until Naomi stepped forward and dropped the platter on the table from enough height the bang startled Laelia. Naomi grabbed two eggs while holding her menacing glare. "I'll be eating in the kitchen. Like a proper servant."

Now who was being insolent? Blindness had left Laelia's confidence in tatters and the old woman's attitude was doing nothing to help restore it. He almost got up and followed her for a much needed talking to.

Laelia angled her face toward him. "I'm sorry she's being so hostile."

Hostility he could tolerate. Open disrespect of Laelia was something entirely different. "You're a very forgiving mistress."

A wry smile formed on her mouth. Knowing he'd put it there felt good. But her smile retreated as she reached her hand out to search for the platter. All wrong. "May I share something with you?"

Her hand stilled and she stiffened again. "What?"

"Place your left hand flat on the table edge directly in front of your arm. Then with only your fingertips, sweep the table back and forth until you connect with an obstacle."

"That's how I spill things."

"That's going to happen sometimes. Even for sighted people. But if you focus on what you're touching and not what you're trying to find, you have so much more information. Feel the table. The texture of the wood. Where the planks meet. When something feels different, explore it until you know what it is."

After a long moment, she did as he asked.

"Good. But raise your palm so only your fingertips sweep the surface. You'll have more control that way."

She raised her wrist a few inches from the table, keeping her fingertips touching. "Like this?"

"Like that."

It still took her a while, but when she found the platter and pulled it to her, peeled eggs wobbled on the plate but none fell to the table.

"Well done, Mistress."

She felt along the edge of the platter and located a boiled egg. With her first bite, bright yellow bits of powdered yolk dusted her chin. The childlike sight made him want to laugh but he pressed his lips together hard instead, thankful in the moment that she couldn't see him. Laelia fared better with the piece of fish. There was so little food on the platter he resisted taking any for himself, but she insisted. The overcooked fish appeased his empty stomach for now. Something more substantial would be required soon or his pains would return.

"Are you ready for wine?"

"Yes, thank you."

"You'll want to move the platter so you have room to work."

Her brows met over her slender nose. "Why?"

"I'm going to teach you to pour your own wine."

Though she couldn't see, her gaze could still narrow. He was pushing her beyond her self-imposed limitations. She didn't know it yet, but that was a good thing. Drusus stood and took the pitcher of wine from the center of the table and held it close to him. "You'll want to move that platter."

She remained perfectly still, the glare fixed in her expression.

"If I set this pitcher on the remaining eggs, it will spill for sure."

"Go ahead. Then at least it will be you who wastes it."

Instead of me. She hadn't finished, but she didn't need to. Drusus set the pitcher down and sat beside her. "Laelia, if you trust me not to lead you into a wall, why do you not trust me now?"

The question hung between them in silence for a long moment. He watched her contemplate the answer, knowing how hard this must be for her.

Finally she released a deep sigh and uncrossed her arms. She set her hands on the table edge and reached forward as he'd taught her. Faster than last time, she found the platter and slid it an arm's length away. "What's next?"

Good girl. He found himself grinning as he reached for the two clay cups at the center of the table. They needed to be replaced with metal as soon as he could speak to the master. Metal survived falls far better than clay. Drusus set them down in front of her. "Tell me what you heard."

"You set something down."

"Correct. Now you find it." He watched as her hand began the back and forth sweep.

After a moment, she located the cup and pulled it closer to her. "Are you sure about this?"

"You can do this. I'm going to set the wine near you. Listen for it to come to rest on the table." Drusus set the pitcher in front of her, and deliberately turned the handle away. "Now find the pitcher."

She kept the cup in her hand and with the other began the sweep in front of her. In two more passes, she found the pitcher. Her fingers slid up the curved side. As he watched, he imagined her fingers gliding up his chest. He closed his eyes and took a deep breath. How long had it been?

When he opened his eyes, she'd located the spout and was using the edge to rotate the pitcher. The wine inside sloshed, and she hesitated. When it settled, she located the handle and grasped it, sliding the pitcher to her.

"Well done, Mistress. Be mindful you're working near the edge."

"How will I know when the cup is full?"

"This I'll need to show you. May I come behind you and take your hands?"

She hesitated a moment. "Yes."

Laelia held still as his chest pressed against her back and his hands covered hers. The unusual crisp scent of his breath filled her nostrils again, and she felt the brush of his body against her back.

"First, put the finger closest your thumb inside the rim. Like this."

He adjusted her finger so it hung over the cup edge just as he said.

"Do you feel that?"

"Yes." He meant the hold on the cup but it was difficult to concentrate on anything other than the foreign sensations washing over and around her. His voice so near her ear. The occasional press of his chest and arms against her back and shoulders.

"Knowing when to stop is the easy part. Making sure the wine falls into the cup is the difficulty. Set the cup flat near the spout of the pitcher. The spout is always in line with the handle. When you connect them, try to imagine placing a bucket beneath a fountain spout."

He released her hands and moved away. This made concentrating much easier. "Now what?"

"Now pour. Slowly at first until the sound of the wine in the cup tells you the position is correct. When you feel the wine reach your finger, you stop."

Determined to at least try, she held her breath and tilted the pitcher.

"Wait." His touch returned and he adjusted her hold on the cup. "This only works if you keep the cup level."

The youngest of children knew how to do this simple task. She set the wine and the cup down, yanking her hand free from his hold. She too was his master, not just her father. "Isn't this why my father brought you here? To tend these things for me?"

"Yes. If you wish to always be forced to rely on others."

If he only knew what she wished. He'd been so kind and patient earlier. It would seem his patience had run out. "You're dismissed."

"Mistress, I—"

"I said you're dismissed."

Chapter 3

Drusus retreated far enough down the hall she would hear him leave. He leaned against the chipped and peeling plaster wall and silently cursed. He was already failing. Laelia apparently had some of her father's temper. But she'd been blind less than two months. The most familiar tasks would have to be relearned. Most patriarchs would have sold her into slavery or encouraged her to commit suicide by now. That Master Ricarri hadn't done so, at least not yet, was the only respectable thing about the man. Because there was only one kind of slavery where blindness could actually be a gift, and he didn't want that for Laelia.

He hadn't wanted it for Julia. Her face appeared in the darkness of his closed eyes. Full, enticing lips beneath her beckoning gaze. But guilt chased the image away, bringing with it the familiar burn of shame. Failure. Regret.

Drusus swallowed and pushed away from the wall, opening his eyes. There was no going back in this life. Only forward.

Only forward.

As silent as a spider, he returned to the doorway to watch Laelia. She held the cup in both hands as if she would crush it any moment. He wanted to pour the wine for her. To hold her hand and assure her in time all would be well. But he couldn't. At least not yet. Not if she refused to even try.

For a long time, she just sat there, bowed over the cup in her hands. His knees were stiff from standing still so long, but finally she raised her head. With slow, sweeping motions, she located the pitcher and slid her hand to the top of the handle.

Please, God, let her be successful. Please.

After two attempts, she connected with the pitcher. She began to pour but not the way he'd shown her and it spilled. She tilted her head straight back and heaved a sigh so loud he heard it from where he stood.

Try again. *Try again.*

Eventually she did, and the smile crossing her face must have been the moment she felt the wetness of the wine reach her fingertip. She righted the pitcher and set it down before taking a long drink. Her hand found the pitcher and as carefully as the first time, she refilled her cup. Rather than drink, she rose with it in her hand and shuffled along the edge of the table toward the doorway as he had a moment ago. What was she doing?

He crept backward, trying to sneak away.

She was faster, finding the doorway with her free hand. "Drusus?" she called out.

The shout punished his already aching head and he flinched. That she was capable of such volume stunned him. Clearly that was a family trait. "Yes, Mistress?"

Her head cocked. Too late, he realized he'd answered too quickly.

"Were you watching me?"

He was tempted to lie, but she was too smart. "Yes."

"You saw the spill?"

"I saw you determined to succeed without help from anyone. Including me."

Laelia smiled again and extended the cup toward him. "I poured this for you."

For him? His hand trembled as he reached to take the cup from her, being sure to grasp it tight as she released it. "Thank you," he managed.

The wine was gritty, likely fouled by a soiled cup or pitcher. Even watered down, bitterness remained in an aftertaste as unpleasant as the scent of mold surrounding them. Even so, the thought behind it was priceless. "That's the best wine I've ever had."

Her gentle laugh filled the small space between them. "Then I pity you."

She didn't understand. The desire to take her face in his hands and somehow make her see the full depth of his gratitude was overwhelming. But all he had were words. "This is the first time someone has served me. Thank you." He swallowed. "Laelia." Her given name still felt strange to use.

She dipped her chin and even in the faint lamplight, her expression said he'd pleased her. "I'm ready to retire for the evening. Please take me to my chamber now."

"Of course, my lady." He set the cup on the floor near the wall and brought her hand to his arm. "The chamber ahead with the open door?"

"Yes." She squeezed his arm, and they began the short walk.

He squeezed her hand and stopped at the doorway. "It's an arm's length from you, Mistress."

When she found the edge of the plastered wall with her free hand, she released his arm and turned toward him. "Good night, Drusus."

"Should I send Naomi to you?"

"No, she'll come when it is time."

"Then sleep well, Mistress."

"You too. Be patient with Naomi. Change is hard for her."

Her tone was more command than request, but her expression softened as he watched her. Again he noticed her strong features and proud angle of her jaw. Her lip was swollen at the corner where she'd been struck, and again the need to protect her flamed stronger than before. "I will do my best, Mistress."

Her smile was warm and then it vanished, replaced by some grave thought. "We both must, Drusus. Or all may be lost."

"I understand." He had much to pray about. But deep in his gut, just beneath his concealed daggers, he feared prayers weren't going to be enough.

Chapter 4

Drusus retrieved the cups and the platter from the *triclinium* and carried them to the kitchen. He found Naomi staring into a dying fire in the large hearth. Her back was to him and though he knew it would startle her, he set the dishes down hard on the wooden table between them.

Her head snapped around. "That's twice today you've startled me."

"My sudden presence alarmed you?"

"Yes, you should announce yourself."

"Laelia feels the same way when she finds herself in someone's presence unaware or when someone touches her unexpectedly, even to help."

She crossed her arms and turned back to the fire. "I don't need some new slave prancing about my kitchen spouting words like an all-knowing oracle. I've cared for Laelia since she suckled at her mother's breast, so don't lump me in the same cart as her father. You don't know anything about this house or me."

"You're right. I humbly ask your pardon. I need your help as much as Laelia. To learn from you how best to care for her and in turn offer what I know. My last master was blind. I served him for thirteen years."

"Why do you no longer serve him? I know the master didn't buy you." Naomi rose from the stool and carried the platter to a wash basin with water so gray, Drusus wondered how she planned to clean anything with it.

"How do you know he didn't buy me?" Drusus rummaged through a basket of utensils, noting none of the knives were of quality and most appeared dull.

"I know him even better than I know his daughter, but I'm the one asking questions here. Why do you no longer serve your last master?"

"He died."

"How?"

The sharpness in the woman's tone brought his gaze to her. "In his sleep, at a good age." And ready to meet the Lord, but Drusus kept that part to himself.

"What are you looking for? If you want to know where something is, ask me."

"I found what I need." He pulled the three knives from the basket, and the longest wooden stir stick and held them in a bundle.

"What are you doing with my things?"

"Taking them to the atrium. I want to have a look at that fountain."

"That fountain hasn't worked in years."

Drusus stopped in the doorway and turned toward her. "Then I can't do any more harm to it. I promise to return your tools."

"You better be through before the master returns, if he returns at all tonight. And don't wake me up with all the noise you'll make putting your things away either."

"I do need to speak to you about that." Drusus tucked the stick and the knives under his arm and approached a wide door off the side of the kitchen. "Is that a storeroom?"

"Yes, but there's rarely anything in it."

"I'd like to make my bed in there. You can keep the slave chamber to yourself, and I'll be closer to Laelia and the front door this way."

"Usually if the master isn't home by dark, he's not coming home. But if he does, he comes to the back entrance where the banging will wake me to unlock the door."

"Where does he go?"

"Don't ask those questions. Not if you wish to avoid his temper."

"It looks to me as if his temper is unavoidable. He struck Laelia today for nothing more than asking a question." Again his wrist twitched at the memory of how close he'd come to drawing his knives to defend her.

"This is what I'm telling you. Don't ask questions and do as you're told, for all of us."

He searched for scars or fading bruises in the older woman's face. "Does he strike you too?"

Her eyes widened for a mere heartbeat, and then the familiar angry set to her face returned. "Stop asking questions. If you want to sleep in the storeroom, do so. I expect my things returned by morning."

Drusus waited for her to leave and made his way to the *atrium*. The fleeting daylight in the atrium needed to be supplemented with lamp light. But there were no floor lamps in the corners of the room. This was a poor house indeed.

He set the tools down, found a lamp and oil in the kitchen, and moved one of the four floor lamps in the dining room to the atrium. With a broom he'd found in the kitchen, he swept the inlaid tiles of the fountain pool free of years of dust and debris. Was that… Surely not. He turned his head and swept harder, hoping he was wrong. But as the mosaic revealed itself, the hideous scene became clear. Bordered in green palm leaves, with surprisingly intricate detail, were six maidens surrounding a couple with exaggerated body parts engaged in various sex acts.

While such scenes were common in brothels and the baths, and he'd performed several of those himself many times in his old life, it angered him to have to clean it to restore the fountain. Though he'd never call such a mosaic clean even if it gleamed. Doing his best to ignore it, he went to work on the supply pipe in the floor.

With knees raw from crawling on gritty tile, the back of his neck slick with sweat, he'd broken one of Naomi's knives. But the force behind the snapped blade had also rewarded him with a faint gurgling sound as whatever blocked the flow of water within the valve shifted.

There was so much rust, he'd need to hit the regulator valve harder to try to break the rust free, and whatever had jammed it. It might wake the others, but that was a risk he'd have to take. He positioned the long stir stick against the fountain's center opening and rammed. On the third thrust downward, water began to trickle over the tile. He pulled the stick out and peered down into the hole.

The low gurgle grew louder, and then a great rush of water hit him in the face. He jerked back, coughing and spewing the stale water from his mouth. He wiped his eyes and mouth clear, and then reached down with the stick to pry the valve wider. With a wider opening, the height of the spray lowered along with the pressure until it was no higher than his waist. But the water beginning to cover the bottom of the pool was dark, with a sour stench. There was no telling how long it would take the water to begin to run clear. Once it did, he would need to close the valve and bucket out all the water to the gardens before cleaning the fountain pool again for the fresh water to fill it.

Thankfully the two drains near the top of the pool rim appeared clear, though he'd still have to wait hours for the fountain to fill before he would know for certain. Only then would he be able to rest without worry of flooding the house.

It was going to be a long night.

He used the small lamp to retrieve the whetstone from his pack in the kitchen and returned to the fountain pool. The broken knife was a total loss, but the other two would be sharp as eagle talons by morning. Drusus rested the blade on his thigh, and drew the stone across its edge until the sound of the scraping sang a long, low pitch. The way Master Pappus had taught him. A skill he'd been given and instructed to one day pass on. The secret to an edge not even a master blacksmith could produce. He'd spent countless nights with the Master, just like this. Sharpening blades and sharing stories.

The ache of the loss remained sharp, and Drusus swallowed against the sorrow clinging to him like his wet clothes. There was no going back. Only forward. He drew the whetstone across the steel again and again, fighting the burn in the inner corner of his eyes. All his strength would be required to endure this new master, who was nothing like the man Drusus still grieved.

A tapping noise was coming from somewhere in the house. Laelia gripped the edge of her blanket and listened again. Was her father home? For a long while she listened, but there were no more noises from beyond her chamber. Just her own breathing in her never-ending darkness.

Perhaps Drusus would be gone in the morning. That's what she would do if in his sandals. Laelia wouldn't report his flight to the authorities to the local *aedale*. That way he would have at least a day or two head start. Maybe longer if Father remained at Lady Fabiola's. Though if Drusus were captured and returned, father would kill him for sure.

The muscle she'd felt beneath his warm skin startled her at first, as did that unusual scent that clung to him. The fragrance reminded her of an herb or a flower of some kind, but neither made sense. She wanted to learn more about him. Was he handsome? Ugly? Somewhere in between? Asking Naomi would only get her Naomi's opinion, not a true description unless she asked for one. But then Naomi would want to know why Laelia wanted to know, and she had no desire to embark on that conversation.

She rolled onto her other side in her narrow bed and bunched her worn pillow. How she'd soaked it with tears so many nights when the darkness first came. She remembered the heat of the fever, the weakness, and the retching—yelling for Naomi to come light a lamp.

Then, the words she would never forget. "Mistress, the lamp is lit."

The next moments were a blur she didn't care to relive—the fear, the tears, and the screaming that brought Father to her chamber. He'd been angry, and as they explained Laelia couldn't see, his first words were a question she'd asked herself every day since.

"Who will want you like this?"

It was still the life or death question. She didn't have wealth and couldn't prove fertility, the two most desired traits among all Roman men seeking a wife. She'd known even before the scandal of her last betrothal had erupted, it might be her last. That was before she'd lost her sight. What a shame that one couldn't see the thread of their lives in its entirety without an oracle. If she'd known then what the Fates had in store for her, her choices would have been very different.

They were going to be different now. With Drusus, if he were still here in the morning, she was going to learn more from him. Enough to prove herself a capable and desirable wife as her mother had. Blindness was a curse to be sure, but her broken betrothal had already destroyed her reputation among anyone noble enough for her father to marry her off to. Perhaps a merchant of small wealth. With Drusus and his unique talents, she could try.

He brought with him more options than she'd had when she'd been about to open her vein earlier today. With him, at least she could make one last great effort to take back some influence over the course of her life. A path that didn't lead to the backroom of a brothel or to the underworld. But instead to children, a roof over her head and enough food for her belly.

Starting tomorrow the search began. She needed a husband. Someone to make her safe and lead her. A savior, as Julius Caesar had been for Rome. The Fates owed her that. Drusus, and all he could teach her, would be the pavestones to make her new path.

Juno, goddess and protector of women, please make him stay. Please.

Chapter 5

Laelia roused to Naomi's fingers pulling on her toes. "Time to awake."

She bent her knee to pull her foot free of Naomi's grasp and a dull ache gripped her calf. "Ohhh."

"What's wrong?"

"My leg." Laelia flexed her foot but the discomfort remained. "My legs hurt." She twisted to sit up and the pain spread to her back and bottom. "Everything hurts."

"You walked more yesterday than you have in a while. The soreness will pass."

Drusus. "Is Drusus up?"

"He's waiting for you in the *peristyle*."

Juno be thanked. But Naomi's tone had been off, alerting Laelia the same way Naomi's expressions used to. "What is it?"

"Nothing."

The dismissive response was a lie. "What is it?" Laelia sprung from the bed to the cool tile, spasms of pain pinching from ankle to waist. "Did something happen? Is Drusus hurt?"

"No. He's well. He...he..."

Laelia hated not being able to see faces. Hated it. "What is it?"

"He repaired the fountain last night. This morning I had the pitcher to go down to the street fountain but when I entered the *atrium*, ours was running. Clean as the emperor's crown too."

Impossible. Unless Juno had done two miracles last night. "Are you sure?"

"Of course, I'm not—"

Blind.

"Forgive me, Laelia."

"It's all right." Laelia had often used that expression too, until she was. She gathered her nightdress and pulled it over her head. "Now that you won't be making three or four trips a day to the street fountain, why did you sound annoyed about it at first?"

Naomi took her night dress and Laelia held out her hands for the arm holes of her tunic and stola. The coarse wool slid over her arms and she slipped the garment over her head and let it fall into place around her. "Are you upset he fixed the fountain?" Which would make no sense at all, but Naomi's way of thinking sometimes didn't make sense.

"He sharpened my knives."

"He took them to a smith?"

"No. He broke one fixing the fountain but the rest he sharpened himself. He said he has whetstones and knows how. But I have never seen edges as fine as these. I don't understand it."

Laelia held her arms out while Naomi tied the sash around her waist. She might not comprehend how he'd sharpened the knives, but she suspected the why. And that made her smile. "I think Drusus means it as an olive branch to you for the squabble yesterday."

"Sit so I can put your sandals on."

Laelia did, content to accept Naomi's command as a dismissal of the topic at hand.

"Do you need me to take you to the *peristyle?*"

"No, I'll feel my way. Has my father returned?"

"No, and with a third belly to try to fill we'll be out of food by tomorrow."

"Father didn't leave any coin yesterday, did he?"

"No."

"Do what you can. I'd like to have mid-day meal in the *peristyle* today. Whatever we have."

"Eat in the garden? You know the shape it is in."

"I want to be outside today." The desire surprised her as it had Naomi. She would thank Drusus for fixing the fountain, and for his peace offering to Naomi. What she couldn't thank him for was the way an eagerness for the day hummed within. A remembered anticipation that had nothing to do with a working fountain and everything to do with the man who'd fixed it.

Soft footfalls cut short Drusus' morning prayers. The sight of her in that stained *stola* infuriated him all over again. Everything in this house bore the rash of neglect, her most of all.

Navigating the wall-less garden would be difficult for her. A perimeter of columns supported the roof overhang on their four sides like a crate. Already she shuffled toward him two or three feet from the nearest column marking the step down from the stone to the path. She held her arm out and paused. "Drusus? Are you here?"

"I'm here, Mistress." He rose from the weeds and started toward her. "If you hold still I will come to you."

A wry smile formed on her bruised mouth as she tilted her head and lowered her outstretched arm. "And if I do not?" She took another step forward.

Drusus grinned. Her fighting spirit reminded him of his own, kept tucked away like his knives. He stopped a good distance away. "Then I accept your challenge and will wait for you to find me."

She grinned wider and raised her arm again in front of her. With the toes of her left foot she eased it forward and searched for the ledge that would show her the single step down to the ground. Clever girl. Her sandaled feet disappeared into the knee high grass as she continued to move toward him.

Something in the grass made her stumble and she pitched forward. His heart jumped in his chest but she regained her balance and drew upright.

"You would have let me fall?"

The disappointment in her voice stabbed. He'd never willfully allow her to fall.

"Drusus?"

Everything in him begged to go to her. Answer her. Take her hand and watch her crestfallen expression fade to reassurance. She would never know this was as much a challenge for him as for her.

"You are insolent, just as Naomi said." The anger in her tone and stern posture made him reconsider. She was his mistress. But she'd challenged him. In doing so, she challenged herself without knowing. He would stand firm. When they bantered a moment ago, she'd heard his voice. He hadn't moved. She already possessed everything she needed to locate him.

She took another step forward, this time with both hands outstretched in front. If she continued straight without reaching to the side far enough, she would pass him. He took two steps left to be directly in her path. The grass rustled around his legs and her head tilted as she slowed. One hand lowered while the other straightened in front of her as she took the final step toward him.

He swallowed to clear his throat and tell her well done. Before he could, her next step brought her palm flat against his chest. The intimacy of the touch through the thin wool of his tunic rendered him breathless.

"I found you." She moved closer while her hand lingered against him.

"Yes, you did."

Her chin rotated up and she stilled. He stared into her eyes, wondering at the woman in their imprisoned depths, and almost bent to kiss her. The absolute most foolish thing he could possibly be thinking, as it could get them both killed. "We should begin."

He grasped her wrist and turned to place her palm on his arm, where it belonged. There and nowhere else. "Today we learn to avoid obstructions like that stone. In the forum, or the market, anywhere in public there are no straight paths or clear routes because the people constantly shift. You'll have to adjust direction with me often."

"I'm ready."

"Then you know what to do."

She squeezed his arm and they went to work.

Laelia's stomach rumbled like unpeeled eggs in a bowl. All this walking built up quite an appetite and compounded the soreness in her body. "Do you mind if we rest a while? Naomi should be bringing mid-day meal soon."

"Certainly. Shall we go to the *triclinium*?"

"No. I thought we might eat here in the garden, though even before I lost my sight it wasn't much to look at. There should be a stone bench close by. Do you see it?"

"Yes, Mistress."

As they approached the bench, she remembered the two stone lions forming the supports beneath the marble seat stretching across their carved heads. As a little girl, she'd stuck her fingers in their ears so they couldn't hear the secrets she shared with her mother. Drusus squeezed her hand and they came to a stop together. She dipped her knees to feel for the low seat of the stone bench and found it with ease. "How many times must I ask you not to call me mistress?"

"I fear I would grow accustomed to doing so when we are alone and then slipping among others. Especially your father."

"He's not my father." The admission hung between them as she waited. Her father had forced her silence for so long, that intentionally breaking it now felt as freeing as it did terrifying. "You don't know what to say, do you?"

"I do not."

"You said I could trust you. I'm going to trust you now. Sit beside me."

He did so, and fully aware of how much she was defying her father and taking Drusus into her confidence, she recounted the second worst day of her life.

"I didn't know until my mother's death. She'd been very ill and while the physicians made promises in exchange for vast sums of coin, we knew she was going to cross the Styx. Father had gone to make another sacrifice, trying to save her. Naomi was with us, and our servant Titus when she awoke. She said she loved me and that Juno would protect me. Told me how much she loved me. That the gods and goddesses would care for me. She wanted Titus to hold her hand, and I remember it was the first time I'd ever seen him cry. She said 'protect our daughter.' Titus looked at me and then at my mother and swore he would. I was only a child but as young as I was, I understood."

Laelia took a deep breath, remembering the moment as if it were yesterday and not eight years ago. So vivid was the feel of her mother's hand on her head and the look in Titus' eyes through his tears.

"Mistress, you needn't continue unless you wish."

The tenderness in Drusus' voice soothed, so counter to the violence in her memories of what happened next.

"Father had been standing in the doorway." She swallowed, letting the scene replay. "My mother died before she realized what she'd done. Titus died by my father's hand. In front of me. I tried to stop him. That was the first time he ever struck me."

"Laelia, I'm so sorry."

"I think every time he sees me, he is reminded of my mother's betrayal. Good Roman women don't bed the slaves and if they must, they take precautions. For my father there was no greater disgrace, and he swore Naomi and I to silence that day if we were to be allowed to live."

She smoothed the course wool of her *stola* on top of her lap and wished again to see Drusus' face. Some clue as to what he must think of her. "So now you know my secret. And perhaps better understand why my circumstances are what they are."

"I am sorry for what you have gone through, Mistress."

"Will you vow on Jupiter's throne to never speak of it to anyone?"

"I will vow on my very life to never speak of it, Mistress."

The title chafed again, as did Drusus valuing his own life above the very throne of Jupiter, but Laelia knew even before she'd told him he could be trusted.

"Naomi approaches," Drusus said.

In a moment, the soft rustle in the thick grass grew louder as she approached. "Some bread and the last of the boiled eggs. It's all we have."

"Eat with us." Hopefully dining together would build on Drusus' gesture from earlier. "There isn't room," Naomi said.

29

Drusus' arm brushed hers as he rose. "Share the bench with the mistress."

"You don't have to leave." Laelia reached out to find him.

His fingers touched hers. "I'm not leaving. Just moving."

The grass rustled again. The squeeze he gave her fingers before releasing them was one of assurance, not direction, and she felt the comfort all the way through her. Naomi muttered a thank you and sat. The chunk of bread she pressed into Laelia's hand was smaller than an apple.

"Should we go for more provisions this afternoon?" Drusus asked.

Naomi didn't answer. After what Laelia had shared with him today, this should be easy. But it wasn't. "We have to wait for Father to leave us some coin."

"Even for food?" Drusus sounded appalled, and why shouldn't he?

"We manage." Laelia bit into her piece of bread.

It was quiet for a long moment, except for the occasional chirp of a bird.

"Since we already have such trust in each other," Drusus paused. "I have a little bit of coin. Enough that we can go to the baths and get a few provisions. Our first lesson outside the house."

Her heart swelled he would confess to possessing some coin, much less offer to share it. By law slaves could own nothing, and any coin they possessed would immediately pass to their master. "I can't let you do that."

"You should know, Mistress, I'm quite irritable when I'm hungry."

She laughed at his casual assertion, but sobered as the reality of the situation returned. "I don't know if or when I could repay you."

"By law you don't have to."

"By rights, I would. It was to your benefit to remain silent."

"Not while you and Naomi remain hungry."

How was it a slave could possess such generosity, and her father none? All the while any stranger would regard her father as the greater man.

"Will you accept this small gift that benefits us all?"

"I think you should accept," Naomi said eagerly.

The crowded forum would be scary. The baths even more. She hadn't been since her blindness, preferring to sponge with water in her chamber while Naomi assisted. But if she stood a chance of eventually securing a betrothal that could save them all, she had to keep pushing past the fears. "I accept."

"Then we're agreed, Mistress? Baths and market after we finish our meal?" His voice was beginning to grow on her. Sometimes soft, but always confident.

"It would seem I have no choice."

"You always have a choice. Always." This time his tone was firm. "We don't have to go to the baths, but I think once we're there you'll find it worth the effort."

If she said no, she would cheat Naomi and Drusus both from a proper bath. And a bath was only a copper, the cheapest thing for sale in Rome. "We'll go to the baths."

"Excellent, Mistress."

She finished her bread, and then her egg in silence. Though it wasn't an uncomfortable silence. They finished their meal and adjourned to the atrium, Drusus leading her as he had yesterday. His unique herbal scent she couldn't figure out seemed stronger now somehow.

"Wait here for us. Naomi and I will return in a moment."

While she waited, memories of her last trip outside the house made her stomach unsettled. She'd endured the ever-present crowds in the streets, being bumped, grabbed, cursed and pushed aside. She and Naomi were halfway to their destination when she'd sat against the wall of a shop to rest. The shopkeeper emerged, yelling no beggars and striking her with a broom. Naomi had helped her to stand and get away, even under the swings of the broom that were striking her sides and backside. They'd made it home, where Laelia had held it together long enough to be alone with her new bruises and scratched skin before sobbing so hard she'd been unable to breathe at times.

If uncertainty was a vicious companion, fear was its three-headed death hound. But she had Drusus now, and he was a strong amulet.

Chapter 6

Drusus feared leaving Laelia alone, even for a few moments, might weaken her resolve to go. They needed the food, his precious few remaining mint leaves were drying out, and she needed to get outside this house. But right now, he needed to get some of his coin and the twins from the storeroom he'd stashed them in last night.

The cool steel welcomed his grasp. Their flat, slender oval shaped blades tapering seamlessly into etched handles as flat as their blades. Anyone would wonder at such weapons, unless he or she knew what they were. Like the Tiber seeks the ocean, the blades glided into the custom sheaths concealed in his belt near his navel. If God willed, he would have no reason to draw them today.

"Hurry up."

The ire in Naomi's tone brought a grin he couldn't suppress. He closed the flap of his pack and shoved the leather bag closer to the pallet of empty grain sacks he'd napped on this morning. Naomi waited in the kitchen with a hand on one hip and an empty basket on the other.

"As much as possible today, please walk an arm's length from the mistress' right side. This gives me unobstructed room to move her closer to you if I need to. Until she becomes re-accustomed to the proximity of others, you'll occupy an area a stranger would otherwise."

"If it will help."

"It will. Thank you. One more thing." Drusus pulled a single *sesterce* from within his belt and held the silver coin toward Naomi. "This is for the baths. Keep Laelia there as long as possible while I take her stola, and yours if you wish, to the fuller. I'll need you to tell the slave at the changing area to bring them out to me."

"Won't you need the change for the fuller?"

"No, and there shouldn't be much change."

"How long have you been in Rome? Laelia and I could have eight days of baths for that."

"Buy you and her both a bathing kit and the best perfumed oil. Pay for a slave to attend you both and use the rest on massages."

"She'll never agree to those luxuries when we need food."

"I will take care of food and I need you to do this for me. Please. The goal of securing a betrothal for her is going to get better the more confident she is in her appearance. I'm counting on you to encourage her to see it that way."

Naomi frowned as she stared at him. "I will do as you ask. But the finest fuller in Rome could not get the stains out of Laelia's *stola*."

He suppressed a grin because she would think him haughty all over again if he told her he did know the best fuller in Rome. "Let me worry about that. You take care of the mistress."

Drusus turned and Naomi followed him back to the hall. "I'm sorry to have tarried, Mistress. Are you ready?"

Laelia held her hand out.

Drusus placed it on his arm and after the light squeeze from her, they started forward together.

"It's strange to hear the fountain again. I didn't know how much I'd missed it," Laelia said softly.

Naomi glanced at Laelia as they approached the door. "When you were a baby and your wet nurse couldn't quiet you, I would carry you in here and walk you around this fountain. The sound of it soothed you even then."

He pictured it in his mind. There was much more to Naomi than he knew. "Do you have the key?" he asked her.

"There's no key anymore. The master lost it and we can't afford to have another made. We can only set the bolts from inside."

That was bad.

"It doesn't matter," Laelia said, almost as if she'd heard this thought. "There's nothing for thieves to take except the furniture that remains. Most assume a few slaves are always present, as it should be."

There was plenty for thieves—and her father—to steal. But nothing he could do about it for now. Naomi shut the door behind them and for a moment he stood in the street with them, letting Laelia get accustomed to the increased sounds.

Her grip on his arm tightened and she closed the distance between them, drawing tight to his side.

"I will never leave your side except at the baths, where Naomi will attend you."

Naomi took her place on Laelia's right side where he'd instructed.

They stood there a long moment, but Laelia didn't signal him to go forward.

"I've been promised a bath," Naomi huffed. "The first proper bath in ages. If you don't start walking, I'll tell Drusus to throw you over his shoulder and carry you like a sack of wheat."

The older woman's harshness rankled, but when her gaze met his over Laelia's head, she winked at him.

Allies at last.

Laelia squeezed his arm and they started forward. After a few steps, she said "Somehow I don't think Drusus is the haughty one among us."

"Who said he was haughty?"

Laelia laughed beside him. "You did."

"Did I say that? I don't recall."

Laelia's unguarded laughter made her a little unsteady, but he loved the sound of it. Naomi swung her empty basket back and forth as they made the corner onto the *Via Ostiensis*. The streets were crowded as they always were and their trek to the baths of Nero would carry them past the pagan temple of Diana, the Circus Maximus where he could never show his face again, through the heart of the city by the forum, and the theatre of Pompey before reaching the baths.

The fuller shop he would bring her stola to would be a back-track a third of the way, but that portion he could run. There were a few things he hadn't done since the master's death, running among them. He'd have pain in his side and fire in his legs, but that was only fair.

He was pushing Laelia just as hard.

Laelia continued to stay focused for only Naomi and Drusus' voices, but listening for them had her actively listening to everything and it was exhausting. Along with how many times Drusus had to adjust their path, start and stop her. And they hadn't gone nearly far enough that an end, and a bath, was near.

"You're doing well," Drusus whispered near her ear as they walked.

She squeezed his arm in gratitude and he came to a sudden halt that jarred her.

"I'm sorry," she said. "I didn't mean to stop."

"What's wrong?" Naomi asked from her other side.

"Nothing. Laelia is testing me to see if I remain alert to her commands among so many distractions. I pass inspection."

Laelia laughed again and squeezed his arm again to continue walking. "You have an answer for everything, don't you?"

He didn't answer. Surely he'd heard her, hadn't he?

"No, Mistress. Sometimes very few."

His somber tone felt out of place and she wished again she could see his face. The noise of the crowd increased, as did how often she needed to respond to Drusus' subtle changes in direction. She felt the muscle of his arm tense beneath her fingers. "What's wrong?"

"Mistress?"

"You're angry, or tense about something. I feel it in your arm."

"I'm fine."

His thick tone said otherwise and further aroused her curiosity.

"We're passing the temple of Diana," Naomi told her. "There are a lot of worshippers for so late in the day."

Laelia could picture them on the temple steps, with their bows and spears. A heavy sigh escaped Drusus and the arm beneath her hand turned more rigid. She wanted to know what vexed him so, but chose not to press him. Private thoughts deserved to remain private. She knew that better than anyone.

The hum of the people about changed as they walked. Like all the voices and sounds around her gathered, but far away. "Is the Circus Maximus near?"

"Yes. You have an excellent ear, Mistress. What color team do you cheer?"

"The one in front."

His sudden laughter was deep and rhythmic, and she began to laugh with him at her own cleverness. They walked on, and it occurred to her she'd never know what color was leading if she ever did go to the races again. Her laughter faded. "My cheering days are over."

"Why?" he asked.

"I'd never know what color was in front now. I don't even know what's in front of me."

Drusus pulled her sideways, changing their path. "Come with me."

His sudden change of direction and stern tone frightened her. She squeezed his arm to stop and planted her feet. "Where are you taking us?"

"Come with me." Drusus kept his stride firm and she had to hasten her steps or else let go. Which she was about to do.

"We're nearly there." He halted and she stopped beside him.

His words resonated like a rebuke. Her repayment for the leniency to slave protocols she knew her father would never have shown. She should reprimand him. Now.

"You're before a bench, on the south-east side of the Circus."

"We're not going in there. I won't allow it." Laelia put her hand to her stomach. All those people, pressed in together, jostling her, shoving her.

"We aren't going in. We don't need to. You just don't know that yet. Tell me what you hear."

"The same things you do," she snapped.

"Good. And they tell you things, if you'll sit down and listen harder to what they are."

Any master would flog him for how he spoke to her, in public, no less, as if she were the slave. But the thought of taking a whip to him, of anyone taking a whip to him, squelched her anger. The sudden spin of emotion unsettled her and she backed away from him until she felt the edge of the bench seat on her legs. All at once, cheers erupted from behind her, sharp and focused. She inclined her head toward the sound and sat down.

"Naomi?"

"I'm still here," she answered.

"You hear them, don't you?" Drusus asked.

"Of course."

"Now do more than hear. Listen."

"People are cheering."

"Close, or far from you?"

She listened to the screaming crowd. "Close."

"And where are we?"

He'd said they were on the south-east side. That must mean something but what? When she'd attended, she'd sat on the north-west side because her father cheered the red. The south-east side was the blue side. She listened closer, picking out individual phrases and cheers. "Blue leads."

"Yes," he answered. "Yes, blue leads. Keep listening."

She did, imagining the small chariots with their spinning wheels whipping around the turning posts behind the four horses pulling side by side. The cheers continued, turned to collective gasps, and then jeers and groans. "Blue no longer leads."

"Well done."

"But I no longer know who does."

"You know who does not. Were we inside and seated in the middle of a color, you would know, from the direction the loudest of the cheers moved to which color now led. You are as intelligent now as when you lost your sight. All that has changed is you must use your hearing to tell you things your eyes once did."

He thought her intelligent. This strong, patient man, smart enough to fix their fountain and befriend Naomi, thought her intelligent. She held her hand out and rose. Tucked securely on his arm once again, they continued on. "Thank you, Drusus."

His arm shifted as he leaned near her without stopping. "I'm your wall," he said softly, so near her ear his breath warmed it for a mere moment.

From deep within her chest, the three headed death hound snarled louder than before.

Juno, goddess and protector of women, please make him stay. Please.

Chapter 7

As the baths neared, Laelia pressed progressively tighter to Drusus' side. He soldiered on, trying to ignore the soft flesh molding against him. But it wasn't working.

Laelia's stride slowed. "It sounds as crowded as the circus."

"It's the baths," Naomi said. "It's always crowded."

"Steps." Drusus approached them straight on. "There are six, but they're two strides wide."

She did well, even though sounds were buffeting her from every direction now. Splashing water, the slap of wet, bare feet on stone, children crying or squealing as they played in the water.

Laelia stopped them and turned her face to him. "I still don't feel right about this. You'll regret this the next time there's nothing to fill our bowls in my house."

"Mistress, consider this a reward for your outstanding progress, if you must consider it anything at all."

Naomi took Laelia's other arm. "Come now, so Drusus can be on his way."

Her fingers clamped down on his arm like a tourniquet. "You're leaving us?"

"I need to take your *stola* to the fuller." That was the truth, though a part. The rest he could never tell her. Public places made him more vulnerable to his past.

"Let's go to the changing room so I can bring it out to him. We'll be fine." Naomi tugged at Laelia again and this time she released him.

"I'll wait here for you."

Naomi nodded as they walked toward the changing rooms. A slave there would give them a towel or wrapper to use. They could wash their garments here at the baths, but he needed to see Otho, who was the very best fuller in Rome. And so did her garment.

"Bathing kit? Only two coppers." A peddler held out handfuls of *stirgils* strung together with *amphoras* of oil the size of an apple. "Only two coppers."

"No thank you, friend."

The peddler accosted the next closest man not purposeful enough in his destination. That man, dressed in a better tunic and sandals than Drusus, bought two kits, including the one made of alabaster. The pale luster reminded him of Laelia's skin. Without permission, a vision of her appeared as she climbed from the bath, water running in rivulets down her bare body.

A run. Yes, he needed a run. Marriage would be the only way he would ever again know the physical pleasures of a woman and Laelia could never be his wife. She was a citizen and citizens were forbidden by Roman law from marrying slaves. He couldn't allow himself to think of her that way and ruin his progress. *Put ye on the Lord Jesus Christ, and make not provision for the flesh, to fulfill the lusts thereof.* Paul's instructions in the letter read at the gatherings in Master Pappus' villa were easier to understand than to follow.

This morning in the sunlight, her fiery spirit and palm against his chest warmed him through and through. He could stay and attend her. After all, he was her slave and men and women mixed in the baths beyond that frescoed wall in front of him. Plenty of others would see her wearing only steam as she moved from pool to pool with beads of water fortunate enough to cling to her bare skin.

Fountain of trouble. He crossed his arms and paced like a caged tiger until Naomi emerged with a bundle of rolled wool in her arms. "What took so long?"

Naomi narrowed her eyes and drew upright. "What has you in such a foul mood?"

"Forgive me. I'm anxious to be on my way. Don't force her to do anything but encourage her as much as you can. She'll protest to treating herself, but remind her I'm also buying food. This is as much for you as her, so enjoy yourselves. You shouldn't finish before me, but wait for me here if you do."

"We will. I know we, I mean she," Naomi frowned and dropped her gaze. "I know how much she'll appreciate this." She thrust the bundle of wool toward him and hastened away.

With Laelia's *stola* safely under his arm, he descended the steps in a fraction of the time he'd climbed them. At the bottom, he broke into a run that would rival a chariot horse, dodging in and around people, goats, and the occasional puddle of filth as needed.

Near Otho's shop, the muscles in his legs burned, but the rest of him no longer did. He slowed to a walk and wiped the sweat from his forehead. Inside the doorway, it took a moment for his eyesight to adjust, and he waved at the slaves treading garments in the water and urine filled trough dominating the room. He recognized two of the five, and both men nodded in greeting.

A tall man with a few wisps of silver hair on his head rose from behind a wooden table. "Come here, let me look at you."

The same greeting he'd been given for years. "Otho."

The two men embraced, and Otho drew back, wiping his face with his withered hand. "It's not that hot out. Why are you bathed in sweat?"

"I've been running."

The older man's gaze flew to the doorway. "Has he found you?"

"No. I just needed the run."

Otho's shoulders fell back in place and he put his hand to his chest. "Praise the Lord. You frightened me."

"I'm sorry. I brought you something." Drusus extended the bundle in his hands toward his friend.

Otho spread Laelia's stola out on his table. Without Laelia in it, the garment looked even worse. "Can you save it?"

"If anyone can, it would be me."

"I know. That's why I came."

Otho's thin lips curved. "And I thought you missed me."

"I do." Drusus cast a quick glance about and came nearer, lowering his voice. "I miss you and the others. I don't know when I'll be able to return to our gatherings, if at all. My new master is worse than I feared."

Otho gripped his shoulder. "Remember God is faithful. Hardships are opportunities to trust in Him more completely."

"Even a master who hates Christians?"

"How do you know he does?"

"His daughter told me."

"Does she also?"

"I don't know." Drusus locked his fingers over his head and paced in circles. What if she did?

Otho pointed to a stool. "Sit. If you're going to pace like that I'll put you in the trough."

Drusus wasn't putting his bare feet anywhere near that trough. He sat, and then hit the floor rump first as the wood burst apart. Laughter spilled from the others, as Otho grinned down at him and extended his hand.

"I suppose that's my fault. You're not as light as you were as a boy."

Drusus pulled himself up and surveyed the broken shards of wood at his feet. "I'm so sorry. I know your son—"

"His memory lives in my heart, not in the things his hands made."

Even with the forgiving words meant to ease his guilt, Drusus couldn't bear to meet the man's gaze. "I'm sorry."

Otho picked up the round, flat seat of cypress and placed it in Drusus' hands. A stump of one of the three legs remained. "Everything must die to live again. This is true of all things, not only men." Otho clapped him on the shoulder. "Put the wood in the fire. It will burn hotter than the coal and help heat what I'll need to get this clean for you." The older man moved toward the shelves along the wall.

Drusus gathered the remaining pieces of the stool in his arms and knelt before the open hearth in the rear corner of the room. The sun-colored flames made him hesitate. Not from the heat, but the finality of what he was about to do. The first broken leg struck the burning coals and sparks of cinder and ash flew up like a covey of pheasant. He turned his face away and closed his eyes for a moment.

When the last piece remained, Drusus couldn't toss it into the flames. Otho's son had shaped this wood. A carpenter like Jesus, and like Jesus, met his death by decree. Otho had escaped when Caesar Nero went rampant arresting those who confessed Christ as Lord, ordering them rolled in pitch, tied to poles and used as human torches. His son had not.

Drusus held the rounded wood in his palms while sweat gathered at the base of his throat. He remembered his own mother running with him clutched tight to her chest through the stench and the screams. He'd been too young to understand what was happening, but old enough to remember. Emperor Vespasian did not actively persecute followers of Christ as Nero had, but Vespasian was old like Otho. When the Emperor's son Titus became Caesar, he might not share his father's indifference. And he, Otho, Lady Pappus and the others had more to fear than Caesar. Every manner of magistrate all the way down to the local *aedale* could have anyone refusing to recognize the Emperor's deity charged and arrested.

Laelia's father wouldn't even need to accuse him first. As his master he could kill him for any reason. The same man who had slapped Laelia for asking a question he didn't like.

Father, grant me wisdom to serve a man I must try hard not to hate. He may be my master, but you alone are my Lord. If the day comes I must choose, give me the strength and courage to follow you, even if it means my life.

Drusus surrendered the last piece of wood to the flames. He rose and brushed the grit of the stone floor from his knees joining Otho who stood mixing liquids in an aged copper pot. The sharp, foul aroma assaulted his nose and he grimaced.

Otho laughed, pouring salt into the pot next. "The worse it smells, the better it cleans." He held up a large amphora with an old cork. "This is for my best customers. Donkey urine, boiled down twice to increase its power."

Only a fuller would be excited by such a thing. "I'm going to buy you a new stool."

"Don't. It was old."

"I want to. Otherwise where will the others sit and wait while you tell them of the True God?"

Otho stirred the pot and glanced sideways. "Your seed took long enough to sprout. How many years did you listen without hearing?"

"But you didn't give up on me."

"No, because the Lord never gave up on me. Now go if you must, so I can work."

The cup of honeyed wine and two boiled eggs Drusus bought on the way helped to quiet his hunger. If he found the stool he sought soon enough, there would be time for a more substantial meal. A sorcerer called out to him as he passed her booth, promising to reveal his future for two *quadran*.

So much darkness, so many who needed Christ, everywhere he looked. He found a carpenter shop but the man wanted twice what each piece was worth and Drusus continued on. The mingled aromas of yeast, wheat, and grain as it baked caught his attention. The other slaves at Master and Lady Pappus' sometimes teased the easiest way to wake him was to pass fresh bread near his nose. Standing outside the bakery up the street was a woman with an infant in her arms. She watched the people coming and going with loaves in their baskets. Her eyes met his and there was no mistaking the hunger in them. He looked at her feet and heaviness pressed his chest.

They were bare.

He went inside and paid for two loaves and a small jar of honey. He had to pay extra for a sack to put them in, and when he returned to the street, she was gone. Scans of both ends of the corridor of shops yielded nothing. There were too many people and then he caught a glimpse of the child in her arms as she turned the corner of a building to another street. He hastened after them, dodging a group of women arguing about something and narrowly missed the backlash of a whip in front of him.

To his right, a man cowered on the street among the shattered pieces of an *amphora* of oil. His master stood over him, bringing the lash down hard across the man's raised arms. "Stupid wretch," his master growled as he drew back for another blow.

Drusus turned away. To interfere would end badly for him and the slave being beaten. Though he wanted nothing more than to take that whip and strangle the man who wielded it until his eyes rolled back in his head.

He spied the woman and child alone in the alley, about to disappear into a doorway. "Wait."

She turned toward him and clutched the child to her tighter.

"I mean you no harm." He approached slowly, extending the basket in front of him. "I only wish to give you this."

The infant reached for the bread and she angled him away. Then proceeded to propose her terms. Not so long ago trading bread for pleasure wouldn't have been so abhorrent. Of course when he'd been that man, he wouldn't have noticed her at all.

"No. It is a gift for you and the child."

Her eyes remained suspicious, so he placed the sack on the ground and backed away. "When you are in need, find the fuller shop on the Via Ostiensis. Tell Otho that Drusus sent you." He turned and walked away. Before moving back into the flow of people on the busy street, he glanced back. She and the sack were gone.

At the next carpenter shop, he found a stool with a band of iron around the bottom of the legs and bartered it down to a fair price. He hoisted it proudly when he returned to Otho's shop. "I have something for you."

Otho raised his head from where he stood working. "I have something for you." He set the stiff boar's hair brush down and raised the stola from the table. He gave it a sharp flick and let the fabric flutter down.

The wool had lightened three shades at least, and only the faintest hint of purple remained in two places. "It's a miracle."

Otho laughed and smoothed away a wrinkle. "Every day is a miracle. This is the work of a man who knows his trade."

Drusus set the stool down and reached for the wool. Dampness lingered, but Otho had combed it and now the fabric was twice as soft. He leaned down and sniffed. Instead of the straight from the fuller smell he expected, a floral fragrance filled his nose.

"I boiled it out in pure water and gave it a perfume rinse."

Drusus stared up into the eyes of the older man. "I don't know what to say."

"That's a first." Otho chuckled, then his expression smoothed. "My spirit tells me the woman this belongs to is very special."

He tried to appear unflustered. Fountain of trouble. "She's my mistress, Otho. Nothing more."

The fuller leaned against the table and crossed his arms. "I didn't mean to you. I meant to the Lord."

"She doesn't know the Lord."

"Do you think that matters to the God who created her? He knows her already, as he did you long before you called on His name."

"Well then He also knows her father."

"Maybe that's why you have been sent. To lead them both into the truth of God."

"I could sooner be Caesar."

"No one thought the shepherd boy with the harp could be king of God's people either."

A loud splash grabbed his attention. The slaves were gathering their work from the trough floor and tossing the togas, tunics and blankets into a pile in the center for rinsing. The togas would be chalked with fuller's earth, powdered clay that kept them white. Several of the togas in the pile were trimmed in crimson, the mark of those who held public office as senators.

Otho handed him Laelia's stola, which he'd folded into a compact roll. "Come, I'll pray with you. Then you should be on your way. The sun will rest soon."

Otho's prayer for him, his mistress and his master, soothed and encouraged him. Afterward, when Otho's back was to him a moment, Drusus slipped a *sesterce* onto the table near the brushes and hastened his goodbye.

In the market once again he purchased a basket and filled it with bread, eggs, and all the vegetables that would fit. Naomi should know how to make a soup or stew with them. He only knew how to boil eggs and roast meat. A pottery peddler allowed him to ride on the back of his cart and dropped him off near the baths. The sun hung low enough above the city wall he'd need to rent them a litter to make it home before dark. Even though riding in a curtained platform carried on poles by slaves was his least favorite way to travel. Trusting six men not to drop him to the ground wasn't something that came easily.

Drusus fought the flow of people leaving the baths and made it up the steps after a few brushes and apologies. Once inside, he searched for Naomi and Laelia but didn't see them, until his second look at an older woman with a striking resemblance to Naomi was actually Naomi.

She smirked as she approached him. "Let me have her clothes so I can bring her out. You won't recognize her either."

Drusus handed over the roll of wool and absorbed his own folly as Naomi walked away. Laelia would be amused he had looked right at Naomi without knowing her. But since Laelia trusted him to be her eyes, maybe not. He waited, bouncing eye contact back and forth between the few men who'd stared at his basket too long. Snatch and sprint thievery abounded everywhere, especially in crowds.

He would have liked a proper bath. The baths were uniquely Roman, unlike most things in their city. He enjoyed the *tepidarium* room best. The warm water would soothe his muscles and surround him in steam that seemed to wash him inside and out before a dip in the cooler *frigidarium*. A sponge and water from the fountain was hardly the same but did the job anyway.

A scuffle erupted at the entrance. Two men argued over something, their slaves poised on either side with raised fists themselves. A tap on his shoulder and he turned, instinctively reaching for his belt where the twins were hidden.

An attacker would have been less of a shock.

Laelia's dark hair curled and twisted into a swirl atop her head while loose tendrils framed her face. A rose tint graced her cheeks and her eyes were rimmed in kohl, making them even more striking. Her lips were colored the deep pink of the evening sky, curved in a smile he wanted to kiss. She smelled divine, like honey and lilac flowers. The cleaned *stola* accented her slender body now rather than marring her appearance with its stains. For the second time in a single day, he could find no words to speak.

"Thank you for the coin and urging me to come. I didn't realize how much I'd missed this."

"Thank you for accepting. I thought we might return home by litter if you don't mind. I don't want Naomi to be burdened with the large basket of food but I can't carry it and walk with you at the same time." Even if he could, Naomi was a much more inviting target for thieves.

"If you have coin for it." She held her hand out and he placed it on his arm.

Naomi picked up the basket and beamed beside Laelia like a proud mother. They began to leave and though the altercation from earlier had dissipated, one of the men remained. He stared at Laelia as they passed. A look Drusus didn't like because it was lewd more than appreciative.

The man's gaze met his and without so much as a pause or misstep, Drusus shot him a menacing glare. For a moment the man returned it, and Drusus feared a confrontation. He'd wanted the man to back off, not start a fight. As they passed him, the man hitched his toga higher on his arm and turned away. His pair of slaves followed.

Thank you, God. "Steps, my lady."

She nodded and he counted them for her as they descended. It felt undeniably good to have been the big dog that stared the other dog into lying down belly up. Until he remembered he was charged with helping Laelia find a husband.

God help him if he had to remain at her side when that day came.

Chapter 8

Motion without fear or needing to concentrate was a new sensation for Laelia. The slaves who carried the litter rarely jarred them or changed pace abruptly. Having to match Drusus' stride and pace wasn't easy at times, so she appreciated the skill required for the eight men to carry them on the cushioned platform between two poles so smoothly.

Drusus and Naomi were both quiet. Maybe they were enjoying the ride as she was. Of course they could be mouthing and gesturing an entire conversation for all she knew. When the litter stopped and was set down, Naomi assisted her to the street where she waited for Drusus. She held her hand out so he wouldn't ask permission to take it, and then led her toward the house. The low creak of the door hinges sounded well before she reached it. Naomi must have opened the door ahead of them.

They entered the house, where the sound of the fountain greeted her. But Drusus' arm shifted as if he'd taken a step back, pulling her to a stop.

"Where were you?"

Father. Laelia's chest tightened. "At the baths."

Drusus' fingers tightened on hers.

"Who repaired the fountain?"

"I did, Master. Last evening."

"Naomi carries a basket full of food and you're wearing a new stola."

"It's not new, Father."

"Don't lie to me." He grabbed her arm, yanking her from Drusus' side. "You were begging again."

"I wasn't."

"You're lying!" He let go of her arm. Oh gods. She threw her hands out to try to brace herself but the blow to her head rocked her unsteady.

Rough arms embraced her and she was spinning until something pressed her against the wall.

"Get out of the way," father yelled.

Drusus was holding her to the wall, putting himself between them. "Master, I beg you to hear me first. If punishment is due it will be mine."

Juno, help us.

"Explain."

"Lady Pappus gave me two sesterces yesterday as I left. We used them today."

The falling water and her own heavy breathing filled the long moment continuing to grow. She moved one arm from its awkward angle at her side to place it flat on Drusus' back. What was happening?

"Two sesterces don't buy a new stola."

"The fuller Otho restored it. I asked Laelia to permit this while she and Naomi bathed, thinking that my lord's interests would be best served if the mistress were to appear to her fullest advantage. If there is fault, my lord, it is mine and I willingly submit to your judgement."

He's protecting me. She saw herself calmly pushing him aside and stepping forward. Telling her father she'd agreed and it had been her decision in the end. Drusus had simply obeyed and handed over his coin. But to her shame, she stayed silent.

"I have six coppers left, my lord, which by law are now yours." Drusus' back shifted. The soft clink of coins and then stillness again. The pain in her temple had begun to throb as she waited to see if more was coming. For them both.

"Join Naomi in the kitchen." Her father's tone remained sharp, and the urge to try to flee was strong.

Drusus hadn't moved and though she desperately wanted him to stay, she pressed her palm into his back. "Go," she whispered.

But he still didn't move. She pressed harder until he took a step forward. In the span of a few breaths, she was alone with her father.

"You do look the better for it. Perhaps a chance at a betrothal still exists that would leave me with some security and a remnant of dignity. If you can keep yourself clean and learn to be of some use to a household. You do know that is the only reason the slave is here, don't you?"

She nodded. He drew near, caging her jaw with his fingertips while she resisted trying to pull free of his grasp.

"Do not make your mother's mistake. He is to be your eyes and *nothing more*. Do you understand?"

Through the resistance of his hold on her face, she nodded again.

"Answer me."

"I understand."

He released her and she put her palm flat to the wall behind her, trying to draw its strength into her limbs.

"Wait for me in the *triclinium*."

Laelia followed the walls and then took her place on the three sided couch she'd shared with Drusus last evening. The pain in her head continued to throb and her entire body felt as if it had been poured into her skin.

Father was home.

In the pitch black silence, the death hound growled.

Chapter 9

Drusus lay on his back in the dark of his store room, but sleep wouldn't come. The evening meal had been a miserable affair. Laelia had retreated into herself again, eating little of her boiled eggs, fish, and bread. She hadn't touched the wine Naomi had poured for her. Master Ricarri had ignored her while devouring food he had not provided, his presence a stifling plague until he retired to his chamber.

Drusus had gone to her, asking is she was all right. Laelia had only nodded and requested to be taken to her chamber. In the short walk there, he'd struggled with what to say. 'Goodnight' was all he'd managed before she shut the door without responding.

Failing. Still failing.

He turned on his side with a huff, pushing the mint leaf in his mouth to his other cheek and tugging at the empty grain sack covering him. The pallet of them he'd made on the floor didn't yield a comfortable position no matter which way he lay. Also irritating him was that he'd lied earlier about how much coin he actually possessed. But he'd rather throw the rest of it into the Tiber than hand it over to Master Ricarri.

Something clattered in the kitchen beyond the closed door. Drusus reached for his belt beneath the sacks and slid one of the twins free. He stood and eased the door open, the hinges grinding in spite of his effort at silence.

"Drusus?"

Laelia.

"Yes." He eased the door further, looking for her outline in the soft glow of the hearth's embers.

"Why are you in the storeroom?"

"I'm sleeping here." He kept his voice low, not knowing how soundly Master Ricarri and Naomi slept in the other chambers. "Did you need something?"

"Yes. To talk with you. Come sit with me."

Drusus carefully made his way around the table between them toward the orange glow. The lamp on the shelf above lit quickly and a tiny flame pushed the darkness to the outer walls. He turned to find Laelia sitting on the floor at his feet, wrapped in a blanket with her dark hair hanging loose around her face.

He should blow out the lamp. Now.

"I'm sorry my father took the last of your coin."

"I'm sorry he struck you again."

"Putting yourself between us was dangerous. I was deeply moved, but you shouldn't do it again."

He held the lamp out and sat down beside her, studying her features and the new bruise high on her cheek. "You're my mistress."

"Yes." Within the blanket she shifted to better face him and their knees touched. But she didn't adjust to break the contact. "And I'm ordering you not to do it again."

The words, the tone, even her posture when she'd delivered them were the most commanding and confident she'd been the past two days. Yet he had no intention of honoring them. "As your servant I'm sworn to protect you."

"I know." From the rim of the blanket her hand emerged and settled on his knee. "And you can't do that if you're dead."

He swallowed, and gently grasped her wrist to remove her palm from his knee. When she didn't resist his light hold, he wanted to tug her into his lap and kiss her.

Fountain of trouble.

Deliberately he pushed her arm toward her own knee and placed her hand there. "I can't do nothing while he beats you."

"If no one has told you yet," she snapped, "this is Rome. He's the *pater familias* and can do whatever he wants."

"Shhhhh," he whispered, trying to soothe her. "I'm aware," he said softly, listening for any sound that might be the master or Naomi.

"Drusus, I need you."

That he heard loud and clear, the admission reaching a place beyond his physical needs.

"I'm not ignorant of my situation. A man in need of a wife, and willing to look past her blindness, is about as likely as the Tiber freezing over. If I can find such a man who is also willing to throw a few coins my father's way now and then, I need you to see for me. You can't do that with two black eyes."

It went against every instinct to protect her, but she was right. "I know."

They sat in quiet for a while until she leaned her upper body toward him and sniffed. "What is that strange scent that always lingers in your mouth? Sometimes it's stronger than others, like now."

"Peppermint leaf. It eases my stomach pains."

Laying the two leaves between his cheek and teeth to suck on throughout the day was something he'd done so many years, he often forgot they were there.

Her brows drew together and her mouth turned down. "Your stomach hurts you?"

"Not as often with the peppermint and since I've learned to avoid spices and *garum*."

"My father puts *garum* on everything except bread. When we have it."

The spicy fish sauce might explain his temper. No, not even then.

"I hope your peppermint helps you. I would be..." she clutched the blanket around her tighter. "It would trouble me a great deal to know you were in pain."

"I feel the same." As soon as the words left his mouth he regretted them in light of their earlier disagreement.

But in the soft lamp light, Laelia half-smiled. "Thank you." From the intensity in her eyes, he would swear she could see him. "I'm stronger than I look."

"I don't doubt that."

She rose from the floor, and he did the same, being careful to bring the lamp up with them. "Should I escort you back to your chamber?"

"No. And I will find a way to pay you back. It's a matter of honor."

He sighed heavily. "Then good night, Mistress."

"Good night, Drusus."

She felt for the edge of the doorway and disappeared beyond it like an apparition.

Drusus extinguished the lamp and returned to his pallet on the floor. He'd be awake for hours now with the memory of her hand on his knee and her hair spilling around her face in gentle waves. Since he'd be awake anyway, he might as well throw the twins if he couldn't run off what ailed him. That was probably best anyway, since he might run straight to the brothels he'd known so well in his past.

He retrieved the lamp and relit the wick. The small flame lit his storeroom well enough to clear an area with a good distance to one of several empty crates. He reached high above his head with both arms, and then bent to touch his toes and stretch his back. After a few rolls of his neck he took up his knives and set his stance as his master taught him. A dark swirl in the grain of the wood became his target. In a single fluid movement as familiar as breathing, he drew the knife behind his ear building momentum from his shoulder to his elbow and then sprung forward to release the knife like a catapult firing.

Too fast to observe, he knew the blade rotated end over end until the point stuck in the wood with a sharp thump. But a closer look stole his satisfaction. The handle angled up with the blade a good half-inch to the right of the knot in the wood.

He hadn't thrown that far off in years.

His second knife stuck flat and true, but still more than an inch off the target. He strode to the crate and yanked them both free by the handles. This close, a mere twelve feet or so between him and the target, should prove no challenge at all. He hadn't thrown since his master's death. Not the longest stint without practice but the most eventful to be certain.

It didn't matter. He'd throw all night or until his blade stuck straight and on target ten times in a row—whichever came first. Missing the mark could get someone killed.

He knew that better than anyone.

Chapter 10

Laelia's empty stomach rumbled the moment she took her *stola* from Naomi to dress.

"While we have plenty, you need to eat better than you did last night. A strong wind might carry you away."

Sometimes she wished it would. "I don't have much of an appetite when father is home."

"He's already gone. He had me prepare his satchel with his toga and extra sandals." Naomi pulled the tortoise shell comb through Laelia's hair in short, quick strokes.

If father had taken his toga, he would be gone at least three weeks on the ships. Her empty stomach sank. "Did he leave coin for us?"

The comb stilled in her hair. "Not a single *sesterce*."

How did he expect them to eat? To buy oil for the lamps and pay the taxes due soon?

Naomi resumed combing her hair. "I'll take a bowl and join the beggars at the temple of Diana."

"I'll go."

"You know what he will do if he finds out, and my face is not as well-known as yours."

Of course she did. The memory of that beating hadn't diminished in any detail in over two years. The cracked rib that ached for months afterward. The bruises on her face that turned an array of colors she would never again see.

There was another way.

Even as she considered it her heart screamed in defiance.

Feeling along the table top as Drusus had taught her, she located her mother's jeweled dagger and slid it inside her dress. The calm resolve surprised her. "Where is Drusus?"

"Still in the store room I think. I'll wake him and make sure he doesn't sleep past sunrise again."

"No, let him sleep."

"But—"

"Let him sleep. Or have you forgotten his kindness and generosity yesterday already?"

"Of course not, but it's improper for—"

"I don't care. Let him sleep. When he wakes have him join me in the *peristyle*. If any of the grapes or bread he bought yesterday remains, please bring it to me there. Do so quietly, and work elsewhere in the house this morning so as not to rouse him." Where had *that* come from? She'd swear her mother had spoken—calm, fully in command and strong. Laelia was none of those things. Or was she?

"Yes, my lady."

After a long moment, Laelia listened to be sure she was alone in her chamber. She closed her fingers around the handle of her most precious possession and brought the blunt end of the handle to her cheek. This knife had been handed down through the women of her family back to the days of the Republic before the Caesars. She cursed her father a thousand times, and then a thousand times more in her mind. She brushed at the corner of her eyes and sniffed, making her back straight as she could. "Forgive me, Mother."

Drusus woke and pushed up from his pallet on the floor. Oooh—that hurt. He rubbed at his right arm and shoulder, knowing they would feel worse tomorrow. Dressing required only his sandals and belt since he slept in his tunic as a rule. With Laelia's father in residence, Drusus slipped the twins into their concealed sheaths within the belt. Laelia might have ordered him not to intervene, but submission was a choice. Not an absolute.

Something Master Ricarri would do well to remember.

In the kitchen, daylight filtered through a small grated window much brighter than it should be. What time was it? The only way to estimate would be to see where the sun stood in the sky. Sundials were somewhat more reliable than water clocks but that wasn't saying much. This house appeared to possess neither but that didn't surprise him.

He spotted Laelia alone in the *peristyle*. She sat just off the paved stone path pulling up grass and weeds with her bare hands. Earth clung to her fingers and dusted her freshly cleaned stola but instead of making him cringe, he smiled. A growing pile of weeds beside her and the small area she'd already cleared down to the dirt told him two things.

First, he'd overslept. Badly. Second, she'd found purpose in a task. He thanked God for that and crept closer.

She hummed a tune he didn't recognize which is why she must not have heard his footsteps. A yellow butterfly alighted on a stalk of grass near her, spreading its wings to her in the sunshine like the Spirit of God Himself. When she reached toward it as if she could see it, he held his breath.

The butterfly didn't move away and when she grabbed the weed by the stalk, she crushed the small animal in a fistful of grass and threw them both onto her pile.

He tried not to laugh and failed. He couldn't stop, or tear his gaze from the sight of the mangled wings flittering in death throes atop the pile of weeds. Even when her body jerked in surprise and her chin shot his direction.

"Drusus?"

"Yes, Mistress."

Her mouth twisted into a scowl as her forehead lined above a severely dipped brow. "What is it you find so amusing?"

He deserved the anger. Tears were beginning to prick the corners of his eyes and he summoned every bit of will he possessed to stifle his dying laughter.

Her hand went to her hip. "I asked you what is so amusing."

He couldn't tell her the truth but had to think fast so as not to lie. Nothing came except a deeper shade of red in her cheeks. He sighed, knowing he would lie. Again. *God forgive me.* "Apologies, Mistress. I recalled a dream I had last night. Forgive me, I meant no offense. I also beg your forgiveness for oversleeping."

Her face softened and the scowl faded—some. "I'm not sure I believe you but now that you're awake you can help me."

"Of course, Mistress." Drusus knelt beside her. "Will your father be joining us?" Like wolves, he preferred the ones he could see rather than the ones he only knew were nearby.

"My father isn't here. He'll be gone some time."

Praise God for that unexpected blessing. He seized a clump of weeds and yanked them up. Dirt clung to the white roots and sprinkled the coarse wool of his tunic. He began his own pile and they worked in a comfortable quiet until a rather impressive patch of bare ground stretched between them. The way Laelia pulled weeds reminded him of the way soldiers raided their secret gatherings. Men and women yanked from their feet in hate for nothing more than following Christ. He shouldn't have laughed but surely after all this time she wouldn't still be this angry. Perhaps something else bothered her.

Women were as complicated as all those laws some in the church thought they all must follow.

Otho told him not to worry about whether or not their meat came from the pagan temples or if he could carry a basket on Saturday. If he believed Jesus was the son of the living God and died so Drusus didn't have to spend the afterlife in torment separated from God, that was what mattered. All those rules came down to two. Love God completely and those around him the same.

Laelia rose and dusted the dirt from her stola but her hands were so caked with the black soil she added more than she shook off.

Drusus cringed and hoped that wouldn't stain. "Are you finished for this morning?"

"No, moving to a new spot and stretching my legs." She crept forward a few paces and paused when her sandaled foot pressed into the weeds instead of dirt. She took a few more steps and returned to her knees again.

"How did you know where to move to?"

"When I'm in the grass and weeds, I feel the stalks and edges tickle my foot through the straps of my sandals and I hear the rustle they make against the hem of my *stola*."

"Well done."

She smiled and grabbed a handful of the green shoots. "Thank you."

When he could no longer reach any more grass, he also moved. Starting in the corner and orderly working around would be his preference, but he wanted to remain near her. He didn't want to miss the floral fragrance of the perfume lingering from her bath yesterday when the breeze stirred.

"I am glad you had a kind master before," Laelia said. "I'm sorry that here you do not."

He read the sorrow on her face as clear as in her voice. "I think I do. In any other house I would have been flogged for sleeping past sunrise while my mistress toiled."

"I meant my father. I'm not much of a master of anything." Her lips flattened and she yanked another weed from the dirt. "Even my own body."

He worked to frame a response that would reassure her but everything sounded wrong, as if she didn't have a right to still grieve her sight.

"I'm trying though," she murmured and returned to her work.

Something told him to remain silent for now and allow her to row through the waters of her thoughts without intrusion.

After they cleared another patch, Naomi emerged from the villa carrying a basket. "Bread, cheese and boiled eggs is all that's left from yesterday." The older woman took the two steps down to the stone path and paused to stare at Laelia. She frowned, no doubt from the dirt now covering the lower half of Laelia's *stola*.

Drusus waved to catch her attention and shook his head side to side with a finger to his lips.

Naomi's frown faded and she nodded in understanding. "You've been working hard."

Laelia rose and scrubbed her hands together to dust the dirt off. "It's long past time to reclaim this garden. Let's eat at the bench."

Naomi carried the basket to the stone bench and left it there. "I'll bring a basin of water from the kitchen so you can wash your hands."

He'd managed to keep his hands cleaner than Laelia because he didn't need to run his fingers through the dirt to find the weeds. She wiped the top of her forearm across the pebbles of sweat gathered on her forehead. "I don't suppose you want my dirty hand on your arm."

He took hold of her hand and placed it on his arm just above the bend of his elbow where it belonged. "Whenever you are ready." He stared at the damp tendrils of hair clinging to the skin of her cheek in front of her ear. He hoped Naomi would think to bring a cloth for her as well.

She applied the slight pressure with her dirt covered fingers and they traveled the short distance to the bench. He squeezed her hand when they reached it and she released him before feeling for the low seat and settling onto it.

Naomi returned with the clay basin half full of water and a towel which she set beside Laelia near the food. "Is there anything else you need?"

"Yes. Take oil from one of the lamps if there's no more in the storeroom and polish this." Laelia pulled a beautiful jeweled dagger from her bosom and held it out to Naomi. He wasn't sure which shocked him more. That she'd also been carrying a blade, or that the handle of it was crusted with precious stones.

Something was happening in the silence between them, but he couldn't understand it. Not even when Naomi said, "Are you sure?"

"Yes." Laelia's tone was firm, which deepened the frown on Naomi's face.

Naomi took it and departed without meeting his questioning stare.

Laelia turned on the bench and began to clean her hands in the basin. "After our meal I need you to take me to see a collector in the forum."

She was going to sell it, not use it. Suddenly her protracted anger all morning made sense. Especially since the way Naomi had behaved suggested the knife was dear to Laelia.

Laelia pulled her hands from the basin and shook the droplets of water away. "Did I remove all the dirt?"

"Not quite. May I assist?"

"Of course."

He knelt on the ground beside her and rinsed his own hands first. Then he guided her fingers back into the water and rubbed at the stubborn dirt trapped between the folds of skin on her knuckles. With his thumbnail he scraped the caked dirt from beneath all ten of hers, careful not to press too deep and hurt her. The towel had warmed in the sun and he wrapped her fingers in the folds one at a time to dry them well, remembering how they'd felt against his chest. He glanced at her, and her expression fired his blood.

Her parted lips and flushed cheeks proved she was no less affected than he, though that hadn't been his intent.

He rose and flipped the towel over his shoulder, taking a deep breath. "I'm finished."

She crossed her arms and a shiver passed through her shoulders he would have missed if he'd blinked at the wrong time.

But he hadn't. And the fountain of trouble beckoned.

Chapter 11

The hard crust cracking in Laelia's fingers was something familiar. Something to distract her from the unease Drusus' rather thorough cleaning of her hands had aroused.

"Do you want me to peel you an egg?" he asked.

"Yes." Boiled eggs and bread were so tiresome, but she remained grateful for the meal. She missed colors. The yellow of an egg, the pink of an evening sky, and the brilliant green of the emeralds in her mother's dagger.

"Here you are, Mistress. Your cup of wine is a handbreadth to the left of your knee."

Laelia held her hand out and felt the cool, slick egg drop into her palm. "Thank you."

They finished the meal in a comfortable quiet before Laelia rose to stretch.

Wicker creaked, which must be Drusus collecting their basket. "I'll return this to the kitchen and let Naomi know we're ready."

"I'll go with you." Laelia held her hand out so he could take it and place it on his arm.

"Apologies, but I need both my hands to walk with you. Do you mind waiting for me while I return these things to the kitchen?"

"No, go ahead."

His footfalls fell fast and heavy on the stone. A smile formed as she listened to him run. Either nature called or he didn't want her waiting long. She would need time alone in her chamber to tend that need herself before having Naomi comb her hair again. The more desperate she appeared, the less coin she would be offered for her mother's dagger. She cocked her head as the heavy thumps resumed. They stopped as the strong scent of his peppermint leaves met her nose.

"I'm ready now, Mistress." He panted. So loud she could almost see his chest heaving up and down in her mind.

"No you aren't. You sound like Pheidippides when he reached Athens."

"Forgive me, my lady, but I don't know who that is."

"Surely you know the story of Pheidippides, the Greek messenger who ran from the battlefield of Marathon to Athens."

"I don't know that story."

"That is the story. Pheidippides ran straight to Athens, without stopping, to tell the assembly there they had defeated the Persians. As soon as he told them 'we have won', he collapsed and died."

"That's rather tragic."

It was, in a way. She'd never thought of it before that Pheidippides had been a man with a story of his own being lived out until it ended in the Athenian assembly. When she held her hand out for him, he took it and wrapped her fingers around his arm and they walked from the peristyle.

"Two steps, Mistress."

Once inside the house, Laelia stopped him outside the door of her chamber. "Please send Naomi to me in my chamber. I'll send her for you when I'm ready to leave."

"Yes, Mistress."

Laelia didn't have to wait long.

She heard Naomi enter and tsk. "Your face is too pink."

Laelia touched her cheeks and found them very warm. "I haven't been in the sun that long since I became ill."

"It's been longer than that." Naomi came to stand nearer. "Are you really going to do this?"

"I have to." Laelia straightened and rolled her head to try to work a knot from her back. "Would you comb my hair again and help me with my color pots?"

"Color?"

"Yes. The less poor I appear the better price I'll garner. And apparently I've burned my face like a vineyard slave."

Laelia assumed her seat at her dressing table where only three days ago she'd been ready to open her vein. So much was different now. So much remained unchanged. Remaining still proved a challenge when the kohl stick first touch her closed eyelid. Holding her breath helped but she couldn't do it for long. After a few tense moments and one slip that had to be rubbed away with oil, Naomi finished with the lip stain. It felt grittier than Laelia remembered, but had likely gone dry in the months without use. Even before losing her sight, she rarely had occasion to apply her cosmetics. When her hair was finished, she squared her body and raised her chin. "How do I look?"

"Like your mother." Naomi's voice held sadness and Laelia reached out, hoping to grasp her arm or hand.

"I know you miss her too."

"I never knew a finer woman in all my life. It was wrong of the gods to take her from you so soon."

The gods. Her mother worshiped the Egyptian goddess Isis until the day she died. Returning to her temple or seeing her prayer statue in the garden, without her mother beside her had been too painful. She'd had Naomi remove the statue, and tried to find the peace she craved in other temples. Diana, Artemis, Juno, even Vesta. Those visits always left her as lost as when she entered and lately, even Juno no longer made her presence felt. "Sometimes, I don't think the gods care."

"Surely they do. They sent you Drusus."

Perhaps. Perhaps it was Juno, or her father Jupiter, that was making him stay. "Let's not keep him waiting. Where's my dagger?"

There was a long pause before Naomi answered. "In the kitchen."

Laelia held back a grimace. Naomi had taken far too long to answer and when she did, she sounded even more sorrowful than before. "Wrap it in our best cloth and give it to Drusus to carry. I wish you to remain here while he and I go."

"But—"

"Do as I ask." She sensed Naomi's reluctance in the following stillness. "Please. We'll be fine."

"Yes, my lady."

Leaving Naomi behind would hurt her feelings more than it would ease the shared burden of relinquishing this part of her mother. But she couldn't be trusted not to cry, perhaps even plead, when the dagger changed hands and was lost to them forever. As it was, she would have a difficult enough time trying not to do so herself.

If the gods were listening and wanted to show her their favor, they could start with giving her back her sight. And if they weren't feeling that generous, she'd take the next best thing—news that her father had met with an accident while on his travels. If he discovered she'd sold the dagger without telling him, he would be livid. He didn't care a potshard about her only link to her mother, but because the only time she'd ever fought him was when he'd tried to take it from her once before.

She was about to willingly hand it over now for as much coin as she could get for it. She had a plan, and as Seneca the stoic philosopher had said, *it is best to endure what you cannot change.* She couldn't change her blindness, her lineage, or her scandalous past betrothal.

Right now, she could change her poverty. Even if her heart stayed with the dagger.

Chapter 12

Something was very wrong with Laelia. She'd emerged from her chamber extraordinarily beautiful, her features accented in the way women sometimes did. But she'd been silent since leaving the house. Her stride constantly hesitated, forcing Drusus to shuffle alongside while she gripped his arm far too tight. Four boys shouted as they chased a cat on the narrow street, rushing past them. She stopped abruptly and drew tight to his side.

Hopefully the orange and white striped cat escaped whatever mischief they planned. He waited for the boys to run past them and patted Laelia's hand on his arm. "You're safe."

"What was that?"

"Boys chasing a cat."

She eased the grip on his arm and turned her face toward his. "I'm sorry for stopping suddenly."

"It's all right, Mistress. But since we've stopped I'm going to retie my sandals."

She released him and allowed her arms to hang at her side.

He would rather have stopped near something, a merchant's table or a wall for her to hold onto so she wouldn't feel adrift, though he'd be an arm's length away at most. His upper thigh kicked in protest when he knelt to untie and retie his sandal strap. He rose, knelt on the other leg for a moment and then massaged the flesh of his upper arm. The returning blood stung like bees beneath the fading marks of her fingers. He spit the well-spent peppermint leaves from his mouth and came to his feet. "Thank you."

Her morose expression remained while she held out her hand for him. They continued on without further incident, though in this part of the city a sharp eye had to be kept above as well as in front. More than once he'd been the recipient of a shower of filth pitched from a window of the floors of the *insulae* buildings above, once with Master Pappus. Tenants were supposed to empty their chamber pots in the central drain leading to the sewer, but the window proved easier, to the hazard of those passing below.

"Are we almost there?" Laelia asked.

"Yes, the booth is about sixty *pedes* away on the right. We need to cross one more intersection." Cross traffic never failed to make him nervous, because he needed to watch for hazards in every direction. They passed through the crossing and he angled them toward a wooden sign with the outline of a sword carved on the smooth surface hanging below a faded gray cotton awning Drusus knew well. The old man who owned this metal shop specializing in weapons had been a long-time friend of Master Pappus. Though why Laelia had wanted to come here remained a mystery. Septimus had two sons but they both had wives and children.

"We approach, Mistress. Two steps and then a right turn." She nodded and once inside, Drusus took a moment to enjoy the sight of baskets full of swords. Most were the *gladius*, a short sword favored by the army and gladiators alike. Hanging from leather thongs on the walls were knives and daggers of every size, shape, and material. A beautiful pair of leaf-shaped steel blades with carved bronze handles sat displayed on a fan of peacock feathers on the table in the corner. When he made eye contact with the man in the corner, his blood turned cold.

It can't be.

But it was Tiberius staring back at him, a sardonic expression on his face as he cleared his throat. "I'm not sure what I want to know first." Tiberius straightened and his gaze lingered on Laelia as his grin widened. "Where you've been all this time or who the beauty is at your side."

Tiberius' gaze stripped her bare in his thoughts every place it traveled.

"Where is Septimus?" Drusus asked sharply, drawing Tiberius' gaze off Laelia's body.

"In his family tomb somewhere along the *Via Appia* would be my guess," Tiberius said with a clear sense of amusement.

"You know each other?" Laelia asked.

"Not anymore," Drusus said coldly, before Tiberius could speak.

Tiberius held his grin in place but Drusus could tell it was requiring effort. "That's not a very kind thing to say."

"My mistress is here on business. Ours is finished." Drusus looked from Tiberius to Laelia, hoping she wouldn't ask questions. Besides Otho, Tiberius was the only other person in Rome who knew all his secrets.

Laelia released his arm and angled her face toward Tiberius. "I've brought you an exceptional piece. My servant will show it to you."

Tiberius maintained that fake smile even now. "Very well then."

Drusus pulled the linen wrapped dagger from his belt and unbound it, holding it out to Tiberius handle first to reveal the array of jewels inlaid in the bone. Tiberius' eyes rounded a moment before he recovered himself and reached to take it. "How did you come by this, my lady?"

If Laelia was affronted by the question, she hid it with the calmness of an assassin. "The dagger was a gift. It doesn't suit me."

Tiberius tested the sharpness of the blade with his thumb and the balance of the weapon on his palm, just as Drusus had when Naomi handed it to him in the kitchen. While no good for throwing, the knife was extraordinarily beautiful. Like its owner.

"I'll give you fifty *denarii* and a tenth discount on a replacement from my collection. One more suited to your tastes."

Drusus was glad Laelia wasn't touching him, for she would have felt the tautness stiffening his frame. Both from the low offer and the way Tiberius' appraising gaze turned from the dagger to Laelia again.

"What would suit me is a fair price for the dagger. The emeralds encrusted in the handle alone are worth that price."

Tiberius' gaze narrowed and he passed his free hand back and forth in front of Laelia's face. When she failed to react, he turned to Drusus. "She's blind?"

"Yes," Laelia answered. "But not deaf. Nor am I unaware of the worth of my weapon so make me a true offer or I will be on my way."

In spite of the tension between him and Tiberius, Drusus wanted to cheer. He'd known there was fire in her and right now, it was blazing.

Tiberius appraised her head to feet and then the dagger he still held. "A hundred *denarii* is my best offer, my lady." Tiberius turned his gaze on Drusus. "But I would give you a thousand right now, in gold, for your slave."

Fear punched him in the chest as their stares met. There was no apology in Tiberius' eyes. Only calculation and greed. Nothing remained of the friendship they'd once shared.

"Drusus isn't for sale at any price." Laelia's voice cut through the tension. "You're closer to my price of a hundred and twenty for the dagger."

Her strongly worded refusal was reassuring. Tiberius appeared less convinced, as he twirled the dagger in his hand. "Everything has a price. Surely if the number were temptation enough, you'd consider parting with him."

To confront Tiberius now would reveal his past to Laelia. But from Laelia's posture she was growing as annoyed as he was with Tiberius' deflection. She stepped up and held her hand out. "Give me my dagger or the hundred *denarii*. That is all I came here to sell and all I will continue to discuss."

Drusus continued to stare into Tiberius' unrelenting gaze. He was not a man to relinquish what he wanted so easily. As Tiberius studied him in turn, he breathed a heavy sigh and looked away first. "A hundred *denarii* it is, my lady. Give me a moment to collect it."

Tiberius walked to the back of the small booth and took a key from around his neck to unlock a wooden chest perched on a low shelf.

"Drusus," Laelia whispered. "Can you count to a hundred?"

"Yes, Mistress," he answered in a low tone. He could count well beyond that, having learned numbers, as well as how to add, subtract and multiply, from the head servant in Master Pappus' villa.

"Make sure all the coin is there before we leave. I don't trust him."

"I'm not deaf either," Tiberius called from the back of the booth. "It's all here, but I'll count it with Drusus to ease your concerns."

He came and poured a leather sack of silver coins on the wooden table. Drusus counted the coins into piles of ten. There were ten piles as there should be. "A hundred *denarii* exactly, Mistress."

Laelia nodded and Drusus reached for the leather pouch on the table.

Tiberius snatched it away. "The leather pouch isn't included."

Drusus' empty fingers formed a fist as he struggled to control his temper. He pulled the scarlet cloth from beneath Laelia's dagger and the knife rolled and clattered on the wood between them. "Neither is the linen."

Drusus collected the coins and secured them inside the cloth, taking care to knot the corners well. He dropped the bundle of coins down the front of his tunic where it would snag against his belt to have both hands free to lead Laelia. "Are you ready, Mistress?"

"Yes." She reached her hand out for him and he placed it on his arm.

"A pleasure doing business with you," Tiberius said with mock cheerfulness. "If I could ever persuade you to change your mind for the slave—"

"No thank you," Laelia said coldly and started forward immediately.

Drusus gave Tiberius a backward glance, as much to threaten with his glare as to guard their exit. On the long walk home, he continued to check behind them often. Tiberius was prone to violence to get what he wanted. At least that they had never had in common.

Laelia was quiet, and he was content to walk in silence except for the few verbal alerts the traffic required. With every step his already strained temper at Laelia's father became more potent. If the man provided for his daughter as he should, none of this would have transpired.

She sniffed beside him. He'd been so lost in his own dark mood and scanning for hazards he'd failed to notice her red-rimmed eyes or the streaks of moisture lining her face.

"Mistress, are you all right?" Of course she wasn't, but he didn't know what else to say.

Her stride broke and she fell to her knees on the cobbled stone street. Strangers on the street watched but none offered to help. He crouched beside her, his every instinct to gather her into his arms. "I'm here."

Without warning, she clutched the wool of his tunic like a lifeline.

He took hold of her wrist to reassure her. "I'm right here."

"I know." A snivel followed her hoarse whisper and the fists holding his tunic tightened, pulling the fabric tight across his back. "I know you are."

She pulled him closer and put her forehead on his shoulder where the tears became shuddered sobs. Corners of his mind whispered warnings. Propriety, uninvited touch, and the slave code of conduct, yet he released her wrist to cradle her head against him, surrounding her trembling frame with his other arm. Her arms encircled his neck and she clung to him like a barrel on the open sea, the tears soaking into the wool of his tunic with every sob.

He wasn't letting her walk home like this. He slid an arm under her knees and picked her up like a child. She tucked the top of her head into the curve of his neck and her whole body relaxed into his hold. Her sobs slowed as he carried her, drawing more stares than before. Twilight had fallen and so would the temperature soon. He quickened his pace, glad she was light and he knew the way without her. The coin trapped between them dug into his already aching stomach, but at least that pain reassured him he hadn't lost it. At the front door of their house, he managed to open the latch without jarring her.

Naomi appeared in the hall and rushed toward them. "What happened?"

"She fell." Drusus continued toward Laelia's chamber with Naomi trailing alongside. "Nothing's broken but her hands and knees are scraped. Bring wine, salt and clean cloth to her chamber."

Naomi ran for the kitchen while he carried Laelia into her chamber. He spotted the outline of her bed in a corner of the dim room and laid her on top of the colorless blanket.

She curled onto her side and grabbed for his hand. "Don't go."

"I'm not." He stroked her upper arm carefully. "I'm here."

Naomi entered the room and he quickly pulled his hand away. The way her gaze flashed to his told him she'd seen. She set the basket she carried on the floor and hurried to light the lamp stand. He reached inside his tunic to remove the bundle of coins and thanked God through all that the knots held and none were lost. He set the bundle beside a small group of jars on her dressing table and picked up the stool to place it at the foot of Laelia's bed.

The light from the lamps revealed a wary look from Naomi when he sat on the stool. He understood the look, and the unspoken accusation behind it. Yes, he was partly to blame for the fall, and the dirt and grit Naomi cleaned from Laelia's hands. Consumed in his own anger, he'd missed that her own emotions were a tangled mess while she walked right beside him. Yes, he should have left this chamber the moment he'd set her down on the bed. And no, he shouldn't be untying her sandal straps right now either.

The thin leather cord unknotted under his nimble fingers and a light tug pulled the shoe free. The other one proved a challenge because the knot faced the blanket underneath her ankle. He considered grasping her leg just above the straps to raise it but he'd touched far too much of her already. As if reading his thoughts, she straightened her leg and rotated her toes to the ceiling. He removed that sandal faster than the first, knowing the angle would be uncomfortable.

When Naomi held a wine-sodden cloth to Laelia's palm, she winced and curled her toes. He wanted to comfort her but knew worse was coming. When Naomi rinsed them with salt water, Laelia whimpered and curled into a ball. Naomi rubbed Laelia's arm with her free hand. "The sting will pass soon, little one."

Drusus rested his elbows to his knees and bowed his head. He prayed for God to take the pain from her body, and her heart, and keep the hatred for her father, and now for Tiberius, from his.

When he opened his eyes, his whole body clenched. Naomi had slid Laelia's *stola* up over her knees to tend to the scrape and the sight of that bare, creamy leg he'd held to his chest drove all thoughts of God away. He looked away and in the edge of his vision, Naomi dabbed at her knee with the cloth and Laelia hissed again. The sound tore through him, breaking the moment enough that he could stand and move toward the door.

"I'll bring her something to eat."

Naomi nodded and Drusus made his way to the kitchen. The cooking fire already blazed and he poured water into the steel pot for eggs. The warmth failed to sooth him and he paced the kitchen like a caged animal until the water boiled. As he did, an idea took root.

A plan fraught with peril and uncertainty, but one that filled him with renewed purpose all the same. He dropped the remaining eggs in the scalding water with a spoon. The steam from the pot pulled beads of sweat to his forehead. He wiped them away with the back of his arm and noticed the bruises. The shape of her fingers darkened the skin above his inner elbow. He was glad she would never see them.

"She's asking for you."

He turned to find Naomi standing in the doorway, the lines of her face etched in weariness that mirrored his own.

"Go to her. I'll bring the eggs when they're ready."

"How did you know?"

Naomi approached and turned the empty basket toward him. "That's all that was left to prepare." She dropped the basket back on the table and stared into the fire. "I'll go to market tomorrow by myself to spare Laelia the heartbreak of spending that coin. I'd give anything to have spared her the heartbreak of acquiring it."

So would he. And that was his plan, but not one he could share with Naomi. "Thank you for tending her wounds."

The older woman closed the distance between them and put a palm to the side of his jaw the way his mother had before he'd been sold. "I may have cleaned her scrapes, but it's you who are tending her wounds."

There was no mistaking the gratitude in her eyes when she leaned forward and kissed him on the other cheek. He didn't know what to say but she pulled away and pushed him toward the door. "Go on, go to her."

"Thank you, Naomi."

"Go on." She bustled past him toward the fire with a dismissing wave.

Laelia sat in her bed waiting for him in the soft lamp light. She wore a night dress and had the blanket drawn up to her waist. That helped, since his nerves were raw and the feel of her in his arms with her head against his chest was etched forever in his mind. "Naomi said you asked for me."

"Come sit with me."

He moved the wooden stool from the foot of her bed to the side, careful to keep an arm's length away. They were about to step out onto a frozen river and he needed to guard his words, thoughts, and actions more than ever.

"Thank you for carrying me home."

"I'm sorry I allowed you to fall."

"That was not your fault. She didn't ask, but I told Naomi so. I think I was overwhelmed with what I'd done, but it's over now. You took care of me."

The silence had nothing to do with the dryness in his mouth and everything to do with the adoration in her expression. The ice beneath him cracked, and God help him, all he wanted to do was lean forward and kiss her.

"I wanted to thank you, but I also wanted to ask about the blade dealer. How did he know you? And why did he want to buy you?"

He felt as if he'd fallen through into the icy waters below. The suffocating chill of his past swallowed his more intimate fears.

Lie.

No.

A familiar battle of wills warred within, but this fight had nothing to do with the desires of his flesh. What would she think of him if he told the truth?

"Drusus?"

He glanced up. The set of her mouth and the tilt of her brow said she expected him to answer. He tried choosing the words that would least horrify her. "Mistress, I—there isn't…"

He couldn't do it.

She raised her knees to her chest and tucked her arms around them. "Forgive me. I'm curious but if it's not something you wish to speak of, I understand."

If only he could. "Thank you, Mistress."

"If managed carefully, that coin will be enough to keep us for at least eighteen months, possibly longer. I want you to keep it safe. I don't want it in the chest where my father will see it. He would gamble it away in days if he were to know I have it. I have known him the sum of my life and you for three days, but I trust you with this task. Will you do this for me?"

"Of course. I'll see to it now."

"Thank you. And take one for yourself to replace what you spent yesterday."

"Mistress, that's more than—"

"That doesn't matter. Take a *denarius* for yourself, I insist."

He rose and gathered the coins from the table, the clink of them against each other loud in the quiet of the room. Her generosity only reinforced his decision. "Thank you, Mistress. I'll see you in the morning."

"In the morning then." She nodded and he took one last look at her in her bed before leaving.

In the kitchen, Naomi eyed the crimson cloth of coin clutched in his hands while she filled a cup of watered wine.

"Laelia wishes me to keep it from her father."

She set the cup and pitcher down and her eyes bored into his. "He's not simple when there's no wine in his blood. He'll wonder how we fed ourselves in his absence."

"We'll cross that river when we reach it. There is something I must do tonight outside the villa. I understand what I ask of you, but there is no other way. Can you ignore my absence for as long as required?"

Naomi's gaze shot to the coin in his hands before returning to his face. "You would run away?"

"No. I would never leave her and you can watch over the coin until I return."

She halved the distance between them, her piercing stare as sharp as his knives. "Swear to me on whichever god you worship you will return and no harm will come to us by your errand."

He set the coin on the table and turned to face her. "I can't swear by Him. I don't have that right, but I beg you to trust in my honor and the strength of my own word. Please, Naomi."

Her breathing deepened as she searched his eyes.

"Please." He lifted silent prayers to God for her acceptance. When her face and shoulders relaxed from a scowl to a frown, he knew he had it, but waited for her to formally say so.

"Use the rear door, and hurry back. I'll not be able to sleep or draw an easy breath until you return."

"Thank you." He headed for his storeroom door to retrieve the rest of what he needed, resisting the urge to run. He could run once he left the house. Knowing Tiberius, every minute mattered. He secured his pack on his back and reached inside his belt to ensure his twin daggers rested at the ready—all the while praying he'd be spared having to use them.

Chapter 13

Drusus slowed to a brisk walk the last quarter mile to Tiberius' apartment, one street from the shop. A fine mist dampened his skin and obscured the half moon. Showing up after dark would be bad enough and being out of breath would further increase the price. As things stood now, he was already short the full amount and couldn't afford to appear desperate.

Even though he was.

Tiberius' apartment building looked the same, though in the past Drusus always approached from the north end of the street he now walked. The vagrant asleep in the alcove of the doorway never stirred as Drusus stepped over him and into the open hall to seek the stairs. The odor of untended chamber pots and stale sweat-filled bedding permeated the passage through the closed doors. His tender stomach reviled the stench and reminded him he'd not eaten or chewed his peppermint leaf since late morning. He knew better, because both honed the ever present discomfort in his gut. If he continued to ignore his body, the dull ache would become true pain in hours.

Retrieve the dagger first. Then eat.

He found the fourth door on the right of the second floor. He'd passed through this doorway many times, and been carried through once or twice. Hesitation stilled his knuckles a moment before rapping the wood. Did he still live here? He readied an apology if he didn't, then knocked. Someone stirred within, a long moment passed, and the door opened.

A woman stood with a lamp in one hand, draped in an unbound toga. She looked familiar and then it hit him. Hard. Her skin used to be darker, her hair black instead of gold. "Is Tiberius here?"

"No." She stood perfectly still, watching him.

"Do you know where he is?"

"No."

The short answers were unlike her. He'd often teased the only way to silence her was to kiss her. Then again, he was different now too. "It's important I find him."

"Then look in the soldier's brothel by the river or the new inn of the gods on the south side of the amphitheater."

"Thank you." He hesitated, and then turned for the stairs as swift as he could move. "Drusus." She'd stepped into the hall and the intensity in her eyes froze him.

Of course she recognized him. He'd been stupid to think otherwise.

"Sometimes I pretend he's you." The lamp lowered to move her face into shadows as she took a step toward him. "In the dark I can almost believe it."

"I'm sorry." More than she would ever know. More than he knew how to give words.

"You should be."

Her reply hung between them in the silence. What could he say so she would understand?

She turned away and closed the door behind her, salting the wound her simple statement inflicted on his heart. He couldn't make her understand back then, nor would he try again. He hadn't walked away from her, but from the man he'd been—no, the man he'd failed to be.

And now? At least now he could run. He flew down the steps two at a time and leaped over the sleeping man at the entrance. God help him if Tiberius weren't at the inn and he had to seek him at the brothel. His restraint had limits, which he'd slammed head first into carrying Laelia home, then put dents in when seeing her in her night dress. His reunion with Julia just shattered what was left. While his sandals pounded the dirty stones of the street and his lungs drank the damp night air, the memories of her returned hard and fast as he ran.

Julia had been his first lover, and the best, though he'd been smart enough to never tell the others that. He'd told Tiberius instead, over too much wine one night at an inn not unlike the one coming into view. From the open doors and the sounds of revelry reaching him this far away, there wouldn't be a vacant room or stool to be had once inside. That didn't bother him. He wouldn't need either, only to find Tiberius and then leave as soon as possible. Several men surrounded one of the large tables where they threw knucklebones. A few patrons dined from wooden bowls but most were there to drink. Would Master Ricarri be among them? A problem he hadn't considered before. He scanned the room, didn't see anyone who looked familiar until he set eyes on Tiberius, who must have seen him first.

The man's stare was strong enough to forge iron, above a mouth flat as a frozen river. Drusus returned the unblinking gaze and waited.

Tiberius said something to the two men, fellow merchants by the jewelry they wore on their fingers and ears. Both rose from the stools at the table and made their way to the game of knucklebones across the room.

Good. If he sent them away, Tiberius knew Drusus was here to do business. He moved toward the table and took an open stool, noting the coolness of the wood on the backs of his legs. Whoever Tiberius' associates were, they hadn't been sitting there for long.

Tiberius raised his cup toward the innkeeper before giving Drusus his full attention. "I'd ask you what brings you here, but I think I already know."

"Then all we have to settle on is the price." Drusus un-shouldered his pack and settled it on the floor between his knees.

The innkeeper refilled Tiberius' cup and turned to Drusus. "Wine?"

"No thank you."

"Leave the pitcher and bring an extra cup," Tiberius said. He then took a long pull at the wine and set his cup down hard enough to catch the attention of two women at the next table. "You might change your mind."

"That's not why I'm here."

Tiberius reached into the folds of his tunic and withdrew Laelia's dagger. "No, you're here for this. It is a beautiful piece." He set it on the table and flicked the end of the handle, spinning the knife on its jeweled hilt. "Almost as beautiful as Julia."

Drusus refused to take the bait, no matter how much he wanted answers. "I'm short twenty two *denarii* but brought my whetstones. I'll sharpen three blades for you to make up the difference."

"A metal-smith would sharpen twenty blades for that price."

"I know. But you know my edges would cut the whiskers from your jaw without oil while theirs would struggle to peel an apple."

Tiberius picked up the dagger and tapped the pointed end of the blade against his palm over and over again. "You're short more than twenty two *denarii*."

Drusus took a deep breath. "You paid my mistress a hundred. I've brought you seventy and offered to put a true edge on your own daggers."

"I know what I paid for it. I also know what I can sell it for. I brought it with me tonight to measure interest. Something so beautiful has to be seen to be appreciated." He smiled and stilled the knife in his hands. "Like Julia."

How did he ever call Tiberius a friend?

Tiberius set the dagger down in front of Drusus. "You don't have enough by half but I'm willing to offer you a trade."

He'd known it would come to this. "No."

"Consider by sunrise the dagger is lost to you forever. This way you perform for one night, hand over the coin you were going to anyway, and leave with what you came for."

Earlier tonight while staring into the flames of the kitchen fire, deciding to hand over all the coin he would ever have was a difficult decision. He'd made it and here he was, ready to follow through. What Tiberius was asking him to do was a much, much higher price.

He stared at the dagger on the table and remembered Laelia's tears and what this weapon meant to her. If he grabbed it and ran, he could outrun Tiberius. But maybe not the thugs that usually were somewhere near.

"You've thought about it long enough to tell me what I need to know." Tiberius rose from the stool and took Laelia's dagger from the table. "You're going to hate yourself, but you're going to do it anyway because you always have to be the hero. That at least hasn't changed."

He was right. Curse him to Hades and back but he was right. There was no point in denying it or wasting more time. Drusus stood and stared him down. "Fine. But you work the crowd alone, and you're the target."

Tiberius' eyes widened in shock. "I have a slave here. He'll do it."

"No." Drusus responded so loud several people glanced at them. "We don't risk anyone else's lives but our own."

"Varus isn't here."

"No but his spies might be." Drusus glanced around, looking for anything suspicious.

"I was never the target."

"And I swore on the blood of the man I killed never to do this trick again, so if you are going to force my hand, the life you risk is going to be your own."

Drusus studied him. His resolve was wavering. If he backed down, which Drusus desperately prayed he would, he'd be admitting his cowardice. If he didn't, he risked a knife in the throat like Varus' brother.

"How do I know you won't miss on purpose?"

Fair question. One he was asking himself. "Because the God I worship forbids it."

Fear and greed warred behind his eyes while Tiberius scanned the crowd again. When his gaze returned, his expression said greed had won.

"I'll make the arrangements with the innkeeper so he can secure the flower and the cherry. Remain seated on the stool I occupied and sharpen your knives where all can see. I'll work the crowd and collect the wagers."

"And you stand target."

The grin fell a shade. "Yes."

Drusus moved to the stool Tiberius indicated and sat down. He pulled his knives and set them on the table. The polished blades reflected the eyes of a traitor. They knew. Somehow they knew the task they would be given and accused him as much as the lifeless eyes of the last man to stand target for him. He pulled the finer textured whetstone from his leather pack and set to sharpening the knife for appearance sake. The edge on them would already skin a grape.

Like new leaves on a spring branch, questions and whispers grew throughout the room. His attention remained on the twins, but the speculations intruded.

"Do you think it can really be done?"

"I hope not, or I'm out a gold *aureus*."

"I bet a month's rent he misses the cherry."

"Those knives look strange. Maybe he'll let us hold one."

He passed the whetstone across the blade and flipped the flat weapon over to even the other side. In a way he pitied this crowd who would soon be parted from their coin and anything else they'd wagered. If Drusus didn't know it could be done, he would think it impossible also. And because people, like all herd animals, do what everyone else does, Tiberius would profit more tonight than in six months of honest trade at his weapon shop. With this exhibition, there were no taxes, no rents, and no purchases required except a single flower, a tiny piece of fruit, and a modest gift to the innkeeper for cooperation and making a few holes in the wall.

But the real cost would be borne by Drusus alone.

Murderer.

Liar.

Failure.

Tiberius made his way through the thick crowd of spectators like a crocodile eases toward a sleeping crane. "Are you ready?"

"Are you?"

"Of course."

Drusus rose from the stool and slung his pack over his shoulder. "I don't know if that's the truth or not. You're a skilled showman and a talented liar."

"So are you."

Drusus paused to meet his gaze. "Was."

"Are." Tiberius approached so close Drusus almost stepped back. "I'll clear over a thousand *sesterces* in a few moments. Don't tell me you don't miss the anticipation of the crowd, the easy coin, the rush of power."

"I don't, and I wouldn't do this now if you'd left me any other way."

The noise of the tavern lulled. Tiberius glanced around them and plastered his showman's smile in place. "Very well then." He leaned close enough that the foulness of his breath made Drusus' empty stomach curl as Tiberius embraced him, his mouth at Drusus' ear. "If you miss, the dagger remains mine. If you wound me, I've made certain you won't leave this inn with both your hands still attached to your arms."

Tiberius released him and stepped away, turning toward the center of the room packed tighter than the holds of the grain ships from Egypt. "Masters, men and ladies, attend me. In a moment you will witness the greatest feat of skill you have ever seen. Make a path, make a path here."

Drusus followed in Tiberius' wake. "Which door?"

"The one in the center."

Drusus stopped and set his pack a few paces in front of him. Close enough to grab if a thief made for it, but far enough to not interfere with his stance. The straps slipped from his hands because his palms were slick with sweat. When did that happen? He wiped them on his tunic and then dried the handles of the twins.

At the wooden door of one of the inn's inner chambers, Tiberius turned to face the crowd. "Bring me the rose and the cherry."

A slender woman with curls cascading down a bared back stepped into the open space between them. Her dress revealed more than it concealed and he looked away. With a dagger in each hand he stretched toward the ceiling for a long moment, and a murmur of anticipation rippled through the crowd.

"Thank you, beautiful." Tiberius' voice.

Drusus waited a moment longer before dropping his arms, and his gaze. Sweat threatened to slip into his eyes and he wiped it away with the back of his arm. He could do this. He'd done it dozens of times before that last time, and practiced it hundreds more.

The noise of the onlookers fell to a hush as Tiberius placed the cherry stem between his teeth and smiled at the crowd. With a nod to Drusus, he turned and placed his ear against the door. The white rose in his hand he held just below the head of the flower at arm's length from his face, also flat against the door.

The image sent Drusus back in time. The dagger in his right hand slipped to the floor and the clatter of steel on stone rang through the room.

Tiberius' head shot sideways, his eyes as wide as coins.

Pick it up. Don't think. Just throw. Drusus reached down and retrieved the fallen twin.

"Is it too late to increase my bet?" someone in the crowd asked. Nervous laughter carried through the throng. Drusus would have laughed too, if he could breathe. Don't think. Just throw. He checked the blade. A deep nick marred the edge, but far enough from the tip to not interfere.

Tiberius stared at him, the cherry still jutting by its stem from his lips.

Drusus nodded and took his stance, his left foot forward and his right angled out.

Tiberius repositioned and now stood ready. Drusus raised his left arm to balance. Don't think. Just throw. A deep breath. Fold the arm back behind the ear, feel the momentum build, and release.

The resounding thump of the blade sounded and the head of the flower fell to the floor. Relief poured through him from head to feet as exhalations rose all around them. They would wait with bated breath for the next one. The real challenge.

Tiberius dropped the headless stem and folded his arms across his chest. The peak of his throat bobbed over and over, his nerves not as controlled as he would have everyone believe.

"Stop swallowing. You'll move the cherry." Drusus transferred his other dagger to his throwing hand and reset his position. He glanced at the crowd again. "Forgive my partner. It's his first time."

A wave of low laughter encircled him. Had he missed this? Holding so many people at once in the palm of his hand?

Yes.

Until he remembered why he quit—the blood, the screams.

Don't think. Just throw.

Deep breath and hold. Raise the left arm. Pull back the right, feel the momentum build. He closed his eyes and let the blade sail free.

Chapter 14

The hush exploded into cheers and groans. Drusus opened his eyes to a grinning Tiberius gesturing to the two knives pinned in the door, the stem of the cherry still in his lips. Alive. Unharmed. Vastly richer than a moment ago. He flexed his hands to fight the tingling coursing through them and weakening his legs as he went to retrieve the twins from the door. But when he grabbed the handle of the topmost knife, the bit of dark red cherry clinging to it froze him in place.

Instead of cleanly severing the cherry from the stem, he'd thrown wide of his mark. Mercifully the point of the blade missed the pit within and pinned the remnants of the small, crimson fruit to the door.

Tiberius clapped him on the back. "You should keep it in the routine. We will call it 'pin the cherry.'"

Drusus pulled his knives free easily. From their shallow penetration and the tight, dark grain of the wood, these doors were made from olive. Not the more common cedar. Not that it mattered to anyone but him. He slipped the twins into their resting place inside his belt. "There is no more routine. I don't do this anymore."

"Yet you just did, didn't you?" Tiberius handed him his leather pack.

"To get what I came for. Now hand it over."

A woman slipped between them. "I've never seen anything like that. It makes me want to appreciate," she grabbed his hand and deftly slid it to her breast, "your other skills."

Drusus yanked free of her hold. "No."

Her painted lips flattened in disappointment as Drusus stepped around her and once again held out his hand to Tiberius. "I need to be on my way."

But the woman wasn't relenting. She moved close and placed her hand on his chest and moved closer. "Are you sure you have to leave?"

He was about to push her away from him when Tiberius laughed. "You're wasting your time, my beauty. Drusus' God forbids pleasure in any form."

The woman withdrew her invading touch. "Pity."

That wasn't true. The opposite actually but he needed out of here. Now. "The dagger."

Tiberius withdrew the jeweled weapon from the folds of his tunic. He flipped the knife in the air and caught it as it spun, extending the handle to Drusus with deliberate slowness. "It isn't the dagger you want. It's the woman."

Drusus didn't look him in the eyes as he took hold of Laelia's knife. "That's not your concern."

But Tiberius held fast, tightening his grip on the other end of the blade. "But it could be, couldn't it? Like Julia is now my concern."

The foulest name Drusus knew almost left his tongue.

Tiberius must have seen it in his eyes. Seen how his words had cut. "She'd be hurt to know you spent your own coin on a knife instead of keeping your promise."

Drusus yanked hard on the handle of the knife, tearing it from Tiberius' grip. It hadn't been that simple then. Or now. "You should free her, as I would have."

"That's the difference between us. I might not have your arm but I'm not plagued by your soft heart either."

Another man pressed in, clad in the purple trimmed toga of a senator. "I hope to see that again, though next time I'll know not to bet against you, young man."

Tiberius straightened and nodded in respect. "Senator Antonius, I hope to see you elected *quaesetor* again this December. Please give my regards to Caesar."

The man snorted. "A common soldier ruling Rome. I've had ten years to warm to the idea and still can't. Of course the fact I'd say such a thing aloud tells me I've had too much wine already tonight."

Delight painted Tiberius' face. "Don't worry, Senator. Your true opinion of Vespasian is safe with me."

"Glad to hear it. Enjoy spending my coin."

The man walked away, oblivious to what he'd just done. Tiberius would keep the secret, for a price far higher than the one he'd set on the dagger. Drusus secured it in his pack and slung it over his shoulder, leaning as close to Tiberius as he dared. "Don't blackmail him."

Tiberius grinned. "That's not *your* concern. Come here again tomorrow. We will find a new inn and I'll split the take with you by half." His expression turned serious. "Half, Drusus."

Drusus turned toward the entrance and pressed his way through the throng of people vying for his attention. The damp air in the street wouldn't cleanse his nose of the stale sweat and cheap wine. Thick fog obscured everything but the glowing balls of torches at the street intersections. He would have to trust the torches to guide him back.

This must be how Laelia felt all the time. At least he had a pinpoint of light ahead. He reached it and aimed for the next without tripping or knocking into anything. A pang of outrage in his gut reminded him he'd allowed an empty stomach far too long. Peppermint leaf would be useless until he ate something. A shape passed through the light of the torch in the heavy fog.

He stopped and listened hard. From behind an arm seized his neck and a thick hand covered his mouth, yanking him backward.

Drusus grabbed at the fingers smothering him and with his other hand freed one of the twins. He flipped the knife so the blade stuck out from the bottom of his closed fist and stabbed. The man's howl made Drusus' grip on his weapon tighten even more to pull back for another stab. His lungs burned and he would pass out in seconds. He jabbed higher this time, his captor screaming and loosening his hold as the shape of another attacker emerged from the mist. *There's two of them.*

Pain exploded along his skull and he went down. The street hit him next, his knees bearing the brunt of his fall.

Get up.

He sprung up, wheeling with knife in hand searching the mist for his attackers. The weight of his pack still pulled at his shoulders, so they hadn't taken it. Muffled groans and a broken cadence told him the wounded one was retreating, but where was the one with the club? Another blow to the back of his skull thundered through him. He dropped his knife and his knees rattled as he stumbled forward.

"Give me the pack."

The straps around his shoulders yanked him backward as the man tried to shake it free. His body resisted but he managed to remain standing and pull his other dagger. *Lord, help me.* He turned and slashed hard and wide.

The man shrieked and Drusus slashed again, going for his belly. Sandals slapped the stone street so fast, he was in full retreat. Drusus ran his fingertips through his hair over the center of the booming ache in his skull. He was bleeding too.

Tiberius had sent his thugs to retrieve the dagger. Of that he was certain. Sending them back without it and with worse wounds than his was the strongest answer he could give. For now. He slipped his shoulder strap off and set his pack down beside him to find the other twin. The one he still held went back in its concealed sheath, blood and all. To find the missing twin, he'd have to search as he'd shown Laelia.

Dirt, mud and animal dung clung to the drying blood on his fingertips as he swept the stone street back and forth. After searching four consecutive areas, moving his pack each time, he found a nail, a dead mouse, and finally his other knife. By then the fog and his own hot and cold chill had dampened the wool of his tunic, adding to his misery.

For the first time, Drusus was glad to reach his new master's villa. The back door's hinges groaned and a door to his left creaked open. Lamplight spilled into the hallway as Naomi's gray head emerged. "It's about time. I— what happened to your head?"

"It's nothing."

Naomi took hold of his arm and tugged him toward her room. The inside caught him by surprise as his attackers had. Dried flowers hung in wreaths on the wall above three beds, the myriad of colors bringing out the rich purple of the only blanket on what must be Naomi's bed.

"Stay here."

She pushed him down onto the middle bed, a scant two feet from hers. The straw-filled wool mattress crunched beneath him. The light left with her and darkness closed around him again. The pain in his skull had eased but enough remained that for the first time since giving it up, he longed for opium. A mistake on an empty stomach, and his was already chewing on his backbone.

Light flickered in the doorway and Naomi returned, carrying a large bowl in one hand and the small lamp in the other. She set the bowl in his lap and held the lamp close to his ear. Her fingers grabbed his chin and tilted his head while she examined the wound. "What happened."

"I fell."

She snorted and released his chin. "This is the wrong house to try to sell that lie."

With the wet rag Naomi dabbed the dried blood from his jaw up to his ear. "The truth. Or I tell her you snuck out."

"I can't."

She wrung the pink-tinged water out in the bowl and soaked the linen cloth again. "Will the trouble follow you here?"

"No."

Naomi took a cup from a shelf above her bed and dipped her rag in it. "Are you sure?"

Not at all. "Yes."

She nodded and her fingers sifted through the hair above his ear. "This will sting."

Her rag pressed the side of his head, soaking his hair, and then—more pain. Lots more pain as he gasped and went rigid, clinging tight to keep from dropping the bowl in his lap. "Salted water is good for cuts." The rag of fire in her hand dug deeper into his hair and the burn intensified. "I'm almost finished."

To her credit, she was thorough, and he kept his lips pressed tight together as the saltwater burned his wound before running down the skin of his neck. She placed the bloody rag back in the bowl and stared at him for a long moment. "Be more careful. She needs you."

He stood with the bowl and the weight of his pack made him unsteady. "I will."

Naomi grabbed him by the shoulders. "You're about to collapse."

"I'll make it to the storeroom after I pitch the dirty water. It's not that far."

She frowned and took a deep breath. "Leave it and lay down."

That was his plan, if his head and his stomach would give him back control for a few more moments. "I will."

Naomi took the bowl from him. "I said lay down."

"*Here?*"

"If you collapse on the way to your room, you'll bust the other side of your head and bleed all over my floors." She picked the lamp up from the shelf and headed for the door. "I mean it. Lie down."

The softness of the bed beneath him killed the last of his good sense. He slipped his arms free of his pack and shoved the leather bag under the bed. The straps of his sandals proved more difficult in the dark, but he managed and they joined his pack on the floor. His fingers located the buckle of his belt but hesitated. There was a chance they'd tried to follow him. He'd keep the twins close tonight.

The straw stuffed in the mattress crackled when he stretched out on his right side and pillowed his head with his arm. Lying on that side felt awkward, but this way his head wouldn't soak the mattress if the wound bled again. Nor would he have his back to Naomi, which even in sleep would give him concern. That woman was as unpredictable as the weather on a summer day.

A faint glow turned his eyelids red but now that he'd finally let them close, they refused to reopen. The familiar scent of his own blanket covered him and his fingers fisted the edge of the thick wool. The whoosh of a soft wind took the faint glow away. He mumbled a frail thank you he hoped Naomi heard before offering a silent prayer to God.

Sleep came quickly, and with it, the true cost of having broken his vow.

The nightmare was back. But instead of the horror of watching his blade fly and sink its tip into the neck of the man holding the cherry stem, this was legions more terrifying.

Because when the knife hit, it was Laelia staring back at him in disbelief as she died.

Chapter 15

This would be a good day. Laelia could buy food. The weeds even ripped from the ground easier. At least it felt that way. She'd made two piles already and if the pictures in her mind were correct, she'd almost cleared the second half of this square. The remnants of the hedge she'd worked around this morning Drusus would have to do.

He slept late again this morning according to Naomi, but she didn't mind. He'd carried her a good distance last night and while she couldn't give him bowls of meaty stew, fine clothes, or his freedom, she could let him sleep.

This handful of grass didn't want to die. The roots refused to relinquish their hold on the hard packed earth. She gave them a good twist, locked her elbows, and yanked again. They ripped free at last and she fell back on the ground behind her. Nothing hurt and as she remained still to take inventory of herself, lying on the ground flat on her back felt wonderful. Her eyes didn't even need to squint against the sun, if there was sun shining directly above her face.

Ten weeks in coming, she'd found the first good thing about being blind. Not only did she not have to squint against sun too bright in her now useless eyes, but she no longer had to witness her father's angry glares either. Hadn't her mother often told her that for the careful observer, there was something of worth to be found in every misfortune?

"Naomi!"

Drusus' voice boomed through the garden like a thunderclap. Before she stirred or sat up, he thumped to the ground beside her. "Laelia?" His hand slid beneath her neck and lifted her head from the dirt while his other hand grabbed her own and squeezed. "Where are you injured?"

"I'm not hurt." With her free arm she pushed up on her elbow and raised her shoulders. "I'm well. I'm sorry to have frightened you."

The other racing footfalls weren't as loud and fast as Drusus', probably Naomi, but were swift nonetheless. "What happened?"

"She's fine," Drusus called out to her. He removed his hold on her neck but his grip remained firm on her hand.

"Then why is she on the ground?"

"I don't know. Laelia, why are you lying on the ground?"

Juno's peacock, they were overprotective. She was in her own house, not some crowded street. "Because I wanted to. That's not a crime worthy of being sent to the arena you know."

Naomi's huff told Laelia she'd just crossed her arms like she always did when making that sound. "Next time tell us, so we don't think you *fell.*"

Her father would never stand for that tone from Naomi. If she were to succeed in her plans, neither could she. "I'm fine. Prepare my midday meal. I'll take it in the *triclinium* today." Not exactly a reprimand, but from the loud intake of breath it caused, close enough.

"Of course, *Mistress.*"

The hiss Naomi put on the end of Laelia's formal title bordered on belligerence. That hurt, but if she were to ever be capable of properly running a house with servants, they were not going to always be her friend or happy in their duties. Her husband would expect her to manage and maintain the slaves. What hope did she have in that if she couldn't handle her own, when there were only two?

Drusus released her hand and somehow she knew he'd moved away from her. "Naomi meant no disrespect. She's only concerned for you, as I am."

This was why her father forbade disobedience. He'd said it spreads like fire. "I've known her my entire life. You've known her for four days."

An oppressive silence followed. Twinges of fear deepened her breathing. Being on the ground suddenly made her feel vulnerable. "Where are you?"

"Four paces from your right shoulder."

His voice carried a hard edge that reminded her of her father. He could be angry if he wanted, so long as he did what he was told. "Will you—" *They aren't requests.* Project authority. She cleared her throat. "Pull weeds with me."

"As you wish, Mistress."

Before she righted herself in the grass to resume pulling weeds, he'd already begun. The sharp, fast rips were so close together she could almost see his hands and arms flying. She tried to keep pace with him and couldn't. Her arms and wrists burned from the effort. This task had been enjoyable yesterday. Today it was a chore. Chores were for the slaves, not the lady of the house she would become one day, gods willing. She wiped her hands against each other and shook as much dirt from them as she could before rising. "Finish this square and then eat something. Have Naomi alert me when you're finished. I need to go to the market."

"Yes, Mistress."

The snapping grass never paused, and now she had a problem. True she could feel her way back to the villa door and down the hall to the *triclinium*. By herself that would take a long time, and she might stumble on the step up. She held her hand out. "After you take me to the triclinium."

The deep sigh she heard pricked her conscience. He cleaned his hands as she had and placed hers on his arm. In retaliation for his silence, she waited a long time to signal him forward. His gait was swift, tense, and almost pulled her along.

"Step."

The harsh tone grated, but correcting him would make things worse. At her seat on the dining couch, she pulled her hand from his arm the moment he brought them to a stop. With as graceful an air as she could muster, she settled on the cushion to await Naomi. No departing footsteps. Only his breathing beside her. Then it hit her. He waited for a formal dismissal. "You may go."

"Mistress."

His departure left her alone with her tangled feelings while she waited an eternity for Naomi to bring her meal of bread and vegetable soup. The soup tasted wonderful, simply because it wasn't boiled eggs. Eating alone however was a forlorn affair. She'd already grown accustomed to Drusus' presence. The loud way he chewed his food, the lingering scent of peppermint leaf afterward, but most of all the reassurance of his presence.

She swallowed the last of the wine in her cup with plenty of bread and soup remaining to be eaten. With a few sweeps of her hand she located the pitcher as he'd taught her and refilled her own cup without spilling a single drop. The second cup didn't taste anything like the first. Perhaps guilt had a taste more powerful than grapes.

He hadn't just taught her to eat and drink without making a mess. He'd spent his own money on food and to treat her and Naomi to a sorely needed day at the baths. He'd carried her home last night, and she trusted him to guard a small fortune in coin. And for all that she'd done her level best to remind him he was a slave. Jupiter help her, maybe she was her father's daughter after all.

Laelia rose and left the half-eaten soup behind. Feeling along the walls, she returned to the garden. "Drusus, where are you?"

"Coming, Mistress." His voice told her what her eyes couldn't. He was still upset.

She sat on the tiled porch floor and wrapped her arms around her knees. "Please sit with me." His sandals scuffed the tiles when he settled across from her. She didn't know where to begin. I'm sorry seemed logical, but that wasn't what came out of her mouth.

"Are you happy being a slave?" What a foolish question. She pictured raised brows while he pondered whether or not to lie. "Forgive me. You don't have to answer that."

He didn't. He didn't say anything at all for a long time.

"I meant if you could have a better life, wouldn't you do anything to try?"

No answer. She couldn't even hear him breathing. This was a disaster. She should have stayed inside. The cool of the tile had already soaked through her wool *stola* and undergarment, making her all the more uncomfortable. He already knew the big secret. Maybe knowing the rest would help him understand.

"Until you came I'd given up hope of ever marrying. Even before I lost my sight, I'd become the joke of the forum. Laelia Ricarri, the wife nobody wants. When my mother died, my father drank himself into oblivion for months. One by one I had to see my mother's jewelry and anything we had of worth disappear. When there was nothing left to sell except me, he tried to betroth me to the widowed or unmarried among his merchant friends. I was ten years old.

"My father dragged me everywhere. To the races, to the theater, to the baths and the forum to hear the orators. Anyone who said anything nice to me would be invited to our house for *cena* and if they came, by the second course, they were solicited in marriage. This went on for three years and then one day, someone agreed.

"Antonius Poetilius, a wine-maker older than my father. He was nice to me but scared me all the same. When my father told me I would be Antonius' wife in a year, I refused and threatened to run away."

Laelia slid the sleeve of her garment up her right arm and felt for the thick scar below her shoulder. "This," she pointed to the short line of raised flesh, "is from that day." She allowed the sleeve to fall back in place.

"What happened next?" Drusus asked.

"I did something dreadful." Laelia hung her head. "I begged Naomi to take me to the temple of Vesta on the first day of Vestalia. She did and when it was my turn, I made an offering of fire before the sacred hearth and asked Vesta and the Fates to spare me. Two weeks later, a servant brought word to my father Antonius Poetilius was dead. He'd died in his sleep and I knew it was my fault."

"His death was not your fault."

"Of course it was. But the worst part was I was happy and it showed." Like the bruises on her arms that night because of it. "Rumors started I'd poisoned Antonius. I'd hear them whispering at the baths, pointing and staring. I didn't try to refute them and after that, no other men came to dine with us. Looking back, I should have married Antonius."

"Why?"

A harsh sound tore from her chest. "Because I already know I can survive a man I detest but at least as a wife, he might not have hit me or called me names. I know odds are as bad for me now as when I was a girl. Maybe worse, but you've shown me I'm not useless. I'm not, and that must be worth something to someone in need of a wife, especially because I'm still young enough to bear children. If for no other reason than that, I have a chance for a life better than this. I have to learn all I can, the things my mother would have taught me about managing a house and the duties of a wife. I'm sorry for being so cold earlier. I tried too hard at being a true mistress and I regret it. Deeply."

"Why do you regret it?"

She sighed and relaxed her hold on her arms. Her Drusus was back; his voice no longer tainted with irritation. "Because you deserve better than to be treated like a slave. So does Naomi."

"I am a slave."

"I know. I am too, more than you know. But if you'll help me, I can get us both out of this house. Maybe Naomi too. I love her like a second mother but I *need* you. I can't find a husband and secure a betrothal without you." She braced herself with a deep breath. "Will you help me?"

Chapter 16

Laelia didn't know what she asked of him. Drusus had known from the moment he set eyes on her, and wiped the blood from the corner of her mouth, she would never belong to him. Simple acceptance came easier than being forced to help give her to another man.

Her expectant expression altered to one of uncertainty the longer she waited for his answer.

He couldn't deny her. Not only because she was his mistress, but because he wanted better for her than the life she had. "I'll always do my best to serve you."

A smile formed on her pink lips that pinched the corners of her eyes. "Thank you." She straightened and for a long moment she stared at him as though she could see. "Have you eaten?"

"Not yet." His appetite hadn't returned since seeing her sprawled across the ground this morning but his stomach would punish him soon enough if he left it empty.

"Please go eat. This afternoon I want to go to the market and stock this house with oil, wine, and grain. Purchasing in quantity costs less for more, and I also want to see what more can be done for the garden."

"Mistress, your father—"

"He never goes in the kitchen, or the storeroom. Besides, he's my problem and I have a plan for him too, not just for us. Now go eat something. You once said I was a fast learner and that you're irritable when hungry. I'm sure a proper wife keeps the slaves well fed and happy as possible, so go eat. Please."

"You are a fast learner." One among many worthy qualities she possessed. "But a mistress doesn't say please to her slaves."

"She does to a friend."

He swallowed the lump of emotion in his throat and stood. "Do you wish to remain here?"

"Yes. I'm enjoying thinking through taking care of myself and my house for once. It feels good to regain some measure of security and independence."

He was sure it did but she was putting her trust in the wrong things. "I'll return shortly."

Her head tilted back so if she could see, she would be looking up at him. "I'll still be here." The mischievous grin on her face from her own mirth made her appear so playful, he longed to drop back to his knees and kiss those wry-turned lips.

He was hungry all right.

In the kitchen, Naomi scrubbed the outside of a bronze pot, attacking a stain only she must see. "I put the rest of the soup in a bowl for you over there." She threw her chin over her shoulder for a second and returned to scrubbing.

"Thank you."

"I don't know what's gotten into her," Naomi said to the pot. "If I had my eyes closed I would have sworn it was her father ordering us about this morning."

The soup had cooled but tasted better than boiled eggs. "Her confidence returns faster than she's ready to wield it."

Naomi huffed and dropped the pot onto the table with a loud bang. "I don't mind confident. I mind arrogant. It's like giving up her mother's dagger took her mother's goodness out of her too, and I don't like it at all." She whirled to face him, hands on her hips. "How's your head?"

"Still attached."

Both of Naomi's lips disappeared as her jaw tightened and her cheeks puffed. She fought the laughter valiantly, but it finally spilled from her and he grinned. In truth his head ached worse today than last night when the thieves clubbed him. The consolation was one would be limping, probably for life, and the other would have a nasty scar to remind him they'd attacked the wrong Roman. He spooned another swallow of soup while Naomi picked up what must have been Laelia's bowl and scrubbed that too. He ate quickly before packing a few peppermint leaves between his teeth and cheek. "Is there any wine left?"

"No. I gave the last of it to the Empress out there."

Laelia had hurt his feelings this morning too, but Naomi's remark would be lethal if overheard by Laelia's father. "You know you can't say things like that."

The older woman scoffed. "You aren't going to tell her."

"That's not what I meant. She was overzealous in exerting her authority but remember she isn't used to using any at all. She'll be all over the place like a newborn colt until she learns to exercise moderation and more importantly, not to back down. She needs to learn no one has the right to abuse her, be it father, slave or husband."

Naomi set the bowl in her hands down and studied him. "You care for her, don't you?"

"Of course. She's my mistress."

Her gaze narrowed above a deep frown. "Your ready answer doesn't fool me. I've seen this before and it will bring disaster if you allow it."

"Like Titus and her mother?"

Her eyes rounded and her glance darted to the doorway. "Say nothing else." She put her back to him and resumed scrubbing the bowl with frantic swipes of the cloth in her hand.

"Laelia told me what happened. I understand—"

She whirled on him, the bowl falling from her wet fingers to clatter on the floor. "You can't understand unless you were there." Her eyes glimmered as she put her hand to her chest. "Unless you had to watch the life drain from the eyes of a friend of twenty years. Unless you had to scrub his blood from the floor and be forbidden from mourning him or ever speaking his name again. Don't tell me you understand."

Naomi turned away from him and gripped the edge of the counter with both hands. "If you think you do then show me," she said to the wall. "And make certain it's not your blood I have to scrub from the floor one day."

He'd been blinder than Laelia. This house held two hurting women in need of God's love and true to his old self he'd only noticed it in the pretty one. *Forgive me, Lord.* He closed the distance between he and Naomi and circled her with his arms.

"What are you doing?"

He wasn't sure, but something told him not to let go. "The best I can." He squeezed her short frame tighter and hoped that pot on the table wasn't about to make a dent in the other side of his head. Naomi's hair smelled like bread and wood smoke and pressed against his cheek.

She stood stiff and awkward between his arms but still he wouldn't release her, unless she told him to. The moment she surrendered surprised him with its totality. She didn't relax in his firm embrace. She nearly collapsed against his chest. Every weary breath echoed the burdens of her heart. How long had she carried them alone?

He pictured his own mother, and prayed if she still lived somewhere someone would be her friend and share the truth of Christ with her. "Do you want to know what I think?" he asked.

"If I say no, you'll tell me anyway."

He chuckled and eased his hold on her to turn her toward him and peer into her eyes. They were grayish brown, like old wood. He'd never noticed before. "Titus and Laelia's mother would thank you if they could for watching over her with such devotion, and being a mother and a father to her when they could not."

"They would thank you. You're bringing her back to life. She won't be able to help but love you for it and that's what scares me."

It scared him too. "Don't borrow trouble from tomorrow, Naomi. Today has enough without it."

She pushed him away and swatted his shoulder. "Now you're giving me orders too."

He would let her retreat behind her wall of crankiness. "No, but I am relaying one. She's ready to go to the market."

"Where is she?"

"Sitting outside in the *peristyle* by the inner door."

"I'll go get her."

"No please, let me. I need to get a few things from my room first and then we'll join you in the *atrium*."

She moved toward the doorway to the hall and turned back at the last moment. "Before you go to sleep tonight, take one of the extra beds for your storeroom." She paused. "I was mad at you that first night. Then you sharpened my knives and I wanted to tell you to come get a bed then, but then I didn't know how to explain why I hadn't the night before." Her gaze met his and remorse twisted her expression before she turned away.

"Naomi."

She glanced back. "Yes?"

"Thank you."

"Just hurry it up. We don't have all day." She disappeared beyond the wall and he couldn't help but grin.

Laelia's back hurt after sitting so long on the porch floor. Once standing, the ache in her back shifted to her hind end. Apparently it had gone numb and was now reawakening with a vengeance.

"Did you hear me coming?"

Drusus' voice startled her. Thank the gods she hadn't yet reached to rub her sore bottom. She pointed her face the direction he should be. "Yes." A lie, but certainly more lady-like than the truth.

"Well done. Naomi and I are ready."

She held her hand out for him and his peppermint scent enveloped her as he assumed his position at her side. "How much coin are you bringing?"

"Five denarii."

"Bring twenty."

He was quiet for a long moment. "Yes, Mistress." His arm slipped from her hand and the sound of his rapid footfalls mixed with the clatter of coin already on him. That he would run made her smile. She put her arm out and eased forward, feeling for the doorway. After a few steps she located it and felt for the pull of the door. It swung closed easier than she expected and jarred her elbows.

Returning footfalls echoed down the hall to her until they stopped nearby. "Naomi waits at the front door."

She turned and held her hand out for him. They walked toward the sound of the fountain and the muted metallic clicks continued, as beautiful to her as a song of the gods. Naomi had their basket. Wicker made a sound unlike any other.

The walk to the market was less a barrage of sound as the past two days. Drusus didn't seem to push and pull her to veer nearly as often, either. "Is it less crowded?"

"How did you know?" Naomi asked.

"It's quieter and we haven't needed to yield the way as often."

"That's an outstanding observation, Mistress." His fingers patted the back of her hand where they already rested as they walked.

Her face turned toward him but when the blackness didn't change, she pointed her head straight ahead again. More coin helped, but what she wouldn't give to be able to see him, just once.

"The *Ludi Apollinares* begin today," Naomi said. "The best time to go to market is when everyone is at the games, though most of the booths and shops close anyway."

Laelia would have to remember that. Once wed, she'd also have to learn to enjoy, or at least stomach, the gladiator games. Anything less was very un-Roman. Being blind would help, and she added a second mark on the advantages side of her list. "Do you enjoy the games, Drusus?"

"No."

The simple answer uttered with the vehemence of an oath surprised her. Neither did she, but she was a woman and of course her memories of the games involved being hawked like a ware to potential husbands. "Why don't you?"

"I don't believe men were put on the earth to kill one another, or for others to take pleasure in them doing so."

Even among the bleating of sheep, children laughing, and cart wheels rolling over the cobbled stone street, the sorrow in his words was unmistakable. As was the way his stride felt off as if he were lost in his own thoughts as she had been this morning. "Are you all right?" she asked him.

"Yes, why?" Naomi asked.

"No... never mind."

Drusus must have known she meant him, because his arm shifted as if he were a soldier returning to attention and his pace leveled off. The chink of the coins when he did seemed louder here on the street than in the house. Hopefully no one with ill-intent heard them.

Understanding flooded her and she jerked to a stop. "Robbers."

"Where?" Naomi asked.

"No, robbers are why you didn't want to bring that much coin." As soon as the words left her mouth, she wanted to slap her own face. If the jingle hadn't already announced their presence to everyone around them, she just had. Her mother would have known better. A coin pouch that full wouldn't conceal in a belt or the fold of a tunic. It was probably hanging from Drusus' belt like a sword, begging thieves with every bounce. "I'm so sorry."

"We're fine, Mistress, but let's not tarry in the street."

"Give it to Naomi. At least in the basket it won't be so obvious."

"No."

She opened her mouth to tell him it hadn't been a request when he continued.

"The coin stays with me. A good thief already knows I have it and the quickest way to get it isn't to try to take it from me. It's to slip a knife point to your side and trust I'll hand it over without a fight."

"Of course you would," Naomi said, grabbing Laelia's other arm.

"No I wouldn't," Drusus answered firmly. "I'd hurl the coin pouch as far as I could one direction and run with you both in the other. Hopefully they wouldn't be a pair, though that's how most thieves operate."

She'd been an idiot and now they were all in danger. "How did you carry the money home yesterday?"

"Down my tunic but we weren't going to need it until we reached your house." His hand on hers tightened. "I'm not going to let anything happen to you. Either of you, but we should be on our way."

She didn't trust her voice and nodded instead. The faster she spent the coin, the sooner they would be out of danger. She would have everything delivered tomorrow instead of today to save coin but couldn't wait longer than that. It would likely be a few weeks still before her father returned from his travels, but best to have everything delivered and put away tomorrow.

"Naomi, we need pickled fish, dried meat, wheat and barley, oil, whatever produce you think will keep well, and anything else you think we can buy in quantity that will fit in the storeroom." She might have made a huge mistake with the coin but remembered a few things about trips to the market with her mother. "Look for empty booths with merchants resting on their stools. We'll get better prices from them, especially in quantity."

That infernal clinking was all she could hear now.

Juno, keep us safe.

Chapter 17

In the past weeks, Drusus had watched Laelia blossom like the lilies they'd planted in the front sections of the garden. She waited for him at the edge of the porch near them, her hand out for him to take. "The air feels damp. Is the fog thick enough I should have Naomi bring my cloak?"

"It's not fog." Drusus glanced above them as he took his position at her side. "I think the sky will open today. The sun hides in the clouds. We should be able to finish clearing the last area before the rain comes."

He guided them toward the rear of the garden, past their bench and the dry fountain whose empty bowls still mocked his many attempts at repair. Unlike the one in the peristyle, he'd been unable to fix this one.

"Naomi isn't feeling well. I told her to spend the day resting. We can go to Marcus' booth for our mid-day meal and bring her something back."

Marcus. He strove to maintain a relaxed arm beneath her palm. She had a way of reading his mood like a scroll with her touch. The soft swoosh of her tunic as they walked reminded him of how they used to sound moving through the garden when the grass was thick and tall everywhere.

"How do the lilies fare?" she asked.

"I think two won't recover but the treatment you and Naomi prepared has revived the others. What's in it?"

"Eggshells, rust scrapes if you can find them, and you know very well I can in this house." Her pink lips curved into that askew grin he'd come to adore. "A bit of honey, though Naomi didn't want to spare it, fish scraps from the *garum* barrel, and fresh water. I'm surprised I remembered how to make it, it's been so long. My mother always made it."

He stopped her at the edge of the last of the weeds. She lowered to her knees, and in one pass found the last of the grass. Behind her, he troubled the dirt with the small rake he'd found in the weeds, along with four empty amphorae, broken parts of other clay vessels, and the bones of a large bird, not to mention insects of almost every kind. The smell and feel of the rich black dirt was always best early in the day. He'd given up trying to keep under his fingernails clean except at night, when he would use one of the twins to remove the thick black lines.

"Did you like the barley soup last night? I think it needed less vinegar but I don't know if Naomi is trying something new or she spilled."

"Ask her."

Laelia twisted her face toward him. He noticed she mapped direction with her ears now even better than Master Pappus had. "Naomi doesn't like her cooking questioned any more than my father likes anything of his questioned. And she's been so happy these past few weeks."

So have you. If only he could find a way to return her dagger to her. She'd been so insistent he repay himself the few sesterces from the day at the baths, he shuddered to think how she would handle knowing he'd spent his entire fortune to retrieve the heirloom.

She paused in her weed pulling to put her hands together in her lap. Her head dipped sideways and she faced him for a long moment, the way she did when she was about to ask him something personal. "Are you happy?"

He didn't want to lie, but the truth was somewhere in the waters between the banks of yes and no. "You're an excellent mistress. Naomi and I could have none better."

Her face colored and she tucked her chin. "Thank you, but don't think I failed to notice you didn't actually answer me." Her twisted grin became a wide smile. "I hear *very well*."

He laughed, raking through the dirt by his knee. "Yes, yes you do." He turned more earth, hoping she would let the question die like the dried weeds they'd burned last week.

"But if you aren't happy then part of you is unhappy. I want to know why."

He closed his eyes and drew a long breath, careful to exhale slowly lest she hear it and frown. Nothing wilted her faster than an audible sigh. She always assumed it was for or at her, even when he was just tired. Telling her why he was unhappy would do nothing. Praying about it didn't seem to be doing anything either.

"Why don't you want to tell me?" The smile was gone now.

He wet his lips and met her eyes, even though she couldn't see him. "I strive to always be content no matter my lot but it is—" The words tangled between his thoughts and his tongue and he sighed in frustration.

"It's what?" Her expression had clouded now as much as the sky above them.

"Difficult for me to accept those things I can't change."

"What do you wish to change?"

Her blindness, her father's temperament and that he and others could worship Christ freely would be first. Then even more impossible things, like his right to claim her as a wife, and that he didn't have innocent blood on his hands or broken promises to Julia on his conscience.

"Why won't you tell me?"

A flicker of motion near her hip sent his heart into his throat. "Don't. Move." He slipped a twin from his belt and in a single motion, coiled and shot the blade forward at the writhing snake as thick as his wrist. The blade stuck a handbreadth below the viper's head and the animal snapped and curled, slapping Laelia with its body. She screamed as the blade fell free and the viper hissed like a cat ready to strike with Laelia its closest target.

He threw himself on top of the writhing creature, feeling its slithery body curling and shifting beneath the weight of his chest. "Move back."

She scrambled back on her hands and heels while the serpent writhed beneath him. What now? He wouldn't be able to reach the twin still in his belt or the one somewhere in the dirt beneath him and the snake.

"What was that?" Laelia still scrambled back away.

"What's happened?" Naomi was running toward them on the pebbled path.

"Stay back! Make sure Laelia isn't hurt."

The writhing beneath him slowed. Now or never. He braced his hands in the dirt beneath his shoulders and pushed hard and fast. He felt the fangs burying in the top of his wrist as his momentum carried him to his feet as the snake swung from his arm.

Naomi screamed while he pulled his second knife and cut the snake's head from its body in a single, fluid motion. The long, black carcass fell to the dirt where it continued to writhe and he pulled the lifeless head free from his skin. The twin punctures were already red, and beginning to pain him, but it was the poison that would kill him if he didn't get it out.

Laelia's eyes were the size of full moons. "What was that?"

"A snake. It's dead now but stay where you are." He cut an X over the twin punctures with the twin still in his hand. "Naomi, get the ribbon from Laelia's hair and tie it around the top of my arm. Quickly."

"Oh gods, it bit you," Laelia stammered as she ripped the ribbon from her hair.

Naomi ran to him and he held his elbow out but kept his arm down, the blood already beginning to run toward his fingers. She moved fast, wrapping the ribbon twice around his arm and pulling the ends taut. The sudden stab of pain told him it was good and tight as she made a firm knot.

He sucked blood from the cuts he'd made, careful to spit away from the women and sucked again, fighting nausea from the foulness of the task.

Laelia grappled to her feet, her face still contorted in fear. "What's happening?"

Naomi moved toward Laelia to take her hand. "Drusus is bleeding himself to draw the poison out."

He turned away from her to concentrate on not accidently swallowing or allowing himself to gag and break the suction prematurely.

"Fetch a pitcher of water and rags," Laelia said behind him. "Hurry."

After ten mouthfuls of his own blood, he prayed God would render harmless any poison that remained. The flesh beneath the wound he'd made was already swollen. The headless body of the snake still twitched, and he kicked it further away as a violent cough tore from his chest.

Laelia moved toward him, her hands out. "Are you all right?"

"Stay back," he rasped, spitting again to clear the bitter film from his teeth. "Stay back on the path. There may be more." He'd been an idiot not to realize a garden neglected this long could be teeming with snakes.

The shade of blue coloring his fingertips and the numbness stealing through his arm reminded him to pull the tourniquet free. He couldn't undo the knot in the thin strip of linen with one hand. He stepped toward her, surprised to find how unsteady the single step made him. "I need you to untie this knot, if you can."

From inside the house came the sound of a crash but he couldn't worry about that until blood flowed through his arm again. The flesh was already as pale as the stone of the amphitheater below where the ribbon buried in his skin. He took her hand and placed it on the knot.

Her dark eyes burned with concentration like he'd never seen as her fingers worked at the knot. In the span of a few breaths, she pulled the ribbon free and rubbed the skin beneath. Then the real pain came. Blood flowed back into the starving flesh, moving like liquid fire through his veins. In spite of his determination not to do so, a low moan seeped from his throat. His fingers spread wide and straightened like arrows as if to escape the coming wrath.

She bit her bottom lip and continued to massage his arm, lower down now, working in firm, rhythmic strokes. "I know it hurts when the blood returns."

So did the thought of how easily the viper could have bit her, somewhere they might not have been able to stop the poison. Laelia's hands stilled, but remained on his arm. Her mouth parted as if she meant to speak, but changed her mind. Her eyes were red and water shone in them as a single tear cascaded down her cheek.

He reached to wipe it away but caught himself before his thumb touched her skin. Never an unannounced touch to the blind, and never so intimate a touch from a slave. "I'm all right," was the best he could do.

She embraced him, her arms locking around his neck as her body pressed into him.

He threw his arm out and away from her. "There's still blood on my hands."

"I don't care." Her head collapsed onto his shoulder and gripped him as tight as the tourniquet she'd released a moment ago. "Nothing can ever happen to you."

It would be so easy to raise his other arm, cradle her to him for only a moment. A moment he couldn't allow.

When she at last released him, her eyes were red and her face drawn. "Where's Naomi?"

"I'll check. Something broke inside a moment ago. I'll be right back." He would take her with him but wasn't about to put his blood-stained hand anywhere near her.

He returned to where the snake lay and gathered both of his knives. When he turned to enter the house, Naomi was emerging with a large bowl with several rags looped over her forearm.

"I'm sorry. In my haste I tripped and broke the pitcher. I couldn't find another but brought a bowl of water instead." She waddled toward him, straining under the weight of the bowl of water.

He slipped the twins in his belt, knowing cleaning them could wait. "Thank you." He took the bowl and raised it to his lips. After a few swishes around his mouth, he spit the water away before taking a long gulp.

Naomi eyed him curiously. "I've never seen knives that flat, or anyone keep them stored in their belt that way. I never knew they were there, though I did wonder about all that stitching in the leather."

"Thank Jupiter he had them." Laelia put her hands out. "What can I do?"

"Hold these." Naomi placed the rags in her hands and kept one to wet and begin cleaning the drying blood from Drusus' arm. "We'll need to bind that and keep it clean until it closes. No more working in the dirt until then."

"That's for the best anyway. Drusus said there might be more snakes."

He wouldn't let this incident, no matter how severe it nearly was, destroy her enjoyment of the garden they'd rebuilt. "Before we weed again I'll pass a stick over the area and make sure, but in the meantime we'll tend the other three sections as before, just more carefully."

Laelia held the strips of cloth for Naomi while she ripped them and tied a folded square over his wound. Maybe it was the gray day or the ordeal of the snake but Naomi didn't look well at all now that he studied her. Her cheeks were drawn and the area under her eyes so dark he thought for a moment they might be bruised. "How long have you been feeling poorly?"

"Nothing a little rest won't fix. I'll be fine tomorrow."

What if she wasn't? "I hope so. Laelia and I both need you."

"Agreed," Laelia added. "When you've finished, return to your room and rest. After you take care of the broken pitcher. I would do it myself but I wouldn't be able to find all the shards."

Laelia bit her bottom lip and frowned.

He knew that look. "What's wrong?"

"Are you well enough for the walk to Marcus'?"

Naomi's gaze met his and he prayed the jealousy wasn't written in his eyes. Laelia might be blind, but Naomi saw everything.

"Yes, Mistress."

"We should leave soon then. I know it's difficult for you to eat later than the time you're accustomed to."

His brow furrowed as he stared at her. "How?"

"Your stomach rumbles like a chariot on a stone street and you sigh every few minutes until you've eaten."

He'd always thought he'd kept the irritability of his stomach out of his manner. At least he'd made an effort to. "Apologies."

She held her hand out to him. "Don't apologize. It's not gluttony, it's your condition. A proper mistress makes concessions when possible for the well-being of all in her house."

Naomi picked up the bowl and poured out the unused water. "Your mother would be so proud of you."

Laelia smiled as he positioned himself beside her. "Thank you."

The bandage didn't allow him to feel her hand beneath his as well but wasn't so thick he wouldn't be able to apply pressure to signal her when needed. "Whenever you're ready, Mistress."

She squeezed his arm and they settled into their smooth cadence toward the front door. Another afternoon with Marcus.

He'd rather starve.

Chapter 18

Laelia knew the route to Marcus' cook-shop so well she could likely walk it without Drusus if she didn't have anyone in her path. They turned the final corner, and the crowd sounded thicker than normal. "Is he very busy?"

"Yes."

The wind blew strong as well. Tendrils of hair kept crossing her face and the awnings fought their ropes with pops and groans. "Is my hair tidy and my *stola* straight?"

"Yes."

She should have had Naomi put color on her lips and line her eyes with kohl. But she'd hated to make Drusus wait after everything that happened with the snake. If everything went like she hoped today, Marcus would see her bare-faced at some point anyway. "Let me have a few of the coppers. I'd like to pay myself today."

He pulled her sideways out of the way of someone or something. "Forgive me, Mistress. I forgot the coin."

She fought the frown. He had almost been killed that morning and it was his first mistake in three months. "Of course you're forgiven."

"Thank you. We can return to the house and I'll do my best to boil some eggs."

He started to turn them but she stopped him. The absent coin might prove an opportunity more than an inconvenience. "That's not necessary. I still want to see Marcus."

Was that a sigh? That's what it sounded like but she couldn't be certain over the noise of dishes on wooden tables and conversations woven together like vines.

"Laelia! You are a vision of Elysium on this dreary day." Marcus' voice was deeper than Drusus', and still sent a little flutter through her anytime he greeted her with appreciation.

She flaunted her best smile on a slow blink and brought Drusus to a stop. "You flatter me again. I thank you."

"Marcus, I need another bowl of—"

"Can't you see I'm engaged in conversation with the lady?"

"Oh please, I wouldn't want to hold up business," she said.

Someone took her by the wrist, presumably Marcus. Her backbone stiffened as he pulled her from Drusus' side. Apprehension flooded her in the absence of her wall.

"Don't trouble yourself, my lady. I could kick them all out right now and they'd be back tomorrow. My stew is the best as you know; though I hope that isn't the only reason you come to visit me."

Jupiter be thanked, there it was. The last encouragement she needed. The tension drained and she clasped his hand that still held her wrist. "I think you know it's not." She smiled and hoped she was facing him straight on. With the clamor of the diners, determining direction proved more challenging.

"Father, we need more wood for the fires." She knew he had a son, Augustus. The boy was reasonably young from the high pitch of his voice, though old enough to work at the cook-shop.

"Forgive me, Laelia, that can't wait. Wait for me in the kitchen. You and your slave are welcome to enjoy anything you like."

"I will. Thank you." She gave another practiced smile and a slight nod before Marcus released her. Before she could call for him, Drusus took her hand and placed it back on his arm. She signaled him to start and when he didn't move, she turned her head his direction and squeezed harder. Surely he would have seen Marcus point to the doorway to the kitchen or be able to see where it was himself. He eventually moved, but the delayed start unsteadied her balance. Her first footfall was clumsy and Marcus probably saw. What was the matter with Drusus? Now of all times, it was necessary she appeared capable.

She wondered for a moment if he was making her look clumsy on purpose, as many times as he shifted and changed direction and stopped her abruptly. The clamor of dishes and conversation faded to the softer sounds of fire. The scent of herbs and savory broth teased her nostrils and enticed her stomach. Splashing water seemed out of place.

"Who are you?" a woman's voice asked.

Drusus signaled a stop harder than he needed to. "Laelia Ricarri. Marcus asked me to wait for him here." Was the woman a servant or a daughter?

"Oh."

The splashing resumed along with the clink of dishes. Dishes, of course she washed dishes. "Are you Augustus' sister?"

"Do I look like his sister?" The *sarkamos* in the woman's biting comment was as thick as the smell of the simmering food all around her.

Laelia angled her chin in the direction of the water and straightened. If not a family member, she must be a servant or hired help since Marcus' wife died last year when giving birth to their second child. This woman was then someone with no right to speak to her in that manner. "In case you are too, I'm blind. Otherwise I wouldn't have asked."

The woman didn't respond, but Laelia put her back to the woman. She had to pivot on Drusus' arm to do it, but she did. His peppermint aroma blasted her now that she faced him, overpowering the fragrance of the stew. She wanted a bowl, and Drusus must since he'd missed his mid-morning snack because of the snake. Marcus did say help themselves. She ought to make that rude woman serve her, but the shrew might one day be her servant also, and making an early enemy wouldn't be good for anyone. "Drusus would you make us two bowls of stew?" She raised her voice on purpose. "Marcus said to help ourselves to anything we wanted."

"Yes, Mistress."

It wouldn't make sense that there would be a table and stools or dining couch in the kitchen but she couldn't eat standing up. Could she?

"Pardon me, my beauty."

She smiled at Marcus' praise, deciding not to tattle on the woman. She stepped back toward his mouthy servant and away from the fires. There were a lot of feet moving now, and she wished to remain out of the way.

"Your slave can bring our bowls back outside now. I've cleared a table for us."

Should she tell Marcus the second bowl wasn't for Marcus, it was for Drusus?

"I'll set these outside and return for you, Mistress."

Wood cluttered to the floor. "Not necessary. I'll bring her. Go on ahead, before someone else sits there and I have to kick them out."

It bothered her Marcus presumed to order Drusus about.

"Mistress?"

Laelia nodded. She would have to start getting used to it.

Marcus took her hand and placed it on his arm. He was hairy where Drusus was smooth. His fingers lay thick and awkward over hers where Drusus' were long and always fit perfectly in the valleys formed by hers.

"Is this right?"

No. She smiled at him. "Yes."

Even his gait when he pulled her forward confused her. His strides were so short it felt like they were hardly moving and made her shuffle—right into the edge of the doorway. Her arm banged the beam and she couldn't suppress a moan of pain.

Marcus must not have heard over the noise of the diners. "Here we are." He stopped abruptly and she fought to keep her top-half from pitching forward. While she straightened, he pulled from under her hand without placing her palm against her seat first. She bit her lip, her shoulder still smarting, and now didn't know where to sit down.

"Mistress." Drusus took her hand and turned her slightly. "Your stool is one pace in front of you and well back of the table edge."

"Thank you." She released him and stepped forward. Mercifully she located the stool and the table with little trouble and seated herself in as graceful a manner as her *stola* allowed. "Marcus, Drusus hasn't eaten yet either. May I impose further on your generosity?"

"You may impose on anything of mine, anytime you wish, my lady."

She felt her face flame and wasn't quite sure how to respond.

"Augustus, bring the lady and I some wine and see her slave gets a bowl of stew in the kitchen."

"Yes, Father."

Laelia began her slow sweep of the table and found the edge of her bowl but not the spoon.

"What are you doing?" Marcus asked.

"Locating my spoon."

"It's in your bowl to the right there."

Why would Drusus put it in her bowl? He always laid her spoon on the right side of her plate. She felt along the rim of the bowl and tried to hide her mounting anxiety.

"No, my right."

Curses! She heaved a sigh and forced a smile. After changing hands she located the handle of the spoon—after what felt like an entire lunar cycle. "How old is Augustus?"

"Ten. He was born in the year of four Emperors, to my first wife Julia."

First wife?

"My second wife decided she preferred the company of gladiators to mine. When her favorite won his freedom, I didn't try to make her stay. She packed the next morning and we divorced that afternoon."

"I'm sorry to hear that." How old was he? Gods she wished she could see.

"I hope not too sorry."

She grinned because it was expected and spooned the stew into her mouth to be spared any more conversation for a moment. A moment of pure bliss, for the rich broth caressing her tongue was hot enough to sooth without burning and tasted of every good thing she could think of. The strong mushroom flavor harmonized the pork. Oh if only Naomi could cook this well. She hadn't been able to even in her younger years, as far as Laelia remembered.

"How is it today? It's all I eat so I hardly taste it anymore."

"It's ambrosia." Laelia spooned another mouthful, this one with asparagus.

The unique texture of the upper stalk tipped her off before the flavor as she chewed.

"Were you ever married?" he asked.

"No. My mother died when I was eight and my father needed me at home."

"And now?"

Oh gods, could this be it? Already? "Now I have to look to my future and where I might best build my house."

"Are there many others besides your male slave in your house?"

The subtle inquiry wasn't from curiosity. The number of slaves in a house is the first indicator of wealth behind *cognomen* and hers, Ricarri, no longer carried anything but shame behind it from her father's exploits. "My father and I find we require only two servants. Drusus you've met and Naomi was my mother's maid. I have known her as long as my father, though sometimes it feels like longer."

"Why?"

She'd spoken too freely. "My father travels very often for his employer. He is home very little." Gods be thanked. She'd thank them more if Poseidon would sink his ship in the open sea.

"What does he do that requires so much travel?"

"He's the overseer for a shipping merchant. On occasion he travels the trade routes to inspect the ledgers and cargoes of the seaport contacts. Corruption exists all over the empire, not only in the Senate."

"You know politics?"

"My mother's father was a senator in the time of Nero."

"A senator?"

She couldn't let him get too excited about that. "Yes, but my mother was his only surviving child and I am hers." And somewhere out there was a jeweled dagger that possessed the history of her family within its emeralds, rubies and pearls. But she couldn't still mourn the dagger. She'd done what she needed to, just like she would do now with Marcus.

"And your father's family?"

She didn't want to talk anymore. She wanted to eat and go home and stop revisiting her chamber pot of a life since her mother died. "My father's family and their villa were destroyed in the great fire. Father was in Ostia at the time, or would have died also."

"I lost a sister and two uncles in that fire. I'm sure I would share your father's pain, though I admit mine is eased considerably every time I see another Christian go to the lions in the arena or hanging on a cross with the other criminals. Vespasian didn't stomp them out nearly as well as Nero did. Perhaps Emperor Titus will do a better job than his father did of keeping our city clean of them and their strange ways."

Something inside her went cold, in spite of the hot food in her belly. Even though the Christians had started the great fire, Laelia didn't share Marcus' enthusiasm for death. Her father however would approve.

"Listen to me," Marcus said. "Apologies, I'm out of practice on appropriate conversation for such a fine lady. You haven't touched your wine. Would you prefer water?"

"No, I'm fine. Thank you." She hadn't heard Augustus return and set the cups down so she had no idea where it was. And as clumsy as she appeared looking for her spoon earlier, she wasn't about to repeat her display of ineptness.

"Your cup is a handbreadth to the upper right of your bowl, Mistress."

Drusus' voice—and close. "I thought you were eating in the kitchen?"

"He's fine," Marcus said, before Drusus could answer her. "If I didn't already know he was a slave I'd think him your brother. Why do you not have him marked?"

Marked? The entire idea repulsed her—especially branding with hot iron. "Drusus would never run away. Neither would Naomi."

"But if they do, how will the authorities know who to return them to?"

"I told you, Drusus and Naomi would never run away."

"You should put a slave collar on them anyway. I have one on all three of my servants."

Suddenly the woman's snide comment in the kitchen made sense. And so did Marcus. She put another spoon full of stew into her mouth but this one tasted like dirt. Three more went down before her stomach threatened to revolt. It wasn't the food. It was the thought of Drusus and Naomi in banded slave collars like the oxen and goats wore—tangible reminders their lives were not their own.

"I didn't mean to offend. I can see how no one would ever want to leave your side."

She raised her head and eased her shoulders back. Marcus had lost some of his luster but he wasn't her father. She couldn't afford to be romantic. The money from the dagger was dwindling. "I'm not offended."

"Is your father home now?"

"No, though I expect him in the next week or so."

"I would like to have you both for *cena* one evening at my house, if you would like."

"I'll let you know once he returns. Is that acceptable?"

"Of course, though I hope you return sooner than last time. I can't remember when I enjoyed a meal so much."

Laelia forced a smile and rose. "Thank you for both, Marcus. I hope to see you again soon." She stepped back and held out her hand for Drusus.

He raised it to his lips for a kiss as she gasped.

"The pleasure will be all mine, my lady."

It was Marcus, not Drusus. She had the overwhelming urge to wipe the dampness of his lips away on her *stola* but couldn't with him watching her. "Thank you."

He released her and she tucked her arms behind her to wipe the slickness away with her sash. If only she could wipe away the image of Drusus in a slave collar. She didn't have an image of Drusus other than the ones she put together herself when unable to sleep but in none of them would he ever be yoked like that. Did Marcus treat his servants so badly he feared they would run away? How could she ask that? Do you beat or starve your slaves and will you do the same to me if I displease you?

She held her hand out again and this time knew it was Drusus who touched her. She wished she could lean against him and have him carry her home as he had the night she sold the dagger. They maneuvered through the street toward the house. The bandage on his wrist rubbed her knuckles. He could have died this morning. He still could, if enough poison lingered in his body. He was quiet, but that was fine with her. She was having her own conversation with every god who would listen.

You took my mother and my sight. You will not take Drusus from me too or so help me I will set fire to every temple I can find.

"Every time I return to this house I find you absent."

Oh gods. He was home earlier than expected. She plastered the practiced smile in place. "Father, I'm so glad you're home. Have you eaten yet? I hope not. I would like to have Naomi prepare something special for you while you tell me of your trip."

The sound of the fountain gurgled while she waited. She pictured her father's face a mask of confusion at her forwardness but for this to succeed she needed to throw him off right away.

"I haven't eaten."

"Good. Drusus, please tell Naomi to prepare the best of everything we have for *cena* this evening."

"Yes, Mistress." He released her hand and she lowered it to her side.

"What happened to your slave's hand?"

"Oh it was dreadful, Father. This morning we were working in the garden and a snake almost bit me. Drusus killed it, but not before the vile creature bit him. He thinks he got all the poison out. I hope if you're not overly tired from your journey, you would like to come see what all we've done in your absence. I think you'll be pleased."

When he didn't answer right away, the fear almost weakened her knees but she held fast. Capable women can suppress emotion. Better ones defy it.

"Is something wrong, Father?"

"No." A long pause. "I'm merely surprised to see you and the house doing so well."

Of course he was. "I'm quite anxious to tell you all about it, but I know you've just returned and may wish to tend other matters first." *Careful, Laelia.*

"If you tell me what it is you would like me to do before *cena*, I'll see to it. Otherwise I'll resume my work in the garden."

"I'll come see what you've done with that weed patch of your mother's."

He could have thought to take her hand but the sound of his footsteps told her he'd left her right there in the atrium. No matter, she knew it well enough by now. Imagining Drusus at her side, she moved forward and when it felt about right, reached out and right where she expected was the edge of the passageway into the hall. She made her way down the hall and knew she was close to the peristyle. She raised her hand and searched out the edge. Not finding it, she didn't know whether or not to move forward or sideways. Sideways. That way she would find the wall and not the unexpected step down. She found the wall and then the doorway into the garden.

"You bought plants?"

The disapproval was expected but she was ready. "No. Most of them were thrown out by street vendors because they didn't sell and weren't well tended. We've been able to save most of them, or at least Drusus tells me we have. He works often with me out here. I thought redoing the garden would be nice if you ever wanted to entertain guests here again."

"Why would you think that?"

"Well I hoped to save this news for *cena* but I've made an acquaintance and he has asked to dine with you."

Footsteps. She couldn't tell if he was moving toward her or away. "A betrothal?"

Laelia attempted her best blush by remembering the tender way Drusus washed her hands. "His name is Marcus Flox and he owns a cook-shop near the forum. I think he wishes to dine with you to become acquainted with you as well because I believe I have caught his special attention."

"Speak plainly, Laelia. Do you think this man intends to wed you? Otherwise I have no interest in him."

That would have hurt her if she didn't already know it to be true. "He's expressed the possibility of marriage."

"Then by all means, I will meet with him tomorrow. I'll have to send Naomi to market to supply a proper meal but—"

"Oh that's not necessary, Father. That's the other news I have for you."
Exactly like you practiced. "When you left last time before you had an
opportunity to fill our coin box, I knew it would be sometime before you
returned. I have found I'm very good at telling fortunes. I think my blindness
adds a certain mystical effect that keeps the coins flowing into my cup. And I
can set up anywhere so I don't even have the expense of a booth or awning.
My only regret is I didn't think of it sooner."

Silence.

Keep the smile. Give him no reason to doubt you.

"How much do you average in a day?"

"On a good day two or three sesterces. On a slow day, enough coppers for
a meal for the three of us." The lies she'd rehearsed a hundred times while
pulling weeds sounded so natural to her own ear, even she almost believed
them.

"I'll accompany you tomorrow."

Juno's peacock. She hadn't expected that. "Of course, Father. That would
be delightful."

"You would likely earn more if you wore a little paint. Does this
acquaintance of yours know you've been earning money this way and would
he approve?"

"I haven't had occasion to mention it but I'm sure he would approve.
Although I have every reason to believe once we're married, I'd have no need
to continue."

"And he knows you're blind?"

Keep the smile. "Yes."

"I look forward to seeing you work tomorrow and meeting this Marcus
Flox."

"Thank you, Father."

"You might have thought to plant some vegetables out here, instead of all
these half-dead flowers. If Marcus asks, tell him you already have and they
haven't yet sprouted so he'll think you'd be a good mistress. Does he have
children?"

"Yes, a son about ten years old."

"Good. With an heir already he won't have need to cast you off if you take too long to conceive."

It still amazed her that his words could leave bruises as good as his hands. "I agree."

"I'll be in my chamber. Have Naomi summon me when *cena* is ready."

"Of course."

Even his gait suited him. In the hastened, but heavy steps she sensed his ever-present temper. She'd succeeded in her performance so far, but now would have to think about how to untangle tomorrow. She couldn't tell fortunes. She didn't even know how to go about getting people to stop. She certainly never did. And suddenly there was the answer. Slowly she turned and worked her way back in the house.

Chapter 19

When the master returned from the garden, he gave Drusus a cursory glance before continuing to his chamber without a word. Drusus took a step toward the garden to seek Laelia, but she appeared in the entrance, following after her father. No signs of injury or distress that he could tell from this distance. He was about to announce his presence when she stopped three paces away, her hand still on the wall. She sniffed a few times, turning her head toward him as she did so. "Drusus?"

He raised his left arm and brought his nose to his shoulder. Definitely in need of a bath. "Yes, Mistress."

"I need you to take me back to the market."

"I'll let Naomi know we're going out. Should I tell her to expect you for *cena*?"

"Yes but tell her delay the meal as long as she can. Then get three coppers from the coin box."

The coin box? There wasn't any money in the coin box. "Mistress, there—"

She drew up straight and angled her nose high. "Do as I say."

The arrogance so unlike her was making another appearance. He'd been subjected to it twice the past few weeks, and always in Marcus' presence. Today Drusus could blame her father for it instead. "Yes, Mistress."

Naomi asked questions he didn't have answers for, beginning with why they were going back to the market. He opened the lid to the small box expecting it to be empty and there were six coppers and one *sesterce* inside. He

127

counted out three and closed the lid. She'd always kept the change from their purchases. Now he knew where she'd put it. Unlike the rest of her coin hidden in his room, along with the dagger he still hadn't decided how to return to her.

"Drusus, I'm waiting."

He almost reminded her he hadn't eaten since this morning and was exhausted from bleeding himself of venom only hours ago. "Coming, Mistress."

For the first time, he needed to lengthen his stride to keep up with her. Once on the street, she strode even faster and upset his rhythm. He couldn't concentrate on keeping her pace and everything happening around them. "This is too fast a pace, Mistress."

She didn't even pause. "Then speed up."

His jaw went as tight as his arm, locking his teeth together. Fine, she'd have it her way. Within moments what he was trying to prevent—happened. A man in front of them slowed, and Drusus didn't have enough time to move Laelia to the side. She bumped into the back of the stranger.

"Watch it," the man snapped.

"I'm sorry, I didn't see you."

"Are you blind or just stupid?"

Drusus resisted the urge to punch the man across the chin, but the snow-white toga and the two slaves with him checked his anger. "The fault is mine, my lord. My mistress is blind and I didn't move her out of the way fast enough. Apologies."

The man gave Drusus a once over that made his skin crawl as he moved Laelia forward. He glanced over his shoulder to be sure they were moving well clear of the man.

"What's the matter with you?"

Her harsh whisper scoured the remnant of his patience.

"You can't walk me into people. I can't appear incompetent or everything I'm working toward is lost."

Walk her into people? That wasn't his fault. He—

"If you're going to allow yourself to become distracted, I'm better off on my own. You could at least pretend to care this is important to you."

Pretend to care? Drusus stopped and she didn't, which swung her around to nearly face him.

Laelia's mouth flattened as she jerked her hand from his arm. "Now you're doing it on purpose. Why?"

She continued her glare with her hands on her hips. Passersby watched them without turning their heads.

Calm down, she's not herself right now. He drew a breath to speak but she was faster.

"You're useless."

That sank deeper than the fangs of the viper and hurt more than the club to the head. "And you sound just like your father."

Her hand shot up and with shocking precision she slapped him in the face. He stood there stunned as onlookers snickered. Heat spread in his cheek and his fists tightened. He couldn't even look at her he was so furious. So he spun and strode away so she could see what useless really was.

What have I done? The pain searing Laelia's palm held nothing to the sickening shame intensifying with every breath. Drusus had accused her of sounding like her father and in her indignation she became him. "Drusus, I'm sorry. I'm so sorry."

No answer. "Drusus?"

Still no answer. The sounds of the crowded market surrounded her, but his voice was missing. Her lungs threatened to revolt as her throat closed and cold dread filled her. She swept the air in front of her. "Drusus, please. Where are you?"

Someone gripped her wrist. "Who are you looking for, sweetness?"

Laelia cringed from the stranger's touch and pulled free. "Leave me alone."

She backed away but collided with something—someone—who smelled like her father after a long night at the tavern. Another pair of hands seized her shoulders and rough stubble scratched the side of her cheek as her heart seized with terror.

The admonishment from Paul's letter rattled through Drusus' head with every step. Slaves were to obey their masters as if they were Christ, whether or not they were harsh and unjust. How many times had Otho told him and the others?

But Paul had never been a slave. And neither had Otho.

She'd slapped him. He'd saved her life, nearly lost his, and she'd slapped him.

Go back to her. Now.

But he pushed through a small crowd of boys herding a pig through the street with sticks. The animal's squeals rose above the general clamor of the marketplace.

Go back to her. Now.

When the sting faded from his face and he'd quelled the anger, he'd go back.

Another cry cut through the sounds of the crowd, slicing through him as it reached his ears. His hands went to his belt even as he turned. A man had his filthy hand clamped over Laelia's mouth and her head pulled back as another pushed her toward an alley. Drusus had the first twin unsheathed but there were too many people between him and the two dead men. All of whom did nothing to stop them.

Drusus started running, flipping the knife for fighting instead of throwing. He used his elbow to help clear his path. Calling out would alert her captors to move faster. The one holding Laelia's mouth made eye contact, and instantly shoved her toward his partner and bolted.

The man turned to see what caused his partner to run, putting Laelia between them. Instantly Drusus flipped his wrist toward him to protect her from his blade as he slammed into them, opening a long slice on the man's arm. Laelia screamed again as she went down, and the man ran. Drusus no longer had a clean throw and let him go.

He sheathed his knife and reached to touch her ashen cheek. "Laelia?"

Another man who wore a simple tunic and rope belt dropped to his knees beside her. "I saw what happened. You were brave to stop it."

"Why didn't you?" It was an accusation as much as a question. Drusus could hear it in his own voice.

The man's gaze met his. "If I'm killed defending another man's woman, who is left to protect mine?" The stranger rose, his knees cracking as he did. "You should get her out of the street." Then he walked away.

Drusus gathered Laelia to him and her head rolled back. He shifted so her chin rested on her chest. He couldn't carry an unconscious Laelia into their house and Otho's was one street over. He walked slowly, her slight weight balanced between his arms. This time there was no pleasure in the feel of her body against his. With every step, his own words came back to him like blows. "I'll never leave you," he'd promised.

He was the worst kind of liar.

Drusus rushed into the shop, and the slaves in the trough stopped their work when they saw Laelia's limp body in his arms. "Where's Otho?"

"He's not here." Alexander climbed out and rushed toward the door. "What happened?"

"My mistress was attacked."

"Take her to the upper room and I'll go for Otho." Alexander ran without taking the time to put his sandals on.

Drusus carried Laelia to the upper room, using the light from a small window. A pallet lay on the floor in the corner beside a table cluttered with scrolls and a clay lamp. Drusus rested Laelia on the blanket-covered straw and knelt beside her. Her eyes were still closed and she wasn't responding. He squeezed her hand. "Laelia, wake up."

His guilt wouldn't let him pray. What then? Go tell her father? The master would beat him for sure. He deserved it, and more, but then her father would likely come straight here. Drusus couldn't bring a known hater of Christians with a propensity to violence into the very home of one of the Lord's most devout followers. He'd put everyone he cared about in danger—again.

The neckline of her tunic had slipped low enough to reveal paler flesh than he should see. He pulled the thin pink wool back up before touching her cheek. "Please wake up."

Someone was coming up the stairs. Otho. Carrying two cups. "What happened?"

Drusus moved out of the way. "She was attacked in the street."

Otho knelt beside him and handed him one of the cups of wine. His gaze cut to Drusus as he slid his free hand beneath Laelia's head. "Where were you?"

Failing. He looked away.

Otho brought the cup to Laelia's lips. "A little water, my lady."

The water ran down the side of her mouth which remained as still as her eyes. Otho set the cup down and began to probe her scalp. "Do we need to send word to your mistress' house?"

"I don't know."

"Will someone at her house be expecting her to have returned by now?"

"Yes, but I can't leave her."

Liar. He'd already left her. The memory of his own terror seeing her pinned between those men, their dirty hands silencing her, dragging her off to violate her wounded him again and again.

Otho eased her head back to the blanket and took hold of her limp hand between his. "Take her foot."

Drusus touched the worn brown leather of her sandal and closed his eyes. Otho prayed in silence. He couldn't. He'd abandoned her in the street. And for what? Because she slapped him?

Laelia's foot jerked from beneath his palm. She thrashed and screamed as Otho pulled back from her flailing arms. Drusus caught a solid kick just before her nails gouged his upper arm.

"Laelia, it's me. It's me!"

She stopped screaming but she was crouched in the corner with scattered straw around her, eyes wild and her breathing ragged.

Tears threatened his eyes. "Laelia, it's me. It's Drusus. I'm here, and you're safe."

"Drusus?" Her voice didn't sound anything like her.

"Is she all right?" Alexander asked. He must have come running when he heard the screaming.

Drusus cringed as Laelia pressed deeper into the wall from the strange voice. "Who's there?" She pulled her knees to her chest and wrapped her arms around them. "Drusus, where are you?"

Her broken plea rent what was left of his shredded heart and he eased toward her on his knees. "I'm here. I brought you to a friend's house. He and some of his slaves are also here, but they're leaving."

Drusus looked over his shoulder and Otho nodded as he shepherded his two slaves who had entered back down the stairs and followed them.

Laelia held her hand out, her spread fingers shaking. "Where are you?"

Her voice trembled as much as her arm as he reached for her hand. "I'm here. It's just me now. I'm right here."

He laced his fingers with hers and her breath left her in a mighty rush as she launched herself against him. His arms closed around her as he shifted to sit on the wooden floor with her in his lap. "I'm so sorry."

Her sobs continued to flow as she clung to him. The blood on his arm dried to a dark powder but that was the least of his wounds. He stroked her back, the top of her head, reassuring himself as much as her she was safe now. She stayed pressed against him, her head to his chest while he held her. In time the sobs became weeping and the weeping turned to an occasional sniffle.

Otho stuck his head up from below, barely visible in the fading light of the window.

"My lady, should I send a slave to your house with a message?"

Laelia pushed closer to his chest.

Drusus rubbed her upper arm and tightened his hold on her. "It's all right. This is my friend, Otho the fuller. We're in his house. It was nearer than yours."

A deep breath swelled her thin frame and she raised her head, almost clipping his chin. "Yes, please. Tell my father we've been delayed but will be home soon and all is well."

It was far from well. Laelia sounded as if someone had sanded her throat.

Otho frowned and eyed Drusus instead. "Are you certain you wouldn't rather spend the night here, my lady? The streets are even more unsafe at night for women."

"I must return home. Please tell my father I'm fine and we'll be along directly."

Drusus didn't like it any more than Otho did, but shook his head to let him know they didn't have a choice. His friend descended and Drusus knew he would do as Laelia had asked.

"Is he gone?"

"Yes."

Her hands slid down her belly and her chin dropped to her chest. "I don't remember anything between them dragging me away and waking up here. Did they…" She held her breath, a tremor ripping through her.

Understanding dawned and he pulled her tighter to him. "They didn't."

She released a heavy sigh and burrowed her forehead into the crook of his neck. "I shouldn't have hit you."

"Laelia, you could have beaten me to the ground and I should still never have left your side. This was *my* fault, and I will never, ever, leave you again."

Her palm came to rest in the center of his chest. "I need you."

He tightened his hold on her, and before his better judgment could stop him, he kissed the top of her head and inhaled the faint floral scent of her hair. *I need you too.* He smoothed the hair back from her face with his bandaged hand. "If you're feeling well enough to walk, we should go soon. It's too late to rent a litter or I would."

Otho reappeared with a pitcher in his hand. "If you insist on leaving tonight, I'm sending every slave I own to escort you."

"Thank you," Laelia said, though Drusus knew Otho had spoken to him.

The older man refilled the cup on the floor and handed it to him. "It's my honor to meet you, my lady, though I wish it had been in happier circumstances."

"Thank you," she said again.

Drusus put the cup against her fingers. "You should drink this water."

Laelia took it and drained the cup before handing it back. Otho refilled it and this time Drusus drank the cool water, surprised at how much he needed it too. If Otho had any thoughts about Laelia still being on Drusus' lap, he didn't show it.

"Master, Amadi has returned," a voice called out from below.

Laelia tensed. "From my father's house?"

A slave entered and bowed before Laelia before turning to Otho. "The lady's father sends his gratitude for the message and asks the lady return as soon as possible."

"Thank you, Amadi. Gather the others. I want you to see the lady and Drusus home."

"Yes, Master."

The slave departed and Otho turned toward them again, kneeling down on one knee. "My lady, if there is anything I can do for you, now or ever, please call on me."

Laelia turned her head toward his voice. "Not unless you can teach me how to tell fortunes and send me patrons tomorrow, but thank you anyway."

Otho raised a brow at Drusus, but he was as lost as his mentor. He took her hand, surprised at how doing so now felt natural and not improper. "What are you saying?"

She bit her lower lip and didn't answer.

Drusus glanced up and thought he might know why. "Otho is my friend. He's trustworthy so you can speak openly in front of him."

She still hesitated.

"Perhaps she has other reasons for caution," Otho said. "I will leave you two."

"I'm trapped in a lie," she blurted. "One of my own making and I don't know how to get out."

Drusus searched her face and saw the fear there. "How?"

"I told father the money we lived on in his absence came from fortune telling. Tomorrow he wants to come with me and I don't know what to do. I was going to the forum to have my fortune read and at least try to look like I know what I'm doing, but I don't. Not at all and if he thinks I lied—" She swallowed and a shudder passed through her and Drusus at the same time.

135

"Can you not just tell him the truth?" Otho looked to Drusus in question.

"No. I will lose everything if I do."

Deceit went against everything in Drusus but what would happen to her if they couldn't fake this? Otho's stare mined him as if he could read his thoughts. Drusus hated to disappoint his mentor, but he wasn't going to stand for whatever twisted punishment her father would dole out for catching Laelia in a lie or keeping her coin safe from his debauchery.

"Drusus?" Otho's tone was a concealed question.

He hoped God would understand. "Didn't the Lord defend his disciples plucking grain on the Jew's Holy Day?"

"He did, but because they were breaking a tradition the Lord's very presence had already made void. Not because the situation affects the truth."

"What Lord do you speak of?" Laelia asked.

The look Otho gave Drusus withered his insides. His gaze returned to Laelia and softened. "Someone I hope you meet soon."

Otho rose from the floor and regarded them both with sadness in his eyes. "I'm grateful you weren't more seriously injured, my lady. Should you ever need a place of refuge, someone is always here."

"Thank you."

Drusus didn't see another way. "If you see us in front of your shop tomorrow, will you send us away?"

"You know I would not."

When he thought he could finally bear the disappointment in his mentor's eyes, Drusus looked up to thank him but Otho had already descended the steps.

Laelia twisted to hug his neck. "You saved my life for the third time today."

"You need to get up now."

She drew back and from the drop of her lower lip, he'd hurt her. But he didn't have a choice. She might not know the fire they danced so near, but he did, and it had to stop.

She remained on his lap, even after he'd pulled his arms to his sides.

"Your father's waiting."

Laelia slid from his lap and rose to her feet with astounding elegance. He climbed from the floor and stood beside her. The distance between them felt like miles instead of a few feet. Her hand extended and her neck stiffened in that regal way she usually reserved for Marcus. "Never leave me again until you've been dismissed."

He deserved that. And the rigid way it had been delivered, though it hurt almost as much as her slap. "Yes, Mistress."

Chapter 20

Laelia turned on her side and pulled her blanket to her chin. She could shove it in her mouth and scrub, but nothing would take away the remembered taste of the hand crushing her lips into her teeth. Fear was a peculiar thing. Her entire life was an ocean of lies. The money she hid, how she supposedly came by it, the reason she got out of bed every day, and the biggest one of all—Drusus was merely her slave.

Walking home surrounded by four of Otho's slaves, Drusus was right beside her but it felt as if they had the Tiber between them. Naomi had met them at the front door and taken charge of Laelia right away. Her father hadn't cared enough to wait up. If she wasn't dead or dismembered, she must be fine.

But she wasn't fine. Not even after Naomi bathed and fed her, dressed her for bed and stayed with her until she'd thought Laelia had fallen asleep. She would never be fine again.

For one unguarded moment in the upper room of the fuller, she'd known what her heart really felt. The part Drusus had breathed life back into from the moment he first came. He'd risked his life for her, and she trampled that gift with the same brutality she reviled. And instead of letting the bad men have her like she deserved, he'd carried her to safety. In the quiet as he held her, she knew she wanted to spend the rest of her life in his arms, not merely on them.

May Juno have mercy on her.

She was her mother's daughter after all.

Laelia's lips were painted and her eyes lined, thanks to Naomi's eyes and steady hands. "How do I look?"

"Beautiful like your mother. I wish I were going with you."

"We'll be fine. Drusus will be with me."

"I'm not sure he got all the poison out from the snake and he wouldn't let me clean and salt the scratches on his arm last night."

Were those from her or her attackers? "How bad are they?"

"Shallow but the skin was broken. He's barely spoken a word this morning and looks like he hasn't slept or shaved since yesterday."

Drusus shaved? Laelia had somehow always pictured him with a beard. "Where is he?"

"In the triclinium with your father."

Her breath caught. "Doing what?"

"Talking."

"I don't like them alone together." Laelia stood and made her way toward the doorway and skirted along the wall toward the triclinium.

"Mistress."

The sound of his voice gave her a new direction, and she strode confidently forward.

"You're right," her father said. "She is walking much better."

"Your daughter is exceptionally intelligent, Master. The fastest study I have ever known."

Laelia fought a grin but felt the blush in her face. Hopefully her father wouldn't make anything of it as she felt Drusus' hand take hers to settle it on his arm.

"I understand you had some trouble last evening. Drusus was telling me two thieves chose the wrong Roman to accost. I'm glad to see you're unharmed."

"Thank you, Father. Are you certain you want to spend the entire day watching me read fortunes? It does get rather dull and boring in between patrons."

"Of course I want to see this. I may see some ways your methods can be improved upon for greater profits."

She would never be good enough, even in her pretend employment. "Whenever you're ready."

"Go on, I'll follow you."

She squeezed Drusus' arm and turned with him. Not concentrating on her father behind her was impossible. "Otho's shop?" she asked in low tones.

"Yes."

Far too soon for her liking, Drusus squeezed her hand and brought her to a stop.

"We're here, Mistress. There's a crate for you to sit on two paces in front of you."

She let go of him, counted two steps and felt for the crate. She found the wood cooler than expected, but sturdy. They must be in the shade. Most of Rome still would be with its crowded buildings and narrow streets at this early hour.

"Master, if you'll permit me, I'll inquire of my friend inside for a stool for you."

"You know this fuller?"

"Yes, my lord. My previous master sent all his garments and linen here for many years."

"Go ahead then. I certainly don't want to stand here all day."

And yet her father expected Drusus to do just that. She wanted to tell him to get two stools, or maybe her crate was large enough to share, but the last thing she needed right now was to invite her father's disapproval.

A soft knock on her left sounded in her ear, and the door groaned open.

"What are you doing?"

The strange, childish voice caught her off guard. The little girl was close. "I'm waiting to tell fortunes."

"My name is Erissa. What's yours?"

"Laelia."

A small hand plopped down on hers where they rested on her lap. "Tell me my fortune."

Laelia grinned and took hold of the little hand, grimacing at the stickiness of the small fingers. She placed her first finger in the center and started to trace a spiral. "Hmmm... I see you growing up to be a very beautiful young woman. A handsome nobleman will marry you, and you will give him many sons. One of them will be a senator."

If only her contrivance could be her own reality, instead of this carefully constructed deceit. Voices carried from inside. Even muffled with a wall, Laelia could pick out Drusus. The other voice must belong to Otho or one of his servants.

"Am I going to get a puppy? My uncle promised me a puppy, but that was a long time ago."

Laelia cringed. Saying yes would be easier, but then she was no better than this child's uncle. Although hadn't she lied to this girl already? "I can't see clearly enough to know for sure. I'm sorry."

"Ugh. I don't want a husband. I want a puppy."

Laelia almost laughed. "You might not always feel that way."

"Will you be here tomorrow? I like you."

Would she? "You'll have to wait and see."

"For a fortune teller, you sure don't know a lot of things."

There was no mistaking the disapproval in the girl's tone.

"I was thinking the same thing," her father said.

"Your stool, Master." Drusus' warm, rich voice reassured her.

"Drusus! Where have you been?" A soft thump followed by giggles. "I haven't seen you in so long."

The little girl knew him?

"I know. I've missed you too, but I have important work to do right now for my mistress. Why aren't you at Lady Pappus' house?"

"It's boring there. Can't I stay with you until Uncle gets home?"

"You heard my slave," her father interrupted. "Move along now."

"But—"

"Erissa," Drusus said. "Go to Lady Pappus' house. My Master needs me, and I need you to go now."

"But I—"

"Please."

"Enough of this," her father snapped.

"Ouch!" The little girl cried and Laelia sensed the scuffle. Had he grabbed her? She hadn't heard a slap. She would know that sound anywhere.

"Master please, she's leaving." Drusus' pleading voice ripped at Laelia's heart.

"Yes, she is."

More shuffling feet, then fast footfalls. The girl was running. Had her father hit her?

"You're mean!" The little girl screamed from down the street.

The sigh of relief Laelia couldn't breathe became a forced calm.

"If you play with street children all day, how do you make any coin?" her father demanded.

"Everything well here?" a new voice asked.

"Master Ricarri, this is Otho. Otho, my master, Brutus Ricarri," Drusus said.

"A bothersome child but she's gone now. When my daughter was that age, I never let her run about unsupervised."

A soft chuckle. "Then I take it you've met Erissa. Sometimes she is too inquisitive for her own good. Her family died of fever last summer and a distant uncle took her in. He works long days and she tends to explore when she manages to slip away undetected."

"That was foolish of her relative to take charge of her if he had no intention of tending to her care," her father said gruffly. "I'm surprised an opportunistic slaver hasn't made off with her."

Laelia's throat closed up and a cough roared from her chest.

"Mistress?" Drusus' hand touched the center of her back, but she kept up a few more coughs for good measure. "Here, drink this."

A wine skin pressed into her hand. Of course he would have thought to bring one. She uncorked it and took a long swallow. The watered wine soothed her abused throat, but not the anger simmering in her thoughts. She re-corked the seal and extended the leather bag for Drusus to take. "I'm sorry. I don't know what came over me."

Warm fingers pressed against her cheek. "Are you feeling hot, or dizzy?"

"She's fine," her father snapped.

Drusus' touch fled and Laelia's knees trembled beneath the wool of her tunic.

"Excuse us, Otho. I need a moment in private with my daughter and her slave."

Her heart sped as she heard Otho retreat into his shop. She could already feel her palms begin to sweat.

"I don't know what bothers me more," her father's hushed tone began. "That you touch my daughter so freely, or that she's comfortable enough with it not to reprimand you."

Her bones were melting. That's what it felt like and she couldn't even make her chin turn the direction her father should be.

"I meant no disrespect, my lord. Only to determine if she were taking ill."

The silence that followed pulled every scrap of fear to the surface. Distract him. "Drusus is overprotective of me. I think he absorbs that from Naomi but will do better in the future. I'm on his arm the better part of the day, Father, and you're right. I've grown too accustomed to his nearness. We'll be sure to be more mindful of what others will think, won't we?"

Say yes. Please say yes. She angled her chin toward the spot Drusus should be and caught a whiff of his peppermint leaf.

"Yes, Mistress."

Laughter sounded to her left and she hoped it would capture her father's attention as well. "I hear laughing. Is it children or adults, Drusus?"

"Three ladies, Mistress."

"Do they carry baskets?"

"Yes."

Shoppers. Please let this work. "Fortunes! Fortunes read. Ladies, let me see into your futures."

The laughter quieted and it sounded like they approached, though it was harder to tell as the street was coming to life with sound.

"See my future?"

A woman's voice.

"You can't even see my face. How could you possibly see the future?"

The laughter erupted once again while heat flamed Laelia's cheeks.

They must have moved along because the laughter faded.

"Does that happen often?" her father asked. There was curiosity in his tone where there should be compassion.

That didn't surprise her.

"No," Drusus said.

By answering for her, she could almost feel his palm on her arm, a simple stoke of comfort and encouragement. She had to keep trying.

"Fortunes!" Laelia called out again and again, but soon she could hear the defeat in her own voice. How had she ever thought this could work?

Snatches of conversation told her people were about, along with a very fussy infant who cried incessantly. Every few minutes she would try again, until she couldn't remember how long she'd been sitting here. Her bottom ached from the crate and no matter how many different ways she shifted, comfort wouldn't come.

"My lady, would you like me to bring you a cushion from home?"

The walk wasn't too long but the idea of being alone with her father without Drusus present didn't sit well with her. "No, that's all right."

"Are you certain?"

She inclined her chin toward him. It wasn't like him to press, and the lilt in his last word and the pause just before it weren't like him either. Something told her to agree. "Yes, a cushion. Bring one for my father as well. Do you need anything else from home, Father?"

"No, but hurry back. I know how long it takes to get to the villa and this isn't free time for you."

"Yes, Master."

There were too many other sounds about to hear Drusus scurry off. He would have hurried anyway without the admonishment. If her father knew Drusus at all, then he would know that Drusus' gave his all to please.

"How is he?" her father asked.

Laelia couldn't imagine to whom he spoke. She hadn't heard anyone greet him.

Two snaps sounded like thunder in her ear. "If you lose your hearing too, we're done for. I asked how is he."

"Forgive me. I didn't realize you addressed me. Do you mean Drusus?"

"Who else would I mean?"

"He's very efficient in his work and is a great help to Naomi."

"What work does he do besides walk you around?"

Smile. Be charming. "He worked with me in the garden every day to help restore it."

"It is nice to see it not quite so overgrown."

She didn't know what to say and hoped the surprise in her face didn't show.

"You must be the fortune teller."

Laelia turned her face toward the masculine voice. "Yes. Do you wish to have your fortune read?"

"I would."

Her palm went out and the stranger placed his hand in hers. She took a deep breath, wondering what to make up as her fingertip found the center of his rather large hand. The roughness of his skin beneath her fingertip spoke of hard work.

"Your continued labors will bring you great rewards." She bit her lower lip and traced a few more circles on his palm. What did men want besides wine and women? "And the gods will bless you with many sons."

She released his hand and folded her own in her lap, supremely proud of herself.

"Your coin?"

Jupiter's thunder, she'd forgotten. Her hand snapped back out, palm up. "Thank you. My slave usually collects the money, but he's on an errand right now."

The man placed two coins in her palm. She couldn't tell what they were but closed her fist around them anyway. "Thank you."

"Thank you, my lady. May I ask you a question?"

Her stomach clenched. "You may."

"Which gods do you believe will bless me with sons?"

"More information will take more coin," her father broke in.

"Of course."

She didn't reach out this time. The stranger placed the coin against her thumb, and she had simply to turn her hand over to take it.

"Jupiter, Juno and Minerva." That seemed a safe answer. Every good Roman knew the Capitoline trio sitting at the temple on the Palentine Hill.

"What about Mars, Apollo, Diana, Saturn, Vesta or any of the others?" the man asked.

Why all these questions? What was her father going to think? "Whichever one you worship. That I cannot see in your future, only the children."

"Not even I can see the God I worship, my lady. Only the things He's made."

Her brow dipped. "Where is his temple?"

"Drusus hasn't already told you?"

She cocked her head. "You know my slave?"

"I thought I did," the man answered in a low tone. Was that disapproval in his voice? Recognizing it in anyone but her father wasn't something she was good at. "Good day, my lady. I will pray for you."

"Thank you."

Drusus had sent him. He must have, and the coins she'd just been paid were probably hers already. She would throw her arms around him for this if her father wouldn't figure it out as well and beat them both. The coins in her hand proved an insufficient distraction from the myriad of questions in her mind. She fingered them again, surprised her father hadn't demanded she hand them over already. If Drusus knew where the stranger's temple was, perhaps it was because he worshiped the same God. Why wouldn't the man name him? There was no reason to by cryptic unless it was one of the poorly kept secret cults like Mithras. Unless they were Christians.

Then it hit her. His refusal to swear on Jupiter's throne. That he'd never asked to visit a temple. Was Drusus a Christian? The gods forbid, that would—

"Well am I not the most fortunate of men?"

Someone seized her hand and kissed the back of it, the touch of damp lips sending a shock through her as she resisted yanking free.

"Do you wish your fortune read?"

"Fortune?" A chuckle followed. "I suppose you'll tell me the gods will bless me with no less than five sons, all intelligent and strong."

His mocking tone prickled the hair on her arms, and a deep breath quelled the urge to send this man away. Where was Drusus? "I don't know what I will tell you without seeing your fortune in your palm first. If you'd like me to, I will. Otherwise, good day."

The frost in her voice should impress her father, if he wasn't going to berate her in some way any moment.

"I don't suppose I can blame you for not remembering my voice."

Remembering his voice? This wasn't Marcus. She knew his fairly well by now.

"As you so eloquently informed me, you aren't deaf."

Aren't deaf? She'd only ever said that to the man she sold her mother's... *Gods help me.*

Tiberius Cina was holding her hand.

Chapter 21

Laelia yanked her hand from Tiberius so hard she rocked the crate she sat on. "I believe you have me confused with someone else. Good day."

"Forgive my daughter. She means no disrespect. Brutus Ricarri."

"Tiberius Cina. A pleasure to meet you."

She sat frozen, like a rabbit in the shadow of an eagle. Where was Drusus?

"Do you know my daughter?"

"No," Laelia spewed. "We've never met. I'm certain I would remember." Her chest heaved, but she couldn't stop it.

"Is that so?" Tiberius' tone was an open threat. "I'm certain I would remember a woman as beautiful as you, with a quick mind and sharp tongue."

"You flatter me." Where was Drusus? Any second her father would learn everything. Should she call out for Otho and beg him to give her sanctuary?

"I'm surprised her husband would allow such a beauty outside the house."

"She's unspoken for," her father answered.

The nausea in the pit of her stomach threatened to erupt.

"Is that so?"

Running would be useless. Without Drusus to guide her, she'd collide into the first obstacle and end up on her knees.

"The gods smile on me indeed," Tiberius' voice droned on, tightening the snare around her neck. "Never before has my walk home been so… rewarding. I hope you might allow me to call upon you Brutus, and explore how this goddess before me has managed to remain unclaimed by mortal men."

The nausea gave way to strangled breaths as her head swam.

"You're welcome at my house anytime. Laelia and I would both be happy to receive you. Isn't that right, daughter?"

Father's tone was explicit.

She would force the words. She had to. "Of course."

"That was fast," her father said.

"I knew you and my mistress would be waiting." Drusus' voice.

"I am Tiberius Cina and—*apparently*—we've never met."

He would keep her secret. At least for now. No sense of relief came, only more questions, and a swelling need to know why.

"My lord." The frost in Drusus' voice could chill a vat of wine. Laelia had never heard him so caustic.

"This is one of two slaves in my house," her father said. "He guides Laelia."

"That must be a pleasant task, accompanying this beauty all day."

Laelia couldn't breathe.

"You flatter my daughter. She does favor her mother a great deal."

"Is your lady at home?"

"No. She's been dead eight years."

"I'm sorry. I myself never married, though recently I have thought that should change. Time to settle down, have children, and make sure this fortune I'm building has someone to inherit it."

"Strong, smart children are a gift of the gods, to be certain. I have only Laelia."

"Your cushion, my lord," Drusus said.

"Pardon me, Tiberius," her father said. "My many years at sea have left me spoiled for a soft seat. Are you free for *cena* this evening?"

"Father, forgive me, but Marcus wished to dine with us upon your return."

"Even if I were not free, I would move the sun in the sky to make it so. I accept with pleasure, and I hope your daughter will accommodate me. As I'm certain she sees the future, she would know how disappointed, and vocal, I would be were she to refuse me."

She wasn't even betrothed to Tiberius yet, and already the traitor controlled her with the secret. The pantheon- sized knot in her throat hindered her reply.

"Are you certain we haven't met before?" Tiberius asked. "I own a blade shop a few blocks from here and you remind me of—"

"I've never been in a blade shop. Before Drusus, I didn't leave the house very much. He's given me a great deal of freedom, but I've never had a reason to visit a blade shop."

"Has he given you anything else besides your freedom?" Tiberius asked.

Her mouth parted at such an inappropriate question.

"Your insult to my mistress is unfounded," Drusus said.

The slap carried over the sounds of the people milling about and the sloshing in the fullery behind her. The absence of pain in her own flesh made her fists clench.

"How dare you speak so."

Another slap. She rose from the crate and angled to the right, determined to move between them before her father struck Drusus again.

"Show mercy, my lord." Tiberius' words ran together. "The slave does forget himself, but he speaks true and for that we should forgive him. For no other reason than I'm certain your daughter would wish it, and already I find myself desiring her happiness."

Liar. But fighting would only add wood to this fire. She and Drusus needed to get out of here now.

"I don't want you to form a poor opinion of me prematurely," Tiberius continued. "I enjoy my wine and the robust conversation of a full tavern. I have no wife at home to tend my hearth and offer me something to come home to. You have your daughter, but I have only my business and a few slaves. One who sometimes also thinks before he speaks."

"And how do you correct the insolent slave?"

Tiberius laughed. "That is a well-kept but effective secret I will barter you in exchange for tales from your travels. Is it too presumptuous to suggest we exchange thoughts on both this evening when we dine together?"

A long pause followed. "I shall look forward to it. You remind me of my younger self, Tiberius Cina."

"Then honor me with a visit to my blade shop this morning. If your daughter can spare you. I have some beautiful pieces I'd like to show you.

Particularly one of the daggers used to assassinate Julius Caesar. It's the prize of my collection."

"I would be delighted. Laelia, I trust you will speak to your slave."

"Yes, Father."

"She's quite adept at managing the slaves under normal circumstances."

"I have no doubt she does everything well," Tiberius said. "Come, you can be the envy of all your peers when you tell them you've held the knife that killed the greatest Roman that ever lived."

"Indeed. Laelia, tell Naomi Tiberius we'll be joining us this evening. I will meet Marcus another day."

"Ah, a second stag on the mountain," Tiberius said.

The insinuation in his tone made Laelia's blood boil.

Her father laughed. "As you said, she is very beautiful. I knew in time the men of Rome would realize all she has to offer. Now come, let's see this dagger of yours."

She waited a long moment, until she could no longer hear her father's voice as he and Tiberius talked of Julius Caesar. "Are they gone?"

"Yes, Mistress."

He'd moved. She turned toward him. "Where did he hit you?"

"It doesn't matter."

"Yes it does. Are you bleeding?"

"No. Let's go home."

She held the coins out. "One of these was already mine, wasn't it?"

"Yes." He took them from her. "I sent a friend. Tiberius was an unfortunate coincidence."

"I know. He knows my father doesn't know about the dagger, and for reasons I don't understand he's willing to play along. Marcus makes some sense to me but why would Tiberius be interested in me to wife? Is he old, or disfigured?"

"Let's go home, please."

"He's your friend, isn't he? Surely you must know—"

"He is no longer my friend. We should go home."

He took her hand and turned her before placing it on his arm. She squeezed his shoulder and they started toward her house. "What about the cushions?"

"They're tucked under my other arm."

They walked in silence, her mind still reeling. Tiberius had admired her in the shop when they first met, and it wasn't unheard of for marriages to be secured and arranged in a day. She wanted to be married, but not to Tiberius. Her father needed to meet Marcus and see how well off he was. Laelia would never win a contest of her wishes against her father, but she might get her way if she played to his greed.

Drusus tugged her right and someone brushed past her shoulder. A narrow miss.

"Are you all right?"

"Yes, Mistress."

He didn't sound like it. "I'm sorry my father struck you."

"Better me than you."

"Don't say that."

"Forgive me."

"You aren't the one in need of forgiveness. He is, not that I'll ever give it. I'm surprised he didn't punish you worse." And he still might, which is why she hoped Tiberius plied him with drink, or her father stopped at a tavern before coming home. If he drank enough, he might not remember. Her mess of a life must be at a new low for her to want her father drunk. Who could she blame for that? Fate? Jupiter? "I think the gods hate me."

"Why?"

A harsh laugh escaped Laelia. "Isn't it obvious? My mother died. My father knocks me about if he remembers I'm there at all. I lose my sight. I find a way out for myself, and it takes a miserable form. I wanted to be married, but something about Tiberius makes me uneasy, though I don't know what. I feel if I could see him, I would know right away."

"Turn."

They made the turn together, and after a few more strides the smaller size of the paving stones beneath the thin sole of her leather sandal told her they were on her street.

"Perhaps Tiberius intends to toy with me for sport instead of asking Father for my hand."

"He's going to ask for your hand. And your father will give it." The blackness in Drusus' voice echoed her own fears.

"I must convince Father that Marcus is a worthier son-in-law."

"And if you cannot?"

She hung her head. Her long history of failures at everything made it likely. "Then I hope Tiberius has a softer touch than my father and I give him a son quickly, lest he divorce me and we end up worse than now."

Drusus' arm became granite beneath her hand and his entire arm trembled as they walked. The air was already warm for spring, so he couldn't be cold. He slowed and she could hear the fountain as they neared the door to her house.

"Is the door open?"

"No, why?"

"I hear the fountain. Faintly, but I hear it."

"Remember I told you your other senses would sharpen to compensate for your sight? That's a good thing."

She'd rather they hadn't needed to, but he meant well. "I suppose so."

The door opened, and Laelia waited for Drusus to lead her through the doorway. Once inside the atrium of her house, she stretched her arms and rolled her neck, trying to work out the knots in her shoulders.

"You're back early," Naomi said.

Laelia hadn't even heard her approach—so much for her exceptional hearing. "We'll need a full *cena* tonight. The man Father is probably going to betroth me to is coming to dine with Father."

"Will Marcus be bringing his son?"

"Not Marcus. Tiberius Cina."

"Who?"

Laelia rubbed at her temples. "I can't talk about it right now, Naomi. Will you please bring Drusus and me some wine in the garden please."

"Yes, Mistress. Where is your father? And does he believe the—I mean, does he suspect at all?"

"I don't know. I don't know anything anymore, other than at the first hint of a husband I became nothing more than some bit of merchandise to be offloaded like something from one of his cargo ships."

"Go on to the garden. I'll bring wine."

"Thank you." She held her hand out for Drusus, and they made their way through the hall.

"Step."

She felt the hard, immovable stone under her foot one moment and then the soft crunch of pebbles the next. The combined scents of roses, jasmine, and lilies bathed her anxiousness in pleasant fragrance. "Take me to our bench."

"Yes, Mistress."

He stopped her near it, and she sat down with ease, the way they had the numerous times he'd brought her to that same spot.

"I'm going to return these cushions to the triclinium. I'll only be a moment."

"All right."

The stir of the gravel made it sound like his feet were dragging through it. Maybe he was as tired as she was already and the day was but half-over. She was exhausted, but not the kind rest would fix. Though not the man she planned or wanted, she'd done exactly what she set out to do, in a way. Perhaps her resentment at Tiberius' haggling for her dagger made her respond to him negatively. That and his willingness to manipulate her, but she'd do the same thing to get what she wanted. She'd been doing it with Marcus for weeks. Maybe she and Tiberius weren't that different. After all, she didn't really know him.

Crunching gravel announced Drusus' return. He would know what to do. He always did.

"Sit with me."

He settled beside her and she reached for him. Her fingers slid down his arm to the edge of the linen wrapping his wrist. "Does this still hurt?"

"No."

She traced the cloth for a moment, wondering if the warmth it held was from the sun or his skin. "Does your face?"

"No."

That was good. He might be lying, but she doubted that he would, especially to her. She inhaled a deep breath of the floral scented air and held it. His comforting presence calmed her long enough to remember the man she'd spoken with before Tiberius. Had she guessed correctly the reason for the man's cryptic manner? There was only one way to know.

"A slap is nothing compared to what he'll do to you if you're a Christian."

A long moment passed, and the garden grew so quiet she could hear herself breathe.

Then it was true. And it was like waking up blind all over again. "Drusus, why? You know what happens to Christians."

"I know," he said quietly. "The why is very simple. I was in need of absolution and a peace that wouldn't come though I made sacrifice after sacrifice to Jupiter. When I finally put my trust in the Christian God, it came. It was at that moment I knew He was real. And if He was real, then his followers' claim that He is the only true God must also be real."

"That's atheism. To deny the gods and the deity of Caesar. You can be executed." How was he remaining so calm about this?

"Very true. We have lost many and will lose more."

"What sort of God sends its followers to die?"

"God isn't killing us. Caesar is." The anger in his voice was clear.

"Then why follow him?"

"He died for us first. So we could be restored to His holiness if we believed."

"Gods can't die. It's what makes them gods." The shock was wearing off and now she was just angry. Angry that Drusus had been deceived into the strange pagan religion.

"He did, Laelia. He became a man and sacrificed Himself for us because of his great love. I kept that truth from you because I was afraid."

"You were right to be afraid." She was trembling now. "My father will kill you."

"I fear my God more than I fear your father. If I didn't, I'd have already run away."

Instinctively her grip on his wrist tightened. "You would leave me?"

"No. I would bring you with me. And Naomi. I've imagined it as many times as there are stars."

"So have I."

"Why don't you?"

"Where would I go? I can't see, and in case you didn't notice, I'm lousy at telling fortunes. I'd end up in a brothel or becomes a slave, which would have the same end result."

"Not all masters are cruel. Mine before your father was not."

Being a slave might be better, or worse, than being Tiberius' wife—or Marcus' wife. There were so many things she couldn't see. "You know Tiberius better than I do. Is he cruel?"

His long, deep breath troubled her.

"Not in the way you mean."

"How many different ways are there to be cruel?"

"Many. He doesn't hit women. At least he didn't when I knew him."

"How did you know him?"

"I was on an errand for my master, to pick up a set of knives he'd ordered to be made. Tiberius refused to release them to me, thinking I would abscond with them or sell them and say he never turned them over. He walked back to the villa with me and we found we had common interests. He became a pupil of my master but through no fault of his own, not a very good one. I had one free day a week outside the villa, and from then on I spent most of them with Tiberius."

"Doing what?"

"Nothing to be proud of."

Wine? Women? Surely not something more sinister, like thievery or worse.

"Laelia."

Her muddled mind sprung to full alert. He so rarely called her by her first name.

"Consider what you truly want. After today, there will be no going back, and no matter what you choose, there will be things I can't protect you from. If you're wed to Marcus, Tiberius or any other man, under the law I'll be subject to them as I am to your father. I will be at their mercy the same as you."

"I know."

"If you don't want to marry him, and your father won't yield, we'll have to run far and fast, and if we're caught…"

"I know." If the authorities didn't kill Drusus on the spot, they would both be returned to her father. He would kill them for sure.

A songbird nearby whistled, and a breeze bathed her in Drusus' scent. The peppermint and sweat that were uniquely him. She imagined them sailing for Carthage or Egypt with Naomi. They would buy a small house or hut. She would never have to suffer her father, a cruel husband, the pain of childbirth that took so many women to the underworld, or being forced to walk a path not of her own choosing. Naomi would lean through the doorway to announce lunch to her and Drusus in their vegetable garden, where they would be working side by side in earth not bordered by a prison of wood and stone. He would eat his food too loud and tell her what was almost ready to harvest and what still needed weeding or watering. She would pour them both wine without spilling any, like he'd taught her. Maybe in time, if she freed him, he would want to stay. Would he want to stay?

"Are you all right?"

His voice shattered the fantasy, like so many clay cups she'd dropped on the stone floor. His bandaged hand grasped hers, reminding her again of how very close he came to giving his life to protect her. She couldn't risk his by running away, and she couldn't run away without him. If she could, she would have done so long before they'd ever met. Fugitive slaves were rarely shown mercy, and even when they were, mercy came in the form of a savage beating, loss of an eye, ear, sometimes even a limb. She ran the fingers of her other hand over the linen strips binding his wound. "We stay. I can't risk losing you. So you will tell no one what you have told me."

"Laelia," he began.

"No one. I'd ask you to swear by Jupiter's throne but I know you won't. So swear on my life."

"I can't."

"You must."

"I can't."

She brought his hand to her face and rested her cheek against his palm. "Please."

The way Laelia held Drusus' hand to the curve of her sun-kissed cheek threatened his restraint. He could survive being condemned as a tool of Tiberius Cina for the rest of his life for her sake. But once Tiberius possessed them both, he would treat Laelia the way he treated all women.

That he couldn't allow.

Tonight, when the house slept, he'd take as much food as his pack would hold, and he would run. He remained unmarked which improved his chances of making it out of the city. *Slaves, obey your masters.*

What other choice did he have? God wasn't doing a very good job of protecting her like he prayed every morning. He was going to have to do it himself.

"Say something." Her jaw moved against his hand when she spoke. Her face could only be the work of God, so beautiful, trusting, and full of inner strength. A face that after tonight he would only ever see in his memories.

Drusus touched her other cheek with his free hand and allowed his thumb to trace the curve of her jaw and the warm, smooth skin he'd spent countless hours imagining beneath his lips.

Her mouth parted and she blinked, long and unsure, like a lone doe in a field of grass.

"No matter what happens, remember who you are. You are strong. You are wise. You are..." He swallowed. "A treasure."

He looked away because he couldn't stand to gaze upon her without taking her mouth and tasting her just once to remember for the rest of his life. Letting go of her was harder, but he managed to bring his hands to his sides.

"You speak as if you're already sentenced to a cross." The rasp in her voice brought his head up, and her eyes glistened with unshed tears. "I will keep your secret. And pray to my gods to keep you safe."

He rose from the bench to put fortifying distance between them. "I should go and see if Naomi needs my help."

She nodded and a tear slid to her lip. "I can find my way back to the house. The sounds of the pebbles tell me I'm not crushing our flowers."

"I know you can. You don't need me half as much as you think."

The corner of her mouth tilted to the sky. "Of course I do. You're my wall, remember?"

He turned and walked toward the house, his heart and his feet warring with every step away from her, like they would tonight. Laelia would adapt, as she had when she lost her sight. She would recover in time.

As for him, Laelia would join Julia and the man he'd killed in the faces that haunted his dreams. Failing. Always failing.

Chapter 22

Laelia held back a whimper and scratched her scalp beneath the braids and twists.

Naomi yanked the hair tighter. "Stop poking at it. You'll loosen the rows."

"But it hurts."

"It'll stop hurting if you stop poking at it."

Laelia didn't think so, but she didn't want to agitate Naomi. "Where's Drusus?"

"Polishing the lamp stands."

"Where?"

"Everywhere. You'd think Caesar was coming to dine the way your father ordered us about when he returned."

"How is father?"

"In a better disposition than usual and not yet dulled from drink." Naomi moved in front and tilted Laelia's chin up. "Close your eyes so I can line them with kohl."

Laelia held still as a statue. It hurt when Naomi would slip and color would go in her eyes. The traitors refused to work but could still give pain.

"Finished."

Laelia massaged her temples, trying to loosen the arrangement of her hair without Naomi suspecting. "Tiberius has only ever seen me with paint. Shouldn't he know what I look like without it?"

"The only time you want a man to see how you really look is never.

Especially not before you've given him children."

Naomi took Laelia's chin in hand again and Laelia puckered her lips for the color that would be rubbed on them. It always came back to children. She remembered the first time she saw blood on the sponge of her toilet stick. Naomi had explained the things her mother would have, had she still been alive. Laelia hadn't felt like a woman that day. She still didn't. The colored cream felt sticky and wet where Naomi dabbed it on her lips. When she finished, Laelia took a deep breath. There wasn't anyone else she could ask.

"Naomi?"

"Yes?"

"What's it like. To lay with a man?" Heat flooded her face and she bit her lower lip.

"That depends on the man."

"How?"

"For some, you will be a goddess they worship with their hands, lips and words until your body sings for them. For others, you'll be a means to their own pleasure and nothing more. Hope for the first, child, but be prepared to endure the second. Most husbands tire of new wives, especially once you carry their child. They'll seek their pleasure elsewhere, and the smartest women know to pretend ignorance."

"Why?"

"They just do. You'll find purpose and companionship in your children, and depending on how pleased a man is with you, he may or may not return to your bed or summon you to his. When he does, do your very best to please him."

"How?"

Naomi brushed her shoulder. "You'll know."

"Shouldn't I know before, well, before my first time?"

"No. Or it won't seem like your first time, and that's very important for new brides."

"There's so much to know. I have no idea how to care for someone who's ill. What if my husband gets ill? How do I—

"Calm yourself, child." Naomi grasped her hand and pulled her to her

161

feet. "All that will come. For now, be charming and attentive. You'll find what you seek, so if you look for reasons to dislike this man, you'll find them. If you look for reasons to like him, you'll find them."

"I already dislike him."

"Then pray to the gods to change your mind or you're in for years of loneliness and hardship."

Laelia frowned. "Like my mother?"

"Raise your arms."

An odd request since Laelia was already dressed. "Why?"

"Raise your arms."

She did, and Naomi untied her sash, and wrapped it higher on her trunk, just below her chest. The ribbon pulled tight against her ribs and she gasped. "What are you doing?"

"Giving you a head start." Naomi wound the long ribbon once or twice down to her waist and then retied it over her hips.

Laelia felt the fabric pulled across her bosom as tight as her scalp was at the moment.

"Can a stola be worn like this? It's so… so indecent."

"Yes, it can. We should join your father in the dining room."

"But I can hardly breathe." Laelia rubbed at the cage the ribbon made of her waist. "Put it back." She reached for the knot that should be somewhere near her left hip.

Naomi's hand stayed her reach. "I can't."

A chill spread through Laelia. "Why not?"

"I just can't. Come now, the men will be waiting."

Fury gripped her from her painful head down to her freshly washed feet. "Why doesn't Father strip me naked, hang a price on me and throw me on the slave block?"

"That wouldn't be better."

"I'm not so sure."

"I am."

Sorrow swept through Laelia. She reached for Naomi but a knock interrupted her apology.

"My lady, your father summons you." The closed door muffled Drusus' voice, but even then it still gave her courage.

Laelia held her arm out for Naomi. "Let's not keep the bottom feeders waiting."

"You'd do best to leave that attitude here in this room. For all our sakes."

Laelia nodded and heard the click of her chamber door and then the soft groan of the hinges in need of oil as it swung in. A swift intake of breath met her ears. Did that gasp come from Drusus?

"Go on, take her." Naomi handed Laelia's arm to Drusus and he placed her hand on his arm and moved to her side.

Laelia squeezed Drusus' arm and they started toward the men who held her future. Naomi was usually right about everything. Laelia would look for the good things in Tiberius. If there were any justice in the way the gods ruled the world, it would be brighter than her past.

Drusus had dredged up every disgusting thing he could think of to keep his body from responding to the vision before him. The smell of rotten meat, stepping in steaming manure, the taste of soured milk, but nothing was working. Not only was Laelia the most beautiful he had ever seen her, but perfumed as well. The delicate scent of jasmine clung to her the way that ribbon did.

Rotten meat. Sour milk.

"Are you all right?" she whispered.

"Yes. Forgive me. You look—" He shut his mouth before any more of his flesh could betray him.

"Ridiculous?" Her curved brow arched along with that side of her mouth. A mouth stained the delicious red of fresh berries.

Rotten meat. Sour milk. "You look very well."

"Thank you. Let's see if Tiberius thinks so."

The man's name proved much more effective at quelling Drusus' physical desire than his silent chant. He turned her into the doorway where both men reclined and brought her to a stop.

"Good evening." Laelia's voice was firm and steady.

Tiberius glanced up from his cup of wine and his eyes widened in appreciation. Lust clouded his expression as he set his goblet on the table and rose. "My lady, permit me to say you are a vision that would challenge the skill of the finest sculptors in Greece. I've never seen a more beautiful woman in all my days."

Drusus couldn't keep his mouth from tightening. He'd heard Tiberius say the exact same script a hundred times to almost as many women in their years together.

Laelia arched her chin in that proud way she sometimes showed. "I hope you'll forgive me if I don't return the compliment. I don't see as well as I once did."

To keep from grinning, Drusus crushed the inside of his lip between his teeth. God help him, how would he ever get through this night? Tiberius glanced at the master, who wasn't laughing.

Her father's eyes were narrowed and his mouth flat. "Come sit."

Laelia tensed beneath Drusus' hand. He guided her to the open side of the three-sided dining couch and a new fear assaulted his resolve. What would her father do when they discovered him missing in the morning?

"Naomi, we're ready for the first course."

Drusus glanced behind him, surprised to find Naomi standing hands together at her waist in the doorway. "Right away, Master."

She disappeared toward the kitchen as Laelia took her seat on the cushion. Drusus stood against the wall behind her, the proper place for him at a formal meal. Tiberius took another sip of his wine and appraised Laelia once again. "You prefer to sit, rather than recline?"

"Yes. I use both my hands when eating, particularly when refilling my cup."

"The slaves don't refill your cup for you?"

"I prefer to be as independent as possible. Because of Drusus I'm able to do many things for myself. He's been an excellent tutor."

Tiberius' gaze turned to Drusus. "I'm sure he has been."

The implication in his gaze begged a punch to the jaw. Instead, Drusus focused on a crack in the plaster on the wall opposite him.

"Brutus, forgive my forwardness, but do you plan to transfer ownership of Laelia's slave once she's married?"

Don't move.

"Of course. Drusus and Naomi are to be her dowry in full. Once she is resettled, I have plans to sell the house and take an apartment near the new amphitheater."

"You would sell the house?" Laelia asked.

"There's no reason to keep it for only me."

"I find apartment living very agreeable," Tiberius added. "And much more cost efficient than maintaining a house, though I do aspire to villa ownership. If not for me, then for my sons."

Drusus flinched at the thought of Tiberius being intimate with Laelia. He could still stop this, and he would. She'd hate him for as long as she remembered him, but as Marcus' wife, not Tiberius'.

Naomi arrived in that moment with a tray of figs, olives and cut cheese. For the rest of the meal, Drusus memorized the crack in the plaster wall.

Laelia responded to Tiberius' incessant flirting all evening with grace and charm that pulverized his heart. Tiberius and the master talked about their respective trades, and the benefits and pitfalls of each. The news of the devastation in Pompeii distracted Drusus from the present agony. The fire mountain Vesuvius rained smoke and fire on the city to the south, burying it beneath ash and rock.

Some among the Romans believed this an omen of the gods against the new Emperor Titus, but Drusus knew better. The simple fact the true God hadn't wiped them all from the face of the earth, starting with Rome, testified to His mercy. The corruption and decay that ran as deep as the sewers in every corner of this city could still astound him, now that he knew the better way. Mankind was a long way from the first garden, and by morning, he would be a long way from this one— and from her.

When second tables were finished, Drusus' neck and knees were in as much pain as his heart. Standing still for that long would do that, and he was out of practice.

"Would you permit Laelia and me a few moments to speak alone?" Tiberius asked.

"Certainly. Why don't you have her show you to the peristyle? Enough daylight should remain and if it doesn't, Drusus can bring the lamp stands there for you."

Laelia rose and Drusus moved aside to take her hand. Her fingers were still wet from having rinsed them after the meal and felt cool against his palm. Tiberius followed, and having the man at Drusus' back made his hand twitch to grab one of the twins.

At the doorway from the hall to the peristyle, Tiberius surged around him to Laelia's other side and grasped her elbow. "I can take her from here, Drusus. You may remain stationed here until we're finished." His tone held no contempt, sneer or malice, but that didn't help. For a long moment, the three of them stood still, both holding Laelia between them. Drusus refused to meet Tiberius' eyes, even in the dim twilight.

He'd survived being taken from his mother as a child. He'd endured the pain of loss and the guilt of broken promises with Julia. He'd survived the guilt of killing an innocent man. He'd managed to relinquish the only wealth he would ever call his for Laelia's dagger. But none of that proved as difficult as letting her go and watching Tiberius Cina lead her straight for their bench.

Tiberius was charming. Laelia couldn't deny that. Along with his honeyed tongue, he possessed a small measure of wealth he boasted of in carefully constructed conversation designed to inform her father without offending him. That Tiberius seemed to already understand her father was favorable. Yet he smelled funny. Nothing like Drusus' peppermint fragrance. Thankfully, the evening scents of her garden offset the unpleasant odor. Look for the positives, she heard Naomi say somewhere in her head.

"I'm surprised you only have one bench," Tiberius said.

"It's a small garden."

"How long has the fountain been dry?"

"Longer than I remember. Drusus fixed the one in the atrium when he first came. He wasn't able to fix this one, but he did try."

When the pebbles gave way to stone again beneath her sandaled feet, Laelia knew they had reached the bench. She let Tiberius stop her anyway. She settled on the seat and in seconds, coolness seeped through the thin wool of her tunic and stola. The marble bench had been shaded a while to already be so cool. "How late is it?"

"Some sunlight remains. Just enough for me to admire you with."

Laelia smiled to hide her annoyance. In the absence of her father, he could stop now. Her hand curved along the edge of the bench until it reached the corner. Realizing she hadn't left him enough room to sit with her, she slid over.

He sat so close his arm brushed hers, and his leg rested against hers once he settled. She wanted to move away, but there wasn't enough room. If this touch chaffed this much, through their mutual layers of garments, how could she ever hope to give him children?

Tiberius took her hand in his and folded his fingers around hers. "Why don't you want your father to know you sold the dagger?"

"Why did you accommodate me, and then pretend you and Drusus didn't know each other either?"

His fingers caressed her hand in some unknown design. "In most circles it's considered unbecoming to answer a question with a question."

"I'm aware."

He chuckled. "Ah yes, there's that fire again. Does it matter why you lied to your father or why I played along? It seems to me what matters is we're both willing to lie if it helps us attain what we want."

His fingertips moved to play on the skin of her forearm now. Should she stop him?

"You know, besides your beauty, one of the first things I admired about you was your fire."

"What do you mean?" Heat was certainly building in her skin beneath a touch that felt less and less obtrusive with each pass.

"The way this stubborn streak within refuses to be quenched by something as petty as blindness."

"You think blindness a petty affliction?"

"You make it seem that way." His fingertip traced a line, maybe a vein she once imagined cutting, all the way to the fold of her inner elbow. "I admire that about you also."

His hand curved around her arm, and the backs of his fingers brushed against the side of her breast. She rolled her shoulder away from him, easing from his grasp and turning her body to face him as much as the bench would allow. "Careful, Tiberius Cina. I am not yet betrothed to you."

"Do you wish to be?"

The question took her by surprise as much as his exploring. It didn't matter what she wanted. She'd heard it all arranged in double meanings and veiled suggestions between him and her father this morning through her disastrous fortune telling. Then again through a meal that would have been perfect but for the presence of the two men who shared it with her and the one who could not, standing guard behind her. Ignoring Drusus as if he wasn't there to maintain convention had left her no appetite. She'd have to grow accustomed to it in the presence of her husband. Tiberius was asking her if she wanted that husband to be him.

"The delay in your answer concerns me."

His tone did sound concerned. If only she could see his eyes to know if the emotion were genuine. "In truth, I don't know yet. I do want to be married, and you've made a strong impression on my father."

"And you?"

It didn't matter. Why couldn't he understand that? If she refused Tiberius, her father wouldn't even need to be drunk to beat her. "I would do my very best to please you in all things, and fulfill my duties as a wife with eagerness."

Naomi would be proud.

"That's not enough for me."

She couldn't stop her forehead from wrinkling and biting her lip. "I don't understand."

"If I wanted a beautiful, dutiful wife who would obey my every command as if it were issued by Jupiter himself, I would buy an exotic slave and then free her so I could legally marry her."

Was he serious? "Do you mean to say you want a wife who is disagreeable?"

"I mean to say I want a wife who knows herself. Who knows what it is she wants, needs, thinks and feels, and who doesn't pretend to be someone else for any man. I see that in you, Laelia, when you aren't performing for your father. You were never more yourself than the day I met you in my shop. I couldn't stop thinking about you. On the street this morning I thought my mind had finally conjured you."

"What happened to my dagger?" That seemed a safe retreat in conversation to give her time to process the boiling mess of feeling Tiberius' words made of her insides.

"You don't know?"

Something in his tone signaled a switch in mood, but she couldn't place it. "Why would I?"

He sighed, and took her hand again. "Laelia, promise me something. No matter what you decide in regard to me, or to Marcus—"

She pulled her hand free of his again. "How do you know of Marcus?"

"Your father told me of him. I have twice the wealth he does and think for that alone I've won your father to my side already, as his primary desire is to see you well-cared for."

"Indeed." Her talent for lies and performance were inherited, so she couldn't very well blame Tiberius for not knowing any better.

"I hope soon that I'll win you over as well, and that you truly want to wear the orange veil for me." He took her hand again. "But promise you'll be vigilant in regards to Drusus."

"I trust him more than anyone."

"And that is noble of you, but I once did the same, as did Julia, a slave of mine. Drusus isn't always what he seems, and I know already of at least two things he's keeping from you."

The death hound snarled, all but biting into her throat. Did Tiberius know Drusus was a Christian? "Are you implying Drusus deceives me?"

"I'm encouraging you to be cautious. With your coin, and please know I mean this in no way as an implication of doubt as to your virtue, but I have no confidence in his and would be very sorry to see you injured, as Julia was."

The idea of Drusus deceiving her further, and involved with another woman, even in his past, made the small bit of food she'd eaten threaten to return.

"Forgive me if I've upset you. That isn't my intent. I want nothing but happiness for you, and hope that you'll give me opportunity to prove so for a lifetime." He touched her shoulder, and this time nothing inside her rejected the touch. "I should go, but I hope I may visit again tomorrow evening to learn your answer. Would tomorrow be enough time?"

"Yes." The fact she could even form a coherent thought, much less give it voice, comforted her.

"I'll send Drusus to you, but remember, be careful of what you reveal you know. He also thinks I will keep his secrets, as you can trust I will keep yours."

"Thank you."

Tiberius stood and stirred the gravel in the path as he left.

Laelia remained on the bench among the wreckage of her shattered hold on her life. If she couldn't trust Drusus, she was truly alone.

Tiberius approached and Drusus forced himself to stare straight ahead, hoping the man would pass by him without a word. Watching Tiberius touch her had been its own kind of agony.

But Tiberius stopped at his side. "It won't be so bad you know."

Drusus wouldn't give the man his gaze.

"It can be like old times, if you'll let it."

Ignore him. You know what you have to do.

"If you haven't realized it yet, Laelia will make the perfect target for you. With her blindness she won't see the blades coming and flinch."

Images from his nightmare returned and weakened his knees. He'd cut his own throat first. But saying so would accomplish nothing. He was running away tonight. It was the only way. So he remained silent, continuing to ignore Tiberius.

Tiberius took his arm in a stern grip. He leaned closer, and the stench of his sweat burned as much as his hold. "Don't forget I know you. If you cause problems for me with her or her father, or resort to heroics and run away or cut off a finger or two," his grip tightened, biting deep into the muscle of Drusus' upper arm, "I'll marry her anyway and spend my anger at you on her, and on Julia."

Drusus closed his eyes and fought to remain standing. "Why are you doing this?"

Tiberius released his arm. "You're profitable. She's beautiful. And if you behave, I'll share Julia with you."

"Drusus, are you still here?" Laelia called from somewhere in the dark of the garden.

"Coming, Mistress," he said in a voice loud enough for her to hear.

"Remember what I promised. Unlike you, I always keep my word." Tiberius left Drusus standing in the shadow—a darkness that had crept into his own soul.

He found the path illuminated by the lamplight from the house and made his way toward their bench. His sight adjusted with each step until he could make out Laelia standing with her arms crossed.

"What took you so long?"

"Forgive me, Mistress. Tiberius wished to have a word with me."

"About what?"

"You'd have to ask him, my lady."

"I'm asking you."

"Laelia, please. I'm doing the best I can. With all of this."

"Are you?"

Her accusing tone slapped his already devastated will to endure. He threw his head back and breathed the night air. The stars overhead surrounded a rising crescent moon. The God who made all of that was still with him. *Help me, Lord.* "Yes, I am."

"Relieve Naomi in the kitchen and send her to my room as soon as you take me there."

"Yes, Mistress." He reached for her hand and placed it on his arm while moving to her side. She shifted away from him, leaving much more space than normal between them before signaling him forward.

Even though Drusus announced the step, he fumbled and nearly tripped.

Her grip on his arm tightened as she stopped him. "What's wrong with you?"

Everything. "I missed the step. Apologies."

Her father approached from the atrium where he must have finished seeing Tiberius out. "You did well tonight. Tiberius wishes to dine with us again tomorrow."

"Thank you, Father."

"I'm going out this evening. Remind Naomi to leave the rear door open."

"I will."

He pulled his toga from his shoulder and gave it to Drusus. "See that is put away."

"Yes, Master." He let go of Laelia long enough to bunch it over his arm. Then he resumed his position as Master Ricarri departed. At Laelia's door, he took his hand from her to open it. She walked straight in, without stopping to turn and tell him goodnight as she had every evening for three months now. He made his way to the kitchen to give the toga to Naomi. He'd never been to the Master's chamber, nor did he have any desire to go there now.

Naomi held a pitcher of oil over the table lamp, the soft gold liquid flowing into the top of the bronze vessel. Her gaze met his and her brow raised. "Is that the master's or the soon-to-be master's toga?"

"The master's. Do you mind taking it to his chamber? And Laelia wants you right away. I'll finish up here."

"All right. There aren't many more dishes to clean and all the food has been taken care of." She set the pitcher down and replaced the lid of the pour hole on the lamp. "Do you want me to re-light this or is the other one enough light?"

"I'm fine." He set the bundle of wool on the table and reached for a platter that still had bits of olive on the polished metal surface. Next, he reached for the wet rag in the bowl of water beside it on the table, but Naomi intercepted his hand.

He looked up and her gaze pierced him. She squeezed his hand in her own damp one. "I know better, but I also know when a man needs to lick his wounds alone." She let him go and handed him the rag. "Be sure you don't miss any spots."

He knew she was trying to make him feel better, but nothing could. He'd relive the horror of the man's death every time Tiberius forced him to throw again. With Laelia as the target his fear would be a thousand times worse; unsteadying his mind and his hands worse than the wine had that fateful night.

And Laelia would pay the price.

He scrubbed at the polished metal, fighting the water in his eyes.

Lord, where are you?

Chapter 23

Laelia tugged at her hair, trying to find where to loosen it.

"Let me help," Naomi said.

"What took so long?"

"Cleaning every dish your father owns."

Laelia sighed and held still as Naomi's fingers worked over her hair. "I'm sorry."

"Tiberius seemed pleased when he left, which of course pleased your father."

"Well as long as Father is pleased," Laelia muttered. A patch of tightness near her forehead gave way and exquisite relief shimmered through her scalp. Naomi continued loosening the braids and twists until Laelia could massage her aching head. "I think I'm going to marry Tiberius."

"I think you are too." A hint of sarcasm seasoned Naomi's voice as she pulled a comb through Laelia's hair.

"No, that's not what I mean. Not because of Father. I mean I'm going to look for the good things. You and Drusus will still be with me. Father won't. And Tiberius seems to genuinely care for me."

"Why does that surprise you? You're a beautiful girl. A beautiful girl who's making a wise choice. Your mother would be proud. Did anything happen in the garden?"

Lots of things happened, but nothing she wanted to talk about. "Like what?"

"I don't mean to tread where I shouldn't. I only wondered if you had any more questions or needed to talk."

Who Julia was and what else Drusus was keeping from her weren't questions Naomi could answer. "I'm fine. Or I will be once I get this ribbon undone. I hope I never have to wear it like this again."

Naomi helped Laelia out of the ribbon and tunic and into her nightdress. "Will you do something for me?"

Laelia stilled. Naomi rarely asked for anything. "Of course, if it's within my power."

"Be patient with Drusus. Unlike your braids, no one can ease what's ailing him. Only time will."

His name swirled her emotions like a strong wind does the sand. "What did he tell you?"

"Nothing. He tells me nothing, but I still know. And I think you do too."

Laelia sat on her bed before her legs collapsed. Surely he wouldn't have told Naomi. "What is it you think I know?"

"If you have to ask, then it doesn't matter." Naomi blew out the lamp but Laelia thought she heard a faint sigh. "Goodnight, little one."

Her door closed and she curled onto her side and pulled her blanket over her shoulder. She rubbed the spot above her temples where the ache in her scalp remained. Tiberius seemed a respectable man, even with whatever sordid history he and Drusus shared in the past. Unlike Marcus, he didn't have children. That would be lesser responsibilities to begin marriage with. She still had some of the coin from her dagger that neither Tiberius nor her father knew about. That would buy her, Drusus, and Naomi passage on a ship going most anywhere if Tiberius turned out to be a tyrant.

Yet sleep wouldn't come. No matter what position she tried or how she placed her pillow, Naomi's cryptic request turned over and over in her mind. What ailed Drusus that only time would ease? It couldn't be his stomach. He had peppermint for that. The only thing changing was her marriage.

She sat straight up, her blanket slipping to her waist. It was impossible—forbidden and impossible. Just like finding out he was a Christian. Drusus was a good slave, and a friend—nothing more. But if that were true, why did this Julia woman bother her so much? She wasn't jealous. She wasn't. And if Drusus were keeping even more secrets, not trusting her with them, he was allowed that. She wouldn't drive herself mad over this. She wouldn't.

But after long moments of restless shifting, she tossed the blanket back and stood. There was only one way to get the answers she craved and settle this once and for all.

Her feet padded much too loud as she crept toward her door. Finding her way to the storeroom took a long time but at last she located the handle. Should she knock? No, this was her house and he was her slave. She needed to start thinking like a mistress again. The soft groan of the hinges marred the silence as she opened the door.

"What are you doing?" He sounded annoyed, but at least he'd been awake already. "Your father could return any moment."

"Then I'll close the door." She shut it behind her and turned around. "I need to talk to you."

She sensed him near and reached forward. Her palm connected with warm, smooth muscle—too flat to be his arm.

Strong hands grasped her wrist and pulled them from his chest. "*You can't be here.*"

The fierce whisper sounded like a command and she jerked free. "I need to talk to you."

"Then we'll talk tomorrow. You need to go back to your room."

"No. Not when you're keeping more secrets from me."

His deep breath heightened the tension she could feel between them. "What did Tiberius tell you?"

"Who is Julia?" Laelia waited, but all she heard was his ragged breathing. She crossed her arms and leaned against the door.

"She's a slave. Like me."

Something in his voice told Laelia there was more—much more. She slid down the door to sit with her knees to her chest. When he didn't say anything else for a long moment, she pressed. "Go on."

Wood creaked. He must have sat on a stool or his bed.

"She belonged to a brothel Tiberius and I frequented."

Then he wasn't a virgin. It shouldn't surprise her really, but her own jealousy grew a little deeper. "And?"

"I promised to buy her freedom one day."

"Did you?"

"No."

"Why not?"

"I couldn't amass the amount the owner of the brothel required for her."

"How did you earn coin?" She waited. A full breath. Two. Still, he didn't answer. "How?"

"I performed knife tricks."

"Knife tricks?" She'd expected a different answer. Harlotry. Thievery. But not that. "What kind?"

"The dangerous kind. But I don't do them anymore." His sigh was heavy enough to sink a Roman galley.

"Why not?"

"Because someone died."

The way his voice rippled with emotion, he must have been responsible. "Was it Julia?"

"No."

"Who?"

"The brother of a very powerful man."

"What happened?"

Wood creaked again and his bare foot brushed hers. He'd risen.

"I'd had too much wine but thought I would be fine." He paused again, a long while. "But I wasn't. My knife hit him in the throat. He bled to death right in front of me."

The sorrow in Drusus' voice cut through Laelia's discontent about his former lover and that everyone else had known this about him before she did. "It was an accident."

"Forgetting someone's name or dropping an egg before its boiled is an accident. What I did was not an accident."

She remembered watching Titus die. How much more painful for Drusus for it to have been by his hand? "Why didn't you tell me any of this before?"

"Because I'm ashamed of it. But now you know. And I need you to go. Please."

"What happened to Julia?"

"She belongs to Tiberius now."

That meant—that meant Drusus would collide with Julia constantly in Tiberius' house. A woman he'd cared for deeply. Maybe he still did. Worse, her future husband owned a woman skilled in the arts of pleasure. How was Laelia supposed to compete with that? She'd never even kissed a man.

An idea sprouted, and then sprung up fast like a weed. "You never lit a lamp, did you?" She hadn't heard a flint strike or smelled a freshly lit wick.

"There's nothing I need to see. You need to return to your room. Please."

He was in the dark too. That gave her courage and she rose from the floor. "Where are you?"

"Beside you. I'll open the door." He must have stood or moved near her because she sensed his presence close enough to touch and his voice had moved.

"Wait. I need to see something first." An odd choice of words her muddled mind chose. She felt a bend in the warm skin and muscle. His arm, and by the pointed end of his elbow, he faced her. Good. But he was still at least a head taller than her. She wouldn't be able to reach and the way her knees were trembling she didn't trust her legs to hold her if she went up on her toes. "Sit down."

"Why?"

Laelia slid her hand down his arm to his wrist and held on. "Sit down. I need to see something."

It took a moment, but his arm moved beneath her and the muted sound of the straw told her he'd sat on his bed. She moved closer, positioning herself in front of him. Her stomach shivered while she ran her hand up his arm, then his shoulder, to stop at the base of his throat.

His swift intake of breath told her even better where his face should be.

With her other hand, she searched for his chin. She didn't want to accidently poke him in the eye with her fingertips, or her nose. The skin she touched, warmer than his shoulder, wasn't as smooth. The stubble of his jaw guided her to his mouth.

"Laelia…" he breathed in a broken whisper.

"Shhh." She couldn't do this and try to talk at the same time. Her head lowered, awkward and unsure, until her lips met his face. Stubble scratched them, telling her she'd missed his mouth in part, but she discovered something else.

Her lips were a thousand times more sensitive than her fingertips. She moved them against his chin, searching with her mouth as she would with her hand for wine on the table, and knew the moment she'd found his.

The heat from his breath stole over her. Her eyes closed, which didn't make any sense. Though she felt them do so, nothing changed in her blackness—except the wilderness of sensation spreading through the rest of her body from the slim contact of their mouths. Of their own accord, her hands moved to frame his face. Her fingers spread below his ears and the edges of his hair tangled them in a feather light caress.

Drusus turned away. She felt when his lips left hers, the growing heat replaced by a sudden chill as his head rotated in her hands. He must have kissed Julia many times. He could kiss her once. Laelia pressed her left hand hard against the side of his face to turn him back toward her. When he yielded, she returned to her exploring. The longer her mouth lingered against his, the more pleasant it became, until salt greeted her tongue—the warm wetness of tears.

The shock was like putting her weight on a step that wasn't there, and she drew back just as sharply. Confused and hurt, she found the door behind her and left as fast as she could. Back in her bed, she replayed everything, trying to understand what she'd done wrong. But the more she tried to understand and couldn't, the more frustrated and angry she became.

The more Drusus tried to drive the memory of the kiss from his mind, the deeper ingrained it became. Never in his life had his mind and his body worked so hard to overpower each another. He sat with his head in his hands in the dark, exhausted like he'd run the length of the city.

He should have tried harder to stop her. Putting his hands on her, even to push her away, would have broken the fingertip hold his restraint held over the passion her kiss ignited.

It would have to be enough, for him and for God, that he didn't kiss her back.

Tiberius told her of Julia, but why? He gained nothing by doing so. Or did he? Drusus turned and lay back on his bed, draping his arm across his forehead. Continuing to serve Laelia, and Tiberius once they were wed, was going to kill him slowly.

He'd be under the same roof with not one, but two women he cared for and could never have. It meant nothing that Tiberius offered Julia to him, because God would only bless intimacy within marriage and Tiberius wouldn't give Julia to Drusus in marriage. Or would he?

His conscience smote him there in the dark. He'd already broken a promise of freedom to her. He couldn't take her as a wife knowing if he allowed himself, he would pretend she was Laelia the way she claimed to pretend Tiberius was him.

Drusus rolled against the wall to free his wool blanket and pull it over himself. How many times had he pulled a blanket over Julia's sleeping body, after finding it from wherever they'd thrown it, and kissed her in her sleep? Much the same way Laelia kissed him tonight. The way Tiberius would kiss her—kiss both of them. He turned into the wall, and brought his knees in, crouching tight beneath the wool.

He knew God allowed hardship, sometimes to the point of death, for greater good. Otho always said it wasn't for men to ask why.

"I won't ask why," he whispered. "But I beg you to deliver me from this."

He wouldn't survive this. He wouldn't survive throwing the rose and cherry for Tiberius again. Especially if it were with Laelia. Every time his knife would leave his hand, he would relive the nightmare. Being in the public, drawing a crowd that often, the man who'd sworn vengeance on his brother's killer would surely find him and cut his throat as he'd promised. Until then, the woman he loved would be the wife of a man he despised. Tiberius wouldn't relinquish Julia, which would hurt Laelia. And Drusus would be a loose sail shredding in the winds of that storm. He would hate and envy Tiberius in equal measure.

Hate. Envy. Lust.

Together they summoned his thirst for wine—potent and plenty.

God help him, he didn't want to be that man again.

"Deliver me, Lord. And if you won't, then make me stronger."

He lay still, willing sleep to come, but the memory of Laelia's kiss refused to cool.

Stronger, Lord. Stronger.

Nightmares drove Drusus to the garden while the moon still shone in a dark purple sky, heralding the coming light of the morning sun. He made his way to his and Laelia's bench. There would be no better place to make a stand than to sit and pray at the very heart of the source of his pain. Night birds, roused too early from their perches among the hedges, chirped and squawked in warning—or frustration.

"I understand," Drusus whispered toward them.

When his foot rose to take another step, the top of his sandal flopped loose and he stumbled. The pebbles of the path bit into the skin of his sole, and he hopped the rest of the way to the bench. He sat and removed the sandal. The worn, thin leather of the ankle strap had snapped near the first lace.

He dropped his head back, closed his eyes and took a deep breath. Without a single coin to his name, he couldn't replace it. He'd have to tie the ends together, though the knot would rub a sore if he weren't careful. The short piece kept slipping free before he could join the two ends together, and the bandage on his wrist from the snake bite kept interfering. After struggling a while longer, Drusus dropped everything on the seat of the bench, pulled one of the twins from his belt and cut away the bandage.

A firm dark scab covered his wound, with no risen flesh or discoloration. He flexed his fingers, testing the movement without the tightness of the bandage. Better. This time he managed to put a knot in the thin leather strap, but it slipped free when he pulled to test it.

"A little help, Lord," he muttered.

By the time he repaired his sandal and lashed it back to his foot, the sky was pink. The master's voice carried from inside the house. Would the man be able to look at him and tell his daughter had slipped into his room last night and kissed him? Drusus shuddered, although he was less reluctant to face the master than to face Laelia.

He couldn't pray. The conversation that always began so easily wouldn't come. In its place, he offered the one Otho first taught him.

Father in Heaven, hallowed is Your name. Your kingdom come, Your will be done, on earth as it is in Heaven. Give us today our daily bread and— he swallowed on the hard part—*forgive us our wrongs as we forgive those who wrong us. Lead us from temptation and deliver us from evil...*

He couldn't finish. The men he was supposed to forgive, Tiberius and Laelia's father, were the same evil he prayed to be delivered from. How was that even possible? And as for being led from the temptation, he led his temptation on his arm every day, so how God was going to answer that was beyond him.

Drusus waited, watching a lone bird that had refused to leave the hedge with the others. The dark, round eyes studied him. If only he could be that bird. Free to go wherever he wished, confined to no one. The longer he considered the bird clutching tight to a branch as thin as its own legs, the deeper the longing became.

"Drusus?"

Naomi's voice snapped his head around as he fumbled to rise. "Yes?"

"Laelia waits for you to take her to the fuller's again."

Thank you, God. Otho could help him make sense of all this. "Thank you."

"How's your hand?" She approached, and took his wrist to examine his wound.

"It's healing."

Naomi's gaze met his and deepened as she released his hand. "And the rest of you?"

He managed a half-smile, though for the effort it required the corners of his mouth should be at his ears. "I'm fine."

She frowned and cupped his cheek with her withered but strong hand. Her gaze bored deep into him, the sympathy and understanding there unmistakable.

Naomi knew.

She patted his face, reminding him of the mother he'd nearly forgotten. He followed her into the house, where Laelia stood waiting inside the doorway.

Naomi continued toward the kitchen, leaving the two of them alone.

Laelia extended her hand, but didn't smile at him in greeting or move toward him as was her custom. Other than the few instructions he gave her as they walked through the house and down the street toward Otho's shop, neither of them spoke.

The street was already awake. Vendors pulled back their canvas flaps and set out their wares. Slaves departed on early errands with baskets or children in tow. Laelia's anger was like a third person, wedged between them and daring him to acknowledge its presence. The stiffness in her gait and tight grip on his arm were almost as unbearable as her continued silence.

He glanced at her as they walked. "I should explain. About last night."

"No."

"It's important to me you understand."

She pulled him to a halt beside her. Her head rotated toward him, but not her body. "No. We don't speak of it. Ever. Just like that *other matter*. Am I understood?"

"Yes, Mistress."

"Very well." Her cutting gaze turned to realign with her body, and she squeezed his arm to continue.

He steered her through the light crowd, an exuberant child bumping into her before he could move her out of the way. The boy scampered off without a word of apology.

She didn't say anything, but her grip on his arm tightened and the scowl on her face deepened. At Otho's shop, the window remained shuttered and the door closed. The overturned crate lay where they'd left it yesterday.

"The crate is in front of you, just to the right, my lady."

She released his arm as if she were glad of it. Her fingernails caught on the skin of his inner arm. The scratch was uncomfortable, though nothing that would draw blood. Not the way her kiss had. He stood beside her, watching the people mill about. A woman stared at him from across the street, a basket on her hip. The wool of her tunic was too thick and napped to be a peasant or slave, but she carried herself like one, even in stillness.

Recognition came potent and swift as she approached. The blonde hair still threw him off.

Julia came to a stop before them, her gaze turning to Laelia. "I'm told you tell fortunes."

"Yes, I do."

"I want to know mine." Julia set the basket down and knelt before Laelia. She withdrew a single copper coin from inside the top of her tunic which she deposited in Laelia's lap. The coin slipped to the ground when Laelia failed to take it.

Julia picked it up and extended it toward him. "Here."

He took the coin from her, hating the way the brush of her fingertips made his skin shiver, even after all this time.

"Give me your hand." Laelia made a cradle with her own, and Julia placed her hand palm up and waited while Laelia traced the lines across them.

"I see a great fortune in your future." Laelia's head dipped as if she were truly concentrating. She probably was, on making up more lies.

Julia's gaze met his. "And what does your divination say of the men in my future?"

"They're in agony," Laelia answered.

His gaze flew from Julia to the back of Laelia's head. Surely she couldn't know that.

"Why?" Julia's tone beckoned him to return his gaze to her, which he couldn't help.

"Because they fear they are unworthy of you. Which they are."

Julia grinned at him with a single side of her mouth, as she'd always done. "Do I give this unworthy man a son?"

Laelia seemed to think for a moment. A moment he couldn't breathe.

"Yes. Three children, Juno be praised. Though I can't see how many are sons or daughters."

"It doesn't matter." Julia rose and pulled her hand from Laelia's. "I wish I could give you another coin for such happy news, but then I won't have enough for bread and a bath and my master would be very cross."

Julia collected her basket and met his gaze again, her own full of amusement. "My future isn't what you promised, but close enough I forgive you. Maybe even Tiberius as well. Until next time, Drusus."

He stifled a grimace as she strode away. She'd used his name.

Laelia turned his direction, though not enough to face him. "Who was that?"

Still tempted to lie, but she would know in time anyway. "Julia."

Laelia's skin crawled at the sound of Julia's name from Drusus' mouth. Her fingertips burned at the realization she'd touched the very hands that had... She tried to drive the images from her mind, refuse them entry, but it was too late. Her mind replayed everything she'd said to Drusus' former lover and nausea welled inside.

Absolutely not. She would forbid it. If Drusus wouldn't permit Laelia a single kiss, so repulsed was he by her ineptness and child-like dependence on him, he wouldn't be kissing, or more than kissing anyone, especially Julia. When Laelia wed Tiberius, she would be Julia's mistress as much as Drusus' and she wouldn't have it. Not in her house.

Had they exchanged knowing glances in place of laughs between them while she described a made up future? Drusus knew Laelia's fortunes were fakes, but not even that satisfied her. The groan of a door distracted her from her anger.

"Good morning, my lady. Where is your father today?" Otho asked.

"My father is at the river today overseeing the barge shipments from the port."

"Well stay as long as you like, though I find it's the nose more than the mind that decides how long one can stand to be in a fullery. Unless of course it's your trade. My sense of smell burned away years ago." Otho laughed, but it didn't sound like Drusus joined him.

"Thank you. I appreciate your continued kindness."

"Would you permit Drusus to help with some heavy lifting this morning?"

"Certainly. Use him as long as you like." She paused. In her anger, she'd chosen harsher words than was like her. But she was going to have to be a stronger mistress than she'd ever been, so she let the command stand. If she'd been a tougher mistress in the first place, he never would have left her in the street to get attacked.

Her head hurt and she massaged her temples as she sank lower on the crate. Things were supposed to be getting better, not worse. Drusus had said the peace he sought he'd only found after believing in his outlawed God. But he certainly didn't seem at peace today. She certainly wasn't and yet she worshipped the true gods.

Juno's peacock. Her life really was a clay cup at the table edge if she were contemplating the Christian God.

Drusus followed Otho into the shop, though it bothered him to leave Laelia unattended. Even in the foul mood she was in. The slaves were heating water for the troughs over a strong fire and could help him listen for her if danger found her. Worse than it already had.

Otho gestured to the stool Drusus had bought for him a few months ago. "Sit."

"I thought you wanted me to help move something."

"Sit."

Drusus did, and was surprised when Otho pulled another stool from beneath his work table and joined him. "Tell me what has you looking like you've dug your own grave."

"Laelia's father has given her in marriage to Tiberius Cina."

Otho looked as if he'd been kicked. "He's going to make you throw again."

"It gets worse." Drusus leaned against the wall behind him and drew a deep breath. "Tiberius now owns Julia."

His mentor leaned forward, lacing his fingers as his elbows moved to his knees. "You're walking right into the fire then, aren't you?"

"Yes. For a man I despise and two women I can't save."

Otho's head shot up, one of his silver brows arching. "When did you ever think you could save them?"

Drusus took the admonition on the chin. "Fair enough."

"There's nothing fair about it. Don't forget that. Jesus washed all of his disciples' feet. Not all of them except for Judas."

"Meaning?"

"You know what it means." Otho rose from the stool. "We're to love our enemies as our Lord did, and serve them as he did. A master is a master. We're to serve them as if they are the Lord, even when they walk in darkness. In so doing we may very well lead them to the light."

A soul-deep sigh escaped him. "Even if it gets me killed?"

Otho closed the distance between them and placed his palm on Drusus' shoulder. "Jesus conquered death with His own. If yours is required, it's no more than He gave for you and me."

"True."

"Of course it is." Otho said. "And truth does what?"

"Makes me free."

"Even though?"

"Even though I'm a slave," one of Otho's men answered as he poured a bucket of water into the pot over the flames of the hearth beside them.

"Even though I'm a slave," Drusus repeated, rising from the stool to help.

Chapter 24

Would Tiberius be this charming after Laelia had wed him? She doubted it. Her father had been on his best behavior again tonight as well. Drusus remained behind her, and she worried he hadn't eaten. She meant to inquire when they returned from fortune telling, but remembered she was still angry at him for refusing to kiss her last night, and didn't. When second tables were finished and fingers and hands rinsed, Tiberius asked her father if he could speak with her in the garden again.

"Of course. She really has done wonders there these past few weeks. I'm embarrassed to say we let it go after her mother passed but Laelia has restored it to a shade of its past glory."

Laelia forced a smile the direction of her father's voice. He'd praised her more to Tiberius in two days than he had since learning she was his daughter in name only. She held her arm out for Drusus, and he led her into the hall. Tiberius and her father lingered in conversation. In the silence between them, something else was different. She sniffed. It was definitely missing.

"I don't smell your peppermint."

"I ran out."

"Why didn't you tell me?" He didn't answer and guilt wound its way through her middle.

"What else do you need beside peppermint?"

"A new lace for my sandal."

Her disapproving sigh sounded so much like her father, it frightened her.

"If you don't tell me, I won't know."

"Won't know what?" Tiberius asked, taking the elbow of her arm on her open side.

"Nothing." She let go of Drusus and without breaking her stride, took hold of Tiberius' arm. That was rather impressive, even for her, but she tried to keep the surprise from her face. Tiberius smelled better up close today. He must have been to the baths. "Did you enjoy your meal?"

"Of course, though in your presence I could eat raw meat and enjoy it."

"Careful, Tiberius." She flashed him a brazen smile meant to look seductive. "There's a narrow river between skilled flattery and outright lies." Her next step—wasn't there. Clinging tight to Tiberius she managed not to fall, though her knee wrenched something terrible when she landed on the garden path.

Tiberius' grip on her arm tightened so fast it hurt as much as her knee. "Are you all right?"

"I'm fine." Except for her face flaming like the eternal fire at the temple of Vesta. "I'm so used to Drusus calling out the steps for me. I forget not everyone knows to do that."

"I'm very sorry."

"It's fine. I can navigate quite well on my own in familiar places. Let me show you."

Tiberius released her and she lifted a silent prayer to every god who could hear her she could make up for the ground she'd just lost—literally. She'd fallen forward, down from the porch edge and her next step forward crunched gravel, so she knew she was on the path toward the bench. Better to be slow than get lost, so she took her time making her way to the bench, only straying into the dirt once or twice. Her plan to walk until she ran into the bench was brilliant, except for being painful. Her knee punished her again when it banged into the stone, but she'd take that over having to stoop and feel for it and appear as incompetent as she had a moment ago. Laelia turned and took a tiny step back, making sure she felt marble edge across the backs of both calves before sitting.

"That was very impressive." Tiberius sat beside her, his leg and arm pressed to hers.

Close. So very close she leaned away before realizing it. "I'm sorry."

"For what?"

"Moving away just now. I'm not used to anyone being that close to me other than my servant Naomi when she helps me dress." Juno's peacock! Had those words actually left her mouth just now?

Tiberius chuckled. "Well, I suppose I'm grateful for that. I am an impatient man, Laelia, so I'll ask you now. What is your answer?"

Yes. Say yes. He's as good a husband as Marcus would have been, maybe better.

"Your lack of response frightens me, my lady, and I'm not a man frightened of anything except Caesar's informants and catching the fever in summer."

Fever in summer—the fever that had taken her sight. "What do you expect of me as a wife?"

"What do you expect as my wife?"

She couldn't stop the grin from spreading. "You know, in most circles, it's considered unbecoming to answer a question with a question."

His laugh was strong enough she felt him vibrate against her side. "I confess I haven't been able to think much beyond the first few days." His fingertips grazed her forearm, edging dangerously close to her lap. "I want to provide for you in comfort, and see the envy of other men when your beauty captivates them from my side. In time I would like sons as smart as me and daughters as beautiful as my wife. I want you to protect my wealth by provisioning the house shrewdly and efficiently, which I already know you won't have any trouble doing."

"How?"

"You bartered me, remember?" The admiration in his tone echoed in the caress his fingertips made on the skin of her arm.

"I would have taken less." Her own admission surprised her. Her inner thoughts became spoken ones around Tiberius too often.

"I would have paid more." His fingertips snaked over her palm until his fingers entwined with hers. She'd never held someone's hand that way before, and the intimacy deepened her breathing. "So tell me now, Laelia Ricarri, do you wish to marry me as much as I wish to marry you?"

Relief, exquisite relief like she'd never known swept over her as she turned her face toward his. "Yes."

"Then permit me to do something I've wanted to do since the moment I first saw you."

Tiberius' hot breath touched her a moment before his mouth. Unlike Drusus' passive resistance, Tiberius ravaged her mouth. She didn't need to think how to respond to him, for this kiss was a conquest. He was everywhere.

When at last he withdrew, she would have melted into the bench if his hands weren't on either side of her head, holding her still while he pressed his forehead to hers. "How soon can you be ready?"

"For what?"

"The ceremony. I'll take care of purchasing the sacrifice to Jupiter and make all the arrangements with the senior priests. The *Pontifex Maximus* owes me a favor so I can name the date."

"*Confarreatio?*" Hardly anyone in Rome, except some of the nobles, still married in this ancient form of union—bound for life, with divorce being nearly impossible. She'd hoped for marriage by *coemptio,* which involved some ceremony, but had been prepared for marriage by *usus,* most common according to Naomi, where the bride and groom lived together for a year before the marriage became binding.

"Your father insisted on it, though if he hadn't, I would have."

This time his voice didn't ring quite as sincere. But before she could wonder at why, he captured her mouth again. The shock this time was less strong, and she found herself moving with him, even raising her hands to his face. Naomi was right. Somehow, you just know what to do.

Tiberius tore his mouth from hers, gripping her face so tight it should be painful, yet wasn't. "How soon?"

Tomorrow, which was the truth, sounded desperate. "Three weeks."

He kissed her again, this time on the end of her nose. "It will be the longest three weeks of my life, but I'll spend it preparing my house for you. What's your favorite flower? I want to have them in abundance."

"Lilies." Drusus would have known that already without asking. So would anyone who could see. The frond-like blooms were everywhere in this garden.

"Come, my lady. If I remain alone in this garden with you any longer, I may not be able to wait three weeks."

Laelia grinned when he rose and took her arm to draw her to her feet beside him.

Drusus watched Tiberius take liberties with Laelia, and the way she didn't discourage him took the scab right off his pain.

"We've done well." Her father's voice startled him. Master Ricarri stood near, watching them in the fading evening light. "Our futures depend on her."

Master Ricarri approached, his arms crossed, as his gaze lingered over the garden. "Like any man, I sorrowed rather than celebrated when her mother gave birth to a girl. I knew she was only the first, and we could have more, but we didn't. The gods would not be so kind to me as to give me a son to carry forward my name."

Drusus studied the man beside him. This was the most he'd ever spoken of himself.

"My name is all I have left. The Ricarri family once owned one of the finest villas on the Esquiline hill, where Nero's Golden House now stands. Did you know that?"

"The mistress mentioned it once, my lord."

"I lost everything in the great fire. The villa, my entire family, all the slaves. If any lived, they never returned. Curses on them, every last one of them, and the Christians who set the city ablaze. Nero didn't do near enough to retaliate for them burning our city. Not near enough."

"I'm sorry for your loss, my lord." Drusus was sorrier for the hundreds who had died by Nero's hand, and the heinous ways in which they did. He could still remember the blackened feet of the boy not much bigger than he'd been, burning on a pole.

The master turned to him, and for the first time, Drusus saw him for what he really was. A bitter man walking in darkness, believing lies as truth, with nothing to live for but pleasure.

"Tiberius may take a sip of his coming feast, but do not allow him to empty the cup. Not until the ceremony. I can't risk him spoiling her and casting her aside before the marriage is binding. I'll be keeping home as much as possible to aid in this but charge you to defend her virginity. From what I've heard from Tiberius about his slave Julia, I don't think he'll be unable to wait, but I need you to be my eyes as much as Laelia does."

"Yes, Master."

Laelia's laughter pulled Drusus' attention from her father. She held her hand out to Tiberius. He took it in his own, but instead of placing it on his arm he laced his fingers with hers and kissed the back of her hand. They approached, and after a few strides, Tiberius slipped his arm around Laelia's waist.

For the first time in his life, Drusus wished he were the one that was blind.

Stronger, Lord. Stronger.

Tiberius took care to announce the step for her this time. She looked comfortable at his side. Everyone beamed but Drusus.

"Good news, Brutus. Your daughter will have me, in three weeks' time."

God help him, this was really happening.

The master laughed. "And why shouldn't she? Come, bid her goodnight so we can visit the inn and celebrate."

Tiberius turned toward Laelia, his gaze bouncing to Drusus before he kissed her cheek. "Goodnight, my love. Sleep well."

"I will."

Tiberius followed the master out, leaving Drusus alone with Laelia. Naomi had yet to emerge from the kitchen. Laelia turned slowly with her arm out, as if to reach for the wall.

"I'm right here, Mistress."

She jumped like a cat that's been splashed. "How long have you been there?"

"I never left."

Her face turned a fiery crimson as her eyes narrowed and chin rose. "Take me to my room."

Gladly. The sooner he could retreat to his own, the faster he could sharpen his already lethal blades and throw them over and over until he couldn't keep his eyes open or his arm steady. Her grip was firm, too firm. When she released him at her door, the finger marks on his arm were white. She turned to face him, put a hand on her hip and grew an inch taller as he watched.

"Whatever I lack in your sight that makes me worthy of a single kiss, I possess in quantity for Tiberius. I tell you so you know I'll never turn to you that way again. I'm sure this comes as a great relief for you."

"It does."

Her mouth fell open like he'd hit her and her lower lip quivered. Moisture shined her eyes, gathering like a filling fountain to spill over any moment. "Then for the sake of my betrothed, I'm relieved to know exactly how much you don't want me."

She turned to shut the door in his face, but his hand arrested the swing, his palm bracing the wood. "You think I don't want you?"

"Don't."

"Don't what? Tell the truth? That I want you the way a man dying of thirst adrift on the ocean wants water. That like him, I'm surrounded by the very thing I need and can't have? You think I can watch you day after day learn and grow, embrace a resolute strength that runs as deep as your wisdom and compassion, and not want you for myself?"

"Then why did I have to force you to kiss me?"

"Because if I hadn't resisted, I'd have wanted much more than that. You would have had to force me to stop." *Tell her the rest.* Before the shame of the truth stole his courage, he confessed. "And I don't know that I would have."

Her mouth became a frown as she took a step back from him. "What are you saying?"

She knew, but not wanting to believe it had forced her to ask anyway. He couldn't have said it any plainer.

"I'm a slave, but still a man, Laelia. My devotion to you is absolute, almost as much as to my God, but it's not without cost."

And right now, the cost was much more than he possessed.

"What comes at a cost?" Naomi asked from behind him. He hadn't heard her approach.

"Nothing," Laelia answered. "Drusus was just telling me goodnight."

Naomi eyed them both as Drusus withdrew his hand from the door and stepped away.

"Good night, Mistress." He left them both in the hall, reaching his room in record time and shutting the door much harder than he needed to. Collapsing on the bed snapped one of the legs and the corner crashed to the floor, dumping him forward and slamming him into the floor.

An oath he hadn't used in two years flew from his mouth. He felt for the lamp on the barrel at the foot of his bed and lit the wick to survey the damage. The leg was severed at the frame, and nothing in the storeroom stood close to that height to replace it. Drusus retrieved the hidden coin pouch and Laelia's dagger from beneath the wreckage of the bed. He was too hungry and frustrated to find a new hiding place, and it seemed pointless with three weeks remaining before they would move in with Tiberius. He shoved the dagger and the coin purse deep in his leather bag and threw it in the corner beside a crate of radishes.

The straw-stuffed mattress he placed on the floor and the three legged bed frame he propped against the large sacks of grain. His consolation for the lump forming on his skull was the wooden bed made an excellent throwing background. And he had lots of throwing to do tonight.

He slipped the twins free, chose a dark spot on the center board, and let the first blade fly. Even as wrecked as he was, the blade stuck perfectly straight in the center of the small black knot of wood he'd chosen.

Tiberius would be thrilled.

Laelia listened to Naomi go on and on about how happy she was for her. A small price to pay to have the tightness of her hairdo undone, though all she wanted was silence.

Drusus was in love with her.

Slave or not, no man spoke from his heart that way unless he was. Gods help her, part of her had rejoiced at his admission, while the greater part had roared in fear. She didn't know Tiberius well enough yet to know what he would do if he learned or suspected. While being married would give her some level of protection against her father, he was still the *paterfamilias*. Under the law he retained the power of life and death over her as long as he lived. Even if Tiberius were lenient of any suspected dalliance with a slave, which was permitted with impunity among men though scandalous among the wives, her father would never be. Her father would kill Drusus as he had Titus, and beat her as he would have her mother if she hadn't died first.

The only thing she knew to do was to bury her own feelings for him, which were now undeniable in the face of his confession. She would bury them like a seed in the ground and cover it with her commitment to Tiberius, hoping in time what Drusus meant to her would die, so that one or both of them wouldn't.

Chapter 25

Laelia was different. As Drusus watched her approach with Naomi from the changing rooms at the baths, he allowed himself a moment to appreciate how much. And that he was a part of why. The past two weeks had revealed her more confident than ever, even in the presence of her father. Last night at dinner, she'd openly disagreed with him in regard to relief efforts for the survivors of the tragedy in Pompeii. From his ever present spot behind her, Drusus had seen three things happen, almost simultaneously. Her father's eyes widened, Tiberius raised his brows, and Laelia popped an olive in her mouth as if she hadn't said anything the least bit controversial.

She really hadn't, in a way. To help the hurting and needy simply because it was the right thing to do was something he agreed with. Right now he also agreed with the way the damp wisps of dark hair framed her flush face, and her arms glistened in the afternoon light from the remnant of oil on her skin. Her beauty still plagued him. More so the inner beauty, the fortitude and compassion Tiberius didn't appreciate. As for having to watch him kiss her, caress her, share *their* bench together, repetition had dulled the ache. That or God was answering his fervent prayer to make him stronger.

Neither of them had spoken ever again about the kiss, or his confession. It was as if it had never happened. Laelia had grown stronger, and not only with her father. She'd insisted Naomi teach her to know a good turnip from a bad one, new wheat from old, and just this morning, how to do her own hair. She'd fouled it terribly, the braids uneven and lopsided, but Drusus had admired her effort, between winks and knowing grins he and Naomi shared over the shoulder of an oblivious mistress.

A peddler approached her and offered her perfumes, which she declined with a certain charm he'd swear she was picking up from Tiberius.

"Are you ready to return home, Mistress?"

"No. My veil should be ready today. I want to pick that up first. Do you remember where the shop is?"

"Yes." He remembered where it was, and how many hours he'd had to wait while Laelia and Naomi fussed over types of wool, colors of dye, and the shape and style of her new stola.

"Good." She let go of Naomi and held her hand out to him. "Let's hurry, so we can be home before Father."

In spite of her haste, he refused to take the steps fast. He sensed her annoyance but guided her with his words and arm, as he always did. Across the street he glimpsed Tiberius with Julia, but neither had seen them yet. He hoped they wouldn't, but Julia's gaze met his and a smile formed as she leaned into Tiberius and spoke.

Tiberius searched until he too saw them, and approached, Julia trailing close behind. "Laelia! Fortuna smiles on me, for I'd just visited your house and was disappointed to find you weren't there."

"Tiberius?"

"Of course, my love. Who else would it be?"

If Tiberius' address of Laelia as my love bothered Julia, she didn't show it. She stood regal and relaxed beside Tiberius, in a snug lavender tunic Drusus had bought for her. The fact she still possessed it, or that Tiberius let her wear it, surprised him. Maybe Tiberius didn't remember helping Drusus select it, or giving him the difference he needed to buy it.

"Don't be silly," Laelia said. "I recognize your voice quite well. I'm surprised to run into you here at the baths, though I've already seen several of Father's friends here who let me know they plan to attend our ceremony next week."

"The day can't come soon enough." Tiberius spoke to Laelia, but looked at Drusus when he said it. "Your father met Julia. He insisted I bring her to dine this evening. I hope you don't mind."

Laelia's grip on his arm faltered. "Father was home?"

"Yes. His employer is in a panic because he's having a feast tonight and his slave couldn't find any pickled herring at the market. Your father thought you all might have some, though I'm certain no one knows how to finish it quite as well as your Naomi. I'm hoping she teaches Julia everything she knows."

Drusus listened in a fog. Her father had been in his room. While he no longer asked questions about where Laelia's coin came from, a chill still passed through him.

Laelia must have felt it also, or had her own, because she stiffened beside him and tightened the grip on his arm. "I'm sure she will. If you'll excuse me, as Naomi and Drusus are both with me, there is no one to attend my father."

"Of course. Tell him I look forward to seeing him this evening." Tiberius' gaze cut back to Drusus as he slipped his arm around Julia's hip and pulled her close to him. "We both look forward to seeing him."

"Julia is here?" Laelia asked, and Drusus thought her grip would crush his upper arm.

"Yes, my lady." Julia's gaze swept Laelia. "Forgive me for not announcing my presence. I forget you don't see."

"Laelia sees very well," Drusus said. "But not with her eyes like the rest of us. Now if you'll pardon us. As my mistress said, we should be going."

"Yes, we should," Naomi added. Though Drusus couldn't see her on the other side of Laelia, he could tell from her tone she shared his concern.

"Of course. I'll see you this evening, my love." Tiberius kissed Laelia full on the mouth, and Drusus had no doubt it was to spite him. His jaw tightened and Julia must have understood, for she couldn't conceal a frown or the sadness in her eyes.

Tiberius backed away, grabbed Julia again, and smiled a victor's smile to Drusus as he led her away, the moisture of Laelia's kiss still glinting on his upturned lip.

Stronger, Lord. Stronger.

"Let's go." Naomi started forward and Laelia signaled him to move as well.

Neither of them spoke the entire way. They all feared the same thing.

Naomi opened the door and Drusus led them in, shuddering to a stop the moment his eyes adjusted. Her father lunged and slapped him hard across the face, knocking him into Laelia.

She jerked to a stop. "What's wrong?"

"Your slave is a liar and a thief." His master threw Drusus' pack to the floor, the coins inside it spilling free with a clatter across the tile.

He's found them.

"Father, Drusus would never steal from us."

The knife. The coin. From the corner of his eye, he glimpsed Naomi move to flank Laelia's other side.

"Silence. Let him answer for himself how your dagger found its way into his possession."

Laelia's head jerked back. "My dagger? That's impossible."

"Say nothing." Drusus squeezed her hand tight beneath his.

Her father slapped him again. "Don't dare give my daughter orders. Was it not enough to cheat her of her earnings because she couldn't see what she'd been paid?"

Laelia's grip on his arm tightened. "Father, please."

"Say nothing." Drusus shoved her toward Naomi and moved away from them to draw her father's attention. His mind warred. Run. Pull the twins. Run.

"Father, wait, I beg you." Laelia tried to move toward him, but Naomi grabbed her arm. Drusus had mere seconds. For Laelia's sake, he could neither run, nor pull the twins. "Naomi, get her out of here now."

"A liar and a thief. In my house!" Her father strode toward the lamp stand against the wall.

Before he picked it up and hoisted it like a club, Drusus knew what he intended. He dropped to his knees, locking eyes with Naomi over Laelia's struggling form. "Get her out of here."

"No!" Laelia struggled harder as Naomi pulled her from behind.

Drusus raised his arms over his head and begged God to spare them as the first blow struck.

Chapter 26

Laelia gave up struggling. Naomi wasn't going to let her go and kept whispering in her ear over and over "we can't help him." With every slur and insult her father screamed, her hatred for him burned hotter. She felt every one of Drusus' cries of pain in her own body. She sank to her knees on the stone porch, and Naomi gathered her close. Not even her weeping drowned the sound of her father's rage.

She would kill him for this. At his age a poison wouldn't even need to be slow. He would never hurt her or Drusus again.

A crash sounded, louder than the others had been. Footsteps approached, and Naomi's arms tightened around her. It was Laelia's turn.

"The only reason," her father wheezed, "I didn't kill him is because," he coughed, and the sound of his panting made Laelia sick, "is because you need him for marriage."

Laelia remained tensed, but he didn't strike her. Instead of sagging in relief, her muscles tensed even tighter. He wasn't going to hit her because that would damage the wares before delivery. She pulled her fists deep into the folds of her tunic, hoping her father couldn't see them.

"I'm going to Tiberius', to cancel *cena* tonight. And think up a reason your slave won't be able to attend you for a while. I can't possibly tell him, it was because the man was robbing us beneath our very noses. But you can rest assured it will never happen again."

Drusus hadn't robbed her. She couldn't explain the dagger yet, but Tiberius would be able to. And he was going to, the moment she could confront him.

"Say something," her father snapped.

I'm going to kill you. "I understand."

"Naomi, see to the slave and clean up the mess before I return tonight."

"Yes, Master."

Laelia didn't stir until she heard the front door slam in its frame. "Take me to him."

They made their way to the atrium, but she couldn't hear anything besides the fountain spray. After several more paces, Naomi gasped and tore her hand free.

The floodgates of Laelia's fear opened. "Drusus?"

No one answered her, so she edged forward. "How bad is it?"

"Stay where you are," Naomi said, sounding angry and scared at the same time.

Laelia's heart pounded as she moved toward Naomi's voice. Something clattered beneath her sandal. Her foot rocked on an uneven surface. She managed not to stumble, but her next step did the same.

"Be careful, don't step on him." The tears in Naomi's voice were as loud as the fountain. "I don't know what to do. He's breathing, but—oh, Laelia."

Her heart couldn't beat any faster as she eased to her knees on the floor. The clatter rumbled again and something stuck her knee. She put her hands out, sweeping the floor to find him as he'd taught her. Her fingers collided with something smooth and hard. Tracing the edges to where they formed a point and recognizing the thin, flat shape made her jaw tighten so hard her teeth hurt.

There was cracked tile all around her. All around Drusus. The shard slipped from her hand and she covered her mouth. Gods. Gods! Her useless eyes grew hot and wet and the screaming swelled in her chest again. More than her eyes were useless.

Laelia sees very well, but not with her eyes like the rest of us. His words from earlier gave her courage. He'd been her wall from the first day, and now she would be his. "Do you know where the fuller shop is on the Via Sacria?"

"What?"

"The fuller on the Via Sacria. Do you know where it is?"

"I, I think so."

"Go there at once and demand to see Otho. Tell him what's happened, and Drusus needs help."

"But your father—"

"I need you to go get Otho." She didn't hear the rustle of cloth or the shuffle of feet. "Now, Naomi. Find Otho. Tell him we need his help, and hurry."

He would come. Laelia was certain of it.

"Yes, Mistress." Naomi ran, judging by the clatter of the broken tile and how fast the door opened and closed.

Laelia crawled forward, searching for him while being careful of the broken tile. She finally felt his warm skin. Arm? She traced the curve to a defined edge, and felt the joint. The round knob beneath her fingertips had a hard bone close to it. His knee. He was on his side, facing her. She put her left hand out and touched the wool of a tunic, not the skin of his leg. His head was to her left and not the right. "Drusus, can you hear me?"

She walked on her knees closer to his head, trying to avoid his arms. Her fingertips paused on the floor and she ran them over the spot again. The tile was cracked here too. It must be cracked all around him. Her father couldn't have used only his hands to do this much damage to the floor—and to Drusus.

She touched… arm, and ran her hand up toward his shoulder, feeling instantly when the warm dry skin turned wet beneath her touch. There was no mistaking that warm wetness, only this time it wasn't her own blood on her fingertips. "Drusus?"

No answer. "Drusus, please."

She shook his arm gently and a low moan mingled with the spray of the fountain. Very carefully, she rose and stepped over him, careful not to kick him or tangle in her clothing. She knelt again, this time behind him. Locating his shoulder this time was easier. She put one hand on his neck to lift his head and with her other hand, pull his shoulder toward her. On his back, his head came to rest on her pillowed knees. He hadn't made a sound, so she laid her palm to his chest.

The coarse wool didn't seem to rise or fall beneath her hand. She brought her other hand up to feel along his jaw, the side of his face, as her gut twisted. Heat and blood covered his face and throat like a second skin. Fresh tears fell as she cradled his battered head. "I'm sorry. I'm so, so sorry."

She wept until her eyes felt as if someone had sanded them and her head pounded.

Feet sounded nearby, approaching fast. A shard of tile wasn't much of a weapon, but she searched for a large, pointed piece in the rubble.

"This way."

Naomi's voice. Laelia uncurled her fist from her makeshift knife.

The shuffling feet stopped almost in unison. "God in heaven," a man said. "Help him, please."

Someone crouched beside her and once again, only the sound of the fountain filled the room for a moment.

"He's breathing, but barely, and needs a physician."

"Naomi, did father take the coin?" Laelia knew the answer but hoped she was wrong.

"Yes. And the dagger."

Someone touched her arm. The hand was large, and the fingers long. "Don't worry about that. The physician will come. I'll send one of my servants here for him."

Otho's voice. "Not here." Her father had been capable of this atrocity while sober, and he wasn't coming back that way. "Will you offer us sanctuary until I can send word to Tiberius Cina, my betrothed?"

"Of course, my lady."

"We shouldn't move him," Naomi said.

The fear in her voice was for more than Drusus. Laelia angled her head toward the direction Naomi's voice had come. "What I do now, I do alone. I understand if you choose to stay. Father can declare you and Drusus runaway slaves, and he probably will. I don't know if Tiberius will be able to reason with him or not but I must get Drusus away from him, Naomi. I will understand if you stay."

"My place is with you."

"And my place is with Drusus."

"Then I'm coming with you."

"My lady," Otho said. "I would rather not move him either but if you believe the greater danger is remaining here, then we must."

"We have to get him away from here. Please."

Even if Tiberius managed to explain the dagger, and Laelia confessed to the coin, Drusus wasn't going to stop being a Christian any more than her father was going to stop hating him for it. He would surely kill him then. But she couldn't explain that to Otho without putting Drusus in more danger. Otho might hate Christians too.

"Please, we have to get him out of here and to a physician. Please." Laelia put her hand to Drusus' chest again, hoping he meant half as much to Otho as he did to her. Harboring a fugitive slave would place the man in as much danger as Laelia for taking them.

"Alexander, you're the fastest. Go to Lady Pappus. Tell her what's happened and to send a physician to the fullery. You find a blanket we can carry him on and something to bind that arm with. Two long stir sticks if you have them."

Otho's orders made her want to fall at his feet and weep. She slid her hand to Drusus' shoulder. *Stay with me.*

"What should we do, my lord?" A new voice. A man, but she couldn't guess his age.

"I'll tell you in a moment," Otho said. "Laelia, how much time until your father returns?"

"I don't know." She didn't want to be anywhere near here when he did. There wasn't anything in her room she wanted to ask Naomi to retrieve. Hopefully Drusus would understand his life was more important to her than anything of his they might be leaving behind.

"Here's a blanket. I have one stir stick, and this is one of Laelia's ribbons to tie it."

"We don't have time to bind his arm if your father could return any moment. Spread the blanket flat here, and we're going to lift him on it. I want one of you on each corner to carry him like a sling, and in the name of the

Lord, be careful and move together. This will not be like treading cloth in the troughs."

A mixed flurry of "Yes, Master" followed.

"I'm going to raise his head from your lap and you move out from beneath him"

Laelia nodded. Otho took the weight of Drusus' head from her lap. She pressed her legs as flat to the broken tile as she could and slid away. A jagged piece of tile sent a sharp pain along her thigh.

"Take his legs at the knees. You two lift his body while I hold his head. Move fast but together, and set him down like a full cup of wine. Ready?"

A few grunts and heaves from the slaves followed, and what might have been a groan from Drusus. She was doing the right thing. They couldn't stay here. A hand circled her forearm.

"We need to rinse the blood from your hands, and throw something over your tunic so it isn't as noticeable on the street. It's not yet evening. People are still about."

"Hurry," Otho said. "We can't wait for you. The less we jostle him starting and stopping the better."

There was no time to waste on modesty. Laelia pulled her tunic over her head and shook it out. Because it never left her hands, turning it inside out and slipping it back over her head again took two breaths. She moved toward the sound of the fountain spray until her shin banged the rim of the pool, and rinsed her arms. "Let's go."

The cut on Laelia's upper leg ached with every step. Naomi wasn't skilled at avoiding or alerting her to obstacles and she stumbled often. She could hear the way people fell silent as they passed, likely wondering at the unusual cargo Otho's slaves carried. Dead were taken from the city by cart if poor and funeral procession if not.

Drusus wasn't dead. And he wasn't going to be dead when they reached Otho's.

Jupiter, Juno, Minerva, Mars, Apollo, Diana, Saturn, Vesta, Venus, and Janus had better all be listening. If Drusus died, she would make good on her threat to set fire to every temple she could find in the city.

"We're here." Naomi pulled her to the left.

"Keep me close to him," Laelia whispered. Naomi squeezed her hand.

"Carry him in the back," Otho said. "Lay him by the hearth. He'll need the warmth and the physician the light."

Another flurry of "Yes, master." How many voices? Three? Four?

Naomi pushed up on Laelia's arm. "There's a step here."

Laelia overestimated its height but avoided tripping. She clipped the edge of the doorframe with her shoulder, but swallowed most of the grimace. The urine odor of the fullery punched her in the nose, but she'd never been so glad to smell it.

"I'm glad you sent word to me. Bring him here." That was a woman's voice, but whose?

"My lady, did you send for a physician?" Otho asked.

Laelia gripped Naomi's arm tighter. This was Lady Pappus.

"Yes, yes of course. I had my servant make him a pallet by the fire. I knew you wouldn't be able to carry him to the floor above." As Laelia listened, the woman's tone grew more confident with every word, until she sounded like Tiberius. "Lay him by the fire and bring me rags and salted water, quickly."

"Do as she says," Otho said.

"Is this her?"

"Yes, my lady."

"You poor child."

Someone embraced Laelia—someone whose jasmine fragrance overpowered the fuller smell. The woman released her.

"What's your name?"

"Naomi, my lady. Laelia is also my mistress."

"I'm glad you've come. Bring her over here by him."

Naomi pulled Laelia forward again, and then stopped her after a few steps. She needed to keep out of the way, though she longed to touch him, hoping to reassure him somehow.

"Water and cloth, Lady Pappus."

"Set it there and go out front to speed the physician along when he comes."

"Yes, my lady."

"Laelia, sit here by the fire."

Naomi guided Laelia down to the floor, but the warmth of the blaze felt too strong. "Am I too close?"

"No, that's perfect. If you reach forward, you'll find Drusus' foot. You can remove his sandals while I begin to clean his wounds."

"I can do that," Naomi said.

"No. Laelia can do it. I'd like for you to take this rag and help me."

"Yes, my lady."

Laelia leaned forward and ran her fingertips along the stone, to the blankets folded and stacked almost a hand high. She located his sandal, and from the shape of them, they were the traditional style. The straps would be tied high on his ankle or low on his calf. Fine hair ruffled against her fingertips as she searched the flat leather strap for the knot. But the knot didn't feel right. The ends were too short and it was much too tight, even for both of her hands.

Splashing water and the low murmur of men's voices kept intruding while she tried to figure out how his sandal was tied. After struggling a while longer, she wondered if they should cut it, but then he would need a new one. Then she remembered. He already needed a new strap. This wasn't the right knot. The leather must have broken and he'd retied the ends together, which must have been uncomfortable. How long had he worn it this way?

Her fingers followed the leather up and found the correct tie. She unwound the strap and eased the lacing to slide the sandal off. She needed to lean further forward to remove the other one, but did so without jarring him.

"Bring Laelia a rag and bowl of clean water also."

"Yes, my lady."

"Do you mind washing his feet, Laelia? I know it's a servant's task but you're already settled and I know will be gentle."

"I will."

"Thank you."

Someone pressed a rag to the top of her hand. She took it and then someone grasped her other hand and brought it to rest on a bowl near her knee. Her father would burn the house down around them if he saw Laelia washing feet, much less the feet of her slave. She wasn't too proud to do the lowliest of tasks reserved for the least slave in the house.

There'd been so much blood—on his throat, his face, even in his hair. "How is he?"

"He's breathing better now that we have his face clean and his head tipped back. The physician should be here soon," Otho said.

"Thank you." She couldn't do anything else for Drusus right now except wait. "I'm sorry to ask more when you've already given so much, Otho, but I need one of your slaves to deliver a message for me."

"To who?"

"Tiberius Cina, the blade dealer near the Esquiline Hill."

A sudden hush fell over the room.

Laelia was unsure of what she'd said or done wrong. "Otho?"

"What's the message?"

"That my father almost killed Drusus and we've fled his house. I need his help, and he'll need to know where to find me. He's my betrothed and we are to be married in a week."

"I will send the message."

"Thank you. I can tell your servant where—"

"I know where Cina lives," Otho said, with an edge to his tone.

"And how," Lady Pappus added, her tone also colored with disapproval.

Otho called a servant to him to go to the apartment of Tiberius Cina and give whoever answers the message that the Lady Ricarri and her servants are lodging at the fullers shop on the Via Sacria near the forum.

"Please ask him to come soon."

"He'll come right away. I'm sure of it." Otho sounded angry. Laelia regretted imposing on him further, but she needed Tiberius. He had the best chance of convincing her father not to involve the authorities, which she knew he would do when he discovered them missing.

"Lady, the physician is here," a man's voice said.

Laelia tensed and someone took her hand and held it—probably Naomi.

"I need to examine him. The women and slaves must leave the room."

"I'm not leaving him." Laelia put all the backbone Tiberius had taught her into her words, and sat stiff and straight as a table leg.

"Nor am I," Lady Pappus added, her tone equally firm.

"Will you permit this?" the man asked, presumably to Otho.

"I don't speak for them."

"At least move out of the firelight. Bring more lamps if you have them."

Otho ordered this done, and Naomi tugged Laelia to the left. She moved away, but letting go of Drusus' ankle made her restless.

"Your servant said he was beaten. With what, if you know?"

"A lampstand," Naomi said.

Laelia's chest clenched as she remembered the cracked tiles on the floor and Drusus' cries of pain that reached her in the garden.

"He shouldn't have been moved."

"I know," Otho said. "We didn't have a choice."

"And he hasn't woken at all?"

"No."

Laelia tried to visualize what was happening in the quiet that followed. Cloth ripped, water trickled and lapped, between murmurs that likely belonged to the physician. She wished she could see his face to interpret them.

Her father would have returned to their house by now, if he hadn't gone drinking, and would know they'd gone. Would he be looking for them already? Would he alert the closest *aedele* in the morning his slaves, and his daughter, were runaways?

"Who does he belong to?" the physician asked.

"Me." A shiver snaked down her spine in spite of the warmth of the fire.

"You don't appear strong enough to have given the beating, so I assume it was someone else. Whoever it was owes you a new slave. This one is ruined."

"Ruined?"

"He'll never recover use of that arm. The bruising beneath his ribcage is most likely internal bleeding. If he does wake up, which isn't likely, the trauma to the skull has probably left him without speech or understanding."

Never recover use of that arm. The arm she held every day? Drusus, unable to utter his own name or dress himself, more crippled than she was? Naomi squeezed her hand.

"The merciful thing to do would be to end his suffering. I can pour hemlock down his throat or open a vein and bleed him out, whichever you prefer."

Laelia rose to her knees. "Drusus isn't some ox in the field with a broken leg or a leaking wineskin to be thrown out."

"Laelia." Naomi took hold of her arm, but she jerked away.

"You're a physician. Act like it." Her eyes began to sting but by the gods she could not cry now.

"Woman, don't address me like I'm one of your slaves. I'm—"

"This man is no mere slave to us," Lady Pappus said. "I ask you to care for him as you did my husband, and tell us what can be done to help him."

"Very little. If his organs are ruptured, they'll flood his body from the inside. These lesions on his scalp here, and here, were likely strong enough to crack the skull. He's never going to wake up again. If by some miracle of Asklepios or Jupiter he does, these broken ribs here will take months to heal.

"You see the arm. Both bones are broken. I'd have to amputate everything below the break. He'll lose that hand and most of his forearm. Without continued treatments, the stump will rot and poison the rest of the body. The cost to even attempt it—"

"Isn't as important to me as saving him," Lady Pappus said.

Laelia couldn't breathe. She'd known her father to be capable of violence, but the brutality required to inflict that much damage was staggering.

"Lady Pappus." The way the physician spoke the woman's name told Laelia to expect more distress was coming. "Please don't think me without compassion. But I won't attempt to save a life I know cannot be saved. I have my reputation to attend."

"Are you refusing to care for him?"

Lady Pappus' tone carried a sliver of Laelia's outrage. She wanted to claw the man's face, and might if she knew where it was.

"I won't risk my reputation any further. The slave should be euthanized."

"He has a name." Laelia stood, her hands curled into fists at her side. "His name is Drusus. He knows how to fix fountains and tell whose leading a chariot race from outside the stadium."

"My lady, I understand—"

"No you don't." Laelia inhaled a deep breath, imagining the peppermint she'd come to know so well. "I might be blind but I see right through you. To you, this is some worthless slave, easily replaced. You talk about reputation, but what kind of physician can so easily disregard a life this way? Only cowards refuse to try because they fear to fail, and he taught me that too."

"Your anger at me is misplaced. I didn't take a lampstand to him like he was a tapestry to be cleaned. I've given you my professional opinion and will hear no more of your accusations. I'm sorry for your slave, but I'm sure with some effort on your part you can find another to equal his abilities, whatever those were you seem so reluctant to part with."

The insinuation infuriated her. She'd never wanted to hit someone more in her life.

"You need to leave now," Otho said.

"Lady Pappus, you are a gentle yet practical woman. Surely you—"

"Otho has asked you to leave. Take this as payment for coming this evening."

The clink of coins sickened Laelia.

"This is more than twice my fee, my lady."

"I know, and twice as much as you've earned after what you've implied about this young woman. I would have hoped you would know how important Drusus is to my family as many times as he worked alongside you in caring for my husband."

"I am sorry, Lady. He was a very good servant."

"Stop saying was, as if he isn't right here." Laelia's entire body trembled. This couldn't be happening.

"Collect your things and leave now, as Otho has asked you," Lady Pappus said.

The man noisily gathered whatever he'd brought with him, and then his footsteps took him away. On the floor, she found Drusus' foot again and didn't care who saw as she stroked his ankle. "What can we do?"

"Continue to pray," Otho said. "I'll have my servant prepare us food and drink and bring you a fresh tunic. Naomi, if you would like to take your mistress to the upper room, send the servants down and there is a basin of water there for washing."

"Come, Laelia." Naomi took hold of her shoulder.

"I'm not leaving him." Three sharp raps at the front door brought her head up. She held her breath, her heart racing in her throat.

The hinges moaned as the door swung. "I'm Tiberius Cina. Where is Drusus?"

Chapter 27

Tiberius sounded winded and Laelia's heart swelled. He must have run the entire distance to reach them. "Thank the gods you're here. My father—"

"What happened?"

"Father found my dagger in Drusus' bag and accused him of stealing it. How did he have it when I'd already sold it to you?"

"Please tell me a physician, or even a *medicus* is coming. Whatever the cost I'll pay it."

For the first time since saying yes, she knew she'd made the right choice in a husband. Unlike her father, Tiberius understood how much she needed Drusus and cared for her more than coin. "He's already been, but he wouldn't help him because he's a slave. He wanted to—"

Remembering the callous man's words made her eyes burn again and clogged her throat. Curse her weakness, showing itself in front of her betrothed.

"To what?" Tiberius demanded.

He had a right to be frustrated, but his harsh tone still bruised. "To cut off his arm."

"Why?"

Laelia flinched. Tiberius asked the question like an accusation. If anyone had a right to accuse it was her. He still hadn't accounted for Drusus' possession of the dagger.

"Why did he want to cut off his arm?"

She drew back, her body tensing. The way he'd raised his voice stripped the assurance his presence brought her a moment ago.

"Answer me!"

She couldn't. This man was nothing like the Tiberius she knew.

"His forearm is broken in both bones," Otho said.

"Which arm?"

"The right." Otho's voice was calm and steady.

Tiberius began to laugh, a harsh, mocking sound that made Laelia's insides quiver. "He broke his arm. The idiot fool broke his arm."

"Don't call him that." Betrothed or not, she'd heard enough. "This wasn't Drusus' fault."

"Not Drusus, your father. Your father is the stupid fool."

She couldn't believe her ears, the one perfect part of her body as dependable as Drusus. "Now you answer me. Why did Drusus have my dagger?"

"He bought it back from me the night you sold it. I would have thrown it in the Tiber if I'd known this would happen."

Laelia's mind reeled. Drusus couldn't have given the coin right back. She'd used more than half of it since that day. "He couldn't have. Where would he have gotten the coin? And why didn't you tell me before if you knew he had it all this time?"

"I didn't ask where he got it. He probably stole it, but it doesn't matter now."

"It matters to me, Tiberius. It should also matter to you because I do."

He laughed again, and the sound prickled her skin.

"You're blinder than I thought if you still don't understand."

She desperately tried to as everything continued to unravel like a wicker basket that had been slashed.

"Careful, Cina." Otho's voice held a hard edge like her stone bench.

Knowing he was near gave her a measure of reassurance. "What don't I understand?"

"I was marrying you to get him, but your idiot father destroyed his throwing arm."

Nausea rose like bile in her empty stomach. "You didn't—want—me?"

"I wanted him, but he's worthless now. Your father has no idea what he's done."

Knife tricks. Dangerous ones. Laelia almost reached into the fire for a fist full of coals to fling at Tiberius. "Get out."

"A thousand curses on you." Naomi's outrage matched her own.

"Losing Drusus and his arm are already a thousand curses, old woman."

"You are just as he described," Otho said. "A man so full of pride and greed you don't know it's enslaved you."

Tiberius scoffed. "You must be Otho."

"I am."

"Then you're as much to blame for my loss as Laelia's father. If you hadn't filled Drusus' head with your strange God and his ways, I wouldn't have lost him the first time."

"You're the one that's lost."

"Hardly."

"You don't think so? How many times would you lash out in anger because you couldn't learn to throw a knife like he could? Then when he finally found the peace and forgiveness he so desperately needed, you envied that too."

"I've never envied a slave in my life."

"Then why do you own Julia? If you'd only wanted Drusus you would have offered whatever price Laelia's father required, but you didn't. You take anything Drusus cares for because you still want to be him."

The quiet that lasted several breaths was its own confirmation. Laelia held her breath against the rage and pain in her chest until the door slammed.

Naomi took her by the shoulders. "Are you all right?"

"No." She leaned against her and drew slow, steadying breaths.

"Master?" The voice carried from the floor above.

"What is it, Alexander?"

"May I approach?"

"Of course."

"Forgive me, my lord but we overheard. Splash knows someone who may be able to help Drusus."

"Who?"

"Scorpio, the *medicus* at the gladiator school near the Temple of Diana."

"Why would he help us?

"Splash believes they were baptized together in the Tiber."

"Does Splash know him personally?"

"No, my lord. He recognized him because he's seen him a few times while making linen deliveries."

Why all the questions? If this man could help Drusus, they should go bring him now.

"It's your decision, Otho," Lady Pappus said.

"I'm willing to take the risk if Splash is. He'll be the one in the most danger if he's wrong. Alexander, you go with him, and take torches. You'll need them on the way back. Have Rathan bring food and wine for our guests. The others may retire for the night but sleep dressed. I may need you all quickly."

"Yes, master."

Laelia needed Drusus in less danger, not more. "What risk?"

For a long moment, the crackle of the fire and mingled footsteps were all she could hear. The urine-tinged air cloaking the room turned oppressive as Laelia waited. Was sending for Otho and bringing Drusus here another mistake among her many?

"Laelia…" Otho began. "Lady Pappus and I as well as Drusus and most of our servants are followers of Christ. We are Christians."

Her mouth went dry. "All of you?"

"Yes. This man is likely well-connected to Caesar through the gladiator games. That isn't dangerous unless he suspects we're followers and wishes to turn us over to Caesar. We respect and obey Caesar but cannot acknowledge deity where it does not exist. I'm willing to take that risk, because I care for Drusus like a son."

"As do I," Lady Pappus said.

Their situation grew more perilous by the hour. Drusus could be dying. More innocent people could come to harm—all because of her father. "What can I do?"

"You've done enough already," Lady Pappus said. "It took great courage to send for help and more to leave your home. Perhaps Naomi could attend you upstairs and find you a fresh tunic. When Drusus wakes, I'm sure he'll want to see you."

"I don't want to leave him."

Naomi took her arm by the elbow. "The lady is right. You wouldn't want him to see you like this, with dirt and blood smeared on you and your garments."

"We'll be here with him." Otho's reassuring tone let her know she had no choice.

Naomi steered her in a large arc. "There are steps here."

Laelia sensed a wall and put one hand to it and after a few steps found a rhythm. When her foot fell too far and she bobbled forward, she knew she'd reached the top.

"Turn right," Naomi said from behind her.

She'd been in this room before, the day the men attacked her in the street. She took a few more steps, following the bend in the wall, to allow Naomi to enter.

"There's a bowl of water but it's not warm. Is that all right?"

Laelia nodded and removed her tunic. When the sodden cloth touched her jaw, she flinched from the chill but stood quietly while Naomi bathed her face and arms.

"Tiberius deceived me."

"He deceived all of us."

"Did Drusus know?"

Naomi's rag paused along Laelia's leg. "I don't know."

"Did you know he bought my dagger back, or how he had the coin to?"

"How did you get this cut?"

The wet rag barely touched the wound on her thigh but the water stung like a bee sting. "From the tile on the floor. How could Drusus have done that without either of us knowing? And why?"

"The night you sold it, he left. He returned later with a gash in his head like the two your father gave him today. He said he'd fallen, but I didn't believe him."

Laelia hugged her arms close, and felt more exposed than she ever had. First Tiberius, now Naomi—who was there left to trust? "Why didn't you tell me?"

"I should have, no matter what he said. I'm sorry."

An unfamiliar sound floated to Laelia's ear. She inclined her head and listened—a groan, and hushed voices. She felt for the wall and headed for the steps. "He's waking up."

Naomi grabbed her other arm. "Wait, you're not dressed."

"Hurry." Laelia stuck her arms straight up and waited for Naomi to slip a tunic over her head. The wool smelled freshly-washed sliding over her face so it wasn't hers.

"Don't rush down those stairs, or we'll need a physician for you too."

"Take me down quickly."

By the time they reached the bottom of the steps, Laelia couldn't hear Drusus anymore. "Drusus?"

"He came to for a moment," Otho said. "He tried to move but passed out again. We need to keep him still. He'll do more damage to that arm if he thrashes around."

Laelia held Naomi's hand and edged toward the voice. The warmth of the fire comforted after the cold sponge bath but nothing like knowing Drusus had awoken, if only for a moment.

"Laelia, you and Naomi come and sit beside me."

Lady Pappus' voice was so musical Laelia was sure she must be beautiful. She no longer sounded concerned, but somehow that reassured Laelia rather than chafed.

"Otho has wine and bread for you both, and I want you to tell me what happened, from the beginning."

Naomi guided Laelia to what felt like her spot before. Laelia swept the floor with her hand, found the blankets, and then Drusus' knee. The knobby joint was bare to her touch like earlier. Had they cut his tunic away?

Someone pressed something bulbous into her hand—a wineskin. Laelia let go of Drusus and uncorked the neck. The first swallow of the wine was sweeter than she was accustomed to, and a long guzzle left the skin limp and nearly empty. "Thank you."

"You're welcome."

Otho's voice was beginning to reassure her as much as Drusus or Naomi.

"Now tell us what happened, and why this dagger is so important."

Laelia did, beginning the day she sold it. She told them everything, except the one-sided kiss she and Drusus had shared and the argument because of it.

"You poor child." Lady Pappus took her hand and stroked the top with her thumb. "All evening I've been asking the Lord to help me understand why He had me send Drusus to you. Now I do."

"What do you mean sent to me? My father bought him."

Soft fingers brushed Laelia's cheek in a sweep that reminded her of her mother.

"He didn't buy him. The night before my husband's funeral procession, I was troubled with dreams. My husband had told me at his death, Drusus was to be freed and given the sum my husband set aside for him. I had no wish to defy my husband's wishes but my spirit was so unsettled. I didn't understand until I overheard a man in the street talking about his blind daughter. I knew then Drusus was to go to you. I argued with the Lord but your father was walking away and the gate was closing on my chance to obey. I made a gift of Drusus to him for his daughter. I know it hurt Drusus terribly, and he was already hurting for my husband, as was I. I'd thought he'd been sent to bring you into the light as a follower of our Lord."

"He was," Otho said firmly.

Laelia's pulse quickened. She was surrounded by Christians. "I don't understand." "Otho can tell you everything he knows about our Lord and when He walked the earth," Lady Pappus said. "All I can tell you is, like you, I couldn't fathom the idea of one God. I dismissed Christianity as another strange religion flooding in along with the slaves from our conquered lands. But I couldn't deny the change I saw in Drusus, and he'd found the peace and forgiveness he so desperately needed. When he shared with me how he'd embraced this God, which I now know to be the true God, I claimed his God as my own."

"Laelia," Otho addressed her again, his tone softer, "we serve the one true God. Jupiter, Juno, Aphrodite, Isis, all the others, they are creations of men and the evil one to lead people astray. There is no God but God. Not even Caesar."

"You can't speak against Caesar." She'd come here for sanctuary, not to be in even more danger.

"Caesar is no more a god than you, me or Drusus. Neither are the statues in the temples. There is only one God, and the only way to be restored to him is through the Son, a part of himself He sent in the flesh to pay the debt we brought on ourselves when we disobeyed Him."

"How can I disobey a God I don't even worship?"

"We're born tainted with disobedience. It's in our blood and part of who we are. There is no escaping it. Every act of disobedience required a blood sacrifice, and this is one of many truths twisted by those who worship the false gods. But our God loved us enough to send Jesus Christ, whose perfect blood sacrifice would forever pay the price of our disobedience. But for you to receive His gift, you must believe there is no God but Him, and in Jesus His Son, who paid the price of your disobedience. Jesus was God in the flesh who came to live among men, performing miracles and wonders, and then died to fulfill ages-old prophecies. He was the only perfect and pure sacrifice for the disobedience of all mankind. And here's where the fights begin. On the third day after His death, He rose again, was seen by many, and then ascended into the heavens where He waits until it is time for Him to return and gather to Himself all who believe."

Disobedience of all mankind? Rising from the dead? One God? "I don't understand."

"Which part?" Otho said calmly.

"All of it. No true father would sacrifice his own child. No one would sacrifice himself, especially in a crucifixion, for something he didn't do."

"That's what love does, Laelia. True love."

"No one takes a beating willingly." She certainly never had.

"Drusus did." Otho's voice was gentle. "Had your father known the truth of the dagger, that beating I suspect would have been for you."

Her heart seized and she felt her eyes getting hot.

"You can't see this, but there are no bruises on his knuckles. He never fought back, and long before your father reached him with that lamp stand, Drusus could have killed him with his knives if he'd chosen to."

"Then why didn't he?" Laelia demanded.

"Because your father is his master. Because to do so would have condemned Naomi to death under Roman law as a slave revolt. Drusus sacrificed himself for you because he loves you, as God loves you. As He sacrificed Himself for you through His son."

"Otho, don't speak for Drusus," Lady Pappus said sternly.

"He loves her, Octavia. Drusus cared for Julia but he *loves* Laelia. I've known for some time, and I think she already knows too. Don't you, Laelia?"

Somehow to deny it felt wrong though her instincts begged her to.

"Laelia, you must trust God with Drusus' life, and your own. Can you do that?"

"How?"

"Believe that He is the One, True God. That there are no others. That He became flesh through His Son Jesus Christ who willingly gave himself up for you and rose from the dead to live again."

"I believe," Naomi said eagerly. "When Laelia's father took her to the games, I saw the Christians among the murderers and arsonists executed in the arena. I saw those that died under Nero's reign. I couldn't understand how men, women and children would die instead of denying their God and worshiping Caesar, but now I do. After what Drusus has done for Laelia, I could never deny his God. I want his God to be my God."

Drusus loved her. He'd sacrificed himself at her father's feet to spare her. Given himself up for her as the Christian God had according to His followers. Drusus followed Him. She trusted Drusus more than anyone else in her life, and Drusus followed the Christian God. Otho and Lady Pappus' and now Naomi's God.

"Laelia?" Otho asked again.

"Don't rush her." Lady Pappus' voice was firm.

Laelia tried to smile in gratitude but her heart was too heavy. If Caesar were a god, then why was he mortal? Why did they die? Especially at their own hand or the hand of others if that were true? Gods wouldn't kill themselves. They would kill their enemies. What she would have done. What Drusus should have done. But instead he'd taken the beating that should have been hers. He must love her. And he must love His God to have done so.

"I believe." Laelia raised her head and felt the heaviness in her heart vanish. With conviction in her voice she said it again. "I believe."

"Praise the Lord," Lady Pappus cried out, the phrase being echoed by Otho and the other servants.

"We rejoice and welcome you to the brethren," Otho said. "I know Drusus will be filled with joy when he hears the news."

"Yes, and we will keep praying for him." Lady Pappus had tears in her voice. "We pray God will heal his body and the Lord's will be done. Take my hand."

The woman's slender fingers gripped hers on one side and Naomi on the other. Otho began to beseech their God aloud, and the words flowed through Laelia as the sweet wine had earlier. When the door groaned, Otho fell silent and Laelia listened, hoping and fearing what was coming.

"Master, Scorpio has come." Laelia could recognize Alexander's gravelly voice.

"Send him in."

Footsteps sounded across the floor as Laelia tensed.

"I greet you in the name of our Lord," a new voice said.

Lady Pappus exhaled loudly beside Laelia and Naomi squeezed her hand.

"Likewise, my friend. Please come. Our brother is badly injured."

"Has he woken at all?"

"Only for a moment."

"Have you prayed for him already?"

"Of course."

"Let me check his injuries. You ladies will need to move away and give me room to work please."

Laelia allowed Naomi to pull her away from Drusus. She listened again to the sound of water, and murmurs the doctor made here and there.

"His heartbeat is strong. His breathing isn't, but I think that's the swelling in his nose and jaw. When I tip his head back and open his mouth like this, see how his chest rises and falls?"

Laelia couldn't, but imagined it.

"I'm going to reposition his nose and stitch closed the cuts in his scalp. You managed to stop the bleeding there very well. A lampstand was a veiled blessing. With a club we would have to worry about wood splinters in the wounds."

"Can you splint the arm?" Otho said.

The physician chuckled and Laelia's fear returned. "Splint. Bah. Remember I treat gladiators. I brought a special metal brace he'll have to wear for at least three lunar cycles. I rarely use it because gladiators are very good at not getting their arms broken, but it's worked two of the three times I have. The third might have worked also but the man died from other injuries before the arm had time to mend. The ribs will take longer to heal and have him in more pain than the arm once it's in the brace, but he's young, with good muscle."

"The internal bleeding?"

Laelia frowned as Otho voiced another of her fears.

"If it's there, only God can heal it, and I pray He will. This bruising along here is more likely the muscle wall than the organs. It will look worse before it looks better as more blood reaches the skin. Warm, wet cloths will speed the fading of the bruising and he must rest. He should be flat on his back for a week and not on his feet again until I've examined him again and given consent.

"I'm also going to leave you an opium-based anesthetic that will lessen his pain. Pour a thumbs-worth into water or wine. Wine helps the taste. Give it to him at sunrise and sunset, but only after he's been awake and spoken for a few moments. We want his mind to recover itself, so numbing him with anesthetic isn't a good idea until we know he's still in there. We'll pray and believe in faith that he is. I can tell by those gathered he has many reasons to mend. Do you have any questions for me?"

"No, brother. Only gratitude," Otho said.

"Ladies?"

Laelia shook her head. Lady Pappus said no and expressed her gratitude.

"Then bring me scalding water in a clean vessel and every lamp you have

224

and I'll get to work on our young friend."

The relief flooding Laelia dissolved her bones, and she leaned into Naomi's side. Naomi held her like a child while she listened to the physician work in the quiet sounds all around her. She'd lost everything but Drusus and Naomi. Her home, her coin, and her betrothed. The real Tiberius, not the deceitful flatterer she'd agreed to wed, was nothing to mourn however. Neither was her belief in the fake gods. From the moment she'd embraced Drusus' and Otho's God as her own, she'd felt different too. Her burdens remained, but the oppressive despair gripping her since Drusus' first cry of pain was gone. Their future was still uncertain, her father a dangerous enemy, she still blind with no source of income, but she had friends, and allies, in Otho and Lady Pappus now.

"The straps of the brace must remain tight. He's going to itch and fuss but do not let him loosen them. Water won't hurt the linen padding but it will stink of sweat soon. Keep it as dry as possible or the mildew will worsen the smell. I don't want to bind his ribs yet because it will hamper his breathing. If I'm able to slip away tomorrow morning, I'll check on him again. Otherwise I'll come in the evening once my duties at the school are finished."

"Thank you, and please take this," Lady Pappus said.

Laelia wished she had something to pay her back with. She hated feeling indebted to others.

"I cannot. My wife would banish me from our home if she knew I'd taken coin from the Lady Pappus. Forgive me, my lady, but I recognized your pearl ring."

"Is your wife named Rebekah?"

"The same, my lady. She served you until you freed her five years ago."

"I wondered why your name sounded familiar to me. She spoke of you often. I'm glad to know you married."

"We have a son named Augustus after your husband, and if we have a daughter, she will be called Octavia."

"You do me much honor. Please tell her to visit, and bring the children. Our brethren gather at my villa on Fridays, when it's safe to do so."

"I'll see she does, my lady, and prays for Drusus. She told me often of his kind deeds to her."

"Thank you."

The physician left, and Otho built up the fire and brought blankets to cover Drusus. Lady Pappus would sleep in the upper room, because night had already fallen and even with servants Otho didn't want her traveling the streets. Otho would sleep near the front door, at his insistence, and Laelia would remain beside Drusus, at hers.

Naomi fixed her a pallet they would share. Laelia pillowed her head with her arm and listened as one by one sounds died away until the crackling of the fire and Naomi's gentle snores remained. The night was quiet except for the occasional muffled voice or oxen lowing as the carts passed outside to restock the booths for tomorrow's shoppers.

She folded the blanket draped over her back and slid away from Naomi. When her snores failed to pause, Laelia searched out the other blanket. She found the wool and slipped her hand beneath the edge to touch him. Smooth skin, warm and taut, and a gentle pass up and down told her she'd located his upper arm, almost on instinct. This was his left arm, not the one she usually held. She traced the curve of his muscle to his shoulder, along his rigid collarbone, and let her hand drift to the shallow valley of his chest. The heat of his body was stronger there, but it was the slow rise and fall beneath her palm that wrapped her in comfort.

A deeper longing filled her, shrouded in warning. Everyone was asleep, and he would never remember this stolen moment, enough her yearning won the battle. Mindful of his broken ribs, she pushed his blanket back to bare his chest, shifted beside him and lowered her head. Her ear came to rest where her hand had been, and the soft, steady beat of his heart warmed her more than any fire ever had. The sound was so much like his familiar gait the corner of her mouth tilted in the seed of a smile. Only a few more moments, then she needed to return to her own pallet. But the muffled rhythm soothed her like a lullaby, and she couldn't bring herself to leave the expanse of his chest she'd leaned into so many times—or the sound of his heart, as constant as the man surrounding it.

Chapter 28

Drusus blinked, but couldn't see anything. Only one of his eyelids moved. The other hurt, like his head, his jaw, his side, and his arm. Heaviness pressed his chest, making it hard to breathe. Tinges of urine tainted the air, but he was breathing.

He flexed his toes and they moved. His fingers moved, but his right arm screamed in fury. He tipped his head forward to see what held him down, fighting the pain in his head and neck. The light of a weak fire revealed a head on his chest and the curve of a slender hip silhouetted against the flames. He'd admired that curve from every angle, and the hand that rested precisely where it always did could only belong to Laelia.

She was safe.

Thank you, Lord.

"Laelia." Like his eyesight, his voice was only half there, a garbled whisper. His head sank back into what felt like thick folds of cloth. He nudged her with his trapped arm. After a few tries, she stirred, and then sat straight up, blocking the small amount of light from the fire in the hearth behind her.

"Drusus?" she whispered.

Speaking would require far too much effort. He slid his hand to her knee, grateful the small movement didn't add to his pain. He needed to see her, and make sure she hadn't been hurt, but she was between him and the faint light source. She took his hand between both of hers, and he squeezed her fingers.

She lowered her head and kissed the back of his hand. A heavy sigh shuddered through her and she held the back of his hand to her cheek. After a few breaths, easier to draw now, what could only be tears wet his knuckles. He turned his hand in hers and caressed her damp cheek with his fingertips. The skin felt smooth and unbroken, but he needed to be certain.

"Are...you...hurt?" The question required as much effort as breathing had a moment ago.

"No." Her voice was firm, like the way she squeezed his hand again. "No, I'm not hurt. Nor is Naomi. She's here with us."

"Where..." Where was her father? And who had carried him into the kitchen?

"We're at Otho's. You're safe now."

Otho's?

"Is he awake?"

That was Naomi's voice, and another silhouette emerged beside Laelia.

"Yes. Wake Otho and Lady Pappus."

Lady Pappus was here?

"How..." He coughed, and his right side punished him mercilessly. Suppressing the groan with a few deep breaths hurt almost as much as the cough. Ribs must be broken.

"Drusus, do you know who I am and where you are?"

He would know Otho's voice anywhere. "Yes."

"Your right arm is broken and is fastened in a metal sleeve to help it heal. You have broken ribs, a broken nose, and two wounds in your scalp that were sewn shut. If you can stay awake for a little while, we can give you something for the pain."

His arm was broken. His right arm. His throwing arm. Oh, God. Tiberius would make good on his threat to hurt Laelia and Julia, and he was in no condition to protect them.

A new light spread above him and Lady Pappus appeared, holding a lamp.

"Lady..."

"Shhh." She handed the lamp to Naomi. "You need to rest. Do not fear for Laelia and Naomi. They are both well and Otho is taking excellent care of them." Lady Pappus knelt beside him and ran her fingers through the hair

228

above his forehead. "Can you take a little water?"

He'd been accustomed to being the center of attention before, but never as an invalid. Otho placed his hand beneath Drusus' head and raised it. Lady Pappus put a cup to his lips and he managed a few sips of lukewarm water before Otho lowered his head. Swallowing had been too much work and keeping his eye open was becoming a struggle. He wanted to go back to sleep with Laelia's head against his chest. He would need sleep before he could figure out what could be done to protect her from Tiberius.

Lady Pappus stroked his forehead, but she was looking at Laelia. "Tell him, Laelia. He'll rest much better if he knows."

Laelia frowned and rubbed the back of his hand. "Tiberius was here."

He knows.

"He cancelled our betrothal."

Through his own fog of pain he could imagine what Tiberius had said and done to Laelia. What her father had done when he learned of the broken arrangement. "I'm sorry."

She squeezed his hand, her brow furrowing. "I'm not."

"Nor are we," Otho said. "But that's not what the Lady wanted you to tell him."

Whatever it was, it needed to be soon. His mind yielded to his weariness with every breath. He squeezed her hand again and his eye closed without permission.

"Your God is now my God, Drusus. Naomi claims Him as well."

Laelia and Naomi believed. The relief sweeping over him like a tidal wave did nothing for the pain in his body. It was far more merciful. Their eternal fates were sealed forever in Christ. For that alone, every blow and broken bone had been worth it.

Someone pulled a blanket over him and squeezed his arm through the thick wool.

"Sleep now," a voice said, but he couldn't pick it out because he was already slipping back into the sweet relief of sleep.

It took a long moment for Laelia to recall why she was sleeping on a hard floor and held someone's hand in her own. She slid her fingers free of Drusus', grateful they were still warm, and hoped no one had seen. Sitting up highlighted the aches in her back and neck.

"Good morning." He took her hand in his again, with a firmer grip than before.

"How are you?"

"Otho says my face looks like the pulp at the bottom of a wine press. I think he's jealous of all the attention I'm getting from beautiful women."

She bit her lip while her head and her heart warred. He'd never said she was beautiful before—because he shouldn't.

"Ignore him, Laelia." Otho was nearby. "The opium has washed away the small measure of restraint he had over his mouth."

Laelia withdrew her hand from Drusus' hold, though she had to pull firmly to do so. He actually had excellent restraint over his mouth. She knew that better than anyone. But how had she slept through him taking medicine, and entire conversations? "What time is it?"

"A little while after sunrise. Lady Pappus has gone to her villa but will return this evening. Now that you're awake my servants can erect a partition so you, Drusus and Naomi can have a small measure of privacy while we work."

"You should have woken me sooner." She hated being an inconvenience, especially after everything Otho had done, and was still doing, for them.

"Drusus wouldn't let me," Naomi muttered. "Even mangled he still manages to act like he's the head servant."

Laelia grinned and touched his arm. "She's glad you're feeling better."

"Whatever they made me drink has me not feeling much of anything, except the urge to help Otho fill his trough."

"Drusus." Otho's reprimand was sharp. "Forgive him, Lady. As I said, it must be the opium. He doesn't usually have the manners of a goose."

Naomi chuckled, and Laelia leaned down, close to where his head should be. "They were nicer when they thought you were dying."

"I still might, if I don't relieve myself soon."

She managed to swallow her embarrassment by biting her lip. She hadn't always been blind and the baths taught her what Naomi and the statues had not. If Otho knew the direction her thoughts had taken, she would get the scolding.

"Come, Mistress." Naomi grabbed her upper arm and tugged her to her feet.

"Go on, Laelia," Otho urged. "I'd hate for you to be here when he has to sit up. He might say more things a lady has no business hearing."

Naomi led Laelia to the front. The door opened and the cacophony of sound grew in strength. "It's already busy."

"We'll go for a short walk."

The prospect of walking a crowded street with Naomi made Laelia cringe. Navigating a crowd and maintaining a smooth pace or adequate space in the path for both of them abreast wasn't something Naomi did well. What Drusus could do was a gift. He was a gift. Not from her father, but from the gods—God. A gift she'd almost lost last night.

"Do you want to talk about it?" Laelia was able to pick out Naomi's question through the barking of a very agitated dog. A large dog, judging by the deep, throaty sound to her left front.

"He sounded better this morning." Laelia tightened her grip on Naomi's hand and tried to match her erratic pace.

"I meant Tiberius."

His name swirled in her mind like the stench of a sewer. "There's nothing to talk about. He meant to use me to get what he wanted. No wonder he and father got along so well." The smell of baking bread wafted toward her, making her stomach tighten. Drusus loved that smell. His pace always slowed ever so slightly when they would pass through the wheat and yeast aroma. "Do you have any coin?"

"No, why?"

"I wanted to get Drusus some fresh bread. And he needs peppermint leaf, but I don't know where to buy that." It didn't matter if Naomi did, because all Laelia possessed were the sandals on her feet and the tunic on her back. Then she remembered not even the tunic was hers.

"He needs more than peppermint leaf. So do we."

"I know."

"Laelia?" A woman's voice called her name.

Naomi jarred Laelia to a stumbling halt beside her.

"Laelia Ricarri?"

"Do I know you?"

"It's Julia, slave of Tiberius Cina. Where is Drusus?"

Laelia's free hand crumpled a piece of the borrowed tunic at her side. "Why do you ask?" She hoped the frost in her voice matched the glare she was trying to project.

"I overheard Tiberius last night. Is he going to be all right?"

The concern in the woman's voice thawed Laelia's jealousy. "He was badly injured but we believe he'll recover."

"Thank the gods," Julia said in a rush. "Could I see him? I went by your house but no one answered there so I came here. It's the only place I thought he would be."

"No one answered at Master Ricarri's house?" Naomi asked.

"No." Julia's short answer quavered and Laelia inclined her ear more toward the voice. That dog needed to stop barking so she could hear more than the words.

"What are you hiding?" Naomi asked.

"Nothing."

Julia had answered too quickly, and Laelia didn't need to see her face to know she was lying. "What's wrong?"

"She's hiding something," Naomi said, putting her arm around Laelia's waist and pulling her flush to her side. "She keeps looking away and plucking at the wool of her tunic, which is far too revealing already. I don't trust her. I don't trust anyone associated with that wretch Tiberius."

Neither did Laelia.

"Please. I just want to see him. Then I'll never bother you again, I swear by Caesar. Please, I don't have much time."

Every reason Laelia had to tell her no couldn't be molded into an excuse. The more she tried, the more she saw her reasons for saying no were all selfish.

Something Drusus was not, nor would he approve of. "If Otho allows it, so will I."

"Thank you. May Jupiter repay your kindness."

"Are you sure?" Naomi squeezed her hand in dissent.

Not at all, but it was too late now. "Yes. Take us back, and make sure it's safe to enter before doing so."

The return walk to Otho's seemed to take half the time. Naomi left them at the door and instinctively Laelia found the wall to rest her hand against while they waited.

"For what it's worth, I would give up my sight to trade places with you."

Julia had spoken so softly, Laelia barely heard her. "To be free of Tiberius?"

"To be with Drusus."

Naomi had been right. This was a bad idea. It also occurred to her she hadn't thought to ask, or have Naomi ask, Drusus' permission.

"You can come in," Naomi called. "Otho had to give him more opium, so he's sleeping. You can see him, but don't wake him."

"Thank you."

The tears audible in Julia's voice washed away more of Laelia's jealousy. She wished it hadn't. It was easier to be angry at Julia than pity her. Naomi took Laelia's hand and led her forward. Thankfully she didn't have to find her own way to follow Julia. She wasn't leaving her alone with him, even asleep.

"I can only give her a few moments before the servants will begin arriving with the soiled wash. He faded so quickly I doubt the sound of them treading in the troughs will wake him, but I'll make sure they don't carry on like they usually do. The partition will do nothing for noise, but will keep customers and anyone else from asking questions."

"Thank you, Otho. I don't know what we would do without your kindness."

"You'll never need to find out."

Laelia nodded in gratitude and took another step forward. Naomi led her toward the back again, pausing to push aside some type of curtain that still tangled Laelia. When she was free of the cloth, she let go of Naomi and sank to the floor with her legs crossed. "Naomi, would you leave us, please?"

She didn't answer, nor did cloth rustle or sandaled feet pad across the floor. Laelia hated to order her away, but it was within her right to do so and she needed to speak with Julia alone. Naomi would probably take two steps on the other side of the curtain and stop, but she needed at least the illusion of privacy. "Naomi, leave us."

"Yes, Mistress."

She waited a few moments, but it was Julia that spoke first.

"What did Drusus do that your father thought he deserved this?"

"He was protecting me."

For a long moment, Laelia listened to the other woman breathe, and occasionally snivel. When Laelia felt she'd stopped, or at least composed herself, she ventured something she'd wondered since they'd stood outside. "Did you know Tiberius was only marrying me to get Drusus?"

"Yes."

That stung, but at least Julia wasn't the liar her master was.

"I thought you knew."

"I thought he cared for me."

"You had something he wanted."

She didn't know how to answer that. Tiberius had had something she wanted to, in a way.

"Drusus was never selfish the way Tiberius is," Julia said. "It's what makes letting him go so hard."

In the long silence that followed, a sudden kinship with this woman formed in place of the jealousy. The same woman she'd so often wished into oblivion since learning of her.

"He's terrified of spiders, though he'll never admit it. Don't ask him to kill one or he'll do it with one of the twins from across the room. When he's sick, don't bother trying to make him rest or see a healer. He won't until he's ready."

Laelia recognized the olive branch for what it was. "Thank you."

"One more thing." Julia paused for a long moment. "I mean no disrespect, but I've seen the way he looks at you. Someday you might... you should know, I mean, if..."

"What?"

"When he wakes from a bad dream, don't ask him what it was about. Just hold him until he's ready to talk about it. Sometimes he won't, but if he does don't let go of him until he's finished. Humming the river song and stroking his hair will help him fall back asleep."

While it chafed Julia would know such a thing, Laelia forced herself to be grateful she'd been given a glimpse of Drusus that, while painful, she would never have known otherwise. "Thank you."

A stew of mingled voices gained strength on her right side until among the low murmur of voices, Laelia recognized Alexander's among them.

"I should leave now," Julia said. "Thank you for allowing me to see him."

"I wish there was something I could do for you." Oddly enough, Laelia found she meant it.

"You can. Take care of him. Should his arm heal, don't let it be known. Unlike me, Tiberius isn't used to not getting what he wants. He was in the worst drunken rage I've ever seen last night."

"Are you in danger?"

"Not as much as your father. Tiberius blames him completely. Be careful."

"Thank you."

As Julia left, she thanked Otho over the soft splashing of the servants who'd begun their work in the troughs.

"She had a lot to say," Naomi said in a huff.

It took her a moment, but Laelia found Drusus' shoulder, then his hand, and held it in her own. "It needed to be said. I think she'll be all right now."

"Will you?"

"When he is."

"Then let me bring you the meal Otho's servant left for you so you can keep your strength up for both of you."

"Thank you." That seemed a tamer reply than "Yes, Mother," though in moments like these Laelia couldn't help but think of Naomi that way. She hoped her own mother would understand, and forgive her. For allowing Naomi to fill that void. And for falling in love with a slave.

Chapter 29

Waking up to Laelia was a pleasure Drusus couldn't afford to grow accustomed to. Her profile as she and Naomi ground fuller's clay together almost lessened the pain aching from navel to nose. He could do precious little for most of it, other than his stomach. "Can I have some bread?"

Laelia's face turned toward his as she dropped the large stone she'd been grinding with in the bowl. "You're awake again. I was getting worried."

"How long did I sleep this time?"

"Past midday meal." She cocked her head to the side, and scooted toward him on the floor. "Your voice is hoarse. Are you thirsty?"

"Yes. And hungry."

A curtain he hadn't noticed until it was drawn back flashed to his right. Alexander, Splash and two other slaves were treading in the troughs behind Otho, who stared down at Drusus with his arms crossed. "How are you?"

"Hungry."

"I saved you two boiled eggs. I'll mash it up for you like I did my son when he was a baby and my father when he was an old man. I might even let one of these two beautiful women spoon it for you."

Drusus turned toward them, and between Laelia's grin and Naomi's eyes as wide as cart wheels, he couldn't help but chuckle. The agony in his ribs turned the chuckle to a moan in less than a breath, and stole the smile from Laelia's face.

She settled her hand on his stomach and bit her lower lip. "You're in pain."

"A little."

Otho huffed as he walked past. "You know what God says about lying."

"I don't, but I want to." Naomi rose and followed Otho into the back room.

From the tilt of Laelia's head, she was listening for their footsteps. After a moment, she leaned down toward his face and her hair spilled over her shoulder so the ends grazed his bare chest above the edge of the blanket resting across his middle. His hunger was instantly forgotten.

"I think Naomi is fond of Otho," she whispered.

It made sense. They were near in age from what he could tell with similar dispositions. "Has your father come?"

"No. Every time I hear a new voice, I fear it's the soldiers. Or worse, he'll come for us himself."

He took her hand, wanting to tell her everything would turn out well and he wouldn't let anything happen to her. That he would protect her from Tiberius and from her father. But it wasn't a promise he could make. Rather, it was not one he could keep, because so much was beyond his power. He'd made that mistake with Julia, and wouldn't repeat it with Laelia. "Pray with me."

She bit her lower lip for two breaths. "I don't know how."

"Didn't you—" Talking required so much air. He drew a deeper breath, as slow as he could to spare his ribs. "Pray to the idols before?"

"Are the stone gods idols?"

"Yes."

"Sometimes."

"It's not so different, except the true God hears you. In time you'll learn to hear Him too."

"He'll speak to me?"

"Not the way I am now, but yes. Do you want to pray with me?"

"Yes. What should I do?"

"I'll start, and then when I squeeze your hand, tell God what you need, or are thankful for, or whatever you want to say."

"All right." She squared her shoulders and drew up straight as if going into battle. She was so beautiful. For a moment he forgot everything but her.

"Drusus?"

"Sorry." This time, he didn't close his eyes. Well, his eye. The other one was still swollen shut. "God, thank you for sparing my life. For the kindness of my brothers and sisters in the brethren, and that Laelia and Naomi know you as Lord."

Another slow deep breath gave him a moment to decide how to phrase the next part. He hadn't told her yet, but he would have to go back. Not only did the law of Rome require it, but so did the Lord. "Protect us from harm. Help us to do what we must, and give us strength for the journey to come."

Drusus squeezed her hand, savoring the feel of the fingers in his. She sat quietly without speaking for a while, so he squeezed again.

"Don't rush me." She bit her lip and her brow furrowed. "He's called God? He doesn't have his own name?"

"He has a name. Several, but for right now you can just call him God. He's the only real one anyway so He'll know you're addressing Him."

Her forehead smoothed and her mouth softened. "God, I'm Laelia Ricarri. I don't mean to offend you by praying without making an offering at your temple first. I don't know where it is yet."

Drusus didn't have the breath or the desire to interrupt her and explain they were the temples. Instead, he rubbed the back of her fingers with his thumb enjoying this moment he didn't think would ever come.

"Otho says you loved me enough to sacrifice your Son… your Son…" She bit her lip again. "Excuse me." She leaned down so her chin was almost on his chest. "What's his Son's name again?" she whispered.

"Jesus."

She mouthed *thank you* and he had to bite his own lip to keep from laughing.

Laelia straightened and cleared her throat. "Your Son Jesus so that I could worship you and know you as the true God." She leaned down toward him again. "Is that right?" she whispered.

"Yes," he said, and squeezed her hand. In all fairness, his first prayers two years ago hadn't been so different from hers. His momentary amusement at the way she thought God couldn't hear her whispers vanished with the sheer joy she now prayed to the one true God.

A lock of her hair tangled on her lip as she straightened again, and she wiped it away with her free hand. "We need help. Please heal Drusus' arm so he can use it again. But not so good Tiberius will try to take him again. Please keep my father away." She paused here for a long time. "And keep Julia safe."

She prayed for Julia. Whom he knew she didn't like, or rather what Julia had been to him once. Laelia's faith was barely a day old and already she followed Christ closer than many among the brethren. And he'd almost laughed at her. *Lord, forgive me.*

"I hear very well, so if—I mean, when I'm not sleeping. So if you would like to speak to me, God, I'm listening."

"Well done, lady," a slave called from the troughs.

Alexander slapped him in the back. "You don't intrude on another's private prayers, you idiot."

The slave recovered and sent water splashing as he shoved Alexander in the chest.

Otho's head slave shoved him back and the man almost fell. "And you're supposed to turn the other cheek."

"You hit me in the shoulder, not the cheek."

"I'll hit you again if you don't—"

"That's enough." Otho swept into the room with a bowl in his hands. "Get back to work and leave these two alone." He knelt on Drusus' other side and as hungry as Drusus was, the white and yellow mush in the bowl looked like roasted venison.

He could move his hand and arm that weren't on his injured side, but as tired as speaking made him, he would be too exhausted to make more than two or three trips from the bowl to his mouth. "Where is Naomi?"

"Scrubbing my tiny kitchen. I think she almost fainted when she saw it."

Laelia's face wrinkled in the start of a chuckle, and then immediately smoothed. "Apologies if she was disrespectful. In my home, she has quite a free rein." She smoothed a non-existent wrinkle from the wool of her tunic. "Of course, I don't know where home is now, for any of us."

Otho's gaze cut to Drusus. "She doesn't know?"

Drusus sighed, the deeper breath sending a spike of pain into his side. "No. Not yet."

Otho frowned and his gaze returned to Laelia. "One day at a time, my lady. For now I need to fold another blanket, and when I've helped Drusus sit up a bit, I need you to shove it under his shoulders. Can you do that?"

"I'll try."

She let go of Drusus' hand and only then did he realize she hadn't pulled it away in Otho's presence.

"You aren't going to like this, but I can't risk you choking." Otho folded the blanket many times until it resembled a thick pillow. He handed it to Laelia, who knelt closer to Drusus' head. "I'm going to put my hands under your arms and lift you toward me. It will hurt less if you don't try to help me."

Drusus swallowed and gave a small nod.

"Ready?"

"Yes." Laelia held the folded blanket near and Otho slid his hands which were cold like snow into the crevices of Drusus' underarms and pulled.

He tried to stay relaxed, but it felt like he was being kicked in his side again. His stomach muscles clenched which only intensified the burn in his side. The whimper he could hear must be coming from his own throat as his face rested inches from Otho's chest and Laelia shoved the blanket underneath him.

Otho lowered him quickly, which hurt the same.

Laelia's hand went to his shoulder. "I'm sorry."

"I'm all right." Drusus hoped she wouldn't pick up on the grimace coloring his tone and glared at Otho with his good eye, daring him to make some remark about lying.

But he'd already picked up the bowl of mashed egg. "Laelia, will you feed him?"

"Me?"

"Sitting him up will have worn him out and I don't think he should move too much until Scorpio sees him again. He's supposed to be resting and I have work to do. Put your hands out."

She held up her hands, and Drusus wondered if Otho saw the tremor in them. If he did, he didn't comment and set the bowl between her hands and let go.

"Thank you, and don't worry about making a mess. Naomi will have something to do when she's done with my kitchen. If that's before the new moon." He laughed as he rose and drew the curtain closed behind him. "Tread faster, men. I want a head start on the linens from the Tarquinius villa."

Laelia stared at the bowl between her hands as if it were a dead bird. "How am I supposed to do this?"

He raised his hand to take it from her but Otho was right. That simple movement taxed him more than it should and he let his hand drop back at his side. It took him a moment to figure out the way, and he was so hungry he almost told her. But once he recovered and returned to her father's villa as he must, she would need the confidence to do even more alone. "You can figure it out without me."

She stared down at the bowl in her hands a long while. The whole time he imagined how that boiled egg would taste, and help ease at least one of his pains. Long enough he almost gave in and told her what to do. But her brows shot up and she scooted close enough to him her knee touched his arm. She set the bowl on her lap, between her folded legs, and found the spoon with her left hand. With her right she touched his shoulder, and slow enough to give him a different kind of hunger, she followed his collarbone to his neck until her fingers rested on his chin.

Just as he'd thought, she kept contact with his chin with her free hand to remain oriented to his mouth, the bowl's position would remain constant in her lap, and she held the spoon in what would be her free hand. "Well done, Laelia."

She smiled. "We'll see. Well, you will." She laughed and put a spoonful of mashed egg to his lips. He swallowed the cool, slick bits without chewing, determined to try to satisfy his belly as he couldn't satisfy any other part of him still making its hunger known.

They both did well. She only spilled three spoon-fulls and put another up his nose. The violent fit of snorting and coughing that followed felt as if his ribs were ripping through the flesh and the bones were grinding together in that heavy brace that was too hot and too tight.

Naomi came and took over, though Drusus wished she hadn't. He'd been savoring Laelia's fingertips so near his lips, but more than that he didn't want her to lose her confidence. But watching her roll her head side to side and massage her neck told him he wasn't the only one suffering discomfort. Discomfort that turned to panic when the soft splashing he'd been hearing all day through the curtain stopped.

"Can I help you, soldier?" Otho called out.

Chapter 30

Laelia couldn't breathe. The curtain wouldn't protect them and they had nowhere else to flee.

"We seek Laelia Ricarri. Is she here?" The voice matched the image in Laelia's mind of the soldier—hard and unyielding.

"Who is asking?" Otho was trying to buy her time, but for what?

Think, Laelia. Think!

"That's our concern, fuller. Is she here or not?"

A hand clamped over Laelia's mouth, crushing her lips against her teeth and snapping her head back.

"I'll be right out." Naomi's shout right beside Laelia's ear pained her almost as much as her hand covering her mouth. "If this goes badly, little one," she whispered, "run and don't turn back."

She shook her head no and tugged at Naomi's wrist still against her mouth.

"You must. Hide until one of Otho's slaves can take you to safety. You must."

Naomi's hand released her mouth and she started to her knees when a strong hand grabbed her wrist. Drusus.

"I'm Laelia Ricarri," Naomi said.

Laelia covered her own mouth now as tears burned. It was too late to stop them.

Drusus' grip on her wrist loosened and he entwined their fingers, but for once she found no comfort in his touch.

"You're older than we expected."

Someone chuckled through the splashing in the troughs that resumed.

"I hear that from every man my father introduces me too, so it no longer offends me. To what do I owe the honor of your visit?"

"Where are your two slaves?"

"I sent them to the baths."

"It would seem Fortuna does not favor your family at the moment, my lady. I bring bad tidings, I'm afraid."

He'd said my lady. They believed Naomi. But was that good?

"A patrolling soldier found your father in a sewer this morning. He'd been robbed and beaten."

Drusus' grip on her hand tightened.

"Is he dead?"

Naomi sounded every bit the fearful daughter, but Laelia hoped for their sakes he was.

"No, my lady. He's badly beaten and unable to walk but told us we should bring word to you here. Now we've done so, we'll be on our way."

"May I offer you some wine before you go?" Otho asked.

"Thank you, fuller, but we'll pass. Long live Caesar."

"Long live Caesar," Naomi and Otho echoed.

When Laelia was certain they'd departed, her fear quieted enough to notice Drusus' grip on her hand was painfully tight. She flexed her fingers and he eased it, but didn't release her. How did her father know they would be here? And he must have returned home to find them gone before he was attacked and it couldn't be a coincidence he'd been attacked last night. Tiberius. Julia's warning, the memory of his anger, Laelia's gut, all told her somehow he was responsible.

Cloth rustled and footsteps swirled around her.

Drusus stroked the back of her hand with his thumb. "It's all right. It's Naomi and Otho."

"Do you think it's a trap?" Naomi asked.

"If it is, what would he gain by it?"

Otho's question was one Laelia was still trying to figure out herself. It would have made more sense to have them arrested and her father had never been one to show mercy. "It doesn't matter. I don't think the soldiers would have lied so we're safer for the moment right here." "What of your father?"

At least Naomi's question was one Laelia already had an answer for. "The soldiers have dispatched their message and will have no reason to return."

"You would leave him to die?" There was no mistaking the disapproval in Otho's voice. She turned her gaze directly into Otho's voice. "Yes."

A heavy sigh followed her answer. Who did it belong to?

"We cannot," Otho said flatly.

"Of course you can. My father is nothing to you. Look what he did to Drusus." To say nothing of the countless bumps, bruises, and cruel words he'd spent on her.

"She'll understand it more if it comes from you, Drusus."

Again Drusus' thumb caressed the back of her hand for a moment before his grasp tightened. "Your father is still my master, Laelia."

"Not after what he's done. I don't care what the law says."

"God requires I obey him, regardless of what he's done."

Laelia ripped her hand from his. "Then your God is unjust and I will no longer worship Him. My father deserves to die for what he's done. To you, me, my real fa—" She strangled the last word from escaping.

"Then you should have left me to die too."

That was a foolish thing to think, much less say. They were nothing alike. "Why?"

"I've killed a man."

"That's different."

"No it isn't."

"Yes it is. I'll hear no more of this." She was thirsty, tired, and angry.

"Laelia, please. There's much you don't know —"

"I know enough. This discussion is over, Drusus. *I command it.*" The words sickened her in her ears as much as on her tongue, but she would not allow this.

"My lady, you are free to do as you like, and are still welcome here as long as you need. But I must go and check on your father and see what can be done for him," Otho said calmly.

The men in this room had to have sprouted long ears and a tail. If they weren't going to consign her father to a fate he'd created, she would have to do it herself. "Then I'm going with you."

"No." Drusus grabbed her wrist. "No."

She pulled from his grip, though it took more effort than she would have thought as injured as he was. "Make up your mind. We leave him or we don't."

"I won't let any harm come to her, Drusus," Otho said.

"Nor will I. She stays," Drusus said.

"I'll go with her," Naomi said.

"No."

"I'm going with you," Naomi argued.

Laelia's teeth ground together like cart wheels on stone. Drusus and Naomi cared for her, as she cared for them, but they were still her slaves. Slaves were supposed to serve and obey. And then she saw it. Saw it as they did. Curse Drusus' honor and his God—their God's rules. She put her fists to her eyes for a long moment and released a deep, shuddering sigh.

"Laelia?" Drusus asked.

She couldn't listen to him anymore. She couldn't hear that deep, strong voice that always brought her as much assurance as the safety of his side. Because right now it wasn't deep and strong. It was unsure and afraid, like she was.

"Enough." Laelia rose to her feet. "We go now, or not at all. And I'll need Otho to lead me please."

"Of course. I'll bring two of my servants as well."

Something pressed the top of her sandal. Drusus?

"Be careful. Please. I can't—" He didn't finish.

"Can't what?" She held her breath, heedless of everyone around her but the man at her feet.

Live without you. "Please be careful."

Drusus could bear to be parted from her, had prepared for it when she'd been betrothed to another man. But only because he believed she would be safe, protected. Not going straight into a lion's mouth without him.

Her expectant expression fell and he forced himself to let her sandal go. He turned his gaze to Otho, who towered over him beside Naomi. "I'm trusting you to bring her back unharmed. Inside and out."

Otho frowned and took Laelia's elbow. "She's not the only one who still needs to learn. You have yet to trust God more than your own strength, even when you have none."

That was hard to hear, because of the truth in it that hit as solid as the lampstand had.

And Otho wasn't finished. "Pray for us. And her father. And for whatever has detained Lady Pappus and the physician."

He had plenty of praying he needed to do. "I will."

One by one they passed out of his field of vision. Otho called Alexander and another servant to accompany them and dismissed the others for the evening. One was dispatched to Lady Pappus' to make certain she was well, and another to sit with him and tend his needs until they returned. He needed a great many things, but above all was for Laelia to return safely.

Father in Heaven, protect them. Take the hate and anger for my enemies from my heart, so that I may show them the love you have shown me. Give me strength to honor You so she sees You in me, as I have seen You in Otho. Make my desires Yours. Please. Stronger, Lord. Stronger.

"I didn't think you'd come." There was pain in the breathiness of her father's voice.

"I didn't want to." The stench of urine and waste was stronger in her father's room than in the fuller shop and made her eyes water. It must be true he couldn't move.

"Where's Drusus?"

"What do you care? You almost killed him."

"I'm sorry."

"Sorry?" Her crossed arms fell to her sides and she planted her feet. "Because you need us now? How did it feel to lay here wondering if you were going to starve to death as I've done for years? Or to feel in your own body the pain you've so freely given me and now Drusus?"

"I'm sorry. I—"

"Stop saying that." Her fists clenched and her voice became as strong as the anger running through her.

Naomi took hold of her arm above her fist. "Laelia, calm yourself."

Laelia jerked free. "Leave me alone." This was between her and her father. Otho would probably interfere also if she hadn't told him to wait in the atrium with his two servants.

"Tiberius' lied to me. To both of us. It was his men that attacked me."

Even now, he failed to see he'd done this to himself. Nothing was ever his fault. Why should it be when there was always someone else to blame?

"I don't feel sorry for you."

"I hoped if I showed you mercy in not reporting Drusus and Naomi to the authorities, that you would repay my kindness."

"Your kindness?" She crept closer to the sound of his voice, the stench in her nostrils gaining strength. "Your *kindness*? You beat the only man who has ever protected me. You were the thief, not him. That coin was mine. I'd sold mother's dagger to feed us and in secret Drusus earned it back for me, and never asked anything in return, except for you to stop when you were breaking his bones for it."

Remembering Drusus' cries of pain beneath her father's brutality set free the tears in her eyes. They made a wet path down her cheek, across skin her father had slapped countless times.

"The gods have punished me enough, Laelia. I'll never walk again. Please help me. You're my daughter."

"No I'm not." She let the silent echoes of her words hang between them. "Or have you forgotten? You think the gods punished you, but they didn't. They're a lie, like your kindness is a lie. So know it's not them punishing you for what you've done. It's me."

For a long moment, all she could hear was her own breathing, still heavy and fast from her anger. She waited for her father to speak, but instead of the pleas she hoped for, he began to weep. The sniffs and muted sobs of his sorrow should be something she reveled in, so why were they breaking her anger into shards like the tile? Why?

She turned around and moved toward the hall. Her elbow banged the edge of the doorframe but she hurried on.

"Mistress, wait for me."

Laelia couldn't wait for Naomi. She was somewhere in the hall when she finally skid to a stop. She retched, her stomach in upheaval as much as her mind, and the coughing and spitting afterward only made it worse.

"Is there wine here?" Otho must have come near to her to sound so loud.

"In the kitchen, that way." Naomi took Laelia's arm. "Come Mistress, sit on the bench."

Laelia collapsed onto the cushions and felt more tears coming. Naomi wrapped her arm around Laelia and sat beside her. Laelia buried her face in Naomi's neck and cried like a child. She cried for her mother, her father—both of them—and for Drusus. She cried for her blindness, for the lies she'd believed from Tiberius and for the death of her dreams of marriage and a family. How long she spent herself in grief she didn't know.

When the tears subsided, her eyes burned and nose clogged. But inside, she felt better, as if she'd cried out the years of fear and despair. She would never have to fear her father again. Now everyone in the Ricarri family, what was left of it, was a cripple.

"I have a cup of wine, my lady." Otho's voice, but from… below her?

"Where are you?"

"Sitting at your feet. Here's the cup." He placed the clay cup in her hand, making sure her grip was firm before letting go. "My servants have cleaned and seen to your father. With your permission, I'll leave one of them to attend him, but he's going to need a physician. Both his knees are badly injured and likely broken."

"I'll stay with him," Naomi said. "He isn't going to hurt anyone, Laelia, and I know he would rather have me than a stranger."

Laelia drank every drop of wine in the clay cup. It helped her throat, but not her problem.

"You saw what he did to Drusus. What he would have done to me."

"I know, but Laelia, you can't see him." Naomi's voice changed in pitch. "If you could, you would know he's not that man anymore."

Otho took the cup from her, and held her hands in his. They were big and strong like Drusus, but rougher. "I know it is not an easy thing to give mercy, but it's what we are asked to do because we have been given mercy by God through Jesus. The harder it is to give mercy, the more God will help you, and the more He will honor it. I know this to be true."

"How?"

"Because today I break bread and pray with the man who killed my son. That's only possible with God. He will help you if you ask, even if you have to ask every day, sometimes every hour."

"You have a son?"

"I had a son. He died for refusing to burn incense to Caesar. A praetorian guard killed him. Today he is one of my closest brothers in the Lord. You will meet him in time."

"I don't want to."

"He isn't the wrongs he has done. No more than Drusus or I am."

"I need to get back to him." And away from here.

"Then allow me take you back. I'll leave one of my servants here with Naomi to assist with your father and send a physician to try to do something for his legs. At least ease the pain."

"We'll be fine, Mistress. There's still plenty of food here. Go be with Drusus. He's waiting for you."

Could she make them leave? Something told her Otho wouldn't, especially after what he'd shared about his son that she could hardly comprehend. "I don't agree with this, but I won't oppose you either. I'm not like you, Otho. I *do not* forgive him."

"That will hurt you more than your father, but that's another talk for another day, my lady. Please, allow my servant and me to escort you back to the fullery."

Laelia nodded, and after some final arrangements, she let Otho take her elbow and guide her from the house. The walk back took longer, which didn't make sense because the street was less crowded and noisy. Maybe it only felt longer because she couldn't stop the sound of her father's weeping from replaying in her mind. Even when they entered the fullery, she still couldn't shake loose of it.

"Where's Naomi?" Drusus' voice. Laced with fear.

"She remained with my father. Of her own accord."

Otho put her hand on the edge of the table and released her arm. "My servant is with her and will let no harm come to her."

"Laelia, would you like to come upstairs with me for a moment?" Lady Pappus' voice. She'd made it after all. "We can wash your face, and there's something I'd like to ask you."

It was coming. She was going to take him back. Laelia didn't want to go with her. She wanted to sit beside Drusus and hold his hand and hear him say everything would be all right. But instead she nodded and held out her hand. Lady Pappus led her to the upper room, washed her face for her, and gave her a cup of wine to drink.

"What will you do once Drusus is recovered?"

The question Laelia had been asking herself since leaving her father. "I don't know. I can't impose on Otho indefinitely. I know better than anyone food, oil, and shelter cost coin, but I know no trade."

"I'd like you to consider helping me with the children at my villa. I care for ten to twenty or so during the day, many with only one parent who is working and has who have no slave or trusted neighbor to watch over them. I'd like to begin tutoring them as well, especially Erissa. She's a bright but precocious girl."

"I've met Erissa."

"Was your father the mean man she told me about?"

"Yes."

"She can exaggerate, but I suspect now she wasn't. I thought her embellishing because she's been smitten with Drusus since the day he cut her fig in half from across the table. I was poised to reprimand him for knife throwing with so many of the children about, but my husband congratulated him and that was that.

"Before I lose myself in memories of my husband, I ask because my other commitments don't provide the time to work with the children, and the two tutors I have hired for them were so overwhelmed they refused to return after only a few days. My sons were six years apart, and I had many slaves to attend them back then. Most of the time the children play rather than learn, but at least at the villa they're safe from those who would steal them and sell them into slavery. Do you think this would be something you might be interested in? I would pay you fairly, and Drusus could remain with you if your father permits."

"My father isn't in a position to permit anything, Lady Pappus."

"A servant told me what happened. I understand your anger, Laelia, but don't let it consume you. I regret not all men are worthy fathers or masters, as my husband was."

"Drusus speaks very highly of him, even still."

"Drusus is like him in many ways. Always ready to act first and pray later. Put themselves in harm's way for others with no thought for their own life, and refusing to accept some things are beyond their control. I think it's harder for Drusus than it was for my husband. As a slave there are a great many more things beyond his control. It's why I'm proud, but concerned, about his decision to return to your father."

"I have no intention of allowing him to. I wouldn't have let Naomi remain behind today unless I'd known my father won't be able to hurt her. Except with his words, but they wound as well as his hands."

Lady Pappus stroked her cheek as a mother would. "I'm sorry for what you have endured, and I won't press you for a decision. I know it's been a long two days. Let's get you fed and then back downstairs. I think Drusus rests better when you are near."

"So do I." She hadn't meant to say that out loud and shivered at revealing so much to Lady Pappus.

But Lady Pappus patted her back and took her hand. "I know," she whispered. "God will make a way for you both. I believe that with all my heart."

They were beautiful words, but Laelia knew better. She'd seen exactly what happens to women who fall in love with their slaves.

Chapter 31

Two weeks of being treated like a newborn child had been too long for Drusus. Between Laelia, Lady Pappus, Otho and the physician telling him what he could and couldn't do, he was certain they were to blame for his lingering headache. After four days, the swelling subsided enough he could see with both eyes again. Three days ago, against wails of protest from Laelia and Lady Pappus, he'd been able to stand and walk a short distance. Afterward, his ribs were punishing him beneath the linen binding them and Alexander had to help him back to his bed, but he'd been outside, seen the sun, and smelled air without the fuller taint.

This morning when Laelia tightened the brace on his arm, only his pride kept him from whimpering. A short nap helped but unlike Laelia who could sleep through most anything, the relentless itch under the linen of the brace tortured him as much as the pain. When blissful sleep did come, the constant grind and clatter of Otho's servants working would jolt him awake.

"How long do I have to wear this?"

Laelia raised her head from the bowl of fuller clay she ground in her lap and turned toward his voice. "Much too long to already be asking when it's coming off. If you're bored why don't you help me? The more clay I grind, the more Otho brings me."

"I didn't say I was bored."

"How can you not be? You've been lying there watching me for two weeks."

"How would you know?" Instantly he regretted his words, even though she was right.

A small grin framed her lips. "I know when you're watching me. Now if you feel like talking, tell me another story. I liked the one about the animals in the ark, except Noah shouldn't have let the snakes and the scorpions in."

He sat up, holding tight to his side with his good hand, and managed to right his upper body without help. "I'll tell you another story, but who's been to see Naomi today?"

"Splash, but he hasn't returned." She turned toward him again so she was going to say something else. The action never failed to warm his heart. Most people without sight didn't make the effort to face someone they couldn't see when speaking. Laelia did.

She frowned and the grinding stone in her hand stilled. "I should go. I should have gone before now, if for no other reason than to see Naomi myself."

"Then we'll go tomorrow."

"You aren't going anywhere. It's enough to have to hear you trying not to pant when you return from your afternoon walk."

"I need to walk. I could make it to the house." His ribs would be on fire and he'd be breathing like a trout in the sand, but he didn't want her near her father again without him. Ever. "Besides, I'm tired of seeing you on Otho's arm."

Her brow raised in unison with the corner of her mouth on a particularly hard smack of the rock into the clay. "Jealous?"

More than he cared to admit, even to himself. "No."

She laughed and smacked the clay in the bowl again, sending a spray of powder into the air. Otho had to know more powder ended up in Laelia's tunic and the floor around her than in his bin to be used. But his mentor gave her purpose and a way to feel like she contributed, and for that Drusus was grateful.

"I'm sure I'll regret telling you this one day." She set the bowl and stone aside and straightened those legs of hers he'd seen far too much of lately. "But when you say no that quickly, and then nothing else, you're usually not telling the truth."

"What else about myself do I not know?"

"That's for me to know, isn't it?" She teased him from the set of her face. "Don't worry. Otho is able to lead me better than most, but none so well as you. Besides, you need to rest."

"I am resting. I'm tired of being on my back."

"I know. You shift around so much that I'm used to the rustling blankets and the leather and metal of your brace squeaking. Between that and Otho's snoring, it's a wonder anyone sleeps."

"You sleep like the dead, Laelia." And she did, which gave him ample opportunity to study her when he awoke from his nightmares. They were now of her father, pounding his flesh over and over with the lampstand until Drusus wished for death himself to escape the pain of the beating. By God's mercy the lamp hadn't been lit, or fire could have started.

Like most Romans, Drusus feared fire. He could recall the smell, the screams, and the horrors he'd seen as a young child in the arms of his mother, running from the flames. The blackened feet covered in pitch and flame, one of Caesar Nero's human torches. How Master Ricarri could possibly believe a man who could order such things done wouldn't be capable of falsely blaming the Christians for the great fire was beyond Drusus' comprehension. A lot of things were.

She hadn't responded to his sleep like the dead comment, and he wondered if he'd upset her. "What are you thinking about?"

"That Lady Pappus isn't here. She's usually here by this time."

Otho appeared, pushing aside the edge of the curtain still hanging between them and the rest of the shop. "I was thinking the same thing."

Drusus looked up at his mentor. "Why keep the curtain hanging? Obviously privacy isn't its purpose."

"Your right, it's not." Otho stepped around him toward his work table. "Hiding Laelia keeps the servants actually working. You aren't the only one who can stare at her for hours."

Laelia blushed and Drusus glared at Otho's back. "Where are they? I don't hear them in the troughs."

"Alexander sent everyone to collect a large order from Senator Aurelius.

The Senator's servants were unable to bring it because half of them are sick with fever." Otho searched the floor until he found Drusus' sandals. "Are you going to walk today?"

"Yes. I'll never get better lying here getting soft and spoiled."

"You mean more spoiled?" Otho took the bowl and grinding stone from Laelia and handed her the sandals. "If Naomi knew Laelia put your sandals on, she'd faint."

"I don't mind," Laelia said. "I never want to interrupt your servant's work to ask for their help, and in Naomi's absence I've become good at dressing myself and lacing my own sandals. This hair however," she grasped a loose end and flipped it up, "is in dire need of her."

Drusus wanted to tell her she was beautiful, but even if Otho weren't present, nothing had changed between them. She could still never be his in that way. Except that she already was in his heart. And sometimes that hurt worse than his ribs when he watched her sleeping an arm's length away.

"I'll let you put his sandals on. When you're finished, call for me and Alexander."

He didn't need Alexander to lean on and hover over him but Otho wouldn't have it any other way. Drusus knew his own body, and it was coming back—slower than he liked, but faster than anyone here was making allowances for.

Laelia walked on her knees to Drusus' feet and the way Otho watched her made Drusus wonder exactly how much Otho enjoyed having Laelia on his arm when they took their walks.

Otho must have felt his inquisitive gaze, because their eyes met. He stared at him for a moment, and then his forehead wrinkled. "Why are you wearing your belt? You can't possibly think you're going to throw with a broken arm. Even if it heals, you—" Otho pulled his mouth closed and remorse painted his expression. "Call for me when you're ready." Otho made a hasty departure and disappeared beyond the curtain.

He'd been about to say Drusus may never be able to throw again. Not like before. Not like when he could hit a cherry the size of his thumb from thirty paces away.

When he'd asked for his belt this morning, Laelia had given it to him without question. She must have understood how much he wanted to return to normal. Even if he couldn't pull the blades free and put them to work, they would still rest where they'd always been. The twins were a part of him, and though his ribs and arm had hurt terribly from working the belt in place by rolling on the floor, he'd positioned and fastened it by himself. Having Laelia lace his sandals was enough of a battle with the lust it aroused in him. Having her buckle his belt would wage war.

Laelia tied off the lace on his sandal and sat back on her heels. "Is that too tight?"

"No. Thank you."

Laelia slid the other sandal on his foot and worked the leather strap around his ankle. He watched her tie the knot, something he hadn't been able to do while lying down before, and realized the other knot was gone. "Did you get me a new sandal strap?"

"Not exactly." She finished the lace and stood.

Even as his gaze traveled to her feet, he knew. There on her left leg, which he'd stared at numerous times the past two weeks, was his broken sandal strap. His throat clogged with emotion. He wanted to take her in his arms, crush her to his chest and never let go.

"Are you ready?"

"No, I need a moment." He needed a lifetime.

She stood still, waiting, and for the third time in the six months he'd known her, he was glad she couldn't see. He blinked furiously, fighting to keep the sting of his blurred vision from becoming tears. He could not cry and embarrass himself in front of Otho and Alexander.

The usual low-toned rumble of activity from the street out front seemed to have grown in strength, and the sounds were different. Laelia seemed to notice also because her chin craned toward the front door and her head tilted and turned. He hadn't taught her to do that, to put one ear forward to gauge and gain direction. She'd acquired that skill on her own.

"Do you hear that?" She angled her head even more, her brow furrowing into a deep V.

"Yes." He clutched his side, and turned on his knees to stand. The ache in his side struck hard and fast, but receded some once on his feet. "Come with me."

Out of habit he reached for her with his right arm but the weight of the brace made him clumsy. The rumble outside grew louder, pigs squealing as if entire herds were moving through the streets. Crying children and shouting, both men and women, but in the medley he couldn't make out what they were shouting.

He took Laelia's hand and brought her to her feet and with his brace pushed aside the curtain. Otho and Alexander were nowhere to be seen and his skin pebbled as fear took root. Otho appeared in the doorway, out of breath and leaning on the frame with both arms. His gaze met Drusus' and for a long moment, he just stared, as behind him, people and animals rushed by.

Drusus tugged Laelia forward. "What is it?"

Otho released the doorway and took two steps inside, their gazes still locked.

"Fire."

Chapter 32

Fire. Laelia gripped Drusus' hand tighter. She could fake brave. She'd done it with her father many times.

"How bad?" Drusus asked Otho.

"At least two districts and spreading according to those already fleeing."

"Which districts?"

"They didn't say, but from the smoke pouring into the sky, it's close."

"I'll gather what I can, Master." Alexander's voice resonated with fear.

"The money pouches only, our cloaks, and whatever bread you can fit in the pack under my bed. The streets will become more crowded every moment we tarry."

She didn't know what frightened her more, being burned or being trampled. Drusus was far from full strength. Between him and Otho she should be able to make it. She had to. Except for the hand she held, everything she cared about was already gone thanks to her father—"Naomi!"

"I know." Drusus released her hand to rub her upper arm. "I'm praying for help."

"I want to also."

He held her hand again. "Lord, deliver us and those we hold dear. Send the rain. Please God, send the rain."

He squeezed her hand. "God, don't flood the whole earth again like in…" she couldn't remember but there was not time to get it right or ask Drusus, "the man who built the ark. Put the fire out and don't let us burn like those men in the furnace in Drusus' story. Help me not burden the others and—"

"You are not a burden." Drusus let go of her hand and took hold of her neck below her ear, his thumb on her jaw. "You are—*not*—a burden." He pulled her to him until she collided with his chest. Both his arms, even the broken one, surrounded her. She breathed deep the sweat and peppermint, the scent uniquely him, and embraced him in return the way she'd longed to for months, careful not to squeeze because of his broken ribs.

"Drusus, we need to go now."

Laelia barely heard Otho over the growing clamor through the open door. Drusus kissed her forehead, infusing her with tenderness and strength at the same time.

But then he released her. "I need you and Alexander to take Laelia to the Emperor's new amphitheater. Alexander needs to carry her. It's the fastest and safest way to move her in a crowd like this."

"Where are you going?" She clung tighter to his arms.

"We have to flee the city like everyone else. *Together*," Otho shot back.

"Listen to me. Both of you," Drusus said. "There are only four ways out of this city through the gates. You'll risk being crushed in the throng at any of them and we don't know where the fire is going. The amphitheater is closer and made of solid stone. Even if the fire reaches it, it won't burn. I'll meet up with you there afterward."

"After what? We aren't leaving you behind." The mere notion was insane.

"I have to go home. Your father and Naomi are there."

Her father deserved to burn, no matter what Otho and Drusus said about forgiveness. But Naomi? "Naomi is smart and strong. She'll escape."

"Laelia, he is still my master."

"No. You are not leaving me." She fisted his tunic in both her hands.

"Master, we must go," Alexander said again.

"Give Otho the pack. I need you to carry Laelia." Drusus' voice was firm.

"Stop it." She gripped him tighter, but he had her wrist and was pulling, willing her to let him go. "You aren't leaving me."

"Listen to me." Now he was almost shouting. "I can't get you there safely even if I wanted to. I have to trust God right now more than I ever have, and

Alexander and Otho with you. You are going with them, even if I have to knock you out so you don't fight."

She went stiff as a statue. He couldn't mean it. The fire was making him crazy.

"We'll meet you at the amphitheater." Now Otho was agreeing with him. "If you aren't there in a week, greet my son and know I'll care for Laelia as a daughter. If we aren't there, find comfort in the Lord and know we are with Him."

"My lady, put your arm around my neck." Alexander took her hand.

She yanked free. "No. No! You are not leaving me!" She grabbed for Drusus again, so fast she pitched into him. If she could wrap her arms around his neck and refuse to let go until he—

Pain exploded along her skull and all the sound died.

Drusus managed to catch her with his good arm before she slid down the front of his body. Pain throbbed beneath the heavy metal brace from striking her, but nothing like the pain inside from having done it. "Take her."

Alexander gathered Laelia like a sleeping child. She looked that way, cradled in Alexander's arms.

"She'll forgive you," Otho said.

"I never will."

"She'll forgive you."

"Whether she does or not is less important to me than her being alive to decide."

"You know that's not up to us, but we will protect her with our lives. You have my word. Remember the Lord. Trust in Him, not your own strength or understanding."

"I'll see you in a week or less at the amphitheater." He hugged Otho with his good arm and then pushed away before his mentor could return the embrace. With fire, every moment mattered. "Go now."

Alexander didn't hesitate. He moved toward the door with Laelia. Otho didn't look back as they entered the river of people, animals, and carts flowing down the street. In seconds, they were gone. Would he ever see them again?

Stronger, Lord. Stronger.

The smell of char hit him as hard as he'd hit Laelia the moment he stepped into the river of people. Smoke filled the afternoon sky from six dark plumes rising to the heavens like long grasping fingers. And they were close.

"Make way." A man knocked him aside, sending fresh pain over his ribs.

He stumbled back into the front of Otho's shop. The plaster covered wooden wall, like so many in the city, would ignite as fast as dry leaves. He trekked in the direction of the house, begging God to protect Erissa, Lady Pappus and the brethren, and Naomi. With every cubit he covered, jostled, shoved about, and cursed, the brace on his arm and his feet grew heavier. He soldiered on, taking breaths in time with his steps.

Up ahead, two horses whinnied and reared up, striking out with their powerful hooves. The chariot they'd been carrying lay on its side, missing a wheel, and two men frantically tried to calm them. Drusus tried to give them a wide berth, impossible with so many people in the street.

"Blind them," Drusus called out. "Cover their eyes with your tunics to lead them, or kill them before they kill someone."

He couldn't help them more than that. The river of people pressed him on, knocking him down twice more before he reached his street. He was closer but now would have to fight against the current.

"God help me. Give me strength like the Nazirite." Even his prayer was strained. He'd never been this winded in his life. He wanted to work himself to a doorway and collapse. Naomi's life, and the master's, wretched as it was, depended on his pressing on.

He pushed forward, leading with his brace. The metal seemed better at making a path, or at least making men reconsider before shoving him aside. He reached the door to Laelia's and leaned against the wooden frame, holding his ground and gasping. There were now too many plumes rising into the sky to count, and they were close. So close.

The door wouldn't open. He clutched his brace tight to his chest, and shoved with his good shoulder. His body screamed at him in pain but the door gave. He stumbled into the atrium. Deeper inside, the missing tiles beneath his sandals assaulted his resolve. *Stronger, Lord.* The fountain was still running, but weakly. Two barrels lay on their side in the pool, one floating like a ship at sea. Strange. "Naomi," he called out.

She wouldn't hear that more than ten paces, he was so out of breath. He made his way toward the master's room. "Master? Naomi?"

"In here." The master's voice carried deep and strong.

Drusus turned the corner, and a tidal wave of rage swept through him. The master held Naomi's braid twisted around his arm like rope. She knelt beside his bed, silently weeping.

"Let her go."

"She'll leave me to burn to death."

"No." Naomi's pleading gaze met his. "No one in the street would come help carry him. I tried. Then I tried to bring water to pour all around us but the barrels were too heavy and pitchers too small. I swear I tried."

Tears streamed from her eyes. He had to do something, and fast. "Master, let her go. Please."

"The two of you can carry me out, or we all die together."

Drusus moved closer. "We'll try, but Naomi can't help me from the floor. You have to let her go."

"She'll run away the moment I do, and you with her."

"Let her go. I give you my word we'll try to get you out."

"Your word means nothing to me."

"It means something to me." Sweat ran down his back and threatened to run in his eyes. They were running out of time. He took a few steps closer. "You already know Naomi can't carry you, Master. Let her go. Laelia needs her."

"Is she safe?" Naomi swallowed as the master pulled her head back, arching her neck. "She's with Otho. They're going to the new amphitheater to meet us."

The wall to his left made a cracking sound. His stomach dropped when he turned. A black circle the size of his head marred the wall. The fire was here.

The master must have seen it also, because he released Naomi.

She shot to her feet. "Help me."

Drusus moved as fast as his weary body could and took the other corner of the blanket beneath the master with his good hand. "We'll drag him on it."

He tried to take a deep breath. The thick, acrid air punished his throat and chest. Flame penetrated the wall, the orange waves shimmering against the blackened plaster.

"Hurry." The master's eyes were wide as he curled on his side and tucked his arms in.

Naomi pulled and strained against the master's weight, coughing in the smoke beginning to crawl above them. Drusus pulled hard, and master slid halfway down the bed.

The pain in his ribs ripped into his side like the talons of an eagle. He cried out as he went to one knee to keep from collapsing, clutching his side.

Naomi took his arm and tried to pull him to his feet, but it was useless. He could barely see, barely breathe, and now barely move.

"Try again!" The master's arms flailed like the flames spreading along the wall.

"I can't," he rasped. He was going to die in this fire. Die beside the master. But Naomi didn't have to. He met her gaze. "Go to the amphitheater. Find Otho. Tell Laelia I loved her as I have never loved another and God will watch over her until I see her again."

"Drusus." Naomi clutched him tighter.

"Go. In the name of the Lord, go now." Violent coughs seized him as he grabbed his chest and sank to his knees.

"Go, Naomi," the master said. "Save yourself if you can."

By the time Drusus was able to raise his head, Naomi was gone. The blackness grew thicker, darkness, smoke, or both.

"You love her?" There was no anger in her father's voice.

"More than my own life." He lay down on the floor. The normally cool stone tile was warm like the bricks of a hearth against his sweat-covered skin. But the air was cleaner there. A comfort that wouldn't last. The smoke above them ignited and became flame, the most beautiful and terrifying thing

Drusus had ever seen. Or would ever see.

The master coughed, the deep hacking mingling with the crackling of the fire beginning to surround them. "If you can reach the fountain," the master wheezed. "Drowning is better than burning."

Not much. If he could get one of the knives free, he could spare them both. *The barrels.* The wood would be saturated. His very own ark. Praying for strength, he crawled like a crab toward the atrium. So dark. So hot. So hard to breathe. His ribs seemed to understand this was their only chance to live, and didn't pain him as much as before. Or God was giving him the strength of Samson after all. Almost there.

A shower of cinder rained down as the ceiling above groaned. The fountain pool hissed like a hundred vipers. He crawled through the soot and found the fountain. The water swirled around him as he curled tight into his damp cave.

His heart poured forth prayers and praise, until the beams above finally gave.

Chapter 33

Laelia came to her senses with sweat and sand clinging to her. Face down on a woolen cloak stinking of smoke. Faint crying and voices surrounded her. She raised her head and a deep ache made itself known above her ear. He'd hit her. She hadn't thought he'd actually do it. She would have wagered her life on it. With her fingertips she rubbed at the tangled hair above her ear. Beneath her scalp was a bump the size of a large grape.

"Laelia."

Otho's voice? It was hard to tell among so many.

"I brought you some water. There's a fountain outside this entrance and by God's mercy, it's still running."

Where had mercy been when they let Drusus smash her head and leave on his own? "I'm not thirsty."

"You should drink to keep your strength up."

She narrowed her useless gaze Otho's direction. "If I refuse, will you knock me out and pour it down my throat?"

"He didn't want you to," Alexander began in his gravelly voice, but Otho cut him off.

"Be silent. When you are thirsty, Laelia, tell Alexander to signal me. There are others taking refuge here also but many have nothing to hold water. I'm going to help them."

"Why bother telling me? You men do as you please." Regret silenced her immediately. This man had risked himself to take her, Drusus and Naomi in.

He'd cared for them for over two weeks, fed them and sent a servant to Naomi and her father every day, yet she'd turned her anger on him in force. An apology was taking shape on her traitorous tongue, but Otho spoke first.

"I tell you so you'll know why I don't answer if you call for me. Alexander will remain with you."

She nodded and curled her knees to her chest. Juno's peacock. She was her father's daughter as much as she was her mother's. Her head hurt. Her nose and throat hurt. That drink her pride refused would be most welcome now. As would Drusus' reassuring voice, the feel of his solid arm beneath her palm and the lingering wisps of peppermint on his breath.

"He shouldn't have hit you," Alexander said.

"Thank you."

"You wouldn't have slowed me down as much as he probably thought. I'm bigger and stronger than you. You would have worn yourself out from the struggle soon enough."

She wanted to take back her gratitude. Why were men so brutish?

"For what it's worth, it hurt him more than you."

The ache in her temple disagreed but she didn't feel like talking anymore. Because Alexander was right, and beneath the pride Drusus had helped her rebuild, she knew it must have. She alone had held the power to spare them both the pain of what he'd done but there was no way to push the sun back and willingly go with Alexander.

Otho's servant couldn't tell her what was going on outside the amphitheater, how much of the city was burning, and every time she asked him if he saw Drusus anywhere, his answer was to keep praying. So she did.

"God, keep Drusus and Naomi safe and bring them back to me. With or without my father, whatever it takes, just bring him back to me."

After a few hundred times, Alexander told her to stop.

"But you said keep praying."

"Yes, but I see they haven't taught you about vain repetition yet."

"What do you mean?"

"God has heard your prayers for Drusus and Naomi. Why not pray for the others?"

267

"What others?"

"Those who do not know the true God. The children who will have no parents and the parents who will have no children after this fire. That God will send the rain, even on this idol filled city to spare His people among them. Pray for the men and women whose blood will soon run in the sand of this arena."

The gladiators and the criminals, he meant. "Why do you think Caesar refuses to accept our God like all the others?" It made no sense, now that she considered it. Rome incorporated the cultures and religions of its conquered lands into its own. It fostered the unity of the *Pax Romana*.

"To accept our God would be to admit he is not one and the Roman way of life is built on a foundation of lies. To face the truth would bring everything down around them, starting with their temples and the coin flowing through them."

"Rome is not so different than Israel."

Otho's voice. He'd returned. "Any sign of Drusus or Naomi?"

"No, and it will be night soon. Alexander and I will take turns keeping watch."

"What can I do?" Besides fret and nurse her tender head.

"You can sleep, and if you can't sleep, keep praying."

"Alexander told me to stop."

"Why?"

"Something about vain repetition."

She heard a smack, followed by a grunt.

"Are you Otho?" A woman's voice. Not one she recognized. In this thick sand it was difficult to hear anyone approaching.

"I am Otho."

"There's a woman, my daughter is with her, she's asking for you or a woman named Laelia. You gave us water earlier today, so I remembered your name."

Laelia shot to her feet but nearly fell when the sand shifted beneath her sandals. If Naomi knew to seek them here, Drusus had made it to them. "Is she alone?"

"I'm not sure," the woman said.

Otho took her arm. "Take us to her, please. Alexander, stay with our things."

She moved faster than Otho but he held her back with a firm grip on her arm. Oh if only she could see.

Arms wrapped around her, bringing her to a colliding halt. "Oh, Laelia."

Naomi's voice. Hoarse and breathy but still her voice. Otho released her and Laelia wrapped her arms around Naomi's neck. "I was so worried about you."

Smoke and char clung to Naomi, but if she'd been strong enough to stand and embrace her, she was well. Laelia continued to cling to her, overjoyed at Naomi's safe return. But she needed to hear him. Touch him. Tell him she forgave him. Finally she could stand it no longer. "Where is Drusus?"

Naomi leaned out of Laelia's embrace and cupped her cheek. "I'm sorry, child. So sorry." The pain was coming, rising from within.

"He said to tell you…"

Unspeakable pain, worse than any she'd ever known, weakened her limbs.

"To tell you he loved you as he never loved another. And that God will watch over you."

"No. He has to come back." He had to. He'd promised never to leave her.

"He's gone, Laelia. Him and your father. I saw the house fall on them. I'm so sorry." Naomi tried to gather her close, but Laelia pushed her away. She would never feel his arm beneath her hand again. Never trust in his direction, smell his peppermint breath or hear his voice. Never plant or pull weeds beside him. He would never again enjoy the smell of fresh bread or the first cool day of a crisp fall when the birds would sing for them in the garden.

She staggered away to keep from screaming. *You promised. You promised me.*

"Laelia, wait," Otho called. He or Naomi grabbed at her wrist but she jerked from their touch. She needed his, not theirs. All she had left of him was the broken sandal strap wrapped tight around her ankle. Her legs gave out, as useless as her eyes now. But it didn't matter. Nothing mattered anymore.

Chapter 34

Laelia woke on stone instead of sand, but didn't open her eyes. Something leather pillowed the side of her head. The earthy scent of the hide reminded her of Drusus' belt, summoning tears behind her closed eyelids. She'd been awake two breaths and already wished for oblivion again. Otho and Naomi spoke in low tones near her, and beyond them, a child complained of hunger and someone wept.

"It should have been me instead of him," Naomi said.

"Drusus didn't think so," Otho answered.

She wanted to disagree with Naomi, and couldn't. If it had to have been one of them, she would have wanted it not to be Drusus. She felt dirty inside now as well as out.

"I'm afraid for her, Otho."

"Pray she will draw near to God and not away in her grief."

Otho's answer for everything was to pray. Prayer wasn't going to bring Drusus back.

"Will you help me?" Naomi asked.

"Of course."

Laelia let the sound of Otho's prayers mingle with the other sounds around her. She didn't want to hear them. They would only remind her of Drusus—of her hand in his as he taught her how to talk to their God. Her eyelids refused to hold back the swelling tide behind them and the leather beneath her grew damp as she cried. He was gone. Her wall, her anchor, was gone. He'd gone to his death to save a man unworthy of his sacrifice, and worse, without ever knowing what was in her heart. He'd never know how much he meant to her. Too late. Unless…

Drusus wasn't here to ask if this was permissible and she couldn't bring herself to ask Otho. Hopefully his—no, their God, would grant her this request. But did she have to say it out loud for her God to hear her? If so, then how did mutes pray? Surely some followed her God. He would have some way to hear their prayers without words. After all, she could always tell, after she got to know him, when Drusus was watching her even though she couldn't see him. Surely this God that created them would hear her unspoken prayer. It bothered her more to remain on her side, which seemed rather irreverent, even for a God without a formal temple. But Drusus had taught her their God was merciful. She needed Him to be plenty merciful for any offenses she'd be committing without Drusus to help guide her.

God, forgive me for asking you to be a messenger, but I need you to tell my servant Drusus something for me. It's important, and since he's with you now and—

My servant lives.

She'd felt the words more than heard them. She concentrated but Otho's quiet whispers and the same weeping from before were the dominant sounds, along with a very angry goose somewhere in the distance. Strange. She took a deep breath, this one smelling less of smoke.

God, I need Drusus to know—

My servant lives.

Laelia froze, terrified to even breathe. Drusus had told her their God would speak to her in time, but she hadn't heard the words through her ears. It was as if they were inside her but either way the message was the same.

Drusus was alive. Her God had spoken to her and Drusus was alive. She sat up, and felt it inside as clear as the sand still clinging to her body and the stone beneath her palms. "Drusus is alive."

"His spirit is with God, Laelia." Otho said. "That part of us will always live and—"

"No, his body is alive and his spirit is still in it."

"I know you want to believe that." Naomi's voice was gentle. "I want to also but the house was in flames and collapsed in front of me. He wouldn't have survived it."

"God told me Drusus is alive." There. She'd said it. She'd been afraid to but now she had, she felt stronger than ever.

Neither spoke for long enough they could only be having a silent conversation with their faces. "You don't believe me?"

"I believe you believe it, but I'm afraid you'll only hurt more because of it."

Naomi's doubt hurt, but she only needed one of them to trust her. "Otho?"

"I know his loss is hard. You'll need time. We all will."

She straightened to better sit up, and nearly rolled off the edge of whatever she'd been lying on. She felt the edges and let her legs down. They must be in the seats of the amphitheater. She stood, using all the backbone she'd learned from Tiberius.

"I've listened for two weeks about how our God created everything, flooded the entire earth, delivered his people from Pharaoh, turned water into wine, healed lepers with His words and the blind with his spit."

"What's wrong," Alexander asked over a yawn.

"Nothing. Laelia had a dream but we're fine," Otho said.

"It wasn't a dream. God spoke to me, like Drusus said he would, and he's still alive."

The eerie quiet descended again. More wordless conversations—she sensed it.

"Shame on you. Shame on all of you. I have more faith in our God right now than the three of you."

The silence remained, but she knew, could feel, they were listening. "Drusus is alive. I have to find him. He must be hurt or he would have come. We have to go to him."

A long pause frustrated her but also meant Otho was considering it. *Please, God. Make them help me.*

"We will go at first light."

"We have to go now."

"I swore to Drusus I would protect you. I can't do that in the dark. Plunderers are already picking over the burned-out areas, and all the soldiers are trying to stop the fires from spreading. We will go at first light, but, Laelia, please don't have false hope."

"I want him to be alive too, child, I do, but he couldn't have survived."

Otho and Naomi weren't going to yield. She couldn't find her way to her house by herself. She couldn't even find her way out of this amphitheater herself. "How long until first light?"

"A few hours. It's best if you sleep while you can."

Sleep. Knowing Drusus was hurt and needed her. She'd sooner drink the Tiber dry but appeasing Otho in this was the only way she was going to get his help. She lay back on the stone seat and pillowed her head with her arm. "Wake me at first light."

"We will."

Was he hungry? Frightened? Burned? Surely their God wouldn't spare him a quick death only to give him a slow one from a burn. That would be like her father. Was his death quick? She'd often wished him dead, but never by fire. Only crucifixion rivaled fire, and maybe being fed to the beasts. But what if her father was alive too? What if Naomi was wrong about both of them?

"Try to sleep," Naomi said.

She'd been perfectly still since lying down. How did—

Eyes. She frowned and closed her eyes. Keeping them closed required more focus than she expected. They must close on their own when she did fall asleep. Or, what if she slept with them open? Juno's peac—

A sigh of pure frustration charged from her chest through her nose. If they would just let her go to him, take her there now and stop—

"It's me."

Naomi's voice had moved behind her, so when a gentle hand stroked the hair over the spot Drusus struck, it had to belong to Naomi. The hand stilled.

"Did you fall?"

"No."

"What happened?"

She'd have to explain why to preserve his honor, because that Drusus hit her sounded as impossible as some of Otho's stories, even to her. "Part of a wall hit me." That was mostly true.

"Try to sleep." Naomi resumed stroking her hair and began to sing.

After a few notes, Laelia recognized the tune. The river song.

She swallowed and curled tighter. *God, wherever Julia is, keep her safe too. Please.*

Otho's gait slowed and Laelia's heartbeat raced. She squeezed his arm and came to a stop. "Are we here?"

"Yes."

He'd been somber from the moment he'd woken her. She sensed it while Alexander and Naomi gathered their scant belongings. "What do you see?"

"The fire is gone, but there's nothing it didn't touch. It's rubble, my lady. It would take days to sift through it."

She let go and reached forward, stepping through debris at her feet. At the wall, no, the remains of the wall from the height, warm char crumbled beneath her fingers. Burned. Crushed. Destroyed. Were they right? Tears threatened and she bit her lip. This didn't make sense. If God didn't want them to lie, He wouldn't lie. He'd told her His servant lives. She listened, not with her ears but with her heart, the way she would when Drusus watched her.

Nothing.

She swallowed, but kicked at the doubt rising up. Their God wouldn't lie.

"He's here." Laelia pressed forward, climbing up and into the debris.

"Laelia, wait." Otho took her arm, but Laelia jerked free and continued, the remains of the house shifting beneath her.

"Drusus? Help me find you." The power of her own voice surprised her.

"Laelia, please, don't do this to yourself," Naomi said.

"Be silent, all of you." She stilled and listened again. Long moments passed, but she didn't hear him. He didn't answer. He'd taught her so many things but she—that's it. Like their first time at the table. She was searching for his voice, not listening to what else was there. How else would she know when it changed?

A bird chirped, how far away she couldn't tell. An occasional pop would spin her head like a chariot wheel in that direction.

"Laelia…"

"Be silent. *Please.*"

A bird took flight, the swoosh of its wings replacing the chirping coming from her left. She listened harder, but there were only more pops and the occasional sigh from Otho, Naomi or Alexander.

My God didn't lie. "Drusus, where are you?" she yelled as if she wanted all of Rome to hear her. Then three raps, so soft she barely heard them. "Drusus?" she yelled again.

Three raps, stronger in her…right ear? She turned her chin a thumb's length.

"I can hear them," Alexander said, excitement in his voice.

The raps continued, in perfect sets of three. She turned her head left a small measure, and the soft knocks evened. She turned her neck further left, almost looking over her shoulder now, and waited for the next set. The quiet taps reached her right ear, but not the left. She turned back to where they had been even and crawled forward. Wood and broken roof tiles shifted beneath her as she moved. A shard of something rigid sliced into her palm. It stung but she yanked it free and threw it aside.

"We can hear you," Otho called out.

She couldn't hear him now over the clatter her hands and knees made in the remains of the house. After a few more lengths, she sat back on her heels. "Again, Drusus. Help us find you."

The taps resumed. She arched her head right, far right. She'd gone too far. She turned her head left, tilting her ear down. Still behind her, but not as strong. He was behind her, and to her right, somewhere beneath this rubble. She crawled forward again and debris shifted beneath her. A gasp flew from her lips as her hands shot out and she dropped deeper into the rubble. She froze, something pressed tight, pinching her knee and pinning her down. She struggled but it made her sink even more.

"I'm coming, my lady," Alexander yelled.

"No. Stay there." *God, help me. Help me find him. I need you to be my wall.*

At last her leg released and she scrambled out of the hole. She went statue still, trying to ignore the pain in her bleeding palm and her wrenched knee. Where were the taps?

There. She arced her head left and right in turn, but they didn't grow or diminish in strength. "Are you beneath me?"

The taps remained faint, but the pauses disappeared. No longer in sets of three, but steady like the hoof beats of a racing chariot horse.

"He's below me. Come help us," she yelled grabbing the first thing her hands touched and throwing it over her shoulder, again and again and again.

Chapter 35

Drusus' last memory of the woman he loved collapsing in his arms played over and over. Long after he'd been able to endure it. Little good was left in this air he'd been shallow breathing. Drifting in and out of sleep, trapped in this black, watery tomb, his ribs and stomach realized the pain they put him in wasn't working to bring relief. They finally gave up and went numb. That or he was so delirious from hunger and thirst he couldn't feel anything. The water he lay in was too full of soot and ash to drink.

But he'd heard her voice call his name. Then his wooden prison rumbled. The water he was half-submerged in rippled, though he hadn't moved. She called to him again, louder this time. She'd come for him.

There was a handbreadth of space between him and the barrel, so he did the only thing he could. He hit it with the metal brace. The intense pain burned away the last of the fog clouding his mind. And she heard him. Thank God, she'd heard him.

"Drusus, hang on. We're coming!"

He didn't have the strength or the breath to answer. It could only have been God's mercy he'd found enough to keep hitting the barrel. There were other voices. Otho? Naomi? His wooden prison continued to rattle and quake, until a single ray of light penetrated the blackness.

"We're over the fountain I think."

Naomi's voice.

"It makes sense. If he survived, this would be the place," Otho said.

"Stop saying if."

Laelia's firm demand made his heart smile. His cracked lips didn't have the strength.

"Are you sure we're not crushing him ourselves?"

Was that Alexander?

"Dig faster," Laelia ordered.

They were closer now. More rays of light, stinging his eyes, but with them came fresh blessed air. He took his first full breath since the roof collapsed and a violent cough tore from his chest.

"I'm to the water. These pieces of wood are wet," Naomi said.

Suddenly sunlight blasted him, so bright he clamped his eyes shut.

"He's here," Otho yelled.

Fingers touched his head, sifted through his hair.

"Drusus?"

He blinked and squinted into the bright light.

"The Lord be praised, he's alive. Quick, here, in this barrel. Move all this so I can pull him out. Quickly."

By the time he could keep his eyes open without pain, Otho's face had never looked so good. But where was Laelia?

"Hold on. I'm going to pull you out. Alexander, hold the barrel."

Otho grabbed him under his arms and pulled hard. He slid half-free of the barrel before Otho pulled him again. This time clear of the water. He lay there on his back, gasping again from the pain of his ribs and arm.

"Where is he?"

He turned his head toward her voice, in the shadows to his left. Her face, arms and tunic were covered in soot, her hair askew.

Naomi held her hand. "He's in front of you."

Laelia crept forward on her hands and knees toward him.

Otho leaned toward her with his arm extended. "Give me your hand."

She reached for him and the blood on her blackened palm made his gut lurch. Otho took her hand and brought her closer, finally resting her fingers on his shoulder. Her hand settled over his heart, moving in time with the rise and fall of his chest beneath the thin, wet wool.

"Drusus?"

He tried to answer her, but a wheezing rasp came instead of *I'm sorry*.

"He can hear you, my lady, and his eyes are open but he can't speak. Likely from the smoke," Otho said.

Another shadow fell over him. Alexander. "Let me go to the Pappus villa and see if the fire reached it. If not, we can bring him there."

Otho nodded. "Go quickly. If she can spare help, bring them."

He tried to cover her hand with his but raising his arm pushed a whimper he couldn't conceal through his lips.

She frowned, and slid her other hand to his, finding it after a moment. "Rest, Drusus. Our God will be our wall. All will be well."

He found the strength to squeeze her fingers. She brought his knuckles to her mouth and kissed them, before laying her ash- streaked cheek against them. "And you should know, before another moment passes, I love you as I will never love another."

He traced her jaw with his thumb, and prayed she understood his unspoken promise.

Alexander returned with two more servants and word Lady Pappus' villa was untouched by the fire. Many of the brethren were already gathering there. Laelia hated to relinquish her hold on Drusus, but kissed his knuckles one more time before letting go. She was done with propriety and hiding her feelings for a slave. Besides, with her father dead, he belonged to her now. Alexander wanted to carry her, insisting it would be faster. This time she went willingly.

At the villa, Lady Pappus was in full command, ordering Drusus taken to her private chamber, and two of her female servants to assist Naomi and Laelia with baths and fresh clothes. So many voices, it was impossible to tell how many people were here, of all ages. They were given wine and bread.

"I know you. You're the fortune teller who doesn't know anything," a little voice yelled.

"Erissa, don't shout," Lady Pappus scolded. "Please go back into the garden with the other children. I'll be there soon."

"But she's—"

"Now."

"All right."

Laelia would have laughed at the defeat in the little girl's voice if she weren't so concerned for everyone. Drusus in particular.

"You see what I mean, Laelia?" Lady Pappus sighed. "That one will do great things one day I'm certain, but for now she silvers my hair."

"She reminds me of Laelia at that age. Very determined," Naomi said.

"I have little doubt. And someone else who is also very determined is asking for you, Laelia. I'll take you to him. Naomi can then help me with the children."

"Of course." Laelia rose.

Lady Pappus took her hand, and then placed it on her arm as Drusus did in the beginning. "I learned to lead my husband as well. Drusus taught me how years ago, when we were still the same height. He was all stomach and eyes then, the way young man are in the last season of boyhood."

"I know Drusus cared for your husband very much and speaks of you both with great esteem."

"He is like a son to me and my own consider him a brother. I pray they are also safe and I will receive word from them soon."

Laelia didn't know what to say. She hoped for children one day, children she would love as much as Drusus. They continued down the corridor a few moments longer, never turning. How vast was this villa?

"This door here." Lady Pappus turned her, and a latch of some kind released. Instead of remnants of smoke, this room smelled like flowers, almost as good as her garden. "We cleaned him and gave him something for pain. He's resting well. As soon as I can locate Tyrayus or another physician, we'll have his arm checked and the padding in the brace changed."

"Thank you, Lady. I don't know what I could have done for him." Sometimes more than her eyes felt useless. What did she have to offer him, besides her devotion?

"He told me how you found him. I'm so very proud of you."

"Thank you." Even with the rasp and weariness in it, his voice flowed over her like warm oil in a fresh bath, comforting her as it always did.

"Here, there's a stool right in front of you." Lady Pappus placed her hand on it and Laelia sat down. "I need to see to the others. Drusus, Erissa is here, and she brought another little girl with her."

"Her Uncle?" His voice. It was still raspy and weaker than usual, but it comforted her all the same.

"No one has seen or heard from him yet. Pray for him, and that God will send the rain."

"We will."

Laelia grinned, grateful to be included. Praying with Drusus felt right, as if it bonded them closer to each other and their God. Would he feel the same way? He'd declared love for her while facing a certain death. Now that he would live, would his feelings for her?

Lady Pappus' measured footsteps retreated and the door closed. Drusus took her hand and her fingers nestled in the spaces between his. Too soon they slid free and he grazed the knot above her ear.

"I'm so sorry."

"I know." She took his wrist and pulled his hand away from her head.

"Please, I never—," a cough shook him.

She tightened her grip on his hand. "Stop."

"I'm trying," he rasped.

"Not the cough. The guilt." When he'd quieted, she stiffened her spine and looked right where his eyes should be. "Tell me what it's going to take for you to let it go. I already have. If you need me to crack a clay pitcher over your head, or punch you in your broken ribs, I will. I'll hate to cause you more pain, but if that's what it takes, I will. And that's why I understand."

He was quiet for a long moment. "I don't deserve you."

His patience with her from the beginning, his tolerance of her Ricarri temper, and the way he'd sacrificed himself in her place traveled through her darkness like a song. "It's I who does not deserve you, but—"

Drusus had done more than enough to deserve it, and it would be unjust not to include Naomi. It was the right thing to do, and more than that, she had no way to provide for them.

"But what?" he prodded.

"Father is dead. You and Naomi are…" *Say it.* She drew a deep breath. "Free."

Silence hung between them. So long it hurt.

"You would free us?"

"Yes."

"Why?"

"Because I must. I'm hoping you won't leave me, but I understand if—

"Leave you?"

Why did he sound angry?

His hand jerked from hers and cupped her neck. Before she could gasp, he yanked her toward him. Old fears raged until his mouth covered hers. This was her Drusus, and yet it wasn't. There was no gentleness, no patience in his kiss—only need.

It frightened her as much as it reassured her. He must have felt it, because a low moan filled her ears that she hadn't made. He pulled away to press his forehead to hers. The peppermint breath in her face made it impossible to think as the grip on the back of her neck eased. She pushed up from his chest with her palms, shocked at the tingles remaining on her lips though the kiss had ended.

His desperate sigh fanned her skin and she placed her fingertips on his…chin and then covered his lips with them. "Was that a farewell or a beginning?"

"Neither."

Neither?

"I've wanted that for so long. And I could never leave you. I want to be at your side as long as I draw breath, and free or not, I can no longer be there as anything less than your husband."

He loved her. He'd said so, never more than in that kiss, but she'd never allowed herself to consider marriage. Never. As a slave it was illegal. Now he was free, and in that freedom able to choose any woman as a mate. One that could see. One that could be trusted to rear his children. She was none of those, and yet, his words made her hope.

"Why would you wish to marry someone like me?"

The fingers on her neck slid to her chin, catching the tears that gathered there. "You are the strongest, smartest, most beautiful woman I have ever known. You are already a part of me and I would give my life to protect you. I can never endure having to share you with another man ever again. I want you at my side every time the sun rises and in my bed every time it sets. But as my wife, not my mistress."

She closed her eyes, drew in a breath so deep it hurt her insides.

"Laelia?" The uncertainty in his voice tugged at her. "Will you wed me?"

"Yes." With her hand, she followed his arm to his shoulder and found his chin. She leaned down, bringing her mouth to his. She wanted to move slowly, explore him as she had Tiberius, but her body wouldn't listen. Her hope and her love poured out into him and in her kiss was *I love you* and *I need you* and *I am yours forever*. Drusus responded in kind, until she had to pull back to breathe.

She tried to regain her breath, like a chariot horse after a race. "Is it always like that?"

He chuckled and traced the shape of her face. "Not always. Let me show you."

He pressed his lips to hers, a feather light touch, before kissing her chin and then the tip of her nose. His thumb caressed her throat as he brushed gentle kisses over her cheek, and even her eyes, before tucking her head against his chest and surrounding her with his arm.

She relaxed against him, enjoying once more the steady thump of his heart beneath her ear. He kissed the top of her head and held her beside him for a long time. Her mother and her father, her true father, would live on through Laelia. She would have daughters with her dark hair and unruly curls and sons with their father's…

"Drusus?"

"Yes?"

She raised her head and pointed her face toward his. "What do you look like?"

His chuckle became a laugh so deep it shook his chest beneath her, and had to be hurting his ribs. But after a moment, she couldn't help but join him.

The End

Epilogue

Laelia awoke and yawned wide enough the corners of her mouth protested. The brazier must have consumed all the coal because the winter chill nipped at her even through the thick wool blanket and thicker fur covering her. She uncurled from the tight ball she always slept in and rolled on her side, sliding closer to her husband.

Her hand drifted to the blunted edge of bone at his hip. She could continue forward to the small, shallow bowl of his navel or to the ribs that had finally ceased to pain him after six months. The brace he'd bemoaned almost every day came off in half that time.

While his bones had healed, Drusus had not.

Erissa had been unusually quiet and withdrawn last week and Laelia had taken her aside and gently coaxed the truth from her. The girl was crying at the end, as was Laelia, who reassured her she'd done the right thing in telling her what she'd seen. For weeks now, she'd pretended ignorance because she knew he didn't want her to know. And she prayed for him—every day.

His arm slid from beneath her cheek and circled her shoulders in a firm embrace, and he kissed the top of her head.

"Is the sun up?" she asked.

"Not yet."

No bold caress followed and there'd been a tremor in his voice. "You're usually happier about that. Is it Brasus?"

"No. Brasus is doing very well. When Lady Pappus and I visited his new master, they were very pleased with him. That was important considering what Lady Pappus made the senator pay for him, a portion of which she gave to us. I tried not to take it but you know how she can be."

"I'm glad the senator's son was more open to the idea of a guide slave than I was."

Drusus tightened his embrace and kissed her forehead. "So am I but I'm saddened the goal is the same for him as your father's was for you."

"Marriage?"

"The senator has only one son. The other two died before they reached their fifteenth summer."

"How old is this son?"

"Why do you ask?"

"Erissa is ten this year. She'll be old enough to betroth soon."

"You think of her as a daughter, don't you?"

She did. In the months they'd shared Lady Pappus' villa, no word on Erissa's Uncle had come. All believed the fire had claimed his life as it had her own father. Erissa was curious, defiant, and headstrong. All the things Laelia had been before her mother died. The only time she could more or less control the girl was when they worked together in the garden. Sometimes Drusus would join them when he wasn't training slaves to lead blind masters. Brasus had been the first once Drusus recovered enough to teach him, and he'd learned quickly. She hoped the next one would also so someone else could soon have the freedom and trust she'd come to appreciate so much. She had to want that for others, or it would make it even harder to be without Drusus for most of the day. This work was important, but she did miss him. Especially in the garden or when Erissa would walk her too close to a wall and clip her shoulder or elbow.

"The senator's son is not right for her. He doesn't share our faith and whoever his father chooses for him to wed will need to have Erissa's strength but your patience. Erissa would drive him to divorce her in weeks, I'm sure of it. She will need an equally strong and patient man, and I suspect God is still raising him up."

She smiled and pressed tighter to him. "You think of her as a daughter too."

"I do. I watched her grow up in this house when I served here, and she looks a lot like you, Laelia. Especially when you're both covered in dirt."

"You used to like that."

He shifted to face her and curved his body around hers before kissing her neck. "I still do. And always will. I only wish I could spend more time with you."

The bold caress came then. Her husband's touch brought a wisp of smoke and heat that would become a flame when he kissed her. Afterward she would smile against his skin as his breathing deepened and his embrace would relax in a satisfied sleep.

And to think she used to disdain marriage.

His full lips traced the shell of her ear and she was tempted to abandon the talk they needed to have. This was important, and time alone with him was rare, especially outside their chamber. The longer she—

He rolled her beneath him, and his kiss returned in the groove of her collarbone. Maybe it didn't need to be now. But it did. *David's sling!* She took a deep breath and demanded her body obey her right now, not his. "When were you going to tell me?"

"Tell you what?" he murmured against her belly.

"About the stables."

The way his body went rigid she was expecting. "She told you."

"Don't be angry at Erissa. She was concerned for you, as am I. I'm also concerned with why you didn't tell me."

The blankets fell away from her as he moved again. In a moment, the familiar sound of the flint struck and in her next breath, she smelled the burning wick of a lamp. She sat up and pulled the fur around her, the leather side sweeping across her shoulders. And then she waited.

He was still there because she could always sense him when he was near, and when he was watching her. How she'd missed his grief is what scared her most. "Drusus?"

His hands took hold of hers through the folds of the fur and she freed the one he held to rest it on her lap. She could feel the fine tremors in his fingers and her fear grew.

"When I tried to throw again, I didn't want anyone to know. Only Cyrus knew because he's always in the stables tending the animals. And the first few weeks when I would miss over and over I told myself it would take time, and the tingles in my forefinger would go away and with enough practice my grip and my throw would return."

But it hadn't. She was tempted to fill his long pause with comforting words and reassurances, but waited. After a long moment, his mellow voice continued.

"Close is not on-target. I learned that from Master Pappus. Tiberius and I both did. And now, like Tiberius, all I can get is close. No matter how much I throw, even at half-distance, I'm not on-target anymore. When I finally accepted it's not coming back, that my throw is gone, I wept as I've never wept before, Laelia."

"That's how Erissa heard you."

"Yes. Cyrus must have also but I never saw him. Erissa thought I'd hurt myself and wanted to get help. I told her I wasn't hurt, just very sad and not to tell anyone."

Laelia squeezed his hand. "Your sadness is my sadness. I would have carried it with you."

"I know. Which is why I told myself I shouldn't tell you. I didn't want to make you upset or fear reminding you of Tiberius or your father. But that was an excuse, and I know that now."

"Then what is the truth?" She bit her lip. She tried not to, especially because he would see it in the lamplight, but couldn't help it.

With his other hand he traced her chin with his thumb. "My pride. I feel less than who I was and am shamed by it. And you were the first and the last person I wanted to share that with. The first because you always make everything better and the last because I was afraid, and still am, you would think I thought you less of who you were because of your blindness."

This was why she loved this man so much. Even in his own pain, he was always protecting her.

"When I lost my sight I was less than who I was."

"No, Laelia. You—

"Drusus, stop." She squeezed his hands. "Listen to me. Please. I was less than who I was. And it took me a long time to grieve that. You're allowed to grieve the loss of your skill. And I want to be there for you as you were for me. And when you're ready, I want to help you and pray for you to overcome it as you did for me. If that means learning to use your other arm or never taking up the twins again, you'll be stronger in time because of this. But I know right now it doesn't feel that way, so let me mourn with you. Please don't keep me from something so important to you because that hurts me more than knowing you are saddened."

"I'm sorry."

She squeezed his hand again. "I won't diminish how painful it is to be unable to do something you could before and I know what it meant as a connection to you with Master Pappus. But you are good at so many things, Drusus. You are the greatest teacher and the most patient man I have ever known. Even with Erissa. I hope in time you find teaching others to lead the blind as fulfilling as you found throwing the twins."

"I already do. It's hard work but I know they will go on to do for others what Otho and Master Pappus did for me. I want to share our faith along with the skill because what good is it if their new master can now travel the city safely if they die and spend eternity in torment?"

"None."

"It is hard to see them go, though I know I have to. Brasus was quite funny as you know and I enjoyed his company very much. Lady Pappus and I will go to the slave market this week to choose another and begin again. I'm already praying God will show us the right one."

"He will. Thank you for sharing all this with me. I want you to know you can trust me as much as I trust you and our God."

His hand pulled free and he hugged her. Too tight, because it pulled her hair and she swallowed a wince from the pain in her scalp.

"I never tire of hearing you say our God. I'm glad that you know now. I don't want secrets between us."

Her stomach fluttered and her mouth went dry but she knew she couldn't keep it to herself any longer. "Then there is something I must tell you."

He still held her, his face pressed to the top of her head. "What is it?"

She gently pushed away and made sure she sat facing him on their bed. This was it. "Can I see you when I tell you?"

"Of course." He took her wrists and brought her hands to his face. Once she had her palms against his cheeks, the heels of her hands at the edges of his mouth, and her thumbs resting alongside his nose just below the inner corners of his eyes, he let her hands go.

This was an intimacy they alone shared, born their first night as husband and wife. With her hands this way she felt every smile, grimace, frown, pant, bead of sweat—everything. That made this all the more special.

"I'm with child."

She held her breath, and after a moment, the tips of her thumbs grew damp and the corners of his mouth rose toward her fingers.

She smiled in return. "I wanted to wait to tell you until after the feast for Lady Pappus' grandson but after what we just shared, I can't."

"Does Lady Pappus know?" The excitement in his voice lifted her spirits even higher than his expression had.

"No."

"Naomi and Otho?"

A small chuckle fell from her lips. "Naomi knew before I did. She helped me to be certain. Otho knows also, but they gave me their word they wouldn't tell anyone until we did."

He laughed, and she enjoyed feeling it as much as hearing it. "That's why they behaved so strangely when they visited yesterday."

"Since they're too old for children of their own, I think they plan to share ours. Would that be all right?"

"Of course. I'm so... I don't..."

She leaned forward and kissed the mouth between her hands. "I know. Sometimes the joy is too much for the words."

He kissed her back and then blew out the lamp. She didn't understand until he took her face in his hands and whispered in her ear. "And sometimes the love."

Laelia touched one of the scars on his arm from the beating he'd taken for her. "The love is what I see the clearest."

"Be of good courage, and he shall strengthen your heart,
all ye that hope in the Lord."

Psalm 32:24

Author's Note

This completed novel sat in storage on my computer for over three years, and would likely still be there were it not for the support, encouragement, and straight talk of several people. To Benjamin, who shows me Christ-like love everyday. You were right, babe. You were right. To Joan Deneve, best friend, author and sister of my heart. Always having you in my corner is life. To author, friend, and life-mentor Lisa Godfrees. For your always wise, frank, and in-love perspective. To author and fellow "rule-breaker" Marc Schooley for the ready hugs and writing wisdom.

To my most avid reader friends whose unwavering support for my writing never fails even after two years: Mary Ellen Goodwin, Angi Griffis, Joy W. Doering, Amy Willeford, Hope Tuttle, and Angela Fox. Those of you who were late to the party but just as supportive and encouraging to my writer heart: Tiffany Halla Colonna, Amanda Geaney, and Amy Robinson. The rest of my reader friends who are too numerous to list here but know your reviews, letters, messages, and especially prayers always find me at exactly the right time.

To authors and reader friends who did early readings for me: Caroline Glasgow, Wendy Loving-Schetski, Kim Jenkins Dietz, Antoinette Harrison, Amy Robinson, Joan Deneve, Joy W. Doering, and Sara Ella. You were and continue to be such a blessing in getting this book out there for everyone else.

Due credit to Mike and Rosa Gross, of One Sharp Marriage. This husband and wife impalement arts team were the inspiration for the rose and cherry trick in this novel. Benchmade Knives U.S.A. for enlightening me to blades so sharp they slice through rows of water bottles with a single stroke.

To my mom and dad. I am who I am today because of your love and influence. To my brother and my sister, who I wouldn't want to do life without. Lastly to my Creator. My wall and the Savior of my heart. You have given me this gift and the grace and strength to use it. Let me continue to use it well. Always.

To the reader, thank you for your interest in my work. To sign up for my email list to be notified of new releases, please visit: http://www.nancykimball.com/newsletter

Made in the USA
Coppell, TX
31 July 2022